# EVANGELINE
## The Seer of Wall St.

a novel

**Clint Adams**

**Credo *Italia***
*San Francisco*

published by

Credo *Italia*
350 Bay Street, Suite 100-124
San Francisco, California 94133 USA

This book is a work of fiction. Names, characters, places and
incidents are either the product of the author's imagination or are
used fictitiously, and any resemblance to actual persons, living or
dead, business establishments, events, or locales is entirely
coincidental.

Manufactured in the United States of America

ISBN 978-0-9768375-7-2 (hardcover)
ISBN 978-0-9768375-8-9 (e-book)

*To those wise enough to know
that yours is the only 'yes' that matters*

# EVANGELINE

# It's All Relative

*I*n the summer of '62—after filling my tummy with paella at the Gates of Spain restaurant in Santa Monica—my great-aunt Pearl told me with pride, "Clinton Dean, you're a direct descendant of John and John Quincy Adams." Not knowing how to react to this info, nor to the sprawling family tree placed before me, I asked, "Can I eat my custard now?" after having studied the kiddie menu.

20+ years later, immediately upon meeting my captive scene partner, Jessica (Paul) Stanton in *The Trojan Women* at Cal, she asked, "So, what are you all about?" Flashing back to childhood for some reason, I responded, "I'm a direct descendant of John and John Quincy Adams." Jessica next said, "No kidding. Then you must also be related to Evangeline Adams." Busy adjusting my too-short and skimpy toga, I uttered back, "Who's that?"

The following year, atop the John Hancock Observatory in Boston, I looked out to the harbor where the Tea Party had taken place. Instigated by Samuel Adams; kin, troublemaker. I liked that. I liked him. For the first time I took 'being an Adams' seriously.

Decades later, now a writer, I reflected on a few back-burner projects waiting to be set free. There she was, my great-great _____, Evangeline Adams. Someone I believed to be a part of me.

From 2012-2015, thousands of hours of research, development and refinement went into *EVANGELINE*'s twelve drafts.

Hiring a genealogist to determine the exact nature of my familial relationship to Evangeline Adams next became crucial. No way could I truthfully refer to Evangeline as my great, great-anything—once, twice or three times removed—if I wasn't certain.

Today I learned conclusively that I'm not related to Evangeline, John or John Quincy Adams. Disappointed? Absolutely. Regretful that I took on this project under false pretenses? Never. In this book, I got to pay tribute to one of America's first female entrepreneurs by relaying a story from a century ago that's equally as relevant today; a total privilege. Evangeline, this is for you.

— *Clint Adams, Spring 2015*
*Northern Nevada*

# Sun @ 28° TAURUS 7'52 (1914)

*S*ix thousand five hundred and seventy days remain in my life, according to my astrological calculations. As a woman of society, now a rather mature woman, decorum prevents me from divulging how many days have come prior. My first began in Jersey City, New Jersey, a locale some might regard as unbefitting a member of America's First Family, but a start to my destiny nonetheless. Nearly three years after the reunification of America's North and South, on an overcast and gusty Saturday, February eighth, at precisely eight-thirty in the morning, the pendulum attached to my internal clock took its initial swing. Its continued movement is something I've learned to never take for granted.

"Make every moment count…as if your life depends on it," my most loyal client, financier J.P. Morgan, always said while straightening the line of his eyebrows with his forefingers. Wise words from an extraordinary man, a titan whose few vulnerabilities, according to him, were divulged only to me. J.P.

never wasted time, or opportunities. This afternoon, I've taken his example to heart. I plan to create a moment that will live on forever. Today, I'll stand firm and show everyone that I truly do matter.

☉ ☽ ✶

"Miss Adams, do you feel that it will be your well-known clientele—royalty, financial barons, moving picture stars—and your luxurious suites at Carnegie Hall, that will influence the judge's decision most?"

On the first of two white marble steps leading to the entrance of the West Side Magistrates Court at 314 West 54th Street in midtown Manhattan, I'm forced to stop. Not yet underneath the twenty-foot archway to this Italian Renaissance Revival structure with its softly inviting terra cotta outward appearance above, my blood begins to simmer under the pressure of cumulonimbus-filled skies above. This is exactly why I've chosen to fight.

The question comes from a stout, broad-eyed, bald man of about twenty-five, impertinent in his demeanor, uninspired in his delivery. He's neglected to offer to share his umbrella on this dingy day, and now he poses questions to me without a proper introduction? "And you are?"

With clammy beads of sweat accumulating on his upper lip he says, "Ralph Slocum, ma'am. *New York Times.*"

"Clientele? Carnegie Hall? You forgot to mention that my lineage traces back to Presidents John and John Quincy Adams. Perhaps it's this fact that will impress the judge most." At that, he has the decency to blush. "Sir, none of these will have any bearing on today's outcome."

Next to me on the slippery, rain-soaked step, my steadfast

twenty-three-year-old secretary and confidante, Bavarian-born Sabine Goldman, agrees with a fierce nod, causing her Jewish Chai pendant to bounce against her ample chest. As is her own unique style, Sabine chooses to wear sheer linen weeks before the arrival of summer, while incessantly humming *I'm on My Way to Mandalay* because she doesn't know the words.

"Ma'am. John Pierpont Morgan. Three presidents of the New York Stock Exchange. King Edward. All those bon vivants?"

"Mr. Slocum, the judge's decision will have nothing to do with those that have selected my services. I am a woman who conducts business. Two hundred Carnegie Hall has been a more than suitable site to render what I do; my address does not make me more credible, less credible, than the next person."

"And how do you feel this decision will impact the future of your business, your 'calling'?"

"My business as an astrologer?"

"Not only that, but the future of astronomy in general."

"You do mean to say astrology, not astronomy. Is that correct?"

"Yes, of course, ma'am. Astrology. Exactly."

☉ ☽ ✷

Two hundred dollars. A petty and simplistic restitution, the cost of the emerald brooch I wear atop my tweed lapel. I could have merely paid the fine, but I requested a hearing instead. When the entirety of one's life's work is under scrutiny, a court case is nothing more than a paltry pittance to endure for unequivocal justice.

So now, like thousands of defendants who have come before me, my fate will shortly be decided in this frigid, second floor courtroom situated on the periphery of Hell's Kitchen. All I can hope is that the marinara sauce I imagine Judge Freschi ate last night left his Italian taste buds satiated, leaving him hungry for nothing more than the truthful aftertaste of my testimony.

The black-eyed bailiff, with one hand mysteriously remaining in his left pants pocket commands, "All rise," seemingly directed to me. My unexpected upward and paranoid stance causes my library of astrological reference books, including my Swiss Ephemeris, my bible, which gives the positions of astronomical objects in the heavens at a given time, to tumble to the floor from my lap like a singular clap of applause. Some pages even become dislodged from their bindings, but my hands quickly regroup them. Although my nerves begin to rattle under the now-piercing gaze of every thief, hoaxer, prostitute and possible Black Hand-extortionist now staring at me, I refuse to be embarrassed. These books are here for spectacle and show, identical to the two hired esquires to my rear. J.P., may he rest in peace, has left me in good counsel. The billions of dollars I generated for him have come back to me in the presence of two of Wall St.'s finest attorneys. The judge should take note, but I'm not wagering on it.

After I've collected my belongings, the bulky bailiff continues, "The Superior Court of New York County, State of New York, is now in session, the Honorable John H. Freschi presiding. Please be seated and come to order."

I feel a stern tap on my right shoulder, ordering me to sit. Then a second. My tactile attorney has earned his pay, twice now. Together, we three behold the parade of criminal horror stories on the docket before us, and we judge for ourselves the defendants on trial.

"Are you nervous?" olive-drably dressed Attorney #1 asks, two octaves above being audible.

"I feel secure about the outcome. Nervousness is felt only by those less certain. Vinci Omnia Veritas," I answer back with authority, while my posterior notices the crude lumpiness of the worn, padded red velvet seat upon which my piles are seated.

In my good man's eyes I can see the absence of Latin within them. Proper English to all present from this moment forward. "Our case is coming soon. Is that correct?"

"Very soon. If the petty larceny hearing preceding ours ends quickly, the judge will surely address you next."

Indeed the theft inquiry ends before it begins when a newspaper dealer fails to appear against his accused. The young man, with hair greasier than a streetcar's axle, doesn't look as relieved as one would imagine. There's an air of disappointment about him rather than elation at the dismissal. What was it that he had stolen? A stack of overpriced 5¢ copies of the Sunday *New York Times*? If practice makes perfect, I'd deduce that he'll re-visit the newspaper merchant until the thief gets the attention he's seeking.

"The next case, the People ex. rel. Adele D. Priess versus Evangeline S. Adams. Will the parties please rise."

This is the moment of my lifetime. My eyes blink shut, then open. Three times. No, not a dream. No one is beside me. Inconspicuously I look behind me to my left, where one attorney gives me a stony grin. I look beyond him and—There. There in the spectator section gazes my trustworthy secretary, Sabine. She always wears a grimace along with a vibrant ruby red scarf, much too seductive for any professional setting. At second thought, a sardonic sneer, rather than a grimace. Sabine's attendance here today comforts me, except when she hums; at any given moment, she can put the fear of God in even the most well intentioned human or pet.

Sabine nods. Yes, I see it. In a split second my eyes move on to her right. There sits the beloved comrade of my Aquarian soul, demure yet conspicuous to me, Emma Sheridan-Fry. In her violet plumed hat and perfect posture Emma doesn't need to grin, grimace or nod. Emma needn't do anything. Seeing her poise, her grace, the way she breathes in air that's always unforced makes my anxiety diminish, my heart full, my being calm, while reinforcing my desire to get these proceedings underway for businesswomen everywhere who fight to be taken seriously. I smile at my Emma and stop searching. Instead, I turn back to the front of the court and cast my azure eyes upon the judge perched at an altar-like rosewood table with russet trim before me. He appears to be a genial man. Still a mystery though what he enjoyed for dinner last night, nor if his stomach found it agreeable or not. If he belches into his clenched hands I'll be certain of my presumption.

Judge John H. Freschi, upon more finite examination, somewhat resembles my diminutive, dimple-chinned and olive toned client, Enrico Caruso. Or am I just being small minded? Perhaps both have origins in southern Italy; perhaps both come from opposite ends of the boot.

"Miss Evangeline Smith Adams?" the prosecutrix, whose overall girth and bulging biceps make her look better suited to coach football, asks.

Thinking all along that it was the judge himself with whom I'd be speaking, uncertainty and confusion take over. "Yes, your—Miss, Mrs." Based on appearance and demeanor, I assume I'm being interrogated by a perpetually unmarried woman. "It is Miss, isn't it?"

"I'll ask the questions. Now, you are the proprietress of the…" Miss Scrum's mouth twists unpleasantly. "…business, shall we say?"

"That's correct, ma'am. It is indeed a business. A consulting business."

"Where advice is given…by you. And do others, within your business environs, provide advice?"

"I am the only one. I have a staff of several secretaries and stenographers. Researchers as well. To be exact, there are twenty-five people under my employ. None but I offer advice."

"And this work takes place at two hundred Carnegie Hall."

"I have several suites there. Ten-oh-three Carnegie Hall is my private office."

"Isn't it true that you, initially, were turned down, time and time again, while searching for these *suites*?"

"Well, yes. That's cor—"

"Your presence was unwelcomed at every building housing office space. Why exactly was that?"

"But, ma'am. As you yourself mentioned, we did locate—"

"Your Honor, please let it be known that the suites to which Miss Adams refers are artists' studios, *not* offices. For the likes of performers and such," the prosecutrix says while tilting her head fully back, now addressing the ceiling.

I looked at the judge, insecurity and indecision hovering outside my mind, the way a child seeks support from a parent.

"Finish your thought, ma'am," the judge says.

"We did locate studios at Carnegie Hall. There are more th—"

The prosecutrix interrupts. "Before we delve into an explanation of what you call 'your work,' 'your profession,' do you understand why you are here? Fraud. Fraud by fortunetelling. A crime."

"I understand. Perfectly. I'm no fortuneteller." Defiance enters my voice. "Rather than pay the fine, I'm here now, to demonstrate what I do."

"At the taxpayer's expense. Do you know how bus—"

While fiddling with his gavel by means of his fingertips, Judge Freschi interrupts Miss Scrum. "It is the nature of your *business* in general. You have chosen to come before me today to, in essence, defend your business rather than yourself. Am I comprehending the nature of your wishes accurately?"

"Yes, and I most appreciate your time with me in this place of law, your Honor."

"Well, I must say, you are standing in the company of two most-accomplished and successful defenders."

"Thank you, Judge Freschi," the polished lawyer behind my right shoulder says mildly, raising his forearm for all to view the diamond cufflink set in sterling silver he attempts to re-clasp.

Hearing his faux-bravado voice, even for a split second, agitates me. I am here to defend myself. Me alone. This is *my* task. I, with all due respect, am the star attraction, in this, the center ring. The price I've paid to attain this standing has been high, with many years of toil and trouble to prove a singular point: astrology is the oldest science on the planet.

"I will like to speak to you myself, your Honor. No one knows astrology as I do. In my humble opinion."

"This is the business to which you are referring?"

Before answering, in my head flash the thousands of charts I've systematically created. The pages and pages of data I've summoned, the computations I've formulated. The azimuths, the progressions, the sextiles as well as octiles. The clients in front of me and those I know only through the post. Not only am I defending astrology; I am defending my entire existence, my livelihood, my life. Trying to convince someone of the legitimacy of this most elemental discipline is like breathing for me now. It's done daily, without thought or planning. An inborn incident.

"Astrology is my business. That's *absolutely* correct, Judge

Freschi."

"Astrology. The interpretation of the stars," the judge says, nodding. "Forgive my ignorance, but how does this differ then from astronomy?"

"Your Honor, time is of the essence. If we—"

Knowing that I may never get this opportunity again, I interrupt Miss Scrum. "Astronomy is the study of all objects outside our world. It, too, is a science. Astronomy, you could say, came from astrology. Yes, you are correct when you mentioned interpretation. Astrology is the oldest, most ancient, of all sciences."

"Beside you, you have the books to substantiate this?"

"Yes, many. Many books have been written on this subject, writings from centuries back by men who are well respected as authorities on this subject, as well as others. *The Art of Synthesis* by Alan Leo, *Liber Astronomiae*, Guido Bonatti, *Christian Astrology* and its subsequent volumes, all written by the Englishman, 17th-century astrologist, William Lilly..." I look over in the direction of the prosecutrix to find her eyes rolling as swiftly as a spiraling pigskin thrown at midfield for a touchdown. I stop.

"To much of the public you are a fortuneteller. Do you intend to disprove this today?" Prosecutrix Scrum asks while looking at the judge, not to me.

"And I will. I am no fortuneteller and I'd now like to tell you why."

"Please proceed then," Judge Freschi tells me, seeming as if curiosity has gotten the best of him.

The precise moment I have been awaiting is before me. I have hitherto collected my thoughts and my words to the best of my intelligence. Before being able to express myself, I hear a distinguishable cough from behind me. I know it came from Emma. No, not strategic, natural. An organic occurrence that provides meaning to me. A sign of sorts, as I believe it to be. Others may not. Either way, the sound from my beloved Emma validates my motives to continue.

"Firstly, I appreciate so much the opportunity to be before you, the prosecution, Detective Priess and Detective Roos today in this Superior Court. My business, my consulting business as an astrologer, comes after years of devoted study, not by chance. I believe I have earned the title of expert."

"An expert of astrology? Not astron—"

"No more interruptions, Mrs. Scrum," the judge commands.

*Mrs.?* Well, you could have fooled me. "Yes. Astrology is the science which describes the influence of the heavenly bodies upon mundane affairs, upon human character and life. To be most clear-cut, it is a mathematical or exact science deciphered via astronomy, which describes the heavenly bodies and explains their motions, etc."

"These heavenly bodies to which you are referencing are planets. Not Heaven itself," the judge says with a wry smirk.

I pause as those in the courtroom chuckle. "It, astrology, is an applied science in that it takes the established principles of astronomy as its guide in delineating human character. It is an empirical science, because its deductions are mathematical calculations based upon accurate data that have been gathered for thousands of years. Are you understanding me, your Honor? Mrs. Scrum?"

"I most certainly am. Please do continue," Judge Freschi says while Mrs. Scrum lets out a sigh.

"Thank you, Judge. Astrology is the oldest science in existence. It is not only pre-historic but pre-traditional, and must not be classed with fortune telling, or any of the many forms of demonology as practiced in ancient and modern times." I still sense reticence and skepticism coming from the man seated before me. Like all I have ever known, this, too, will be a challenge.

"Your presentation is quite proficient. Please do carry on with your defense, Miss Adams."

Gracious be. Another good sign.

"Astrology is the science of the effects of the Solar Currents on all living things, especially human life. The earth, in revolving around the sun, passes through twelve different currents of Solar Fluid, thus causing the great diversity in human life."

"Currents. Like wading down a stream to discover others unlike ourselves? Diverse others?"

"Perhaps so. A path, so to speak."

I proceed to tell his Honor more and more of what I have learned to be intelligent information. As far as I can determine he is able to absorb its meaning and ponder what I am saying as the truth.

Mrs. Scrum next bolts to her feet. "Your Honor, we cannot hold up the proceedings of the day any longer with—"

"You're entirely correct, Mrs. Scrum."

"Thank you, your Honor," she says sweetly. "Now then, time for your demonstration, Miss Adams. Take this data, look it over and divulge your findings," Mrs. Scrum tells me while handing me a piece of paper folded neatly in quarters. "Everything on it that you need?"

The moment of truth has arrived. Upon finding the contents within, no name appears; only a birth date, including year along with location and time of birth, nothing else. All the ingredients I'd requested beforehand. "Yes, indeed, ma'am." My heart pounds identically like the jackhammer I hear on the street outside.

"If your demonstration does take beyond the agreed-upon allotment, we will have to continue onto another case. Yours will be over," the judge reminds me.

Before responding, my eyes jut over to my left without a flinch. There, staring at me sternly in polished almond wood, so matter-of-factly, a Comtoise longcase clock ready to strike three. "The chart I cast will take no more than a few minutes and I will then explain it."

With little more back and forth, Judge Freschi and Mrs. Scrum allow me to do my work in front of them, in their presence and that of everyone else in the courtroom. Although I dare not look back, I can tell that Sabine and Emma are holding their breaths.

I take out my ephemeris, my compass, my writing tools and begin cyphering and scribing. Is it interest or boredom on the faces of the twenty-or-so spectators behind me? I focus only on the task at hand, knowing no more than ten minutes will be needed to chart this anonymous person's life story. It turns out to be a challenging, sorrowful tale to tell. But, when complete, I convey all back to the silenced courtroom.

"This is a younger man. A boy with slightly longer hair the color of flame. Clear green eyes. Skin freckled from the sun. Athletic. Playful. Obstinate. Bold in front of others, uncertain by himself. Frequently misunderstood by family members. Discontent with their misjudgments. A somber face worn in private. Sadly, this hapless lad will live a very short life. Water. A watery grave. Water, water all around him that will take his life so early…"

First a gasp is heard during my words, then a few whispers and murmurs from those awaiting their turn at trial, then nothing. Mrs. Scrum, a look of astonishment on her face, remains silent. Her eyes search out the judge.

"That was my son." Judge Freschi's voice cracks. He next looks down at a metal-framed object indistinguishable to me atop his desk. "He drowned recently." The judge's relative speechlessness leads the prosecutor to ask more questions of me regarding the fees I charge, income, taxes paid, business licenses, my previous employment in Boston and any prior criminal activity or incarceration. I respond succinctly, accurately, truthfully with a clear conscience. Mrs. Scrum discovers nothing blameworthy. Everything I do, professionally and personally, is thoroughly legal and above board. Abruptly, Judge Freschi cuts the prosecutrix off mid-sentence and orders a brief recess.

The courtroom erupts in chatter.

⊙　☽　☆

When the judge returns, I stand.

"The defendant has given ample proof that she is a woman of learning and culture, and one who is very well versed in astronomy and other sciences. I say she violated no law."

The judge glances to the prosecutrix, then to me, then to the courtroom at large while holding the paperwork I had given him in his right hand—his son's chart. As he waves it in front of us all, he declares, "I am satisfied that the defendant has not pretended to tell fortunes, and she is accordingly acquitted. Defendant dismissed."

My good humor is magnified when he adds, "Today, this defendant raises astrology to the dignity of an exact science."

⊙　☽　☆

The same reporter is waiting in the foyer of the courthouse, and this time he follows me as we both head out of the building.

"The judge, in his most honest appraisal of me and my

efforts, has done astrology a great favor. My business goes on. I applaud the way he conducted himself today. Judge Freschi could have—"

"What do you think this decision will lead to? For you? For others?" the stout reporter asks.

"I don't know about the others. For me, professionally, it means that my quest in life remains intact, alive."

"Which is...?"

"To thrust astrology from reading rooms into mainstream popular culture, and to be remembered, in perpetuity, for having done so."

"To some, you've already achieved this. The former anyway. Doesn't seem like much of a challenge. And personally?"

At that, Mr. Slocum displays his first show of fine manners: he opens the front door for me. Outside, my eyes see only sunshine, no more clouds, no rain. The late-afternoon yields nothing but brightness and blue skies ahead. "To see if I can accomplish this all, indisputably, and then some, before November 10, 1932."

"What's so significant about that date in particular, ma'am?"

While contemplating my answer a waft of noxious air indistinguishable to my senses invades my being, causing me to briefly lose my breath. Fecal odor via the sewer? Illuminating gas? Fumes from the tenements and shanties that line Eighth Avenue nearby? Ninth? The smell of death? "Oh," I say, "it's just a private goal I've set for myself."

☉　☽　★

As I walk down the steps of the courthouse, nothing in my life, my career, will ever again be the same.

# Sun @ 19° PISCES 13'22 (1899)

*I*t was the spring of 1899 when the preliminary transformation of my life occurred, seemingly overnight. As I boarded the southbound train with my first-ever secretary, Mrs. E. P. Brush, a devoted Virgo, I was filled with uncertainty. "Nearly three and a half million inhabitants. Teeming with immigrants now. Mightn't we become lost in the shuffle?" Mrs. Brush said, while taking her initial final step into the twentieth century. Being in the company of a naturally worrying Virgin and her tightly-bunned brown hair did little to ease my fears.

"You shouldn't be handling those bags, Mrs. Your lumbago will flare up, leaving you in great distress before we've even arrived."

"That's true. I'll carry only the smallest."

"We'll need to walk to the third carriage. You must conserve your strength. Once inside the cabin, I'll prepare your Milk of Magnesia."

"Thank you, Mrs. Brush, I'm not yet decrepit. Days ago you

celebrated with me only my thirti——, twenty-ninth birthday."

Sometimes I wondered to which position Mrs. Brush was employed, my secretary or my nurse. We did find our way to our cabin, which contained the clearest of windows, and made ourselves comfortable for the ride to New York City. What a joy it was to find no other passengers among our compartment. A scent of juniper and perhaps cinnamon lingered in the air, presumably from previous occupants. Other than the after aroma, Mrs. Brush and I remained unaccompanied. The solitude gave me time to ponder and contemplate where I'd come from and where I was headed. Boston served me very well for my first thi——twenty-nine years, but I felt I had accomplished all I could there. No more challenges to conquer, no more dreams to actualize.

Mrs. Brush appeared deep in thought in her seat across from me. With her eyes scrutinizing the rack above us, I'm sure worrying if our luggage would topple onto ourselves whilst in transit, I loosened the belt surrounding my midriff. Next, I took off my tweed hat and removed two gray hairs I found inside. I wasn't sure if they belonged to me or to Mother. It was her hat that I was borrowing. I let the now-lifeless strays drop to the floor.

How odd it felt to be away from her, and at length—a first. Although she disapproved of my vocation, provincial as she was in her outlook, I still felt as if I owed her so much. I was determined to prove her wrong. Astrology is *not* demonology. And it *is* befitting an Adams, I felt assuredly. My three older brothers had distanced themselves from me years prior, never really getting to know me at all. Now, it was their time to share in the responsibility of caring for Mother. My turn at life was finally presenting itself to me; and I, after having waited three decades, decided to take it.

Early on, trying to eke out a living as an unmarried secretary in Boston had been ripe with limitations. Mother was thrilled when I'd announced my engagement to my employer Mr. Lord in 1894, but our marriage was not to be. I chose astrology over stability. Working as an apprentice here and there only gets one so far. For years I'd made minimal income with my palmistry practice, but with most people afraid to admit they even knew me, growth by word-of-mouth became an impossibility. Boston is a place that's not governed by City Hall; it's instead run by Roman Catholicism, where in church the men sit in the front pew and the women and children sit behind. An environment where men are superior, women are inferior, and any single woman who practices astrology and palmistry would do best to run far from town before she's thrown out of it.

A new setting also meant a new business strategy. In Boston, the few clients I'd had expected theatre with their readings. Drama. Against my nature, I'd painted brightly colored stars onto my clothing, spoke melodramatically the best I could and even threw what I referred to as "celestial dust," that was nothing but wheat flour, up into the air for effect. In New York, I would engage in nothing but pure professionalism.

As I felt the train accelerate to its maximum speed, and smelled the mouth-watering deliciousness of braised beef wafting into the stagnant air of our berth, I said, "The dining car must be nearby. I'm rather excited. Are you, Mrs. Brush?"

"About what?"

"This adventure. Starting anew. Trying things differently."

"Call me conventional, Mrs. I miss Boston…and Father, Mr. Brush, already."

I never asked why Mrs. Brush always called her husband "Father" and me, despite being an unmarried woman, "Mrs." Although I'd asked her first name when we initially met, she's always been "Mrs. Brush" to me. Decorum. Habit. Monotony. I also never asked why she chose to work for me in the first place— a traditionalist employed by someone so very non-. As she reached for her burgundy bound *Book of Isaiah, Volume II* and pearl tone fountain pen from her handbag, Mrs. Brush crossed both legs and then wrapped her right foot around her left ankle from behind, something only a thin person can do. Next, she began to underline with black ink passages that, I can only assume, appealed to her most.

Looking to contemplate material of substance myself, I elected to cast my own astrological chart with the resources that were kept in the empty seat to my left, tools I never, on any occasion, kept far from me. Having done this for so many others prior, this was only the second time I allowed myself this luxury. Mother always used to tell me, "It's a sin. Best not to know." Somehow, I never followed this credo while divulging to others what the future held; I had to make a living. But I never felt as if I deserved my own predictions. Or, maybe I was afraid. More appropriately, maybe I'd been taught to be afraid.

The near-springtime, all-in-bloom freshness of the countryside whizzing by my window at one hundred miles per hour added to my enthusiasm about New York City and the prospects that came with it. But for the next twenty minutes, my eyes stayed glued to my ephemeris, the mightiest of all astro-reference books. Translating the data I'd found into practical knowledge via my mathematical calculations took another twenty minutes. Another ten to make notations while corresponding them to dates and times in the future.

Upcoming astrological transits, when compared to my own horoscopic natal chart, bared a litany of landmark activities in the near future and in the decades to come. Career successes, deceit, sabotage, greed, fear, illness and much more.

Through my chart I foresaw great change coming soon; I found myself settling into a full-time life in New York City in or around 1905, contrasted with the momentary one I was living now, due to familial obligations. But it was the imminent turn of the century that held the most progress, change arriving nearly simultaneously with the New Year. I couldn't wait.

I took all of this in stride, and yet there was one element in my chart that I had difficulty understanding. Close to midyear 1903, I was to meet a woman with whom I would feel a soul-connectedness, a dramatic woman. The chart alluded to, much later on, a profound and quite intimate union. Perhaps I'd made an error in my computations. How could this be? A most definite closeness, attachment with a woman, not a man, was what I saw in the stars. I'm sure it will make more sense the minute I establish roots in New York, I thought. My plan was to cast my chart once more while there.

"Tea and assortments are coming forthwith, ma'am. Will you be partaking?"

"Yes. That's perfect. Mrs. Brush. Pardon me, but may I ask, how long is it that you've been married to Fath—Mr. Brush?"

"Four years now, ma'am. Nearly five."

"And, your interests. Do you happen to be enchanted with dramatic theatre? In Boston?"

"Why, yes, Mrs. Adams. I most certainly am. I attend performances at the Boston Museum as often as is possible. *Twelfth Night*—"

"That's wonderful for you. But it was your attraction to performing I was indeed inquiring about. Were you ever a dramatic actress?"

"Me? In the theatre as an actress, ma'am? Oh, my heavens. That could never be. The entire concept, as abstract as you've presented it, terrifies me. I cannot think of anything that would initiate panic in me as much as something as that."

"Mmm," I replied. Outside the window, the bouncing boats in the harbor, the white-capped waves and the ominous sky above the

Atlantic Ocean as we passed New Haven and New London, filled my imagination with water. It must have been my ascendant in Pisces at work. Daydreaming was a luxury I relished when not working. How better to take advantage of this feeling than a slight day nap. I felt that if Mrs. Brush uttered no words, this could easily be accomplished.

Looking across to her, I could see that my conversation of her as an actress has set her fingernails in motion as she fidgeted about her face, fostering perpetual red scabs and bulbous protrusions that would forever go unhealed. A nap, posthaste, would sober her as well.

☉   ☽   ✯

"Mrs. Mrs., please. Wake up," I heard Mrs. Brush calling at me. I could feel her hands firmly grasping my upper arms, jostling me forwards and back. I woke up.

Staring me in the face was not Mrs. Brush. It was one of the notations, a date I'd jotted down on paper while constructing my chart. Still, my imagination was at work. Reality had not yet approached me. "Nov—"

"Mrs. Adams, you're not right," Mrs. Brush said, now manhandling me, progressively more violently. When I squinted my eyes, the real Mrs. Brush took shape before me.

"Oh, Mrs. Brush. It was... a horrible dream."

"For the Lord's sake. Take a deep breath, Mrs. Get hold of yourself."

I followed her advice. Then, rather quickly, I could see Mrs. Brush gathering her belongings. That was my cue to follow suit. My astrological tools were the first I collected. Atop the pile was the sheet of paper onto which I'd scribed a particular message, one that frightened my subconscious more than my conscious, it seemed.

*November 10, 1932. End.*

While Mrs. Brush was busy smoothing the creases from her starched dress that had been seated too long, I took the single page into my hand, crumpled it, and stuffed it in between the bottom and rear cushions of the seat, never to be glanced at again. Like all things horrid, I chose to, for the moment anyway, forget that this experience had ever occurred.

The bucolic scene outside the windows had been replaced by bustling and under renovation Grand Central Station in New York. No longer Grand Central Depot. Jackhammers and drills everywhere were streamlining its former three floors into six. Each and every voice, belonging to travelers and laborers united, reverberated like a hum inside its main concourse. The train was perfectly punctual and Mrs. Brush already had her coat on, sensing my eagerness to forge our next adventure amid the city.

"The porter is on his way, ma'am. Not Irish. I summoned him just a few minutes ago. I didn't want to waste a moment."

"Extremely efficient of you, Mrs. Brush." The exact reason I'd chosen her for my secretary—a typical Virgo, precise and fastidious in all they do.

The well-mannered porter speaking with an Italian accent collected our bags, along with his three-cent tip, and Mrs. Brush and I proceeded to depart the train and seek out a coach for the Astor House. I felt like a child once again, full of vigor and enthusiasm, seeing a new life full of opportunities before me.

I hoped that the room I had occupied so many times before would be mine this time around. I knew how much Mrs. Brush would love staying there, with its many rooms facing the hospital across the street. Born not only a health-obsessed Virgo but a Florence Nightingale aficionado, my secretary would be free to observe the sickly and infirmed come and go at will.

Upon our arrival we were greeted by the hotel's most-proper proprietor, Mr. Van Amstel. The Astor House, and its decades of splendor and refinement, was where the Adams family had been staying for generations.

With a half-smile, half-cordial demeanor and fully crossed arms, our host said, "Your usual suite awaits you, Miss Adams."

"That's most pleasant news, Mr. Van Amstel. And my travel companion, Mrs. Brush?"

"Yes, hello, Mrs. Brush. How kind to know you. Yours is the adjoining room at the end of the hall. It has a lovely view of the river."

"Not the hospital?"

"Well, yes. Now that you mention it, you will be able to see the hospital from the side window. Correct."

"I'd also like to mention to you that I'll be conducting business here as well. A consultation business. A few of my local clients will be paying short visits." The moment I uttered these words a strange feeling came into my stomach. I shouldn't have wondered what I would hear next.

"A business. A business of what sort, ma'am?" Mr. Van Amstel asked while placing his fingertips to just beneath his nose, noticing what I can only imagine to be a clump of beeswax he hadn't yet thoroughly combed through his thick black and grey moustache.

"The business I perform in Boston. Palmistry and charting astrological diagrams. I'll be doing this here."

Instead of looking right at me, Mr. Van Amstel next chose to peer directly at the floor. His expression reeked of embarrassment. Then, his moustache began to twitch back and forth. "I beg your pardon, ma'am. You said *palmistry*? An interpretation, telling of the palms of the hands."

"Yes. That's what I do. I could show you, if you like."

"Ma'am, that's out of the question. Excuse me, I appreciate the offer but that's entirely unacceptable. If this is your objective, I'm so sorry but you'll not be permitted to stay here."

"But my family—"

"The Adams family has been coming here for decades. Yes, we're honored to have them, you. And, you're more than welcome now…but not if you bring this witchcraft with you."

This man and his objections provoked me in a way that was becoming all too familiar, giving me a much heightened desire to instigate a change in the way in which I, astrology, was viewed. Yet I said nothing, only attempted to retrieve my bags from the doorkeeper.

"I can, at the very least summon you another porter to help with your transit to another hotel."

"That won't be necessary at all, Sir. We can do it ourselves."

"Mrs. Adams, we'll surely need help. We—I cannot move these myself," Mrs. Brush interceded. "The cobblestones."

But we did. On this day, I felt possessed of an enormous might as we traversed down one perfectly paved, not stony, street then up another. It felt good to be in such control, not needing to rely on anyone else to attain our goals.

"Begging your pardon, Ma'am. People are staring at us. It shames me to be seen like this, transporting our own bags. Ladies…doing such a thing," Mrs. Brush told me in a whine. Then she whispered, "Makes you appear mannish. What shall they think of us?"

"Mrs. Brush, carrying luggage doesn't make us any less ladylike. We'll soon be at the entrance of the Windsor. Strength demonstrated bodes well of our character."

"And the Windsor will take us? What if—"

"What if you imagine you're not a Virgo for a moment? Worry only brings the expectation of naught."

Apparently my comment silenced Mrs. Brush long enough for

her to focus on carrying her single bag.

Approaching East 47th Street, Mrs. Brush and I found our way to 575 Fifth Avenue, the Windsor, a hotel that advertised itself as "the most comfortable and homelike hotel in New York." I kept imagining the peace that came with the notion of being home.

The staff at the Windsor welcomed Mrs. Brush and me as if we'd stayed with them repeatedly. The hotel owner, Mr. Warren F. Leland, with his tie askew, its clasp uneven and no greasy moustache to twitch, even came by as I signed the register.

"Today, it is the Sixteenth. Yes, Ma'am?" Mrs. Brush asked while inscribing her name.

"Of course. The day before St. Patrick's Day, the Seventeenth of March."

"Miss Adams, it's wonderful that you've chosen the Windsor. We'll make sure this visit is a pleasant one for you. How long will you be staying here?" Mr. Leland inquired.

"I'm uncertain. I plan on moving here, temporarily at least, to New York. Mrs. Brush is my secretary and we'll eventually be relocating our business here from Boston."

"That's lovely. And which type of business is that?"

"My vocation is palmistry and astrology."

Mr. Leland didn't respond right away; no chart was needed to tell me that an argument was about to ensue. The pause in his reply spoke volumes to me. Mr. Leland next began scratching his head. Then he abruptly stopped. What a relief his well-creased face gave me as it blossomed into a rosy smile.

With nothing but adoration exuding from his sea green eyes, and seemingly paternal devotion from his undemanding voice, Mr. Leland said, "My daughter, Helen, is quite interested in the celestial. Her birthday is coming up soon. A week or so."

Hurrah. A believer, I said to myself. "In March. When exactly?"

"Towards the end, the Twenty-Seventh."

"Aries. They're quite delightful. It would please me to create your chart, and hers too, if you like."

"Oh, how very interesting that would be. Thank you, ma'am." But his mind already seemed to be diverted elsewhere, and he began scribbling notes at the front desk and calling instructions to his staff.

After a host of excuses, cancellations and full schedules, Mr. Leland did provide me with his birth date, time and location, and we, in turn, set up an appointment to meet that afternoon inside his office for my interpretation of his chart. I could tell that he was only humoring my invitation, as he seemed to be focused on the St. Patrick's Day parade that was to take place the next day in front of the hotel.

I nearly regretted having offered to cast the chart, for I was astonished at what I found. Very rarely did I question the deduction of my data, but this time I began to cast his chart all over again. Unfortunately, the same result.

"My dear Mr. Leland. My heavens, I'm so sorry…to tell you. It's with great regret that I now forewarn you of imminent, catastrophic danger for both you and your family, including your daughter, Helen. A personal disaster of some sort. Please be prepared."

Mr. Leland's eyes, tired and swollen, bugged out of their sockets. Not absorbing one word of my warning, he couldn't understand that my sole desire was to help him. A believer when I'd checked-in, a non- during his moment of truth. Throwing his hands up to the sky aloofly, he declared, "Why do you tell me this, Ma'am? Now? With all that's going on? Misfortune?"

"I warn you, Mr. Leland. I've never been more sincere. Instantaneous. Danger coming in this place, your place of business immediately. Entailing a *personal* disaster. You must be made aware. I'm sorry to have told you this, but please do be very mindful of what is going on before you here. Inside this hotel."

Bobbing his head up and down furiously, Mr. Leland said, "Certainly, ma'am. I'm gra—" He didn't finish his sentence as a tall and handsome dark-skinned bellman entered our presence unexpectedly. "Dexter, what can I do for you?"

"The chairs we are to bring outside. Wood? Or pad—"

"The cushioned seats, Dexter. Only those."

The bellman tipped his brown Windsor Hotel cap with its gold embroidery and shiny black brim to us both and departed. "Ma'am, as soon as the parade is over, we'll examine every nook and cranny of this place and make sure everything's up to snuff. Don't forget, half the city will be outside our doors tomorrow. Not a one in. No disaster," Mr. Leland said cheerfully, reassuringly. "Now, wouldn't you care for a nice cup of tea?

# Sun @ 26° PISCES 12'04 (1899)

*O*n March 17, 1899, as the St. Patrick's Day Parade wound its way up Fifth Avenue, the Windsor hotel caught fire. In just ninety minutes the entire hotel was completely destroyed. Tragically, a disaster of some sort was what I had foreseen for this day, but never had I envisioned myself and Mrs. Brush being susceptible to it. The fact that I'd spent the entire night prior nauseating without knowing why, should have tipped me off. My ill stomach took so much of my time and attention that I had none left to unpack my luggage then. No chart calculations were needed to tell me that danger was forthcoming.

Everything happened so quickly. Alarm bells clanging. Flames and pandemonium everywhere. Fire escapes too hot to make use of. Normally able to see years into the distance, this time my eyes burned blind by searing smoke and scorching ashes. The bloodcurdling screams became deafening. Children to their mothers. Husbands to wives. Mrs. Brush to her Heavenly Protector. Never was I more engulfed by peril than those moments as I felt myself being herded away from a hotel on the verge of destruction. Fear consumed me, just as it did many times in childhood. Like then, I thought my life would soon end.

Although cut, scraped and existing in a nightmare, Mrs. Brush and I were two of the fortunate few. Located in rooms on only the second floor, and being situated nearest the front entrance, Mrs. Brush and I were able to escape relatively unhurt minutes after being evacuated. Unlike others, our luck provided me with that added insight to tote along my most valuable possessions upon exiting, my astrological paraphernalia. Mrs. Brush clutched onto her bible and never let go. We weren't able to observe much from the outside. Instead we were ushered away, far away from the mayhem. My instinct guided our feet to the somewhat nearby Continental Hotel.

Poor Mr. Leland. His daughter, Helen, never did make it to her twenty-first birthday the week later. Instead she perished after jumping from the sixth floor. Her body was so badly burned that Mr. Leland found it impossible to identify her.

About ninety people succumbed in all. This was indeed the worst hotel fire disaster in American history. More would have died had it not been for some of the off-duty firemen who happened to be marching in the parade on the avenue out front. At first investigation, it was believed that the fire was related to a theft that took place. But others alleged it was a lit match thrown from a second-story window that had blown backwards instead, causing lace curtains to ignite.

Dozens upon dozens of people were first reported missing. Spectators came from everywhere to view those wretched ruins. As firemen sifted through the rubble, Mrs. Brush and I sat as peacefully as possible in our new home away from home, the Continental. Neither of us being stable enough to remain alone, Mrs. Brush and I shared a lavish suite and did our best to comfort one another. Three dollars a night was worth the extravagant price to pay for our attempt at regained sanity. Little to no full sentences were exchanged the next morning as we anxiously dined at breakfast in the banqueting hall that resembled the interior of a French chateau. Raspberry jam, and scones with butter, for us both. I sipped my Indian black tea slowly as I contemplated my future in New York City. Was it the right move? A correct decision? Why was I spared? With such an inauspicious beginning, how could I not wonder? Perhaps divine destiny had granted me yet another second chance.

But I needed not ponder much longer. Copies of the morning's *New York Times* were delivered to us in the dining hall, and I placed mine down on the chair next to me, with the front page facing the stiff, cement-like cushion. Too much painful grief and misery to be reminded of so early in the day. Food would soothe me, I felt. But, with nearly hysteric exclamation, Mrs. Brush interrupted my meal by saying, "Mrs. Adams. You must see."

I expected another horror story related to the fire. But my eyes witnessed a headline that would end up catapulting me and my career into a yet unfamiliar sphere. Mrs. Brush removed the waving newspaper from my eyes and she began reading aloud.

*"'According to Mr. Leland, an astrologist, Evangeline Adams, had forecast the entire disaster to him, privately, only the day before'."*

I couldn't believe my ears. My hands picked up my copy of the paper, but Mrs. Brush proceeded with her recitation. *"Miss Adams was completely certain of impending doom, so close by, imminent. Danger near you in the place of your business, she had told me. She even mentioned my family. Danger to them as well. Miss Adams knew all this'."*

The headline in *The New York Times* would offer two articles of significance, I immediately imagined. The first was that people would see validity in my reading of palms; people of all types in a wide variety of locales. The second was that some skeptic might believe that I'd had something to do with creating the fire in order for my abilities to be proven accurate.

And indeed, some did speculate, especially those who not only dismissed palmistry and astrology, but those who felt hatred for it, associating it with witchcraft, demonology, evil. I was torn in my feelings. I felt nothing but sorrow for Mr. Leland and the losses he had to face, the losses of many others. But for better or for worse, my own fate had taken a turn that day as well. For Mr. Leland's mention of my name proved to be most providential to me, bringing next to all of New York's finest to my doorstep in one fell swoop.

☉　☽　★

"What's to become of these horoscope requests, ma'am?" my ever-dutiful Mrs. Brush asked, visibly reeling from the catastrophe by continuously constricting the slack that existed between her scalp and the tips of her hair.

"I still don't know how they all knew I was here. At the Continental."

The pandemonium of the previous days had spilled onto the aftermath of my newspaper mention by Mr. Leland. Mrs. Brush excused herself to her room next door to mine and returned with a copy of *The New York Times*, dated March 20, 1899.

"I think it's going to be in your best interest to read the news more regularly from now on, Mrs."

"What is it this time?"

Thumbing through the middle of the first section of the newspaper, Mrs. Brush focused on print too small for my eyes. Reading the bolder subject titles was easiest for me, words difficult to escape my vision. I saw two that were most noticeable. 'NO MORE DEATHS REPORTED' in one column on the left, and

'FUNERAL OF MRS. AND MISS LELAND' on the right. I hadn't known Mr. Leland's wife had died as well. How doubly sad. Twice the tragedy.

At the exact same time I found another title appearing in the middle column that read, 'REACHED STREET JUST IN TIME,' Mrs. Brush recited the typescript appearing below. *"Dr. Evangeline S. Adams of Boston and her private secretary, Mrs. Brush, who were reported missing, are safe and stopping at the Continental Hotel'."*

"Oh."

*"Mrs. Brush.* They mentioned *me,"* she said in awe.

"Yes. But now, people are going to think I'm a medical doctor."

"When we checked into the Windsor. Don't you remember what you'd told them? 'I'd done extensive work in homeopathy.' '*My* patients'."

Mrs. Brush hadn't quite yet learned the art of truth-stretching. Yes, I did work for two homeopaths in Boston, but Mrs. Brush and I'd just come from being expelled at the Astor House. I *had* to make myself look more credible, more respectable in front of Mr. Leland and his Windsor front desk staff.

"Let's get back to our chores at hand. Shall we?" Sifting through the stacks of correspondence one more time left me dizzy. "Yes, there *are* so many of them. Just like the Astor House, the management of the Continental here will soon demand our departure if my business creates a burden for them."

As my secretary and I plucked away at the requests by post, written on every kind of stationery imaginable, we also found ourselves besieged with visitors to the hotel, prospective clients who were never invited, sometimes making their way beyond the confines of the lobby. A multitude of strangers, mostly comprised of what seemed like fashionably clad and stylishly coiffed society doyennes, freely helped themselves to the knocker attached to the door of my room.

"This one, Mrs. Adams, comes all the way from California. Seeking a chart. It appears to be much like the rest. Shall I read it to you?"

"No, Mrs. Brush. These all have to be sorted out in the most strategic and fair fashion. There must be at least a hundred here alone."

My calculations were remarkably quite off though. If Mrs. Brush and I were to have counted the requests we would have cyphered into the night. Hundreds turned into thousands, and just as we both suspected, the owner of the Continental Hotel, Mr. H. S. Duncan, informed us that it would be in our best interest, as well as his, to seek a business location elsewhere.

After having scanned the terrain on foot for opportunities in mid-Manhattan, I sent a variety of follow-up appointment requests by post to about a dozen office building administrators. What a perfect spot midtown would be, the place where the best opportunities in town intersect. Well, that's how it also appeared in my chart—a most favorable location and the most favorable time to procure an office, indeed.

Mrs. Brush was eager to accompany me at our first scheduled meeting of the day in Murray Hill. But as we walked through the lobby of the Continental Hotel to exit, we encountered a woman outfitted in a variation of powder blues who must have been in her late-twenties.

Without a "hello" or "pardon me," the fair-headed woman stepped immediately before Mrs. Brush and demanded, "You must help me. I've been frantic for weeks. My husband—"

"*I* am Evangeline Adams. Is it I with whom you wish to speak?"

"Yes, oh…" Not even an apology to poor, startled and already- and always-fragile Mrs. Brush. "My husband, I'm certain of it, has developed interest in one of my closest friends. Highly inappropriate. You must tell me what you see in my future. Madame Lavinia, on West Eleventh in Greenwich Village, told me my husband will be apt to stray because his second toe is longer than his first."

Mrs. Brush and I just looked at each other in amazement. Not long after that Mrs. Brush glanced down at her own feet, covered in shoes, unseen corn pads underneath; perhaps pondering the length of her own toes and the peril that comes with disproportion.

The intrusive woman with her shrill voice, demonstrating nothing but fright like so many I've encountered before, looked at me as if insisting upon a reply.

"Maybe your husband should buy larger shoes because of his misshapen toes." I couldn't resist.

"You're not taking me seriously. You must help me. I am at my wit's end. What if he decides to leave me? I can't live without him. I do cherish him so. Please tell me my fortune, Miss Adams."

"But Mrs. Adams is not a fortuneteller, ma'am. She's an astrologer."

"My birthdate is December 12, 1875," the young woman said while patting the upper regions of her protruding stomach, making sure I'd notice the beads of iridescent aquamarine dangling from her wrist. "I pray every night to the Greek goddess Demeter that it's a boy."

Stomping my foot down, while still possessing enough fortitude to do so, I said, "Now's not the time, nor place. You can make an appointment if you like. I'd be happy to help you then. I'd also need to know your birth time and location of birth. We can take care of this later."

"But his toes say he'll cheat."

"I'll be able to tell you all you need to know about him and maybe even his toes. If you can come back to this hotel, I can see you before dinner at four in the afternoon."

Mrs. Brush and I seemed to find it more urgent than we thought to establish a suitable office environment. By the time we'd scoured the bulk of midtown Manhattan both our toes and feet were exhausted. All three of our morning meetings were brief; however, the slurs that building management spewed at Mrs. Brush and I not only dismayed, but entertained, us greatly.

The first, at a small, boutique-style building in the Murray Hill area: "No, no wizardry here. We go to the circus for that. Try the Village."

The second, a variety of warehouse spaces in seedy Hell's Kitchen. Two scurrying cockroaches on the floor made Mrs. Brush nearly faint. Still, we were unwelcomed within two minutes upon entering. "Witchcraft! This isn't Salem, ma'am. Be off. And take your broom with you."

We found no luck at the third, a small building close to Gramercy Park. But we were treated with respect during our visit, albeit a somewhat insulting respect. The young manager, a blond-haired man with perfectly round ringlets, greeted us with tea and biscuits, and said, "You know, I was told I was a trapeze artist in a former life. Men do it too, you know."

"Oh, I'm sure."

"By Countess Esmeralda. She hails from Transylvania. Front teeth filed down to a point. Maybe you know her."

"More than likely not," Mrs. Brush told the man. "Mrs. Adams doesn't consort with that type."

"What Mrs. Brush meant to say is that I'm seeking office space for my professional consulting business. It's quite different from…anything else."

"Oh, a consulting business. Many of our tenants here do that, I think. But I've never rented to a female businessman before."

"Correct me if I'm wrong, but that would make me a

business*woman*, now wouldn't i—"

"I've never heard that. Business*woman*. Clever. Did you coin that one yourself?"

Yes, what an entertaining day this was, to be sure. The young man, despite his impromptu faux pas, meant well when he told us that he couldn't accommodate our request for space. He even offered other solutions. "Greenwich Village is just the place for you," he exclaimed. No, it most certainly was not. Trying my best to distinguish myself, my astrology, from fortunetellers would do me no good if lived and worked immediately next door to them. Lower Manhattan, never.

"Hasn't Mr. Alexander been charming, Mrs. Brush? Thank you fo—"

"Oh, one more. Didn't you say you're also seeking a residence?"

"Correct. A residence *and* office space. Perhaps temporary. Until I relocate permanently from Boston. In a year or so."

"Carnegie Hall. Why didn't I think of this sooner?"

At that moment, had there been a bell inside me, it would have clanged. Although it made no sense, I had to ask, but Mrs. Brush beat me to it. "Carnegie Hall? That's a concert venue."

"Oh, it most certainly is. But it also possesses the choicest private artists' studios. Prestigious. With apartments attached. Musicians. Actors. Artists. What do you call what you do again? When you first walked in? *Cerebral* arts?"

"Celestial arts."

"I'm getting chills. You're a celestial artist. C'est une fait accompli."

Once we left the company of Mr. Alexander, something about the crazy notion of Carnegie Hall appealed to me. Worth checking into, I thought. Mrs. Brush found the concept to be too "Bohemian" and wanted no part of it.

☉ ☽ ★

Like career-driven Capricorns, though neither of us were, Mrs. Brush and I re-examined all options prior to our final appointment of the day close to Times Square. Having wearily strolled twenty-or-so blocks up Fourth Avenue, my eyes next became magnetic once they came upon a theatre marquee, and I don't know why exactly this occurrence struck me and my intuition so hard. Like a bolt of electric current. Right there, near the crossing of West 45th Street and Seventh Avenue, my sore feet were forced to stop directly in front of the Lyceum Theatre.

"Why are we pausing here, ma'am?"

"I'm not entirely certain."

Upon peering upward where my eyes were already focused, Mrs. Brush said, "Oh, what a coincidence. I have seen this myself. A pleasant production. It was in Chicago at the Schiller Theatre there in the late summer of '97."

"This was a novel first. Am I correct?"

"Yes, indeed, ma'am. Captain Charles King's novel…brought to the stage."

"*Fort Frayne*. Indians. The cavalry. Brawls and such."

"Yes, you may recall Mrs. Sutherland, the dramatic critic of *The Boston Journal*. She and another woman were responsible for the adaptation and subsequent production."

"I was introduced to her once, of course."

"The play's co-writer is a lovely and charming lady. I'd seen her in numerous dramas when she was an actress at the Boston Museum, Emma Sheridan."

Both my intuition and my curiosity drew me to look closer. I didn't know what made me focus so intently on not only this name but the woman herself, this woman of the theatre. "Emma

Sheridan. Yes, I've heard her name many times as well. She's no longer an actress?"

"No, she now writes. From what I'd read in *The Herald*, she retired from the stage shortly after marrying an engineer. She was exceptional, high spirited, kept me most entertained." Mrs. Brush smiled and shut her eyes. Fulfillment seemed to sweep over her being.

"Married, to an engineer. Well, maybe I'd like to experience this production."

"And I'd love to see it once more, Ma'am. Perhaps I'll accompany you."

The sight of that marquee, and the story that now surrounded it, left me as Mrs. Brush and I regained our pace en route to the intersection of Seventh Avenue and West 57th Street. Much too tardy now for our final appointment, and not wanting to yet again experience disasters like the previous, we decided to head directly to Carnegie Hall, even without a scheduled meeting. Once we arrived, my instinct told me that we'd found our home.

The seven-story brown structure with its few meek masonry steps, built eight years prior by Scot-American philanthropist Andrew Carnegie, was one I'd never really paid attention to. But, this time, I wanted to explore every inch of it, inside and out. We were shown three studios to let on the ground floor, but it was the first we were shown on the second that captured my attention most.

"This has five windows instead of three."

"Is five more fortunate for you, Miss Adams?"

"No. Not necessarily. I'm no numerologist, I'm an astrologer. Five windows allow more light in than three."

"Yes, of course."

Actually, it was Mrs. Brush that did the window counting. She brought it to my attention while I was being given statistics related to interior square footage. Our new studio at 200 Carnegie Hall provided ample room for a secretary's station, a welcoming waiting area and a quiet and private office from which I could create charts. My fee of five dollars was somewhat high for a half-hour session, but it sufficiently paid the higher rent that would be assessed for such a convenient space.

Before long the contract was signed. I'd made perfectly clear the actions I would be undertaking as a consulting celestial artist. The management officer of the Hall, a tired looking older gentleman with bluish bags under his eyes, made clear that as long as payments were made timely and dutifully, gestured no complaints. I assured him that all business conducted by us would be thoroughly professional. All was now complete for me to grow my business into an endeavor of hopeful significance.

⊙　☽　★

"I'm not an astrologist. Not even a palmist, Ma'am. But don't you think the fire at the Windsor may have been an evil omen?" Mrs. Brush inquired that night as we packed our bags, preparing to check out and move into Carnegie Hall the next morning. "Recalling it, having to rush away in such haste, gives me shivers."

"You see it as inopportune. With regard to our departure. I see it as providing my calling with an open invitation to success. Without Mr. Leland's proclamation, none of these requests for my services would have manifested."

"Mrs., the tragedy of it all. Injuries, deaths. Gives me nothing but bad dreams. We could have easily succumbed alongside the others."

"But we did not. Don't you see it as part of our destinies that we escaped such plight? I most certainly do. I feel the heartbreaking losses. The calamity of it all. I feel them deeply and I have sorrow for those left without their loved ones. But I'd be a fool not to recognize good fortune. Mr. Leland and what he had said thrust my destiny into an immediate and easily accessible spotlight."

"I see omens and you see life in the limelight."

"I see good fortune for you as well, Mrs. Brush. It's your choice if you'd like to share in the beam of my spotlight...or fear it."

"Fear. You had told me once before that Virgos innately feel more fear than others. I must correct you, Mrs. I am *not* afraid."

I knew after this brief exchange that I must reexamine Mrs. Brush's chart. At that moment, I understood a bit more clearly what some of those positions truly meant. The transits and progressions, her upcoming Saturn Return crossing paths with her inflexibilities and reluctance to change. Not at all easy for her. Her routines, her lifestyle not necessarily meshing with *my* goals. Her husband in Boston. Her time with me might be coming to an end within a short period.

But after conducting a full examination of my chart compared to Mrs. Brush's, I tossed my conclusions aside. It became clear that, despite Mrs. Brush's planetary configurations, it was *I* who needed to exercise patience. Compassion. Some people possess more fear than others. Mrs. Brush was delightfully efficient and dutiful, a superb worker. These were all standard traits of a Virgo sun person, but they might also be qualities that Mrs. Brush had cultivated on her own, manufactured. I'd always believed that each and every fear within us has been learned—that not a solitary one is present at birth.

In little time, Mrs. Brush and I created an office and living space at 200 Carnegie Hall. The delivery of my cherished vintage carved rosewood rococo parlor table I used for my desk, complete with a framed photo of Mother atop, made my untested workspace familiar to me. Our new environs ended up being most suitable and pleasing, except for the constant cloud of cigarette smoke coming from the tuba, oboe and saxophone players in 202. Not once though did I allow their addiction to overshadow mine—antiquing. Nothing brought me greater joy than discovering treasures cast aside, then making practical use of them once more. Being able to fill my apartment and studio with vintage furnishings and porcelain elephants satisfied me deeply.

Much work lay before me; scheduling office hours, selecting stationery, setting prices as we began sorting the many postal requests for charts. Two topics dominated the interests of my clients: love and money. Never have I been one to divulge identities, but a sampling of the questions I received are as follows: *What is the best time to create a child? What is the best time to marry? When will I find my true love? Was I wrong to decline that proposal of marriage? Will we have enough money to purchase a country home?*

Another topic, of course, found its way to my eyes: health. Although I'd learned much from my previous employer, homeopath and unprofessed visionary Dr. Adams in Westborough, Mass.—no relation to John and John Quincy—and the way he approached medicine via the assistance of astrology, I was no doctor. Reminding my clients of this was always of paramount importance to me. I did feel that astrology could help though.

For the majority of these requests sitting before us, we first sent out a postcard telling of the cost involved and a brief statement removing liability in the case of clients who were chronically ill. To my surprise though, Mrs. Brush placed one request on top of the stack.

"You would be wise to read this one now, Mrs."

The envelope was already opened, and at first glance I saw everything I needed in order to proceed. Day, time and place, in addition to the fee of five dollars. In this letter, a woman mentioned being quite ill with a blood disorder. She had seven children, with the youngest being eleven months and the oldest nine years. Her husband was deceased. She wanted to know if, not when, she would become well again.

"How sad, Mrs. Brush."

"Did you see the blotches there?" Mrs. Brush said, pointing to certain smeared areas of dried text, touching its texture briefly.

"Yes."

"Those must be from her tears." Upon saying those words, Mrs. Brush began to tear up herself. "In what way will you reply, ma'am?"

"Well, yes, I'll surely go to my desk now and cast this woman's chart first."

Only a few minutes were needed. Yes, so very sad indeed. From the facts I was able to gather, I could foretell that this woman had already died two days earlier; July 07, 1899 at 2:31AM. In the brief time that had passed, having dispatched the post from Missouri to New York, this woman had crossed over. How quickly the tide can turn made me recall that violent dream I'd had aboard the train. Mrs. Brush, looking just as panicky as when she'd awoken me then, came into my office to hear my results.

"Please do send these five dollars back, Mrs. Brush. Along with my deepest condolences."

"Oh, so tragic. Poor children…though they'll be divinely provided for," Mrs. Brush said, while making the sign of the cross with her right hand just above her heart.

This was a view I could never comprehend, what was divinely provided for. What can be understood is what the stars have in store, the free will we possess and how it affects our destiny. But the ways in which the Almighty intervenes is a concept that left even me baffled. Speaking to clergy had led me nowhere, since every member I'd ever sought out had refused interaction with me.

This was what upset me most, for my beloved astrology to be confused with demonology, in addition to me time and time again being written off. How very unfair.

Trying to bring hope to those who had lost it, I believed, would be doing what God had intended for me in my time on this earth. With my devout faith in the infallibility of the stars, I doubted I could extend the forecasted date of my departure, and so I must endeavor to accept it and make best use of what's left. The goal bred my own brand of faith inside myself and there's nothing immoral about that.

# Sun @ 26° CAPRICORN 56'51 (1901)

"*M*rs. Adams, there is a messenger in the waiting area and he's most eager to speak with you personally."

"Did he tell you why?"

"He won't say a word. He told me he was instructed...by someone else to speak with you only. The gentleman appears quite refined, makes a very fashionable impression."

"I'm in the middle of a chart at this moment. Please inform him that he can meet with me in ten minutes time for about five."

Before exiting my office, Mrs. Brush stroked her index finger sideways upon the area between her upper lip and beneath her nose just like a telegraph signal, intended for me to notice without a word having to be spoken. Once again the beet-juice and ginger vibrancy tonic I'd discovered in Chinatown had left its indelible mark on the hair above my lips. Having stained my mouth red so frequently, sometimes I just left the residue, assuming people would think it to be cosmetic lip rouge. The proof of the Oriental concoction's life-affirming attributes though, was yet to be seen;

still I sought to extend my projected lifespan during my fleeting moments of whimsy.

My mood that day was not the most courteous or inviting, mainly because of having eaten beef too rare the night prior. Being forced to dispose of belches underneath my breath began to take its toll on my patience. As usual, I focused on completing the chart before me, and calculated the most favorable time for a woman to seek a husband, a chore I seemed to have been doing daily, something I didn't ever seem to weigh up for myself, pursuing a mate. No time for that. No interest. If the truth be told, now that the calendar pushed me beyond my thirtieth—yes, I had to admit it—year, my professional goals came before all else. Just as my chart had indicated many years earlier, my age itself combined with my unmarried status now demonstrated that, indeed, I'd unlikely bear children.

The days of my entertaining suitors, as few as there were, had ended in my twenties. Once my heart recognized its calling, while under the tutelage of Dr. Smith in Boston, I knew that my life would be consumed by nothing but astrology. Those first forecasts, proven correct later on, were the only validation I needed for me to realize that I was on a path that would lead to great fortune. I knew even in my earlier years that spending an afternoon, an evening, in the company of a man only wasted my time. How could I achieve greatness if I were attached to a man who would want me to fulfill only traditional feminine duties? How could I focus on creating success if, as society believed, I was supposed to be spending all my time seeking a husband?

"Mrs. Brush, this one's ready to go out. I'll see the gentleman now. Please send him in," I said through the open door.

A young man of twenty-or-so years, with his edgy jawline and dimpled chin, entered my office, his shined black boots illuminating the floor beneath them. His entire appearance was regal and he spoke with eloquent diction. To most women that write to me, this man would be a most appealing prospective husband.

"Please do have a seat, sir."

"Thank you. You are Miss Evangeline Adams?"

"Yes, that's correct. And, you? What is it you wish to tell me?"

"My name is Mr. O'Malley. And I am the courier to a rather, let's say, prominent financier in the commercial sector downtown. May I ask you a few questions?"

"Questions? I thought you'd be delivering information unto me."

"I understand you are very busy with your work, but I have only a few queries. I respect your time. You'll, of course, be paid for this conversation."

Quick on the mark, my mind calculated the sum total of "prominent financier" + well-dressed courier + "paid for this conversation," prompting me to say, "My fee for a half hour is twenty dollars," a figure equaling four times my standard fee.

"Oh, I'll provide you with one hundred dollars for a much briefer amount of your time."

The man's words became music to my ears. They could hardly wait to hear more. "That's certainly agreeable to me. Please then, go right ahead."

"These services that you provide, are they specific to one area or another? Love? Money? Travel?"

"It's the client who poses questions. I look for times that are most favorable or least favorable to undertake certain endeavors."

"And you do this while looking at the palm of one's hand."

"Also, the stars. In terms of somewhat specific times, I find that creating an astrological chart is most accurate."

"Do you happen to be working for any clients in the financial district at the moment? Financial experts?"

"No, not experts. I provide information having to do with finances, but not necessarily financial speculation for those who are experts."

"My employer would like to meet with you, on a trial basis."

"That's no problem whatsoever. He's welcome to come for an appointment anytime. Perhaps—"

"Oh, no, ma'am. That wouldn't be possible. You must come to him."

"To *him*? I'm sorry, but that's not feasible for me. I'd have to transport papers, my tools, books."

The young man smiled benevolently. "This gentleman is well aware of that, ma'am. He'll certainly make it more than worth your while."

"This is all so mysterious. Who is this man? And where is he located? You haven't yet been able to identify either of these. *Where* downtown?"

"Mr. is located on Wall Street and he will pay you five times your rate for travel from midtown to downtown once and once again for the return to your studio. In addition to this, he'll be paying you five times your rate for the consultation."

"If I my calculations are correct that's three hundred dollars."

"Gratuity not included, ma'am."

I'm not usually provided one. "Oh, but yes, the gratuity. Of course."

This person who had invited me should have been a writer of mystery novels, because my curiosity had become thoroughly aroused. My knowledge of Wall Street and its inhabitants was lacking, but I could most certainly suppose. Money made the proposition appealing. Becoming familiar with another segment of the community as well. Clout. Credibility. Cachet. Not to mention the fourth 'C,' "cash." The harmonious sound of all four 'Cs' combined was like the cha-ching of the cashbox at Chase National.

From the trifling few hundred I had been earning in the backrooms of Boston, to the modest-to-medium income now in the low thousands I was bringing in at my studio, will in no way compare to the future prosperity I'll capture from the banking sector, I imagined. This magnate with whom I was yet to be acquainted could be my invitation to a life that only, thus far, existed in my dreams.

"Ma'am, I'll need to know your decision. Mr. is awaiting an entry into his appointment calendar. He is quite a busy man, to be sure."

"This afternoon could be a possibility."

"Miss, his schedule books two to three weeks in advance. He was thinking two weeks from today, after lunch, three o'clock or thereabouts. If that suits your timetable."

As if via a telepathic observation, Mrs. Brush knocked upon my door. Rather than the two-to-three sort, this knock lasted a full five seconds.

"Yes, Mrs. Brush."

With her paranoid raw nerves and bugged-out eyes in full view, my secretary blurted out, "A matter that requires your expedient attention, ma'am. Here…in front of me. Paperwork. Critical paperwork. Documentation needing your signature."

I humored Mrs. Brush, mostly in an effort to discover her hidden agenda and to prevent her from doing further damage to her already pockmarked face. Politely, diplomatically I said, "Will you please excuse me for a brief moment, sir."

Departing my office seemed somewhat inappropriate. What could be so urgent? What could possibly be more important that three hundred dollars? I must speak to Mrs. Brush one day regarding the correct orders of procedure, I thought.

"What is it you find so pressing?"

"Mrs., have you examined this man's credentials in the most

thorough manner?"

"No. I assumed you did."

"I saw nothing. I examined nothing. He could be a complete and utter fraud. Out for no good. An imposter leading you astray. His looks are alien."

"Mrs. Brush, did you remember to take your anti-anxiety elixir this morning?"

"Ma'am," she hissed. "This possible charlatan could be leading you down a veritable path of doom and destruction. Here in New York, lunatics are known to wander the streets with hopes of luring the most unsuspecting."

This time the succession of rapid fire whacks came from the reverse side. It was Mr. O'Malley who did the knocking. Much more acutely, succinctly and loudly than Mrs. Brush. I shuddered to think that he'd heard a word of what Mrs. Brush and I had spoken to each other. Perhaps I should have practiced whispering more often, and tested it thereafter.

"Come in. I mean, please do enter," I said.

Mr. O'Malley looked dismayed. The impatient and twisted contortion he now wore on his face made him appear twice less attractive than when he arrived. A mean grimace took over his lips.

"Mr. is a busy man, a rather impatient one, and has no time for those who question his stature or moral make."

Nothing Mrs. Brush could have told me would have dissuaded me away from three hundred dollars spent for a paltry few minutes with me. Still, to humor her, I said, "I beg your pardon. Please demonstrate that you or he will be able to pay me as prescribed."

"I won't demonstrate what I can do. I'll therefore do it. Here is the three hundred dollars, minus the gratuity. Does this convince you of the legitimacy of my calling?"

As I seized the money from Mr. O'Malley's hands, almost playfully, I began to count it immediately. I nearly felt like a child, one that grabs onto the brass ring of a carousel effortlessly without having to lean over. Luck was mine; no more iron rings. I had never seen hundred dollar notes before. One. Two. Three. I relished this sensation very much, much more than I ever thought I would. And there'd be a gratuity as well? My, my.

"You can carry on, Mrs. Brush. I'll be making this appointment myself with much pleasure. Which is the best time exactly two weeks from today? Three? Four? Two-thirty?" My speech was now in a race with my dreams. Eagerness led me to say, "Or even sooner. I find myself to be a morning person. Is he as well?"

"Well, the Stock Exchange commences precisely at eight o'clock. Mr. often partakes in the ritual of the morning bell, you know."

"Oh, the bell. That's wonderful. How much time after…that? I can be available all day."

"Again, after lunch is best, ma'am. If lunch involves a few libations, Mr. will be your most agreeable client. That's a certainty."

"Three it is. You give me the address and I'll be certain to be there."

⊙　☽　✶

I never did find out the identity of this mister with the bell from the courier; it was only the day before our arranged meeting that I learned his illustrious identity. My frenzied imagination took me all the way to heaven and back during the hours that preceded three o'clock. Steam yachts in Nantucket Sound, an Oriental excursion, a canvas-back duck dinner at Delmonico's; not a single luxury was disregarded inside my head.

The carriage ride down Seventh Avenue would be uneventful and calm, I assumed; I don't think I heard a single word its driver told me. But just as I was in the middle of imagining a way to open a Swiss bank account without having to actually be in Geneva, a thick, grainy wad of spit from a grey mare next to us traveling in an uptown direction landed on my face. Reality had just slapped me. Disgusting. Humiliating.

"Driver. Young man, please let me off at once," I insisted as I reached for any available handkerchief inside my handbag.

"But this is Chambers Street, ma'am."

"Yes. Fine. At once." How utterly horrid. As I wiped off the last glob of mucousy brown slop, the carriage stopped and I got out. I could barely find space to walk. Rather than putting the rag back into my bag, I let it drop onto the already grime-laden street below.

Downtown was bustling with activity. Passersby, smartly dressed for business appointments, were much too preoccupied with stocks, bonds, commodities and such to notice my slimy mishap. Wall Street and its environs had always possessed a strange allure for me, so utterly unlike midtown and its predictability.

In front of the New York Stock Exchange, the people coming and going gave me a thrill unlike anything I'd ever known. As they scampered about to complete transactions, not a single soul seemed to take note of the impressive statue of George Washington across the street at Federal Hall—one of America's first capitals. Inside the Hall's Greek Parthenon-replicated exterior, Washington was sworn in as first President, John Adams as first Vice-President. I felt myself needing to view this statue up close. As my fingers touched the raised bronze letters, "Sculpted by John Quincy Adams Ward," on the plaque below the statue, chills ran up and down my spine. Somehow I just knew that I was in the right place at the right time.

Since I was a child I'd wanted to experience this rush of adrenaline, something I was never allowed to do, nor felt worthy of. My feet took me on a tour of this place I knew I belonged. Wall

Street, I could feel, would soon craft my fortune.

The massively sturdy granite structure with its few windows, known as "The Corner," addressed at Twenty-three Wall Street was immediately before me, but I was still one hour early.

Spontaneity, next, guided my feet to see with my own eyes Lady Liberty, the one-hundred-fifty-one foot tall neoclassical gift from France everyone was still discussing. Dedicated on October 28, 1886; a Scorpio. I strolled over to the harbor through Bowling Green onto Battery Park, and from there I had an unobstructed view. Lady Liberty was larger than life. A symbol of all of America. Liberty and freedom; the calling cards to our illustrious country.

The immigrant experience and its hardships were something my family knew quite well; my father, mother and brothers had come to Jersey City from Andover, Massachusetts before I was born. Father's hopes were high for a fresh start; manufacturing paper railroad-car wheels was his dream. Then I came into this world unexpectedly, the funds disappeared, and Father died well before I'd reached my second birthday.

Was it my extra mouth to feed that put us under? Some would say that the guilt I felt caused the lengthy illnesses to which I succumbed as a child; never precisely diagnosed, but forever hospitalized. Our move back to Massachusetts after Father's death was, predominantly, for one reason. "That's where Adamses belong," Mother said. Although only an Adams by marriage, Mother held our birthright dear; it gave her hope, a presumed leg up from those named Smith or Jones. I was reminded of this constantly.

Gazing at the clock on the tower nearby made me realize that I'd have to quicken my step if I wanted to appear at 23 Wall Street on time. Being the daughter of parents educated at Phillips and Dartmouth, not to mention being an Adams, I did my best to act according to what my upbringing, my heritage dictated. Literate, respectable people are always punctual, never late.

The reception gallery of the building was magnificent, as if the entirety of it belonged in a European museum containing the finest works of the Post-Renaissance. The art pieces housed therein were exquisite; each with a white and black identification label underneath, educating passersby like me, art lovers by proxy, those least in-the-know. My eyes gazed upon *The Adoration of the Magi* by Giotto di Bondone, *The Battle of Issus* by Albrecht Altdorfer and *Figure of the Heavenly Bodies* by Bartolomeu Velho, all side by side. "I have an appointment at three o'clock with a Mister John Pierpont Morgan."

"You are Miss Evangeline Adams?"

"I am indeed."

"Please proceed to the top floor where you'll be escorted to Mr. Morgan's private suite."

What was the make of this man? And what exactly did he want with me? Soon I'd find out. As I made my way through the four-story Morgan Building, a fortress-like structure known by the locals as the House of Morgan, my palms began to sweat. I didn't want to get my scaled-down pile of reference books soggy, so I wiped my hand upon my conservative dark-grey tweed suit while no one was looking. Adjusting my black silk cravat removed the remaining moisture from my fingertips. I'd worn my favorite rose-colored pin with opaque cameo pierced through it, delicately indicating femininity in a neighborhood where all women were either administrative staff or visitors. Wall Street was a man's world and the musty air that surrounds it could have very well been caused by the disproportionate, detectable levels of testosterone.

At the end of a long, art-filled hallway, I found a waiting area as grand as the lobby of the old Windsor. May she rest in peace.

"Please make yourself comfortable, Ma'am. Would you like me to hold your...material—" A youthful red-headed, rail-thin secretary appeared before me. Face, body and haute couture that, all put together, resembled those belonging to a French fashion model.

"Oh, definitely not. Not necessary at all, but thank you just the same. I am Miss Evangeline Adams here to see—"

"Yes, ma'am. Mr. Morgan has been anxious to meet you. As far as I can tell, he's never encountered a woman such as yourself before. Mr. Morgan finds such pleasure in trying out new things."

'Trying out new things?' What was I...a chemistry experiment? New Yorkers were undoubtedly a bit different from Bostonians; they didn't seem to embarrass easily after revealing their offensiveness.

"Please, if you will, take a seat over there. Mr. Morgan will be with you shortly," the office assistant said, as I passed inspection, now for the second time. My decision to dress less heterogeneously, as I do for my in-studio clients, and more "financial" for Wall Street, was indeed the right one.

On every wall, it appeared, was a family tree of each and every Morgan that had ever lived. Most with the first name of John. I wonder which edition John Pierpont was within the Morgan lineage. The world of finance surely was an idiosyncratic one, something I knew little about. Stocks, bonds, commodities. Buying, selling. A bear market, a bull market. No, nothing much about it captivated me.

Plenty of time had come and gone since I first sat down. Perhaps close to one half hour. Endless amounts of minutes for me to sit daydreaming about things I'd never understand. I much preferred my time staring in wonderment at the Statue of Liberty. The water in the harbor soothing my Pisces rising, the air above it satiating my Aquarius sun. Calmness had taken over me until I heard someone, a male voice, blaring like a bullhorn or perhaps a subdued Coney Island barker.

"We cannot have it. Not again. Re-think your proposal then get back to me."

I could hear no response. Perhaps the recipient of the lashing had none, or wasn't allowed one. Then the bullhorn voice, a bit more hushed, muttered something to the woman who'd greeted me, then disappeared into an office. "No. Not today. Out of the question," he commanded, as if through a brick wall.

The door to the interior office opened and the same blood red-headed secretary approached me with an envelope in her hand. "Miss Adams, I'm terribly sorry. I realize you've come from midtown and your time and travel here is most appreciated, but Mr. Morgan is unable to see you today after all. Please take this."

I accepted what the woman had offered me. I didn't bother looking inside. "I take it this is compensation for my time."

"Yes. Mr. Morgan would like to reschedule his appointment with you at your convenience."

"Tomorrow? Is that a possibility?"

"Let me check and confirm with you," the woman said, stepping to the desk and glancing into her calendar. "Closer to mid-morning will be most suitable. Ten-thirty. May he see you then?"

"Ten-thirty is fine."

"Your transport will be summoned and waiting for you at your studio one half hour prior. You'll be recompensed the same for your journey and services when you arrive. Until then, a pleasant day to you."

The mystery of it all mesmerized my senses immensely. As I left the Morgan private office, instead of exiting the building, I approached what I'd assumed was a little-used, out of the way stairwell behind what I thought was a storeroom door. There, absent from any onlookers, I opened up the envelope and inside were five one hundred dollar notes. Paid so handsomely for having done absolutely nothing! And, the same the very next day. What a whirlwind discovery this financial district had been for me. Covering up this money and placing it into my modest brown crocodile tote satchel became my top priority.

Again, taking myself off-course on purpose led me to more discoveries. The exterior façades housing the offices of Charles Schwab containing Germanic gothic spires, the more modernistic-looking E.F. Hutton building with its abundance of silver-toned right angles and back to the entrance of the New York Stock Exchange again. A fantasyland for those who cherished money and where it's kept, where it's made and multiplied. So disposable. Yes, most intriguing. Never before had I given so much thought to the many things I could soon procure. Travel. A country home. The finest of clothes.

Somehow, at the corner of Wall St. and Broadway, my carriage ride north was tardy. Waiting and staring was all I could do. Through the fence to the Trinity churchyard there and its hollowed out white gravel pathways before me, I read the gravestones of those I could clearly see. In the dismal wintry setting of bare-limbed Bradford Pear trees and brown lawns, I noticed ice. Cold, frozen-over tundra formed by the lack of steady sunlight. The specifics of the signage were indistinguishable, but one term was repeated over and over, the word "rest," on a good variety of the granite slabs.

John Winthrop Chanler. U.S. Congressman, b. September 14, 1826 d. October 19, 1877. Age: 51. Charlotte Milton Thornberry, Socialite, b. March 21, 1763 d. May 26, 1795. My age exactly. Emeline Fletcher Jones, Rest in peace. b. April 01, 1804 d. July 19, 1833. Three years younger than me. For the second time, chills ran up my spine, while my left eye began to twitch.

Wall St. and its possibilities consumed my attention for the duration of my return trek to 200 Carnegie Hall. My mind was anything but at rest.

"How serious you look, Mrs.," Mrs. Brush told me. "Why are you in such a hurry?"

"Much to do. Much to accomplish…before it's too late. Tomorrow mid- to late-morning, do I have an opening?"

"What a coincidence, Ma'am. There was but one appointment then. At ten-thirty and the young woman just now cancelled."

"Back to Mr. Morgan's office. Please schedule no one here. I'll be most indisposed."

# Sun @ 18° AQUARIUS 33'32 (1901)

"*M*r. Morgan will see you now. Please follow me to his study. May I bring you a cup of tea?"

"Heavens no. Venom. Nothing shortens one's life more than caffeine," my heavy-handed internal voice said, while meekly my mouth uttered, "Oh…no thank you. The effects of caffeine alter my judgment, impair my sensitivities. Maybe just half a cup."

Of course I never drank tea anymore. Roasted-grain Postum had become my new brewed beverage of choice. Still, etiquette guided me to accept the Paragon gold Fleur de Lis teacup containing Earl Grey White graciously, while afterwards pouring it into the potted palm when the secretary's eyes were far from view. Thinking about the prospect of drinking it already made me jittery.

Walking down the hallway, carpeted in crimson, beyond the reception area was like taking a stroll through the Great Hall of the Metropolitan Museum of Art. Every artist known to mankind, from van Gogh to Gauguin, from da Vinci to Degas, from Monet to Matisse, was displayed on the walls. The frescos there contained every pigment of the rainbow. In every corner was a statue depicting the most notable of Greeks and Romans. I sat on a red velvet divan and I felt most regal. What an ill-fated time though for my dyspepsia to be flaring up. I knew I should have taken lesser portions of cabbage last dinner. Oh, the consequences of my taste buds' desire for Germanic cuisine.

Crossing my legs tightly was the only solution. How much must I wait this time? Any much longer and I'd have to reschedule the meeting myself. Fortunately, not having to linger at length, the woman entered and invited me even further into the fortress. "Mr. Morgan will greet you now," announced the secretary.

Lifting my papers, tool and books, my ephemeris slipped from the pile and landed on the marble floor before me. As I bent over to pick it up a bit of air passed from my posterior, but, thankfully no one noticed. "Excuse me. I don't usually carry these around with me."

The woman only nodded and, like a tour guide with index fingers pointing forward, delivered me unto Mr. Morgan's office. The grand stained-glass doors opened and there he was, looking rather dyspeptic himself. I wondered if he'd eaten cabbage the night before as well.

The gentleman before me didn't rise immediately. Instead he examined me. From head to toe. Then, from toe to head. Was I welcomed by him? Or not?

Seconds of silence passed as I caught this fellow staring at my faint moustache while I couldn't help but gaze at his purple nose and flushed cheeks. "You're the seer. Imogene Adams?" he asked.

"Yes, I am, Sir. Well, to be most accurate, my name is Evangeline Adams and I'm not necessarily a seer."

"You're not? I was told—"

"I'm an astrologer and a palmist."

Mr. Morgan scrunched up his face like an ecru-hued, prickly

wad of paper made from ticker tape and said, "No matter. Take a seat and we'll get things underway."

Without asking any further questions, I merely followed his lead. Somehow my instinct told me that I was in the company of an Aries man. Commanding, impatient, impulsive, insensitive, bold, selfish, domineering and highly outspoken. It was all too obvious. The positive character traits of the first of the zodiac's twelve signs, Aries—clever, courageous, dynamic and romantic—were still to be detected. Feeling a sudden bout of bloat coming upon me, I abruptly switched positions in my seat one, two, three times. "Yes," I said. "Let's. Please, where and when were your born?"

"Do you need a cushion? What in blazes is wrong with you?"

"I'm merely excited to meet you, Sir. Please, when and where were your born?"

"Why?"

"That's vital to my forecasting. The date, time and place of one's birth. This is why I'm here, isn't it?"

"Seventeenth of April. Hartford, Connecticut." He smoothed his fingers over his eyebrows, a habit to which I'd become reasonably familiar in a matter of a meagre few minutes.

"I'll also be needing the birth time and year."

"1837. The time? Why on earth would you need that?"

"Precise planetary configurations, of course. It's most essential, Sir."

Abruptly, but so timely, a barely audible knock came on the door. Before the series of three knocks had completed, Mr. Morgan bellowed out, "Yes?"

Through the keyhole of the closed door whispered a soft but authoritative female voice, "Three in the morning, Sir. Precisely at three."

Since Mr. Morgan did not respond, I said, "Thank you," to the anonymous eavesdropper.

"I now have all I need to know. If I may sit at that empty desk to make the necessary calculations?"

"Yes. Well, then. If you're going to do that, then I'm going to do this," he said, opening up a copy of *The Wall Street Journal.*

Neatly, and yet most precisely, I looked up the birth data in my ephemeris, a publication akin to the Farmer's Almanac, a veritable must-read for any astrologer. Since J.P. Morgan was a man of obvious fame, much of what I was discovering, scientifically, had already been known to me. For the next ten to fifteen minutes I calculated and constructed a biography that would make even the most accomplished man green with envy. At the same time, as happens with everyone, I saw misfortune. In addition, through the pages of this document that provide the positions of astronomical objects in the sky at a given time I discovered a concealed gem. Luckily, Mr. Morgan's ascendant was in Aquarius, conjunct my Aquarius sun; an unlikely but most welcomed bond between us, an astrological crisscrossing that breeds trust. He should listen to what I have to tell him with very little skepticism, I presupposed. Gathering up my paperwork, I prepared my presentation to Mr. Morgan inside my mind.

"Shall we commence, Mr. Morgan?"

"No, not right now. I'm in the middle of some numbers. Give me a few more minutes."

I did. Mr. Morgan was living up to his impatient Aries-sun "My-concerns-take-precedence-over-yours" profile perfectly. Perhaps I was the one who needed to exercise a tad more leniency.

As I obeyed my orders to tolerantly wait like a schoolchild ready for recess, my eyes drifted to a grand discovery: one of the finest pieces of polished-pinewood furniture in the office, positioned in an unobtrusive, dimly lit corner. The stunning longcase clock, an antique Comtoise from France, most likely from the late-seventeenth century, stood at least eight-feet tall.

The intricate ornamentation in its center depicted a delicate countryside or farm-like scene in rich green, red, silver and bronze tones.

The homesickness I suddenly felt nearly stole my breath. Oh, how I longed to return to my history, my time past, in Boston. The soothing sight of the River Charles as it flows under the Longfellow Bridge before emptying into the harbor, the streams of fashionable New Englanders strolling through Copley Marketplace during springtime to purchase red tulips and yellow marigolds, not to mention a few salty taste treats. The office where I'd apprenticed under straightforward Dr. J. Heber Smith, the man who'd cared for me while I was so ill in my adolescence. If time permitted, I'd visit the mental hospital where I trained under empathetic Dr. George Adams in Westborough, casting charts for his patients. Perhaps even a visit with Mother and, what I can only imagine to be, her inadvertent nonchalance towards me and my work, at our modest Beacon Hill abode, before she passed on. Home.

Much of me sensed that when I reappeared in Boston with Mrs. Brush, she'd not return to New York in my company. Inside the back of my head I'd always felt that…and her chart had said something to that effect as well. New York, it seemed the signs were telling me, was still the place of daydreams for me. My reality lay to the north.

While having thought about where I'd come from, I glanced over at Mr. Morgan who was still deciphering his numbers, perhaps as I did. "May I?" I asked as my hands grasped the handles of the plush seat that contained me.

Mr. Morgan motioned with his own for me to proceed to the window where I was already headed. From it, imagining it to be Boston Harbor, was a view that resembled Monet's *The Seine at Giverny*, scenery that must have been created to take one's breath away. There she was once more, though this time marred by obstruction but from a more flattering angle, Lady Liberty, with her torch outstretched. "Amazing," I said, not realizing my utterance was aloud.

"New Jersey?" Mr. Morgan was looking up from his paper.

"Oh, my no. The Statue. What a glorious welcome she must provide for those seeking better."

"Opportunities come to those who work hard. Endless hours of devotion to success and attainment."

Mr. Morgan's response brought me back to the task at hand. With authority, I walked back to the more inferior, much smaller, what seemed like a padded secretarial seat across from his mighty brown leather Larkin Morris Royal chair with dark quarter sewn oak armrests and said, "May we now begin, Sir?"

Placing the newspaper upon his desk without re-folding it first, Mr. Morgan said nippily, "Yes, this is what I've been waiting for. Let's get to it."

"Well, I must say, there are many favorable opportunities coming to you and your company. In a very, very short time you will be engineering a coupling, a merger of gargantuan scale. I see one industry, but two independent companies, coming together to form one. I see it creating, what looks to be, the largest corporation in this country and it will make you more prosperous than you've ever imagined. Your first effort though, that you believe to be securely structured, an agreement, will fail at the last minute. It's the second that will succeed. All having to do with a metal and a non-metal, iron and carbon...steel."

Comatose would have been the most correct way to describe Mr. Morgan in my presence. Staring at me as if his eyes were paralyzed. Crossed limbs strangling his circulation. Expressionless, like an insecure apprentice actor playing King Richard III once he's put upon a stage for the very first time. Then, he began shaking his head. After that, back to paralysis again. I'd not go on until I heard a reaction of some sort. Certainly I didn't want to shock the man into a state from which he could not return. Next, I recalled the numerous occasions he'd made me wait.

"The time when this is most favorable being next year. The first attempt I mentioned will begin to take shape in the latter part of this year. It will also involve someone near me, connected to me, where my business is conducted. I'm not entirely positive, but I believe it to be Mr. Andrew Carnegie. Have you accordingly met with him?"

Now, Mr. Morgan scowled. "Who have you been talking to? Who have you told that you and I will meet here today? You must have spoken to one of your neighbors there. Carnegie?"

"I do not know Mr. Carnegie, Sir. I only rent out the space there...for my work. I speak to no one there. Only my secretary and your messenger knew of this meeting."

"That'll be all. Thank you very much for coming here today, for your services. Mrs. Lukens will pay you on your way out." Mr. Morgan then used his appendages to speak for himself. Like a dust broom he swiftly brushed me out the entrance with his left hand. Just as I was about to close the door to his office behind me, I heard, "Halt!" My feet froze. Without moving an inch, there I stood as Mr. Morgan re-opened the door. "One more thing," he said, while ushering me back into his office, this time securing the deadbolt afterwards. Towards the hidden Comtoise clock we crept, away from the prying ears and eyes of the keyhole.

"What is it...you'd like to know, Sir?"

In a hushed voice softer than I knew he was capable of producing, Mr. Morgan asked, "Tea. Is it true? What you told Mabel?"

Appearing to be the all-seeing, all-knowing authority, I put my deductive reasoning skills to work without needing to ask, "Tea?" and "Who's Mabel?" This is when I knew I had him. Trying to replicate the same decibel level he'd just demonstrated, I leaned over after a lengthy pause and said, "My lips never touch it. Caffeine."

"Cuts back our lives, doesn't it?" Mr. Morgan asked in a boisterously bold voice that had now become a whisper. Next, outstretching his right hand to me, then scanning the room to the left and right, he turned his palm facing upward. "How long have I got?"

I was taken aback. I didn't know how to answer. The more I hesitated to deliver a response, the wider his desperate eyes grew. "That's not for me to say, Sir," I answered finally.

"Tell me. I can take it. When?"

My calculations could have very easily predicted the date of his death, but my pink floral steel beaded pocketbook told me not to utter a word. "People usually depart close to the day of their birth. That's all for now. Perhaps I can tell you more next time."

Somehow the desperation in Mr. Morgan's eyes vanished. Like a gentleman, he escorted me back to the door, unlocked it and I walked out while saying no more. It wouldn't have been right. Never was it my intention to manipulate with fear, but if it's legitimate for the insurance industry to do so, why should it be any different for astrology?

After collecting my pay at the reception desk, I exited the outer office of J. Pierpont Morgan & Sons with a smile on my face, realizing that the budget for my next antiquing trip to Boston had just grown tenfold.

☉   ☽   ✶

Summer seemed to arrive before spring had come to an end, and I traveled home. A wondrous time to spend walking the perimeter of fashionable Copley Square after the morning fog had lifted. It was a place where everybody knows the name Adams, and every out-of-towner receives a scolding after they refer to our fair city as "Beantown." How perfectly gauche. A decadent dinner of lobster croquettes along the Long Wharf pier, smelling the brine-scented air and looking out onto the harbor the night before, confirmed that I was indeed home.

Only minutes beyond tending to Mother and her needs, I was now free to contemplate nothing more than my own. Endless hours of "I'm doing this" and "I'm doing that," with never a query about me, my life personal or professional, had, for the moment, come to a pause.

Stepping into the Boston Museum and Gallery of Fine Arts, an icy, off-season Atlantic gust entered the building unexpectedly, leaving me with chills running the course of my spine. I tightened my buttoned up sweater and collected my warmth as I approached a stagesmith entering the empty theatre.

"I'd be most appreciative if you could show me the way to the scenery department. Is that how it's known?"

"Oh, yes, ma'am. I'm on my way there right now."

"I'm to retrieve a lamp that was used in your last production. A Tiffany lamp. I bid on it at auction, and won."

"I know that lamp. Unfortunately, it received more compliments than our last production. Right this way. Over there," the man wearing overalls said as we strolled past rows and rows of painted-over canvas flats depicting urban Boston. The scenery shop was like a village unto itself; platforms, wagons, curtains and the finest contemporary furnishings dominated my view until I approached the beauty. "Good afternoon, Mrs. Fry," he said to a woman packing up bric-a-brac, from a parlor-like setting, in a most delicate manner.

"Jakob. You know me too well. Emma," the woman, wearing subtly feminine pink lace around her neck, said while making clear their level of familiarity. Welcoming me with a handshake most sincere and silky soft to the touch, she said, "You've bought yourself a very fine lamp, Mrs. Adams. We're going to miss it here. It's become part of our family."

The way the woman spoke, it was as if she aimed to entertain with her melodic tones. It would have been rude to have stared much longer without speaking, but her air of not only wisdom but relaxedness left me dumbstruck.

"I'll bring back a carrying crate, ma'am. Please excuse me," the workman said to her.

"Have we ever been introduced before?"

"No. I don't think so, ma'am," the woman told me with more conviction than uncertainty.

As she began polishing the lamp with a cloth, I asked, "You are a director here?"

"Oh, pardon me. I have been involved with this theatre for decades now. My name is Mrs. Emma Sheridan-Fry. You may, too, call me Emma."

"I know you. Your production. A drama you had written. At the Lyceum in New York. Recently on stage. My secretary had seen it in Chicago."

Still intent on polishing, Emma's green eyes lit up. "*Fort Frayne.* I hope she liked it."

"She said, absolutely, she did. I am Evangeline Smith Adams."

Without moving the hanging black curl from between her girlish eyes—she appeared no more than thirty—Emma said, giggling, "Well, yes. I already know that. You had the winning bid." Looking back down at the lamp again, she went on to say, "I also read in *The Herald* what you'd forecast, if that's the most accurate word. That horrible Windsor fire."

"Oh, yes. So sad. Horribly tragic." Next, I did something most uncalled for. I reached for another rag taken from the railing of a workbench and began polishing the other side of the lamp. Both holding onto it, but my strokes were brusquer, harsh and rigorous. Emma's buffing resembled a massage, gentile and careful. Her middle finger lifted up, the only one not touching the scouring rag. She looked at me as if I were molesting the fragility of the lightshade. As I continued, Emma moved her cloth away from the glass lamp itself and onto its bronze base.

"Isn't that silly?" she said. "Some there stated that you were involved in starting the fire, or had an accomplice, so your prediction would be proven truthful."

Hearing someone so attractive voicing such ugly speculation, rumors I'd been hearing for nearly two years, offended me. There was no way I could respond. Instead, I offered a stern glance and stepped back from the lamp.

She grimaced sheepishly. "It's merely hard for me to believe in the stars, their powers. How—"

"The stars possess no powers, Mrs."

"Oh, please Mrs. Adams. I didn't mean to offend you. I should correct myself by stating that it's all beyond my comprehension. Maybe I'm a dimwit."

"It's science pure and simple, Mrs. Fry."

"Oh, no. Emma." Changing the subject abruptly, Mrs. Fry said, "You're going to love this lamp. I think Tiffany's garnered praise every night we've used her here onstage."

"I'm so fond of decorations. Usually antiques catch my fancy, but when I'd heard that you were auctioning this one off, I had to be privy to the bidding." Still feeling the sting of Emma's words, I attempted to bite back sarcastically by saying, "I do my best to make practical use of devices that illuminate."

"My heavens. I didn't mean to insult your business, Mrs. Adams," Emma said while touching my right hand briefly. Her movement caused the scent of sandalwood and Lilies of the Field coming from her to float its way to my nose. The fragrance exhilarated me and left me sniffing for more. "It was my spiritual upbringing. I was brought up to believe that events in the future are not meant to be known. Left as mystery, a surprise. A 'lesson,' my grandmother liked to call them."

"It's Miss. I'm an unmarried woman. In my business I simply, routinely, point out the most favorable and the least favorable times for an undertaking. Just the other day—"

With a broad smile hard to ignore, and eyes that caught the light from every lamp inside the shop, Emma interrupted first with a raised finger, then said, "That's just it. I *adore* least favorable times. Those are the moments from which we are to learn, choose to learn. Or not. How can we possibly learn from adversity if we know exactly when, where and how it's coming?"

"Your arguments are difficult to follow, ma'am."

"If I may…are you not spiritual? Religious? Do you believe in any God or Supreme Being?"

"Begging your pardon, Mrs. That information will remain confidential. I also fail to view its relevance."

"Prove it to me, if you please. I value scientific insights…and I love to learn. Please do tell me something you feel I should know…and I will tell you if I already know it. Perhaps I don't need to be told what I already know or what I already recognize as being one of my own life's lessons."

Always relishing an opportunity to prove myself, the edge to my stance suddenly softened. In a tone more dulcet than mere minutes prior, I told Emma, "So be it. I am at your disposal, it would be an honor. My days here in Boston are not so full, I'd be happy to give you my guidance."

"I graciously accept your kind offer. When? Where? My priorities are my husband and my boy, but other than that, I'm entirely yours."

"My studio here in Boston is more than suitable. It would be my pleasure to cast your chart. Complimentary, of course."

"How kind of you, Miss. Please, then, name the place, time and day and I'll most assuredly be there."

Knowing that I kept every Monday afternoon free from clients, this was the day I chose for my meeting with Mrs. Fry—Emma. I wanted to select a date when my mind was most at liberty. Theatrical people can be amusing, but Emma seemed to be coming from a much deeper place than some of her superficial contemporaries.

"I haven't a writing instrument, I'm afraid," I said.

"My mind is like a safe. From memorizing pages and pages of script as an actress. Nothing leaves it. Please tell me instead."

"This coming Monday at one in the afternoon. Extremely close to King's Chapel on Tremont Street. Fifty-two, to be accurate."

"It's as if you read my mind. I can think of no better time and location." When she smiled, both sides of her face created dimples of perfect proportion. I couldn't help but stare at them.

The wooden crate for lamp transport arrived immediately after our appointment was set. Perfect timing. "I shall pack it for you gently and you can be on your way, ma'am," the man said.

"Yes, and I'll let you be off as well," Emma said. "What a pleasure. And, thank you once more for enlightening me. I look forward to our visit on Monday. Good day, Miss." She curtsied politely.

As Emma walked away from me, I felt the same sensation as when I first saw her: closeness. Her gait was one I'd never seen before though: feet pointed outward, deliberately, when taking strides, like a Russian ballerina performing *Swan Lake*. In some way, everything about Emma exuded vivacity. Being in her presence made me feel more alive...up until the moment though when I happened to rest my hands upon my hips; I couldn't help but squish my fingers into the fat that masks them. Being a woman of petite height, every one of my additional pounds seems magnified by ill-proportion.

Forgetting that my newly-acquired lamp was before me, the stagehand interrupted my own physical fixations by asking nonchalantly, "You and Mrs. Fry are old friends from New York?" while hefting the wooden crate.

"No, not at all. We just now met."

"It looks like you've known each other for years."

# Sun @ 17° CANCER 31'03 (1903)

*F*ifteen minutes before one and my fingers could not stop fidgeting. As sunbeams shone through my color-stained windowpane, I was reminded of the times I'd attended church in my younger years. Destiny had been a foreign concept to me then. So was the Holy Spirit. It's not that I believed I could manipulate what was intended to be, but I did see what I did as helping those who felt they possessed no choices. Nothing wrong in that, nothing whatsoever.

With a sigh, I picked up *The Boston Herald.* There on the front page was an article about the proposed merger involving J.P. Morgan and Andrew Carnegie, just as I had foreseen. After meeting Mr. Morgan, I'd known enough to guess that he'd dismiss my warnings and go ahead with this mission that's doomed to fail. Maybe someday he'll learn, I thought. Either way, it didn't matter to me. I was more than willing to accept another thousand-dollar payday from him anytime.

Exactly at ten minutes prior to one the bells chimed at the

King's Chapel next door. This was a happening to which I never gave notice, but something that Mrs. Brush found intolerable. A bell striking not on the hour. "Perfectly horrid," she'd always say.

As my ears absorbed the faint buzz following the final clang, there came a knock at my front door. Most precisely, a total of five knocks with a slight hesitation in between the second and third, a pattern that sounded more than vaguely familiar to me. How oddly memorable. Emma had arrived early, eager to have her reading, I thought. The anticipation of seeing her unblemished, cheery face again made me feel giddy. Walking past the cracked looking glass now tarnished in my musty entranceway gave me a brief moment to see if anything about me, my form or dress needed re-adjustment. No. Well, not in the scant few seconds that existed between the mirror and the front door. A relaxing breath was taken in, prior to grabbing onto the door handle. I exhaled while pulling it open.

"Good day, Mrs. We were on our way to pray. You live—"

"Mrs. Brush. Mr. Brush..." I couldn't think of what additional to say, I was too flabbergasted. But I'm sure the panic that existed on my face must have spoken for me.

"We came from Quincy Market and picked up some peach preserves for you and your mother. I hope she's convalescing well." White- and crisply starched-gloved Mrs. Brush handed me the spotless glass jar, leaned over and told me, "They also aid with digestion."

"...How thoughtful."

"I knew you'd probably be in. Father, here, thought it best not to intrude, but when I saw those peaches, I knew they must be yours."

"Thank you so much. They look wonderful. I'll hope to make use—Emma!" I said, noticing her street-side arrival, energetic stride and lavishly-brimmed organza rose hat plumed with an assortment of peacock feathers. Now, even more panic graced my face.

"Miss Adams, I'm right on time. Perfectly punctual, just like those Virgos you'd told me about. Good morning."

"Why, I'm a Virgo." The minute Emma brushed the draped plumage to her left side, now exposing the fine details of her beaming face, Mrs. Brush said, "My heavens, you're Emma Sheridan," while beginning to fawn. A spontaneous congregation of artiste and admirer at my front doorstep was something I hadn't anticipated, nor necessarily welcomed. "Father, this is Miss Sheridan…from the theatre, an actress."

"I used to be. I'm now a dramaturg."

Appearing to be confused by the term, meek and mild-mannered Mr. Brush, an ordained deacon, squinted his eyes directly at Emma, then to Mrs. Brush, then to me, then back to Emma once more.

"A writer of plays, Father," Mrs. Brush answered with arched eyebrows. "Oh, my. I already know that. I saw one of your productions in Chicago."

"Miss Adams, this is the woman you'd spoken of. *Fort Frayne* at the Lyceum."

"Most correct, Emma. This is Mrs. Brush, my secretary, and her husband, Mr. Brush."

"How delightful to know you. Miss Adams is going to draw a chart for me this afternoon."

"An astrological chart? But you don't work on your free day," Mrs. Brush said while recollecting my daily calendar letter-perfectly.

Again, without invitation, a rather tardy Nor'easter from the Atlantic blew directly into my face, causing goose bumps to form on appendages visible and not. "Monday is the only day that is suitable to Miss Sheridan. The others were already full."

"Oh, that cannot be. I…" Mrs. Brush, rather than finishing her thought, stared directly at me, dressed in my more-vibrant-for-Sunday clothing, from top to bottom. Eyes alighting on the crème ruffles below my amethyst flare skirt then onto the sterling silver Edwardian hair comb atop my head. With a puzzled look to her face, Mrs. Brush continued by saying, "Miss, you know what a fan I am. Why didn't you tell me? I could have easily assis—"

Not being able to hear even the faintest word of dialogue from his mouth, Mr. Brush whispered in the direction of his wife's right ear, something that made her say, "Yes, Father. We *are* intruding on Mrs. and her appointment."

"Oh, please don't leave because of me," Emma exclaimed.

"Our holy sacraments await us in church. Come, Father." With all of Boston's conservatism ostensibly rolled into one person, Mrs. Brush turned to Emma and somehow gushed no more. Instead, she was cordial, polite and orderly when she said, "What a privilege to have met you...*Mrs.* Fry, is it now?"

How astute Mrs. Brush is of proper decorum. "My gratitude for the gift, Mrs. Brush. Delightful to see you, Mr. Brush."

Mrs. Brush waved to us both, rather half-heartedly; Mr. Brush, not at all, as they departed. It was only after they were several steps away that the meek Mr. Brush opened his mouth a second time. I can't imagine what else he had to say. I, in some way, sensed it was only a reaction to something his wife had told him previously; a tidbit, most likely, divulged in a murmur.

"Good day to you both," Emma shouted out in their direction down the street.

Mr. & Mrs. Brush didn't look back. Mrs. Brush, I had a feeling, was eager to move on.

"How sweet of her to bring you such a treat."

"Yes, wonderful. I'm so indebted to Mrs. Brush. A by-the-book Virgo. The martyr. I chose her to be my secretary because of it, a married Virgo. Dedicated to her work above all else; no husband-searching to get in the way."

Emma responded with a nervous chuckle. "Well, at least her husband allows her be employed. That's a blessing these days, isn't it?"

Next, it was my turn to snicker—knowing that Mrs. Brush was in fact the sole income provider in that family.

I placed the preserves in the cupboard of my kitchen, and Emma and I proceeded to exchange pleasantries over tea and cakes. Tea for her, cakes for me. Our time was one of the most delightful I'd spent in months. For someone I'd only known a matter of minutes really, I felt nothing but at ease, at home, with Emma. While I brought up the scientific subject of the Langley aerodrome launch, Emma next mentioned reading *The Souls of Black Folk* by W.E.B. Du Bois. I'd talk, she'd talk. She'd speak, I'd speak. The way Emma let me finish my sentences without interruption; the manner with which I listened without adjudication. Emma and I blushing at the same moment we simultaneously manufactured gooseflesh on both our forearms. Chatting about this, that and the other almost made me forget that I'd invited Emma to have a reading.

While seated on the divan together, with a black pillow situated between us, I asked, "May I have your right palm?"

Without hesitation, Emma placed it into mine after taking off only one of her violet-toned, pearl-beaded gloves. Her skin, just like last time, felt silky soft to the touch. "It doesn't matter if I happen to be left-handed, does it?"

"So, you're left-handed."

"No."

This time it was Emma's forehead that was beginning to develop sweat. Being able to demonstrate my skills without calculations always seems to amaze my clients. But it's the fine details that come from the charts that cement comments offhandedly made (pardon the pun) when merely reading palms.

"Your decision to leave acting was the right one. Drama is a great passion of yours, but you see it as a means of expression for the player. Not necessarily for the exclusive purpose of entertaining an audience."

"Yes."

"You had wanted to move to New York in the past. Living there." I said no more, but was waiting for a sign that I'd mentioned something she recognized as being correct, valid.

Emma scratched her scalp for a full five seconds before saying, "I'd never told anyone that in an interview. Not ever."

"Your family. You stay in Boston because of your husband…and a son. You have only the one?" I said, looking more into Emma's peacock feathers than to Emma directly, fearing I may be intruding.

"Yes, Sheridan. I've mentioned him several times in interviews."

"It matters not what has been brought up before to anyone. Please trust me, everything I'm telling you now comes from what I learn and see at this very moment."

Emma nodded and we proceeded. I went on to tell her much about many things that seemed important, some things that were incidental. "I'd have to say that I'm content with the details you've provided," she said. "Very edifying. I'm eager to give my feedback on your…what I've experienced today. But I'd most certainly like to see your astrology demonstration, if you please."

"I'd be happy to. So, no questions about—"

"No. Astrology…if you please."

"Now is the time when you tell me your place of birth along with the date and time."

"Painesville, Ohio. The first of October, 1864. Three thirty-five in the morning."

"If you'll excuse me, I'll now need to glance into my ephemeris and make some citations. You look as if you'd like to step into my garden for some fresh air. You may do so now if you wish. It's quite enjoyable there."

Emma did just that. Her demeanor was not what it had been. Not nervous, but not as carefree either. As she walked away, though, she gave me a look of trust. Exactly the opposite look I recall from Mr. J. P. Morgan when I'd been dismissed so rudely. Something about me had no fear in telling all I saw.

While compiling the necessary data, I found something, one piece of information that made the protractor fall from between my fingertips, onto the chart itself. How shall I put this into composition? I wondered. Which words shall I use? Within a few seconds I knew it best to focus entirely on all the other aspects of the chart, rather than on one small portion. A quarter of an hour was all it took for me to complete my scribing. Emma apparently needed more fresh air than I had predicted. Twenty-or-so minutes were needed in order for her to come back to my desk, revitalized.

Before I began with my recitation, Emma decided to give one of her own. "As a Libra I am to be optimistic. Isn't that right?"

"Librans are indeed considered to be the optimists. Yes."

"I'd imagine most people come to you to know more about love and money. To most people, that's what they consider to be most important in life, in *their* lives. For the rest of mine, I will know that I create the life I want, the one that I believe I am meant to live. I don't think there is anything you've told me, will tell me, that I'd have to disagree with. I see what you do as being exactly what I do, entertainment for those that are seeking a journey outside themselves, for at least a moment or so."

I frowned at being on the receiving end of Emma's spontaneous soliloquy. Maybe some do think of astrology as entertainment. I'd never be one of them. Still, there was something exciting about the way Emma enjoyed putting forth her opinions to me. As Emma pursed her lips into a locked position, I sensed she was withdrawing her trust in me in order to protect herself from feeling exposed by my insights. Yet at the same time, I admired her forthrightness and confidence in herself. Many of my clients are frantic when they appear before me. Somehow, Emma made it all seem so much less serious, more tranquil.

"I appreciate your analysis," I said. "And, just as you have done, there is nothing you've said that inclines me to disagree with you either. May I now proceed even further?"

"By all means, please."

"Your moon is third degree Taurus. Written communication over spoken stands out. Shakespeare was a Taurus. From much of your chart I can see that your literary skills supersede your passion for acting. It is through your writing that you'll be making the fullest use of your faculties."

"I know that, yes," Emma said, smirking.

"Many planets in Sagittarius. Throughout the rest of your life you will travel for your work. You will teach. You will teach others, in colleges and universities, a new and welcomed approach for actors entering into dramatics. You will write a book about this, but I see it being published in the distance, nearly two decades from now. You will continue to have fewer and fewer friends in dramatics and more in the literary world. Sometimes you trust, too much, those in the dramatic field. Like you did with your audiences, your aim to please remains quite high."

"Entirely correct. Everything."

"Especially your husband. In the coming years, you two will have a more liberal understanding of each other. Once your son is grown. Your husband will travel as well. But you may not travel together. You will always love each other. And, despite what I'd said earlier, you *will* be moving from Boston. Just as you'd previously desired, you will most likely be living in New York City."

"I can see that happening myself. What a pleasant adventure that will be."

In a rather muddled fashion, I did my best to be as clear as I could about what I saw in the distance. My stance open, inviting at the start, next turned frozen. My hands went clammy.

"About twenty-or-so years from now there will be a woman who plays a prominent role in your life. You will become quite close to her." At this point in my delivery I, myself, became insecure in my speech, had difficulty choosing the right words. I wasn't so sure why. I couldn't understand my hesitation, but I continued anyway.

"With this woman you will share a… Well, *more* than a sisssterly bond. Not just as one confidante to another. You will become as one."

Nearly a full, tension-filled minute passed before Emma responded. It's as if the script inside her mind were redrafted a hundred times before she was able to say, "Well…it's always nice to have new friends, isn't it? I look forward to making her acquaintance." She said this without looking directly at me, while rising from my prize mahogany captain's chair so abruptly that it fell over the second she stood.

Without picking it up from the floor, I immediately said, "I hope I haven't disturbed you in some way."

"Of course not. Fabulously entertaining. What great conversation these facts will make when I bring them up this evening to my husband at supper."

My heart sank. I felt as if I'd failed miserably with my demonstration. All hopes for fostering a newfound friendship shattered. "Thank you for coming to see me today, Emma."

"Thank you for coming to see me today, *Mrs. Fry*," Emma said, the way an English professor corrects misused grammar. "Bostonians exercise proper etiquette at all times."

"Of course. My mistake. Thank you again…Mrs. Fry."

"And thank you, Miss Adams, for sharing such an exquisite performance."

☉   ☽   ★

Back in New York and away from Mother, with the sun soon approaching Virgo, my work became the sole focus of my life. I did my best to promote my services any way I could. Lecturing to small groups in and around town, nearby ladies' clubs from the Catholic Daughters of the Americas to the Daughters of the American Revolution, Manhattan social circles and the like helped spread the word, and as a result, a wider array of clients entered my doors. For some reason, a good number of them had come from two very diverse fields, the arts and finance. Charles M. Schwab became a frequent visitor and always seemed to take immediate action following our visits together. Although born in Pennsylvania, Mr. Schwab still acted and re-acted in ways that very much reflected his German heritage. Every time I spoke of his cusp placement at the time of his birth on February eighteenth, he insisted that he was indeed an authoritative Aquarius, not a weak-willed Pisces.

Mr. Schwab, contrary to his colleague, J.P., forever took me seriously.

"November of this year, late November is when it's most favorable for you to speak with Mr. Morgan. After you have conversed with him, there is another man with whom you'll share a better, more promising association."

"That would be Mr. Carnegie. You and I have spoken about him before."

"Yes, because his sun conjuncts your rising in Sagittarius. Much better. But Mr. Morgan is essential in these talks and your interaction with him must come first. It's natural for you to intellectualize your communication with Mr. Morgan, but that will not work in your favor. He's an Aries, playful, child-like. Treat him as such; give him toys to play with."

"All we ever talk about is money...and steel."

"Find an expensive toy made of steel and give it to him. He'll enjoy that. It will entertain him. Don't forget that your sun in Aquarius conjuncts his rising. You seem to have a valid bond to both of these men, but it's you who's needed to bring the other two together. You are the catalyst."

As my most recent session with Mr. Schwab was coming to an end, it was he who brought up the subject of his financial obligation to me. He didn't appear to be concerned with any particular amount that would be most pleasing to my ears. Instead, Mr. Schwab, out of nowhere, asked, "How much does Mr. Morgan pay you?"

Involuntarily, my entire body jerked back several inches. "I beg your pardon?"

"Mr. Morgan. J.P. He's your client, isn't he? I assume so."

"J—, Mr. Morgan? A client? It would be disrespectful of me to disclose that information. I'm sure you can understand."

"It's no secret. I know we discuss him, but he talks openly about you. Brags. From what I've come to know, J.P.'s paid you handsomely not only for your services but for the expense of your travel to his Wall St. office. Whereas I come to you here."

"Well, he has... That's correct. I can validate that my travel time was paid for by Mr. Morgan, J.P. Very professional, respectful of him to do so."

"I'll pay you the very same. No, it would be a privilege to pay you the same plus twenty percent in addition, because of my deep respect for your fine work."

"All I feel comfortable mentioning at this time is that J.P. has paid me several times more than my standard fee."

"Three? Four? Five? I shall pay you six times more than your standard rate of twenty dollars...in addition to the twenty percent added on. A bonus, so to speak."

I couldn't answer straight away. The fee Mr. Schwab was mentioning was outrageously inflated. I'd be a verifiable idiot to turn it down though. These men happened to be two of the wealthiest in the country. They could easily afford it. They could easily afford any amount.

"If you insist, Mr. Schwab. I will graciously accept the compensation you are proposing."

"Charles. I'd be honored if you addressed me by my first name."

"And, Charles...I'm just curious. Does J.P. know that you visit me? Here?"

"No, the subject's never come up."

Just as a poker player never shows his hand, colleague-yet-competitor Charles Schwab never displayed his to J.P. either. His Venus in Sagittarius assured me that he never would. It would mean catastrophe to me should J.P. Morgan ever discover that I had violated our oral exclusivity agreement. "No other money wranglers," he'd insisted, pounding his clenched fist onto my office rolltop after my fifth or sixth time meeting with him. But any gambler knows that two jackpots are better than one. How could I *not* up the ante?

# Sun @ 27° SAGITTARIUS 56'52 (1903)

$A$s early winter loomed, with icicles forming on bare-limbed tree branches upon my most recent return to Manhattan, a bout of mind-numbing melancholia captured my mood and wouldn't let go. A paralysis that sometimes left me and my body bedridden. Listlessness, despair and deep, deep contemplation consumed me over matters entirely meaningless, like the scarce amount of curd cheese left in my kitchen.

During these moments of down time, creativity, such as the formation of rhyming couplets entered my mind every now and again, but not until November did I feel the need to take literary, epistolic action. Although I'd never considered myself much of an essayist, it was true that as a teen I used to love composing my thoughts on paper.

Nineteen-oh-four was fast approaching. The stars professed that this was an overwhelmingly favorable period to make my move to New York final and permanent before spring appeared. Then again, Mother still needed my care. Her emotional dependence upon me will likely do her in should she know my move has become long-lasting, I presumed. The guilt I'd still felt over my father's premature demise was overwhelming enough at times. I didn't need more. When in New York, on numerous instances I did find myself missing many things about Boston, like the carefree sensation of those endless trolley rides I used to take on Blue Hill Avenue, but it's my mind that took me back to the reading I had done for Emma Sheridan-Fry. Although I'd believed the stars to be infallible, I could have conveyed my interpretation of them to her a bit differently, been a bit more subtle, less direct in my method.

A written letter was in order. How advantageous that my two o'clock appointment, "Mrs. Gadabout Town," had not shown up. Much free time to gather my thoughts and remedy these feelings of guilt and self-reproach. "Oh, Mrs. Brush. Would you kindly bring me the fine clamshell, personal stationery from my cabinet, a fountain pen and an ampoule of blue ink?"

Mrs. Brush took no more than thirty seconds to enter my office with the needed tools. While still in the doorway, we both could hear that someone had just come into my studio, the waiting area. More than likely a messenger.

"Probably another beggar. From Russia. Poland. Or Germany," Mrs. Brush said, shaking her head in disgust.

Footsteps approached us with no appointment, no warning. The man who stepped through the hallway shocked me. "I must speak with you immediately. Very important indeed."

Barricading the doorframe with her two arms outstretched, Mrs. Brush exclaimed, "Mr. Morgan, well. Again you visit without notice. I'm not exactly certain Mrs. Adams can accommodate you at this very time. She's—"

Mr. Morgan raised his hand as would a policeman conducting traffic at the intersection of 42nd Street and Broadway during the luncheon hour at Times Square. Mrs. Brush recognized the halt sign and her expression displayed great insult. I feared the two would come to blows within seconds.

"Thank you, Mrs. Brush. I'm sure Mr. Morgan won't be but a moment. You can close the door behind you."

Mrs. Brush gave Mr. Morgan a stern look while he made a point of admiring his polished fingernails. As soon as the door shut, he demanded, "What did Schwab tell you?"

My heart skipped a beat. Terror filled my pupils and J.P. noticed it before even I did. Barely able to get out two words, I miraculously managed three. "Schwab? Charles Schwab?"

"No time for dilly dallying. I know he comes here. He told me so."

"Well…yes, as a matter of fact he does. He…discusses matters of a personal nature. Family and such."

"Liar."

In my head, I knew my life was finished. Soon I'd be telling fortunes with my hands hovering over a crystal ball in Greenwich Village.

With bulging eyeballs yet a normal tone to his voice, J.P. said, "I'm not angry. I just gotta know."

"What?"

"Are we on the same page?"

Not knowing what he was talking about, I yet sensed no anger. As usual J.P. was only obsessed with getting ahead. Being as fast as I could be on my feet, I quickly endeavored to turn defense into offense.

"The merger. If Mr. Schwab takes my guidance, it should happen effortlessly."

"What about our business with Old Man Carnegie?"

"Mr. Schwab and I haven't spoken about Mr. Carnegie in many, many months now."

Expecting J.P. to say, "So, Charles has been seeing you for months, has he?" just never happened. Business, business and more business.

"What about Rogers? Frick? Farrell?"

"I recognize none of those names. Mr. Morgan, please don't forget that any information exchanged between Mr. Schwab and I will remain confidential. Just as the words I share with you, whether it be here or at your office on Wall St. There's no way I can destroy that confidence. Mr. Morgan, I'm a professional."

"Aw, shucks."

"What?"

"Aw…from *Huck Finn*. We've been reading that to our grandkids every once in a while. Now, they repeat it all the time," J.P. told me, a warm smile lighting his face.

Rather than chastising me for seeing Mr. Schwab as well, J.P., without verbalizing it, had made me aware that I'd done exactly what he would have, had he been in my position. "It's the American way," he told me many times. J.P. helped me understand that making the most of an opportunity is the way to live life. As a result of this mutual appreciation for more, we bonded.

Mr. Morgan—his impatient, nearly comical, gruff mannerisms combined with his child-like colloquialisms—kept me entertained every time he came into my office. No longer did I perpetually accommodate him by taking away precious time from my own schedule to travel south to Wall Street. It was he who, for the most part, did the commuting. Mr. Morgan had come a long way since his days of skepticism. It wasn't so much that he'd become overly open-minded; he just enjoyed the endless dividends my readings had produced for his bank accounts. Not an erroneous prediction yet.

Each time we met, J.P. divulged more of his personal life to me. His wife, Fanny, was doing such-and-such; their children, Jack,

Louisa, Juliet and Anne were doing that. The way he spoke, more slowly and more peaceful than normal, when mentioning his offspring made me feel that he was a good father. As J.P. relaxed around me, his inhalations appearing to be deeper, more prolonged, I relaxed around him.

Pleasantries aside, whenever Mrs. Brush scheduled an appointment with J.P. and his name emerged in my calendar, I looked forward to the meeting. Despite the illustrious clients, my family had failed to be impressed with my prosperity. "An Adams would never consort with astrology. It's unbefitting," my mother continued to say.

I could imagine John and John Quincy might have agreed, but I've oft-times wondered how Abigail, America's first feminist, may have looked upon me. Being a Scorpio, she would have been direct and honest in her appraisal, while still being sensitive of my feelings.

"Evvy, are you with me? The Standard Oil stock?"

"Oh, I beg your pardon, Sir. I was contemplating...the most fortuitous time to sell. Late-March will be best. Early November even better for buying more."

"You didn't look into your book."

"Oh, but I already did, Sir. Sell late-March, buy more early-November. I'm certain of it."

Mr. Morgan raised his eyebrows in a way that told how he felt about my computations. But all he cared about was what I voiced to him; he cared not about how I came about my conclusions.

"Next week I'll be in Europe again. Any thoughts?"

"Which is the date you'll be leaving? Is this for pleasure? Or business?"

"It's always business. My family's coming along, my wife's idea. But...yes, business as usual."

"The day next week?"

"I think Wednesday."

"Wednesday for one week exactly. Let me research that."

"More like a week and a half."

A mere few minutes were needed for me to ascertain exactly what his itinerary was in for. Thumbing through the pages of my ephemeris gave Mr. Morgan ample time to examine his cuticles and admire the luster of his lacquered claws once more, after biting off a stray hangnail from his pinky. Just as he looked up from his left hand, I had finished my assessment.

"So sorry to tell you, Sir. Not the most auspicious period for negotiations. I assume this is the purpose of your travel."

"No, the Missus's. Her idea. I thought I'd throw in a meeting or two."

"I don't see the people you'll be meeting with to be very receptive. Or, they or you will cancel."

"Then Mrs. Morgan is getting her wish. Uninterrupted time in Europe with me."

"And your family."

"Yes," J.P. again said, smiling. It seemed, by looking away from me, that he attempted to camouflage the warmth coming from the mention of his wife and children. J.P. continued by saying, "I forgot about them. The family too."

☉   ☽   ★

My free day once again left me with yet another estate to scavenge, this time on the East Side of Central Park. Carrying around my clutch filled with cash reminded me of the time Mrs. Brush and I arrived in town, having to transport our own hand baggage from hotel to hotel. An assortment of vintage pink crystal glassware from early-nineteenth century Holland was on my agenda—the spoils of an estate auction—and I had already cleared several spaces for it in one of my most refined Viennese softwood credenzas at home.

Serenity was my companion as I strolled through the park for the first time in nearly a year. Many imagined me being a woman of action, and I suppose my chart verified this. But, on a fine crisp day such as this, I was determined to not only tell myself to stop and smell the roses, but actually do so…at length.

A newly painted green bench all to myself next to the lake drew me forward—until my shoe sauntered onto a pile of vile dog dung. With nothing at all to wipe it off, I dipped my shoe, delicately, into the lake as a bath of sorts. This action helped, but it was not nearly thorough enough to cleanse my footwear of debris.

"Please allow me, ma'am," a stranger, who had been to my rear, said while approaching my right foot.

"How polite of you."

"I always carry a shoe brush with me every time I enter this park. Stepping into—unpleasantness—seems to be my destiny."

"It's funny you phrase it as such."

"You don't remember me, do you?"

How bizarre. To be rescued in the park by someone I've seemingly known before. I stared at the prematurely gray-headed younger man, who lifted up his pants leg above his right shoe. His brown, nearly black eyes showed shrewdness. After being thunderstruck by his own overtness to me, the gentleman's subsequent handshake transmitted peace.

"I'm sorry. We've met? I don't say that I recall."

"You're the seer. At Carnegie Hall."

"Yes, I am. Miss Evangeline Adams."

"I remember rather vividly. Your reading, or forecast, I'm not so sure which term is most appropriate, but you warned me."

"Please refresh my mind. My memory is so full."

"Touch my ankle," the man commanded. I became

dumbstruck—the nerve he possessed! As my temptation to strike him passed, he lifted up his pants' leg further above his shoe, then his sock. This young man in his early twenties revealed that his right calf was made of wood.

"I'm so sorry. What does this have to do with…?"

"You told me that peril was coming my way. Immediately. From a large animal. You must… It was about a year and a half ago. You had a full waiting area of the upper crust, ladies, and you made reference to me being the only man. You told me that very few men seek out your services."

"Oh, yes. I do recall now. You seemed to be in despair at the time."

"Very much so. I was terminated from my employ. My fiancée had died a few months earlier. It was a mare gone mad that hurried into me on the street. My leg was crushed and it had to be removed."

I shook my head. How terrible to have experienced all three disasters at once. "Yes, I warned you about the horse. So tragic, all of it."

"But none of it could have been prevented. You spoke of favorable and less favorable times. Everything that happened was God's will. Absolutely none of it could have been avoided."

"Well, I, too, believe in *free* will. I must have mentioned that as well. But your disposition is not one of dread. You appear to me to be in rather fine spirits."

"Spirits. Destiny. This is what I speak of. Everything that happens; good, bad, during the best of times, the worst. If I had been focused on an impending accident of some sort, I wouldn't have had this, these, experiences."

"You're so optimistic about everything."

"I, for a fact, don't believe we're to know from anyone which time is best or worst for the actions we intend to take." He smiled, and his gray hair seemed to disappear when he did so. "I'm grateful I saw you today, so I can relate this story to you."

"It sounds, though, that you're in much opposition to what I do, to my own destiny, calling."

"Pardon me for saying so, Miss Adams, but every scientist on Earth has the capacity to keep learning. I know you believe devoutly that the stars are infallible, but we're here on Earth, not up in the stars. God is with me now. Before, every day of my life before, I was angry, bitter, in the worst of moods, a drunkard even…and other things I'd rather not indicate to you now. From these challenging experiences I learned, I chose, to be grateful for the fullness I feel. I may have only one leg and little money, yet I decided to believe, to realize my life is complete. I'm rich, not poor. If I were continuously told what is to come, what would I learn from?"

"That's a wonderful recitation, Sir. My deepest and most sincere felicitations. The only way I can reply to you is to say, 'Astrology's not for you.' For others, it just might be."

"A more than fair reply. I'm grateful I'd met you before. No disrespect, but I'm grateful I quickly dismissed the lot of what you'd told me."

This time I merely nodded my head in response. If this had come from anyone else I would have lost control of my temper. How disrespectful, I would have thought. All my years of study, all those countless hours of providing service…and this man's most grateful for having dismissed my work, rejected what the stars told me, forewarned me about him and his life.

In all honesty, I had heard this all many times by now. Sometimes they laughed when they spoke about it afore me. The most irritating was when they scoffed not to my face but in the face of others. Hearsay was what I hated most. Never would I gossip if I felt it would jeopardize a person's livelihood. Damn those non-believers.

The man with the wooden leg bowed in front of me after having cleaned off my right shoe, as if he'd been knighted by King Edward VII himself. As the man walked away, I paid most attention to his profound limp, rather than the words he'd just uttered. How sad indeed, his crooked walk. So many of the people who had come to me would have been shattered by having experienced such calamities. This man gave me cause to notice a different perspective about life; things, people, situations for which to be grateful.

Enough pontificating. My precious antiquing awaited my presence. Onto Fifth Avenue once more to discover a collection of hidden treasures—the perfect potion for even the slightest bout of downheartedness.

As I continued walking down the gravel footpath east, in the distance in between a grove of birch saplings newly planted with splints attached to support their standing, I saw someone on the ground. Then, I heard a male voice calling out for some reason— somebody perhaps in jeopardy. Several men and women before me rushed up. Enough people were there to help by the time I had arrived, and just when I felt I could be of assistance, the bellowing had stopped.

Upon closer examination, it was the man with whom I'd just spoken. The wooden-legged man must have tripped or been knocked over, and he was looking straight at me. It seems so insensitive to even call him that now. I felt embarrassed that I had not asked his name. As I passed by, I found that I couldn't look directly back at him. Only a portion of me could comprehend the enormity of the pain he must have felt for the multitude of misfortunes that have been bestowed upon him. Absolutely no part of me could feel gratitude for those many miseries, despite his claims.

Once exiting the park I was in no mood to feel agony, and I found Fifth Avenue bustling with distraction. It was as if the entire city of New York had descended upon it. A sea of black clothing coming, going. The same shade for everyone in Manhattan, with only the make of the fabric distinguishing the rich from the poor. Seeing so many of the same, knowing I was yet another in black, made me feel indistinguishable from anyone else. All the same, for a moment I had to close my eyes ahead of stepping along any further. I wanted to forget ever having laid eyes upon that man in the park, the one I had given the warning a year and a half prior. I wanted to forget what he had told me. I wanted to go back to the time when I knew for certain that the stars are infallible and I was meant to interpret them for a worthwhile reason. "My life's work is not, and has never been worthless, inconsequential. I *do* matter," I said to myself.

My anxiety attack lasted a mere second or two. Another deep breath. Exhale. And I continued onto my destination.

The entry to one of the many palatial estates in the neighborhood of Fifth & Seventy-first was magnificent, unlike anything I'd ever seen. The Statue of Apollo water fountain, the ten-foot-long Lalique crystal chandelier, not to mention the gold lamé welcome mat out front, would have made even the Palace of Versailles jealous. I knew I was in for a major haul at bargain-basement prices.

"May I escort you to the next room, Madame?" the prim, white-gloved head butler asked.

"By all means, yes. It's all so breathtaking."

Being surrounded by artwork of the Italian High Renaissance was like going back in time, sitting alongside the shores of the Arno in Florence, admiring nothing but all things ornate, meticulously crafted.

"But what's that doing there?"

"Madame?"

"That lamp. It's in stark contrast to the period artwork."

"The Tiffany. It was Monsieur's favorite. He cherished it every day until his last. Such a shame it has to be sold."

"Yes. But why is it among antiques? Something so contemporary."

"You're entirely correct, Madame. Monsieur, in his later years, added only new accoutrements to his collection. They made him feel young. The antiques that surrounded him made him feel old, too close to death."

"Death? I'm thrilled when I come upon a gem from the past."

"You see, Monsieur feared it. Death. Perhaps he was on a mission to alter the inevitable, his destiny."

A perfect partner to the lamp I already owned. I had to have it.

☉   ☽   ✶

"This city is sinful. Too permissive. Heathenry around every corner."

"Mrs. Brush, you're just having a bad day. I could pour some brandy into your cup, if you like. To soothe your nerves."

It was not even the end of a long work week and, as Mrs. Brush returned from her lunch alone, there were still a multitude of tasks before us.

Mrs. Brush looked at me in a way my mother used to. From love to hatred in a mere instant. Her gaze made me fearful, like my life was at stake. "Satan's elixir," she sneered.

I backed away a step. "What…happened?"

"Heathen lust. The man downstairs. That Jew."

"Mr. Kaufman? The doorman? Did—"

"It makes me want to wretch. The sin in his filthy immigrant eyes."

"Quiet down here," I said to Mrs. Brush as I led her to the divan, closing the door behind us. Resting my hand on her shoulder made her flinch, so I removed it at once. Her sneer remained. Rather than sitting on the divan next to Mrs. Brush, I instead walked over to my bookcase and retrieved the bible she had given me the previous Christmas. Expecting her to treasure its possession once I handed it over, she surprised me by slapping it onto the glass table in front of her.

"You wouldn't know. You can't imagine how I feel."

"Did he touch you?"

"All desires of the flesh are evil. Yes, that filth touched me," Mrs. Brush answered.

"I'm so sorry this happened to you, Mrs. Brush. I'll personally make certain this matter is addressed."

"You'll *never* understand. Your disinterest in men comes close to being unnatural."

Much too confounded to respond, I paused.

"Father told me so. That time in Boston. I prayed to the Holy Ghost for it not to be true, but…your look to Mrs. Fry then. The same way I look at my husband. Not right." Mrs. Brush just shook her head.

Immediately I blushed upon hearing those words.

"Whatttever do you mean? I have never—"

"God knows." Rather than a glance above to all that's sacred, Mrs. Brush instead seethed with hatred as her cheeks became enflamed and her lips turned ashen. "The Lord Almighty knows all."

I couldn't believe I was hearing any of this. "Mrs. Brush, I feel for your regretful encounter, but I also can't help but feel offended." After taking a moment to try and digest what had just taken place, Mrs. Brush got up from the settee and began to walk out the door. As I saw her leave my presence, like a flash of lightning, my mind took me back to my forecast of Mrs. Brush's impending departure, late-October, 1904, a time when my patience with her would no longer be warranted.

The next day, first thing in the morning, Mrs. Brush provided me with her resignation. The two of us were as cordial as we could be. Without saying any extraneous words, Mrs. Brush collected her belongings from my office and her residence quarters, and I never saw or heard from her again. All that remained was the fear, my paranoia, of the idle gossip she'd implanted in my mind.

# Sun @ 11° AQUARIUS 15'42 (1910)

*S*uccess had come swiftly at the turn of the century, and by 1910, the destiny that had brought me to New York City at the right time had fulfilled its promise. My annual income, now in the hundreds of thousands, made me, to my knowledge, the most successful businesswoman in town, in a country where banks continued to issue no loans to women, for business or otherwise. There may have been other women as successful or more so, but my business was self-created, not inherited from a dead husband or any other male family member. Having beaten the odds, I'd succeeded in a man's world rather convincingly. Everyone who's anyone had by now sought out time across from me at my desk in what the press deemed "the seat of the mighty."

My ailing mother sadly passed away from dementia in 1905. A diehard Bostonian to the end, Mother never forgave me for becoming an astrologer. She never forgave me for breaking off my engagement to my previous employer, Mr. Lord. Both had brought scandal to me, to her, and most in particular, to anyone directly descended from John and John Quincy Adams.

Mother's death was heart breaking to me, but only a year later transformed itself into a blessing in disguise. Tears and sorrow caused by grief became, to a certain degree I imagine, the kind of elation felt by slaves after the 13th Amendment was passed in 1865. Emancipation. Freedom. That churning knot that lived inside my stomach for decades dissipated into nothingness. No longer would I feel my heart, my loyalties torn. And her death was yet another reminder that one has limited time on this earth. Choosing to favor risks over fear, electing to learn from those who are different—these became my mottoes, my ways of making the most of my life.

The two goals merged on a beautiful spring day in April of 1906. I met my new secretary on the promenade that fronts the Battery Park waterfront, both of us staring at Lady Liberty at the exact same time. I had just come from a prosperous meeting with J.P. at his Wall St. office. Sabine had just stepped off Ellis Island, her first moments on American soil, looking to create a fresh life in New York City, just as I'd done. She was an immigrant from Germany, a Jew, someone Mrs. Brush would, most likely, choose to despise, and the contrast seemed to further confirm fate's hand. Sabine was proud of her ability to master English well enough before her arrival, and her accent diminished as time passed, but, somehow, my self-effacing ears that were never adorned with gemstones, always chose to hear Mizz rather than Miss, whenever she addressed me.

☉　☽　✶

"Miss, the jewels. Why are you collecting so many? You don't wear them."

We were standing at the base of three travelling chests; much too many for a single lady. Best to be better prepared than less, I thought. Stately visits to Buckingham Palace happen seldom in one's life and must be taken seriously. "I know. This occasion's different. When I'm presented to the King I must look my best."

"It's important to him that you are wearing jewelry?"

"That's what's done. All women do. You must know that, Sabine."

"I won't be packing any, Miss. For myself. I have none. I don't need them."

My blunt and truthful Scorpion secretary told no lies. Her kind of beauty needed no embellishments. Sabine's sleek torso, long limbs, stalk-like neck and absence of jowls about the jawline made her magnetic presence stand out above all others. But it wasn't she who was to be presented to England's reigning king. "The emerald brooch. You must—"

"What is emerald?"

"The green one. Do you know where it is? It must be packed with my emer—, my green-colored dress."

"Smaragd when noun. Smaragdgrün when adjective."

"Yes, thank you, Sabine."

"The one you hide behind the toilet tank. I shall bring it."

"Please dust it off. Then scent it with Subtle Orchid after."

Sabine looked at me with her usual slant of the head, sideways. Why I'd picked a Scorpio to be my most-trusted assistant, I'd often wondered. Scorpios and Aquarians were never meant to know each other, I was certain of it. Yet there must have been something about her obstinacies that I found charming. Or her impetuous and unpredictable Aries rising that I found amusing. Oh, the two added together, mon Dieu.

With nearly every trunk packed and ready to go, I ticked off items on the list that existed in my head. How ridiculous though, all these clothes, jewelry, hats, bindings, clutches and not the necessary ingredients I used for my trade.

"Sabine, I nearly forgot—"

"Your compass, protractor, ephemeris, paper and pen."

Now I remembered why I'd hired her. Scorpion, the most thorough. Mrs. Brush had always been more than competent, being so efficient. But Sabine didn't possess her nervousness. She was supremely in control at all times—and forever created a positive impression when in my company. The numbers of men that flocked to her during the times we made entrances together defied count. Yet she showed interest in none of them.

Any time I gazed upon Sabine, I was again reminded that the stars had bestowed her with perfect proportions, the rarest of natural good looks. Long golden hair that was reflective in the sunlight. Eyes that made the water off the coast of Crete look unclear. Teeth in exquisite alignment, their color whiter than porcelain. An attitude so confident that compliments offended her. Sabine knew she was beautiful and didn't need to be reminded of it.

"Sabine, you do think of everything."

"Again I know what you were thinking. Maybe it's telepathy."

Perhaps. But no reason to inflate her ego—*that* was already as large as a Zeppelin about to take flight. "Please then. Tell me what you believe I was thinking."

"Why you hired me. But you forgot about my Capricorn moon."

Right. A Capricorn moon: goal-oriented with relation to career. I'd better watch my back.

☉   ☽   ✶

In the company of our travel luggage, Sabine and I boarded the carriage that would carry us to West Twenty-Fourth Street alongside the North River, with droplets of morning dew still coating its padded bench seats. Although I had taken this voyage numerous times, it was never for the purpose of being transported to an event such as this. Presented to English royalty. Of all my worldly possessions it was my astrological tools that I most valued. This is part of the reason I am being summoned, I assumed. Having been over-worked as usual, I'd had no time, previous, to create King Edward's chart. But I knew there would be plenty of opportunities aboard ship in the privacy of my cabin to perform such a task.

"Why does your nose sniffle, Sabine?" I asked.

"A slight head virus, Miss. It's not the grit."

"Grippe. Not grit."

An exaggerated sniffle came my way as an indication of a rude reply. There's nothing viler than anyone born in the eighth house when they're in pain. It's the one time they no longer obsess on their privacy. When a Scorpio is ill, everyone must know about it and suffer along with them.

Not much of consequence was said on the carriage ride to Pier 64. Something told me that much of my time during the week-long voyage was to be spent alone. Sabine needed to recuperate, and I wanted nothing to do with her un-wellness, her disposition included.

"There will be entertainment on this ship?"

"Oh, most certainly. A music saloon and a complete orchestra."

"I will find pleasure there. You needn't worry about me."

"I wasn't going to."

Boarding the twin-Steamer ship Columbia brought back my excitement. It was a sunny at daybreak and the sea below was calm. No umbrellas, no wobbly legs. My cabin was on the first level and it was sublime. The finest of the finest was laid out before me.

Delicately twined linen containing gold leaf around its frame. Even a Satinwood kidney shaped writing desk to do my work when the time to earn my keep came about.

On the first night, I was asked to dine at the Captain's table in the First Cabin Dining Room. What an honor. Especially convenient as well. Being unescorted due to Sabine's convalescence in her compartment, I was accompanied by other single passengers. The captain, Crawford, still handsome with teeth disproportionate to his face, was a dashing host and a clever conversationalist, even ending sentences containing more than seven words in melodic rhyme. Before the meal he made a noteworthy speech, in English *and* French, about travel and the enjoyment of living the high life. How right he was.

Each of the seven courses was delectable, from the warm Camembert with wild mushroom fricassee hors d'oeuvres to the cold Crème Caramel dessert, a feast befitting even the most discerning palates of polite society. As others joined their companions while en route to the ballroom, I received a tap on my right shoulder.

"Miss Adams. I didn't recognize you without your Tiffany lamp."

The single glass of Hiedsieck 1907 Diamant Bleu cuvee champagne must have already gone to my head, because I failed, at first, to recall the woman who did the tapping. She was in the company of a confused-yet-cocky-looking gentile man. "My Tiffany lamp. Oh…in Boston. I was thinking—"

"Mrs. Sheridan-Fry," she said, before whispering, "Emma."

"My heavens, of course. Thank you for coming over to introduce yourself."

"This is my husband, Alfred. It's our twentieth anniversary and we're taking a three-month tour of Europe."

"How magnificent. Wonderful to meet you, Alfred."

"Mr. Brooks Fry."

"Yes, to be sure. You came from Boston to make the trip?"

"My husband did. I spend most of my time in New York now. Educational dramatics for young people."

"I recall having read about you in the paper. Your theatre company. Some sort of conundrum though having to do with management."

"Always a struggle. I left and was reinstated. But never mind about that. Who is your companion on this trip?"

"My secretary. She's a bit under the weather at the moment."

"Well, please do join us in the ballroom. We've brought along our son, Sheridan. He's already there, I'm sure. He'll be happy to dance with you."

Mr. Fry next let out a hoarse choke for the entire dining hall to hear. Emma then looked back at him. I made things a whole lot easier by interjecting, "I don't dance much. I'm afraid your son would be left most displeased by my abilities. Thank you just the same though."

Something told me that there was a subtext to Mr. Fry's demeanor. Recalling back to that conversation with Emma that ended so awkwardly on the footsteps of my Boston home, perhaps Mr. Fry was looking at me with some sort of formed prejudice. Either way, I was able to excuse myself. Fatigue was setting in and I wanted to accomplish much work the next day. Emma had been more than cordial, just as she was that day at the theatre in Boston. Unruffled and open.

Mr. & Mrs. Fry strolled their way into the ballroom before bidding me goodnight. An odd coupling. If I'd cared more, I'd be tempted to create his chart and see how it compared to that of his Libran wife. Questions filled my head along with a headache that had grown larger and larger.

In my stateroom I found that I could not sleep, tossing and

turning in unison with the turbulent waves beneath me. And the few moments I was able to doze off didn't last long once I'd faced another one of my devastating death dreams. The ache in my head needed attention. Every type of beverage existed above my basin, but no seltzer water, the elixir that soothed my sore head every time. It would be disrespectful to awaken Sabine in her room next to mine. Walking to the kitchen area myself would be the surest remedy. Fresh air smelling of the salty sea and my seltzer.

Removing my bed clothing came swiftly. It was still early enough for late-night persons to be savoring cruise-line cocktails, so I dressed appropriately enough. There were several kitchens on my deck, but I knew the location of only one. It was just past the Music Saloon. Fewer people were out than I'd imagined.

Just as I relished the thought of sipping my soothing seltzer, my eyes happened upon the crowd in the saloon. Many, I could tell, had consumed a good variety of nocturnal potations. In the dimness of one corner I saw a familiar yet somewhat garish silver necktie I had seen before. It belonged to Mr. Fry. There he was, looking much happier than I'd last seen him. Emma, wearing a stylish wide-brimmed hat, had her back turned. She, now more animated than I had seen before, also seemed to be enjoying herself.

When her white handkerchief landed on the floor, she leaned to her side to pick it up, revealing a bevy of cleavage at mid-slant. That was when I discovered that the woman with Mr. Fry was not Emma, but Sabine. Never have I been more a gassed! "Move swiftly," I told myself, afraid of being spotted by either of them. Perhaps Emma had been with them and had only excused herself briefly. That's what it must have been, I told myself.

Retrieving my seltzer from the kitchen staff was effortless, but it was geographical information I was next after. "May I reach the outdoors from here, another way than traveling through the interior?"

"But, Miss Adams, you're not wearing an overcoat. You'll freeze out there."

"The music coming from the saloon bothers my headache. I'd like to avoid it completely if there's any possible way."

"It may even be too late, Miss. The captain may have already ordered doors to the exterior locked."

Back the way I came turned out to be the only option. As swift as a jack rabbit I'll be, I thought to myself. With my seltzer in hand I pulled up my navy blue cable stich woolen sweater as high above my neck as it would go.

But as I passed the Music Saloon, unfortunately I managed to come upon exactly the person I was hoping to avoid. Not appearing at all nervous, Mr. Fry was almost boastful when he said, "Goodnight, Miss Adams," while tipping his hat.

Not stopping, I replied back, "Goodnight, Mr. Fry," then I corrected myself by blurting out, "Mr. Brooks Fry."

Upon his exit, I rested my hand upon my heart softly to harness the rambunctiousness of its beating and returned to my room. What a fool was I. Sabine was nowhere to be seen. Something about Mr. Fry's brash, all-knowing glare frightened me to death. What did Sabine tell him about me? My private life? Which questions did he ask her about me? And how personal were they? For the first time in a long while, my intuition was overcome with paranoia. My secretive twelfth-house ascendant became worried. As I unlocked the door to my room, I opened the bottle of seltzer, took down a mean swig then pressed my ear to the wall of Sabine's room next door.

No rustling, no scurrying, just snoring. Louder than an Irishman having been on an all-night bender.

What motivated me to sleep was my desire to awaken the next morning, imagining it all to have been a dream. By the time I did rise my headache was gone. A bit of work was laid there before me, but when I began my preparations to cast my first chart there was a rap upon my door.

"Good morning, Evangeline. Forgive me if I've disturbed you."

"My heavens, no, Emma. Please do come in."

Emma remained in the doorway, as I noticed her entire daylight wardrobe coordinated in soothing shades of sea green, and she said, "I'll be dining in the hall soon. Would you care to join me?"

A small amount of panic set in at the sight of her exquisiteness. My body couldn't help but tense up just a bit before asking, "You are dining with your husband? Your son?"

Her expression was completely carefree. "Oh, I'm not entirely certain where Sheridan is. Alfred isn't feeling so well this morning. He'll be remaining inside a few hours more."

"Yes, what a pleasure it will be."

"And, your secretary. Will she be joining us?"

Again, back to the night and my witness to all sights unsavory. "She..." After pointing to the door to the adjoining room I discovered the words I was looking for. "We haven't yet spoken today. She's on her own, knowing that I have work to do at my desk."

"Just the two of us then...if I'm not taking you away from your astrology."

"No. A more than pleasing way to initiate the day."

After gathering my wrap, Emma and I walked together to the dining hall. Upon being seated we proceeded to talk about trivial matters, notions that stimulate the simplest of minds.

Once we'd clearly differentiated the winter weather patterns in North America versus Europe, Emma said at last, "I'll forever recall that conversation in Boston."

"The stars never lie."

"I now find myself more and more drawn to New York, just as you mentioned to me. After our return, back to Boston though. For about a month."

"I'm thinking of going up myself. Perhaps I'll call on you while there," I said cautiously, while casting my focus on the floral centerpiece that separates us. "Your husband...travels?"

"Now that you remind me, yes, he does. As do I. Educating and such. This twentieth anniversary trip is more for our son." She smiled proudly. "He's seventeen now. Soon he'll have his own life. Once we're in Europe the three of us, inevitably, will go in three different directions, different commitments. It's this cruise that bonds us, yet here I am, paradoxically, spending time with neither of them."

Emma's eyes seemed to hold mine for too long, and so I looked away. "What a lovely bracelet. Made of ivory," I said as I noticed the delicateness of her wrists.

Emma nodded, then rested her chin in her hand. "If I may, why is it you're not married, Evangeline?"

So matter of fact was Emma. Only a person of the theatre could presume to be so bold. She was still somewhat of a stranger, yet it was this characteristic that I liked most about her. She was as direct as Sabine, without the abrasions that followed her German wrath. "I was once engaged," I admitted, "but *scandalously* terminated my relationship with the man."

"And when was that?"

"When I was much, much younger. In Boston. I thought I loved him, but it never felt quite right."

"Calling off an engagement in Boston. That's practically punishable by law," Emma said, breaking into a laugh.

I laughed too. My engagement *had* been laughable. In retrospect, not one honest instant during the duration of it.

"Just as I believe for myself, the same is maybe true for you.

Perhaps we just haven't yet met the right ones," Emma said cryptically.

I offered no reply because I couldn't think of any. Instead, I gazed at my hands containing a plethora of wrinkles and folds that had long gone unnoticed. As I clasped them together out of habit, I felt only dryness and scrapes, along with callouses and two warts I don't remember having detected prior. These same hands, so lively when they created my chart in 1899 aboard that train. Panic was beginning to set in. If I truly did want to meet my soul mate, I'd better hurry.

November 10, 1932 was now only 8,159 days away.

# Sun @ 1° PISCES 29'29 (1910)

*H*aving already met the King twice earlier, much of my nervousness had subsided upon my arrival in London. Balanced breathing, complete with its full inhalations, reminded me and my vanity to stop sucking in my stomach. His Majesty's visit to my studio at Carnegie Hall in 1907—the day after a party thrown by New York's élite the night before—was one I knew I would remember forever. As much as Scorpios give me the shivers sometimes, it mystified me how magnetic they, and their eyes, can be to the opposite sex.

Being presented to His Highness on this occasion at Buckingham Palace was an experience to be savored by every sense of my being. Walking up the right side of the Grand Staircase on its vermillion velvet carpet leading to one of the main State Rooms, along with so many fashionables, took my breath from me. Everything from that point on became a gold-leafed blur, and I failed even to mix with any of the other notables who were present, it was the King himself that captured my attention most throughout the evening. Like a child whose mouth salivates upon seeing a sweet and succulent plum pudding, this is how I pictured His Royal Highness.

As planned out in advance, I was wearing my emerald gown and emerald jewels. Sabine helped dress me, yet divulged no interest in my evening to come. A coincidence that she and the King share the same birthday, November 9. Both enticing to their carnal counterparts; seemingly in control of all that happens, yet at the same time, the very ones that create their own demise.

My knees shook with intensity as I was officially announced to King Edward. Because of our less than formal encounters that had taken place in Manhattan, fewer conventionalisms existed between us now.

Appearing just as mighty in physical stature as J.P. Morgan, but infinitely more gentile in manner, much less vociferous, the King said, "Miss Adams, such a pleasant sight." Now in adulthood, it's easy to see how he was once referred to as the "playboy prince" during his youth. Strikingly dressed in his regal blood red cape with white fur trim complemented the King's natural magnetism perfectly.

"Your Royal Highness, an honor to greet you here. My gratitude to you for the most generous invitation."

"You must enlighten me with a consult while in England. They present me with such fascination."

"It would be my pleasure, Your Highness."

"Please do speak to my right-hand man, Butler Halliday. You two can compare diaries and arrive at a suitable day and time for us to meet."

"As always, looking forward to it with delight."

"Until that time, Miss."

Returning to my hotel to tell Sabine, who was giving herself an eyelid massage as a pampering treatment, of my opulent evening, I had to laugh at her lack of awe. In my room she was business as usual.

"You meet with him in two days. You've created his new chart already on the ship...or you do it when you see him?"

"No, soon. Tomorrow morning I will do it. He has no time to wait for me to draw it up in his presence."

"I will prepare your desk, Miss. I'm sure you remember his birth time."

"No, I'm not so sure I do," I said, given that I've made mental notes of at least two hundred-or-so thousand birth times, dates and places.

Sabine, famous, as is every eighth-house soul, for possessing the memory of an elephant, forgets nothing. "Ten forty-eight in the morning."

"You're positive of that, I assume."

"You assume. I know. Ten forty-eight in the morning, Miss. I only need to see it once to remember."

"The rest I recall clearly. No need to ask. The ninth of November, 1841 at Buckingham Palace."

The next morning, still feeling inebriated from my royal evening out, my fingers flipped through the pages and my calculations began.

Struggles seemed to far outweigh triumphs in the king's days nearby. His chart indicated that he was already ill, yet no one knew about it. The more I delved into his future, the sadder I became. When having last cast the king's chart in 1907, I'd vaguely seen some sort of hazard before him. I'd asked, "Do you still smoke regularly?"

"My heavens. I no longer have the time. Nearly never."

I'd taken him at his word, and chose not to pursue health-related forecasting, nor divulge whatever information I may have found. Doing my duty this time, remaining professional, treating the king's chart as anyone else's, sobered me up from the night before immediately. Reality set in. And I now had a major responsibility before me.

King Edward VII, who did his best to remove himself from all things political, would continue to be embroiled in disputes with those more conservative. His stand against discrimination would cause him to be involved in public battles. His condemnation of the use of the word 'nigger' would generate contempt from those obsessed with strict maintenance of class structures. This full list of struggles would only lessen his resolve, diminish his precious energy reserves. I felt this for certain.

Still, his ultimate passion, his horses, would bring him great pleasure in the very near future, winning a good variety of races and steeplechases. Unfortunately, they might do this after-the-fact, victories too late for him to celebrate.

In between writing, I found myself stopping to reflect on this charming man of girth. Someone who took full command of a room without even uttering a single phrase. Parties had been invented for King Edward. He was a private man, but someone who found great ease and satisfaction benefitting others in their social aspirations. My sixth sense showed me water, a place that would bring the King tranquility; big water, a place where he would convalesce as best he was able.

As I was about to continue with my transcription, I was interrupted by Sabine in the most polite way. Rather than speaking, she handed me a brief note on gold-emblazoned letterhead, written by one of the King's men. All I had envisioned was coming so soon. How deeply regrettable. The note stated that King Edward could not meet with me in the coming days. Instead, he, along with a few of his men, had left for Biarritz on the Bay of Biscay in southwestern France. It was no secret that His Highness was quite fond of the casino there. Smoking a dozen cigars and twenty cigarettes a day was confirmation of the fate that lay before him.

It was in Biarritz on the shores of the Atlantic where he would suffer disastrous effects stemming from a lung disorder of some sort. He would convalesce by the seaside resort and would make a return to London in the second month of spring. It was his heart, though, that would fail, several times, while at the palace. Lamentably, I felt positive that King Edward would die during the first few days of May, closest to the sixth in the afternoon, in the company of his wife, Alexandra, and his son, successor to the throne, George V.

Since I knew I'd no longer be meeting with the King, nor ever see him again, I now had to figure out how to distribute this blunt information. Even when deaths are foretold, I don't waste time for the most appropriate moment to arrive to reveal my discoveries. I had to do my job. Sabine would know the appropriate liaison, I was positive of it.

I closed my books. Sealed the chart within an envelope and stood up. Apparently my mobility must have been too abrupt, as my head began to spin and I felt myself becoming lightheaded. I reached for the windowsill with both hands to steady my stance. Outside, I could see nothing but blackness, doom for what was to come, and my own reflection in the windowpane. But was I seeing the king's doom or my own? The passing of my forty-second birthday had happened days earlier. The whites of my eyes, now always red and strained. A pale color limned my complexion. Fame. Fear. As I stared intently at my reflection, I, for the first time, regretted saying, "The wise man cooperates with the stars, the fool thinks he rules them." A quote mentioned in print every time I'm interviewed, one that would presumably appear on my own headstone. Yet what an injustice it sometimes seemed, for free will to have its limits, and for me to be occasionally known as the prognosticator of death.

Once I felt secure on my feet, I walked into the sitting room of my hotel suite. There, waiting for me patiently, with a bicarbonate, teacakes and a prune scone perfectly placed on a lace linen doily and shiny cylindrical silver tray was Sabine. Compassion seemed to be oozing straight through her eyes. She somehow knew that tragic news was mine to deliver.

"You see his death. Don't you, Miss?"

"Yes," I said. I then shook my head but shed no tears, although I'd wanted to. What a travesty. A Scorpio whom I so admired, a man full of life, yet who had gambled too recklessly with fate.

"His heart. It will stop."

"Again, Sabine knows all."

"I don't need the astrology chart. I see his largeness, eating fat, doing no calisthenics. Liquor, smoking all the time. No surprise at me. I have seen this before."

"Now I have to deliver this information. But to whom? This is his fate, it can't be altered."

"The man, Henry, the one that gave me the note. I can summon him. You can give him the information. He can decide where it should go from there."

And so we did. It wasn't long before the King wrote back to me personally. He didn't seem the least bit worried. He was most encouraged that I'd told him his horses would continue to win. But he did seem to have the strangest wish. King Edward requested that one more, additional reading be done, this time for his son, George. He provided his son's birthdate and time and asked me specifically how his ascension to the throne would be received. 'Will it be an easy transition for him? Is he sufficiently qualified to perform the necessary duties?'

It was pleasure to ease the concerns of King Edward. June 3, 1865, Gemini, the communicator—on the surface, all seemed most favorable for George to reign effectively. But it was to be the period at the beginning of his leadership that appeared the most complex. The least favorable time for him was to be the very start of his new life. Because circumstances were strained with Parliament and his father, this would continue. Primarily due to his ascendant in Aries, the stubbornness George possessed would make it doubly difficult to forge compromise and resolution with his cabinet members.

His narrowness came from a variety of factors in his chart. And his health would suffer as a result; a nervousness, a severe nervous condition would haunt him on a daily basis.

During the time George was King, the most notable event would be the strong likelihood of the eagerly-anticipated formation of the Republic of Great Britain before his death. The new King was also likely to have many children with his wife. George would live to be seventy.

I sent this new chart off with much respect and admiration for King Edward. I remained in England only a few days more, having accomplished all I'd set out to. Reflecting on King Edward made me think deeply, perhaps too deeply, about the duration of life. It does seem to come and go quickly, I knew for a fact. My work kept me satisfied though. My work, my antiquing, my collection of porcelain elephants. And, Sabine continued to bemuse me. So very honest, but just as private at the same time.

The cruise back to New York was less mysterious than the former. Sabine and I never spoke of those nighttime goings-on while navigating the high seas. And perhaps it was all best left a mystery. I did wonder though how things turned out with Emma's husband and son. If they'd completed their separate itineraries. How lovely it would be to visit with Emma once more. Both her calmness and delicate appearance appealed to me. If our schedules allowed, perhaps a meeting could be arranged. When I arrived home, I'd write to her.

☉　☽　★

Only a few weeks after being back in the U.S., newsmen of the world inauspiciously confirmed that Edward the King had passed. What I hadn't expected along with the bulletin was the torrent of ill will I received from the English. Somehow, someway, it was made known that I had not only predicted the death of the King, but the stormy reign of his son as well.

I hid from my grief and the backlash, spending time in New Hampshire and Vermont for a few days amid nature and the soothing comforts of quiet. I headed back to Boston initially, while Sabine and the entirety of my staff stayed in New York. Just me alone on the train, to enjoy time away from being Evangeline Smith Adams.

Mentally, in the comfort of my private mobile cabin, I added an endless amount of entries to the To Do list that lived inside my head. My newest strategy for longevity, something I'd learned from a doctor in England, an exercise given to those who live with terminal illness…keeping a To Do list full. The simple logic behind it: the fuller one's list is of things they want, desire, need to do, the longer they'll have to stay put to get them done. I liked that.

I must have added over a hundred on that train ride. None more significant than, "Be bold when meeting with Emma. Unafraid. Let nature guide you. Seek out a fresh experience."

☉　☽　★

Unlike the last time inside my home, Emma and I next met at a tearoom we both knew in Beacon Hill as the fog began to lift over Boston Harbor. Potted Saintpaulias, in shades of pink and lavender, adorned each and every quiet table for two. Stillness and a sense of familiarity surrounded our reunion. No Tiffany lamps this time; merely a convenient meeting place for us both. For someone who believed not in astrology, I wondered what interest she would have in me.

"Oh, my. It's amazing what a European jaunt can do for the soul. How lovely it is to see you once more, Miss Adams. Evangeline." Never before had I seen such a genuine smile.

"It's funny to think that you ever referred to me as Miss Adams, as you initially did. Yet you've forever seemed like Emma to me."

"Then, my friend. Evangeline it is, will always be." Emma, this time, appeared to me as an old friend, a new old friend. Not someone I was still getting to know. The words I chose to use in her company were not as heavily scrutinized in my mind before letting them loose. Some of my fears were disappearing inside without effort.

"Much, much better. You appear so different. A new style."

"More sizeable than that. A new attitude."

"Well, whatever it is, suits you perfectly."

Along with Emma's openness, there was a comforting quality I found in her, just as I first felt when we'd met before. Emma was stimulating, not only with the topics she chose to introduce but the depth from which she spoke.

"Do you still believe there's no escaping your destiny?"

"As always, unwaveringly. I believe devoutly that the stars are infallible. Even with poor King Edward, it was most—"

"Isn't that sad? Ill-timed. Heart-wrenching... No, I'm not necessarily talking about end results or outcomes. To me, that's not destiny. Those are facts on a timetable. Destiny is what we are meant to learn, to accomplish in this lifetime."

"One's purpose in life."

"Just as you noted much earlier, events in my future, you see happening. How can I come close to experiencing those if I don't voluntarily learn, or I should say, choose to learn, about my present? What you had told me then doesn't seem so outlandish now, some of it anyway."

Hearing this made my brain immediately flash back to that crippled, one-legged man I'd encountered in Central Park. How he'd learned to be grateful as a result of his adversity. "If I were continuously told what is to come, what would I learn from?" I recall him telling me.

Before being able to respond, a mature-looking, primly attired woman seated next to Emma and I turned around in her chair, exposing the three identical gunmetal necklaces she was wearing. With crucifixes attached. After wiping both sides of her mouth precisely the same with her crisp, spick and span snow-white handkerchief, she flagrantly threw it down upon the table before her. "Miss...Adams, is it not?"

"Yes, I'm Miss Evangeline Adams."

"You are that seer, the woman who enraged all of England with your demonic divinations."

It's easy for anyone to imagine that this encounter was not a new one for me. But in front of Emma. In a civil teashop, where delicacies were cast aside and replaced with the whispers of curious onlookers. The rage coming from the woman's eyes terrified me. As the woman picked up her handkerchief from the tabletop, she also knocked a full teacup onto the floor below. Its shatter was deafening and created a dead silence in a room chock-full of propriety.

"I practice no demonology, Madam," I replied softly.

"Proclaiming doom to the vulnerable and unsuspecting...for prrrofit."

I didn't know how to respond to that.

Just before the proprietor arrived at our table, Emma took my hand, held it and with the greatest of ease, exorcised all fear from me.

"It's best if we go now," she said.

As I arose from the table, I felt I had to say one more thing, anything. "I help people, Madam. Help with their problems," I again said in a hushed voice.

"You heathen. You're the furthest thing from God-like. You help no persons. You rape them!"

"Come, Evangeline. Come. Don't look back," Emma said.

Upon exiting the tearoom, Emma still held me by the hand and led me down the narrowest of streets along a brick sidewalk to Louisburg Square, a medium-sized park nearby. The majority of it was quiet. There we found a bench with chipped green paint situated before a deserted pond containing no geese. "It sickens me that you had to witness that spectacle, Emma."

"It's nothing to me. Much ago, when you told me that I'd be moving to New York from here; this is the reason why."

"An antique city with relic-inhabitants."

"My husband is one of them. He despises all things different, different from him. Our marriage, as you may have already speculated, is not what it appears."

I dared not tell her what I'd witnessed—her husband and Sabine. "But your trip to Europe, your anniversary there."

"As I said earlier, we took this trip only for Sheridan. My husband and I made an agreement aboard ship that would, how shall I say, leave us open to others."

"Oh, my—"

"I loved him at first, I thought. Part of me always will. It's no longer genuine though. Together we created a son, and I'm most grateful for that. This was my purpose...with Alfred."

This time it was my turn. I placed my hand onto Emma's and she appeared to be relieved. Without warning, a charge surged through my bones. Consoling Emma wasn't my objective. Her show of teeth and deliberate gaze into my eyes, I believed, were confirmation of her receptivity towards me, my gesture and the notions I had floating around my mind since the day I'd first met her. I smiled back and couldn't stop while my imagination ran wild. Thinking back to my list, I chose to cast decorum aside and go for more. My right hand still on hers.

With my other hand, I reached up to touch Emma's cheek softly, briefly. "So very lovely," I told her.

Emma chose to do the same. Her hand touched my cheek, a cozy sensation it had never experienced, and she said, "Beautiful. Just as nature intended."

# Sun @ 3° LEO 48'15
# (1911)

"Miss, your next patron has kept me laughing as long as she's been here."

"I can't wait then. Send her in."

"Miss Adams is ready to see you, Madam," Sabine said with an immense grin, beaming all the way to my office from the waiting area.

"You must call me 'Schatzi'…everyone does. Everyone in Deutschland," a jubilant woman said, nearly shouting, with a foreign accent and the kind of painted-on rosy cheeks I'd only seen by actresses readying to appear onstage. Billowy blue harem pants worn in the daylight? Her hairstyle was the most unique I'd ever observed; most of it ruby red, with porcelain-tone highlights interwoven evenly with the former at quarter-inch intervals.

"But I cannot. You are not mein Schatz." It was nice to see Sabine interact so freely, warmly with one of my clients. I'd noticed that it was only non-Americans that she patted on the back, ushered into my office by the shoulder and greeted with genuine affection. Those Fifth Avenue-ladies, the most regular of my regulars, received the opposite treatment. I considered how difficult it must be for immigrants, and the paradox they face of not really fitting in and missing what's most familiar. I knew Sabine many times pined for her homeland.

"I take it you're too from Germany," I said, joining in the gaiety.

"A little bit west of there, Miss A. London south, Croydon. Surrey, England to be exact."

This woman was the most exuberant I had witnessed within my workplace in ages; no visible worries whatsoever shown on her face. Hair dyed like a candy cane and a translucent turquoise blouse that looked tighter than the skin on a poached knockwurst. Her fingernails were coated in the color of a fire engine ready to extinguish a raging inferno. "Do you live here now?" I asked. "Or do you happen to be visiting?"

"Well, make your diagram by the light of the silvery moon and you tell me."

With pleasure. The woman, named Gwendylspire Boughchamp, divulged her vitals and let me go about my business. But as I did my research, and made my calculations, she interrupted at every opportunity to poke her nose everywhere it didn't belong.

"You've been here long, have you?"

"Something like twelve years now. It's home."

"From Boston."

"Yes."

"Ya' gave the King some bad news. You ain't too popular in England these days, I take it."

Her now-animated and somewhat schizophrenic-sounding comments coming from an altered personality were beginning to interfere with my reading. They also annoyed me. The woman's amusing quality had vanished and been replaced with relentless questioning.

"I'm just about done with my preparations."

"Take your time, Miss A."

"For the most part, very favorable conditions having to do with just about everything personal."

"So…I *will* meet a tall, dark, handsome stranger. Isn't that the script you ladies like to use?"

Her cynicism had next become rudeness. I kept forcing myself to recall that she was a paying customer and the customer is always right. "I have never said that to a single soul. That's a stereotype."

"Go on then."

"In present time I must say that I see deception. You may be deceived by someone. Or you may be perceived as having deceived someone else. This is all surrounded by justice, the law. I don't know why but I see it being connected to the legal system."

"Oh, is that so? And I'd heard that you use to dress up like a gypsy and sprinkle powder on your clients just before all the hocus pocus begins."

"Miss, I'll now give you your full reading and then we'll be done. My next client awaits me."

☉　☽　✶

As soon as I could, I dispatched with this stranger. My next client arrived and was similar to so many, a tad nervous worrying about losing the love of her life. By the end of my working day it was, as J.P. would forever say, business as usual.

While at home the same evening my mind flashed back to the backlash that was created from my English predictions. I began to worry some myself. Although adept in my abilities and in possession of a full list of loyal clients, I recalled that it was my self-promotion skills that had gotten me to where I was. I worked hard to make myself known as the world's leading astrologer. Negative publicity would be my ruin as there are next to no remedies for bad press.

After my mind returned to present circumstances, I don't know why, but it reverted over to the face of Alfred Brooks Fry and his upturned at the ends, over-waxed black moustache. The very same second I was contemplating the aftermath of negativity, bad press, scandal, I saw him in my own head, Emma's "husband." A foreboding energy took over my movement. "Step lightly," I was told from my stomach.

The following day, it seemed like one by one my client list was filled with nothing but Pisces, the most naturally gifted psychics in the zodiac, making for an easy day at the office; they do my work for me, all I have to do is validate what they already know. Also, a match made in heaven for me personally; their sun conjunct my ascendant. After a while though, I was beginning to witness an obvious pattern after having to call out one of their most negative traits, making up new truths in order to perpetuate airs.

"Is this correct? The birth year you have provided?"

"Oh, without a doubt. The time I had trouble retrieving, but the year I cannot forget," my current female client told me while wearing a tightly wrapped tangerine-colored turban atop her head. My instinct told me otherwise. Most Fifth Avenue ladies, who change clothes not the customary one-to-two, but eight-to-ten times a day, invented new birthdates, and this was a Pisces élite, a woman who must have lived out the majority of life via her imagination and creativity.

"I do see a most turbulent time ahead in your chart, in the area of romance. A man is, or is about to be, disloyal to you…with someone you know. This will take place in the near future, the next few months. The outcome doesn't appear to be in your favor."

"And you would see it differently if…I were born in, let's say, another year?"

The truth always comes out. Pisces fib as often as they take breaths. I should have offered a disclaimer to every one of them that enters my studio under false pretenses.

In due course, the woman gave me her truthful birth year and all was solved, a chart that much more accurately depicted her life and the events that were to take place. She left my office beaming as she adjusted the new light-boned, long corset she'd spent nearly ten minutes talking about. Now that her bulges were more firmly concealed, Mrs. R.i.E., I shall call her, "Romance is Everything," knew that all would turn out perfectly fine in the coming months. That she was a little older than what she'd first admitted made no difference to me. Her chart, however, suffered the consequences of vanity.

Next into my studio came a woman nearly identical to the last, yet her stony, highbrow air somehow took me back to that conservative woman I had encountered in the tearoom with Emma. My peaceful day seemed to be transforming into aggravation before my very eyes.

"My guest list. For my next dinner party. Is it diverse enough?" Mrs. "Fridays-at-Four," wearing not a turban, but a hat big enough to live in, containing its own tropical fruit salad, asked intensely.

"That's what you want to know?"

"I pride myself on the parties I plan. They must be perfect every time."

"The date?"

"Fourth of March, 1852. Precise—"

"No, the date of the party."

"You didn't state that, Miss. You merely asked, 'Date? *The* date?' One must be absolute, thorough when articulating. If I come upon one more faction who utters an incomplete sentence I think I will—"

It was as if Aries had taken over my spirit. "One more faction *that…*"

"I beg your pardon."

"Oh, I'm sorry to interrupt."

As the woman's curvaceous vein began to bulge forward between her left temple and her receding hairline, she said, "No, by all means. You seem to derive pleasure in correcting me. Continue, please."

"A common mistake. *Who* would follow a specific person, persons or name of a person. *That* would follow a group or faction."

With fifteen minutes remaining to our session, one of my staff members rapped on my door. Whenever I was working with a client I took no interruptions, ever, under no circumstances. The door didn't open, so in a raised volume of voice I said, "We have several more minutes."

Another rap. Was I not quite loud enough to be heard? I thought.

"This is highly improper. I have paid you dearly for your services," the seated woman in need of an English lesson roared out to all of Manhattan.

"Let us continue, Mrs."

Now a third rap. "Please do pardon me for one moment. I'll gladly extend our meeting once I resolve this inconvenience."

As I opened the door I found, to my surprise, one of my ten stenographers holding the knob, Margaret, a single lady who usually attended to nothing more than my thousands of requests by mail. Immediately next to her was a uniformed police officer standing behind another holding a piece of paper.

"You are Miss Evangeline Smith Adams?"

"Well, yes. I most assuredly am, but what—"

"Take this. Please."

I took the single-page document from the suited man and still knew nothing. "But what—"

"This is your order to appear before the Superior Court of New York, ma'am. You're in violation of Penal Code 165.35. Purporting to tell fortunes for a fee. A class B misdemeanor."

"This is outrageous," should have been my words, but they instead came from the seated party-planner.

Needless to say, the stiff, veiny woman abruptly fled my presence, did not pay and I was left alone in my office to read the official letter I was holding. My staff, which had witnessed this spectacle, remained silent, awaiting a reaction from me.

The quiet didn't last beyond the moment Sabine came back from her beauty appointment along with her newly crimped locks. She didn't need much of an explanation from the others. She bolted into my office. "Was ist los, Miss?" She'd reverted back to her native tongue.

"I have charges against me. A violation of some fortune-telling ordinance. Here in the City of New York. I can't believe this is happening. The authorities do this all the time in Greenwich Village. But to *me, here*..."

My mind, already plagued with a migraine, couldn't comprehend it. My career, all I had worked for, all of the ways in which I'd promoted myself, my legacy, the validity of modern-day astrology. Now at risk.

Just as I was about to place my fingertips upon my forehead, Sabine fully entered my office, shut the door behind her and walked in back of me in my seat. With no hesitation she said, "Close your eyes, Miss."

I did as I was asked. "Put your head back. A little."

After tipping it backwards, Sabine began massaging my forehead exactly where the most tension could be found. She was silent and so was I. No sounds coming from the outside could be heard anymore. The palms of her soft, moist hands, forming concentric circles to the sides of both my eyes became therapeutic, medicinal and tender. How did Sabine know that what I needed most was the human touch? The caress of another woman? Within a very short period of time, the tensions dwelling in my mind became absent.

"It's good. The feeling?" Sabine murmured.

"Wonderful."

I had nearly forgotten how good it could be to be comforted so lovingly. My mind drifted to Emma and the soothing caress of her hand.

Before long, Sabine softly began humming a lullaby I recognized immediately. To *me* though, a grown woman. A sing-songy melody composed for infants ready to capture their forty winks. Not until she reached the tune's second verse did she begin singing it. "*Guten Abend, gute Nacht, von Englein bewacht, die zeigen im Traum dir Christkindleins Baum. Schlaf nun selig und süß, schau im Traum's Paradies.*" As she finished, I thought I could see teardrops forming in Sabine's eyes. Then, seeming to know that I'd noticed this, she looked away from me hurriedly.

Never in a million years would it have occurred to me, but Sabine and her seldom-seen softer side, I believed, would make a very caring mother to a child.

"It's important to have lady-friends, Miss."

"Yes, that's true."

Once more, Sabine knew much, much more than I'd ever divulged to her. "I have some. But it's men I like best."

I had never been touched like this by a man, any man. My personal life was also something I rarely had to explain. I was alone because, well, because my work would always come first.

"When I do this, you're thinking of your—Boston. Yes?"

Hearing such an odd comment brought me back to reality

immediately. Sabine also knew that it was time to stop. Although I was indeed grateful, I couldn't muster the words, 'thank you.' Acknowledging what had just happened just wouldn't seem right. Not appropriate. Maybe Germans were naturally more liberal, more laissez-faire than the average American.

Sabine went back to work. And so did I.

☉   ☽   ★

"Balderdash!" J.P. shouted.

"I've never been so worried. My career, my future...all I've done to get to this point."

"You think I don't know about all the others that wish to do me in?"

How true. Being as successful as J.P. was, there must have been many, countless others that have been jealous. Competitors. Friends. Enemies. Saboteurs. But my resilience, my resolve was nothing like his.

"My life will be in ruins, J.P.," I told him with resignation.

As if they were witnessing a miracle, my fuzzy eyes next saw J.P.'s left hand reach out and touch my right shoulder. Perhaps he didn't know what he was doing. Perhaps instinctual. In the following moment, it was gone. Back to waving his hands in the air, J.P. shouted out, "No, none of it I want to hear. We're wasting time. I'm here to discuss substance. The company I've asked about...good or bad?"

"Of course, sir. I see it most favorable in...six to eight months. Any time prior to that would be much less. A failure of sorts."

"I never fail. I always win. Being unafraid is what separates me from my colleagues. I never fear them, yet they're ever afraid of me. I'm the winner. They lose."

"Fear is the key. Isn't it?"

"Not that simple. 'Cause you're a woman, a successful one. Folks don't like that."

"It's wrong, J.P. Whether the world's ready for a successful businesswoman or not, I shouldn't—"

"Enough. It'll take no more than a minute for me to direct one of New York's finest defense attorneys to you. He'll represent you. The judge will make note of this and will dismiss the whole thing."

"I don't know—"

"You don't know what to say. Well, that's why I said it. All on my dime, naturally. End of discussion. Oh…on one condition. Stop seeing that kraut, Schwabbie."

J.P. didn't elaborate, nor did he allow me to acknowledge his directive because he was, of course, joking. Wasn't he?

# Sun @ 2° CAPRICORN 49'08 (1912)

*J*.P. was entirely correct, as he always was. Nobody takes action better than an Aries after they've become impatient. I'd grown quite fond of that man and the loyalty he'd shown me. The hugs that sometimes ended our sessions at first surprised me, coming from such a manly giant, but then became expected. Not soft, tender and cuddly; still business-like with a somewhat subtle familial tone about them. Fatherly, and most appreciated because J.P. initiated each and every one. Our brief embraces conveyed approval, acceptance from someone I considered being a near-family member, responses I had been seeking since my earliest years.

It was arranged that I never even had to appear in a court of law at all. Everything was handled outside. As days passed, one after the other, I awaited the damaging residual effects of gossip, imagining I'd become the negative talk-of-the-town. Thank my luckiest star this incident never made its way into print. Not one word about it was published in *The New York Times*. Not earthshattering enough, I presumed. None of my worries had come to pass, but the whole experience of being ordered to court made me utterly more cautious than I had ever been previous.

I learned from J.P.'s attorney that that eccentric-looking and enthusiastically enigmatic English woman named Gwendylspire Boughchamp to whom I'd given a reading, was in actuality an American actress who'd once starred in the *Ziegfeld Follies*. It was her testimony implying fraud that had brought this matter to the attention of the City prosecutor. My instinct told me that she hadn't arrived in my office of her own volition. But rather than becoming paranoid about the host of culprits who may have hired her, I went about my daily duties.

☉  ☽  ☆

As my business continued to grow by leaps and bounds and my waitlist for individual appointments increased from days to weeks to sometimes months, my steadiest steady customer remained my most faithful. I always thought of my connection to J.P. to be one where either was there for the other when needed. One of the best professional-turned-personal relationships I could have ever envisioned.

Even though a brief lull in my calendar did end up occurring— secretive society ladies now too afraid to enter my premises for fear of exposure—syndicated newspaper columns began carrying my predictions all over the world by 1912. This meant a huge increase in requests by post. My staff, now having expanded to twenty-five or so, conducted my business in not one but several suites at Carnegie Hall: more secretaries, more stenographers, more researchers, mail openers and readers, apprentice astrologists, schedulers and a host of others.

Each and every one seemed to hover around my office, like

honeybees over a hive, whenever they knew J.P. was coming. Hands rested aimlessly upon the 19th-century mahogany teapoy table, faces stared into the Italian Gilt Wood Grapevine mirror blankly, and mindless chatter took place around the Baroque "Putto Face" cast iron wall fountain. Mostly all these antiques were, in part, financed by J.P. and his numerous visits, and each and every worker bee in my employ knew it.

As J.P. passed them by, providing no "How do you dos?" or second glances, it was only business in Europe, international companies that he had on his mind. As always, I was more than ready to accommodate his queries.

Wearing a straight face and his let's-get-down-to-business demeanor, I knew I had to keep my words short. No time to waste in the presence of His Majesty, the King of U.S. Finance. As economically as possible, while taking no more than one second to do so, I asked, "The dates again?"

"The first weeks of spring."

"Where exactly?"

"Well, arrival in England, obviously. On the twenty-fifth. In London for four or five days. Then onto Paris for about the same. You need more?" J.P. said as he attempted to wiggle his index finger within the non-existent space between his bounteous neck and starched hard linen collar.

"No, that's fine."

Merely a minute after being seated, J.P. loosened his grey steel-colored tie and unfastened the black leather belt around his waist. This relaxation ritual had now become regular in my company. "Only around you, Evvy."

As usual, just as my eyes alit onto the pages of my ephemeris, J.P. lit up another one of his cylindrical Cuban Montecristos. During these times I always remembered to do my fresh-air inhaling in the direction of an opened, smoke-free window, and to exhale while turning back to J.P. "Did I tell you about the fire inside my house?" he said.

"No. How awful. Was anyone—"

"A small one. Cinders on the floor of a broom closet."

"Prob—"

"A maid. I fired her on the spot," J.P said after letting out a tension-filled puff. Appearing contemplative upon his next intake, J.P. afterwards said softly, "Is that how you see me going? You can tell me." Next, a nervous and oh-so-rare look of insecurity came over him.

"We've discussed this so many times. Not to worry about such a thing. But accidents do happen. Let me—"

"Yeah, yeah, yeah. Get back to your cyphering. Remember, not one word to about this. To any living soul."

"Not a one, J.P. Never."

My calculations showed that business during late March and early April with virtually any company domestic or abroad would be promising for J.P. and his business associates. But somehow not during those days while at the Aix-les-Bains resort in southeastern France.

"If time permits, I'm thinking of placing Rome into the mix. But I can't miss an important P.R. opportunity in England. An I.M.M. subsidiary. The second week of April, I think it is."

"Staying in Rome may be fine, England as well. But…there is a sign that travel itself during that time is not wise. This promotional opportunity has to do with travel?"

"One of the companies I own, the White Star Line. The maiden voyage of its newest ship, the Titanic. Leaving from Southampton."

"When?"

"I've got to see my schedule," J.P said while examining his itinerary. "The tenth of April. Calling in Cherbourg and Ireland before New York. I may catch it in France if that suits me better."

I looked hard and long into this idea. Never had I seen a more negative time for any endeavor. Upsetting aspects affecting this chart.

"All else looks fine, but it's the timing of this crossing itself that appears disastrous."

"How about boarding ship at a later time?"

"No, it will be during the space, the time, between Ireland and the U.S. that it all appears so bleak."

"Everybody who's anybody's going to be on it. Fantastic P.R., individually, and for business. Americans *and* Europeans."

"This voyage will still generate attention, but for all the wrong reasons. I feel sick to my stomach, J.P."

"Evvy, you are looking a little green around the gills. I'm not going to lose any money, am I?"

At this point I had to be frank, more than frank. So many times I'd provided information and guidance, but I still encouraged each individual client to make their own decisions. I didn't know if it was my own personal feelings toward J.P., my concern for him, or my sureness about what I was seeing.

The words just came out of my mouth. "J.P. under no circumstances should you be aboard that ship, ever. No boarding at a different port. Please avoid this ship. There will be other opportunities for you to promote what you do. Your travel on this ship will be catastrophic."

J.P. twitched his plum-pigmented nose, looking a bit bewildered and indecisive. "Evvy, if I'd heard this from anyone else, I'd still go anyway. I'm taking you at your word because you've proven yourself right every time."

"Even if there are moments in Europe when you re-think, don't!"

"Alright then, I absolutely won't go."

As J.P. uttered that statement, the sickness in my stomach subsided a tad. I knew that he would keep his word. This somehow validated to me that J.P. had become more than a client, he was a loyal and true friend. He'd stood up for me during my legal dilemma and I hoped my words of caution would see him extend his life by avoiding calamity.

⊙   ☽   ✫

And calamity it was—a catastrophe that affected the whole world. J.P.'s brand-new ship, the Titanic, struck an iceberg and sank. The news trickled in as more names of the dead were revealed—over fifteen hundred in all.

My heart ached for those I had known, those I hadn't and the families that were left behind. And a large part of me felt so irretrievably guilty for not having been able to see more, though I knew it would have been impossible. I'd never been able to establish specific details that unambiguously when other information was absent from my scope. To know of every tragedy coming before us all would be like being able to pull one needle from every haystack. The same had been true for those seeking my financial advice: With J.P., I was able to see when the times were best compatible with the data provided about particular companies. When people asked me which stocks would be most profitable, I hadn't a clue.

Despondency dominated my days after the Titanic accident. I began to give much greater credence to the notion that nature shall overpower man every time, at every opportunity. It was pointless to dispute the fact that my powers of insight were insignificant compared to what the Almighty was capable of stirring up. In so many ways, Emma's talk of fate, destiny and life's lessons and that story about God's will from the wooden-legged man I'd met in the park, seemed to make more sense.

During a free moment in between sessions, I took a stack of paper from my desk and began composing a letter. I no longer desired to suppress my true feelings. So many times I had thought about Emma and longed to see her again, but I was never able to articulate the depth of my emotions. Yet as I had heard so many times before, as I'd been reminded of multiple times in the present, life is indeed fleeting. We are here for only so long and perhaps we were, as Emma insisted, obliged to do something with it; purposeful objectives prescribed by an "Order much Higher" than anything I could ever imagine.

Although my career was at its pinnacle, in so many ways I felt I had advanced no further than childhood. Melancholia, and the stifling after-effects, had had their way with me on so many occasions in the past, but this time they seemed insurmountable. What difference had I made with my life? In which ways was I truly able to make a difference in anyone else's? I had made them all weaker for having to rely on me for their own decision-making. I'd provided no comfort whatsoever. Just like those gypsy fortunetellers I'd been so often times compared to, I had exploited those most vulnerable that came to me. I'd served no purpose whatsoever.

I was never able to finish writing that letter to Emma. In its place, I stared outside through my window facing Seventh Avenue. Unable to make out expressions of the people passing by, I saw nothing but blurs. Indistinguishable images rather than humans. Each and every one so very sad.

"These are for you."

Not hearing my door open and not having expected anyone, I thought, at first, that I was imaging the presence of a ghost.

"Daydreaming again?" I heard in a whisper.

I turned around in my seat to face a very welcomed sight.

"How good to see you, J.P."

The timing of his visit couldn't have been more perfectly plotted. My friend, J.P. Morgan looked somber, sincere and somehow perfectly at peace. He was carrying the most precious display of horticulture I'd ever seen.

"I had these custom made for you, you know. Lilies, dyed black."

"I don't know what to—"

"For chrissakes, stop saying you don't know what to say. Take these damn things."

"Put them over there, on the marble table. They're stunning. But why?"

"Evvy, I wouldn't be here if you hadn't helped guide me. I owe you my life. What you've done for me…"

"The papers mentioned you, you know. *J.P. Morgan changed his plans to board the Titanic at the last minute,'* they said." I didn't feel the least bit slighted at J.P.'s gain in publicity while my name was not attributed to his decision. "Is that how you see it? I helped you?"

J.P. had an astonished look on his face, like he couldn't believe what he'd just heard.

"You're making a joke. It's obvious. You've helped me in so many ways, with my mergers, investments, buyouts, and now saving my life."

J.P. didn't need to explain more, because the emotion coming from the language of his body, his open physical stance and his right hand positioned atop his heart, spoke for itself. Warmth seemed to be emanating from his every pore, absorbing it was inescapable.

"Sometimes I see it only as 'doing my job.' Doing it all for a living. That's why people come to me, for my job."

"Evvy, but sometimes the two go together. When I step into this studio, it's you I look forward to seeing most, not what you have to tell me."

Because of my rare sensitive state, my eyes welled up with tears and I didn't try to stop them. Never had a living soul seen me cry before, but this time I was willing to let nature take its course.

J.P. reached inside his breast pocket for a crisp and clean handkerchief and I took it from him. I chose not to use it as my pride didn't want to admit that it needed to.

"Thank you, sir."

"Is that what you call a friend?"

"J.P. Friend."

It was at that moment that my emotions got the best of me. In all my decades of dedication to astrology, predictions, I had spent so much time promoting myself, my career; never in a million years would I have thought that my profession and my personal life could be intertwined.

"When we first met, those first few times, I was your client. You were my advisor. Now we're friends. How lucky I am."

"I'm the one that's lucky, J.P. Today, I needed a friend."

"We all need friends, Evvy. Ain't no point in making billions if there's no one to hold your hand at the end of the day."

$$\odot \quad \math{D} \quad \star$$

"It's cute when Mr. J.P. blushes after he flirts with me," Sabine boasted, while failing to comfortably adjust the vast contents of her brassiere and modify its monumental task.

"Your ego is simply amazing."

"It's the truth. He likes watching me...then his face turns ruby red."

"He has rosacea. It's a skin disease. He's very self-conscious about it."

"Oh, I didn't know. But he does like to watch me walk,

especially when I'm not looking."

"If you can't see him, how do you know he's watching you?"

"My caboose. I can just feel him watching me when I walk away from him. Just like you do. I don't mind."

"Sabine, I have never—"

"I know you for many years now. It's only natural to be curious, Miss."

I began laughing out loud at the absurdity of it all. Perhaps, aside from her moon, Sabine had excessive amounts of Capricorn in her chart and I'd neglected to notice it. Vanity and ego come in all shapes and sizes, and Sabine made full use of both whenever given the chance.

"Can we get back to business, please? Who's coming in next?"

"No, nobody's coming in. Now, time to do a few by mail."

Eager to let my social skills take a break, I said, "OK, bring them in and I'll get started straight away."

"Please try to control yourself as I leave the room."

All I could do was gasp at the nerve of her. Scorpios are now, and will always be, shamelessly oversexed, I knew most assuredly.

Sabine brought in a pile of chart requests by mail and the stack was arranged by those who'd included payment on top, the others on the bottom. Barely able to find room on what had become my second, "post-only" desk, Sabine too exuberantly pushed aside hundreds of other, pre-existing requests. As the newest tower of white, crème, beige and camel colored envelopes tipped over the moment it was placed on my desk, I noticed one in the middle. It was addressed incorrectly, as the majority of them were, to *Mrs.* Evangeline Adams. Nothing new about that. But numerous stenciled crisscrosses adorned this particular packet. Some were blue, some black, others were green, and the largest, most exaggerated one was bright red.

As I lifted out the letter, a heavy pewter St. Andrew's cross fell from the envelope and landed onto my desk with a clang. How incredibly odd, I thought. The handwriting was most precise and delicate, leading me to believe that many drafts of this same letter had been made prior, before styling it just right.

The word God and Savior appeared to have been placed in every sentence—written as a protective measure, it seemed. The letter had been composed by a twenty-two-year-old housewife from Minot, North Dakota. Having received a wide variety of pleas for help, this one I'd seen only a few times earlier. Before composing the chart I could already imagine its outcome.

*Jimmy never comes to me the way the Almighty intended. As soon as he gets home from work I feed him supper. When he's done he gets a sinful lustful look inside his eyes when he speaks of his friend Seamus a man. Forgive me but I love my Jimmy and I don't want his soul to be delivered unto Satan. My Jimmy comes home soiled and sweaty after his times with Seamus. God help us for our sins. Mrs. Adams why was I born not good enough to please him? When will he return to the Lord God Almighty? You must answer back before I end my suffering.*

The woman was thorough in her delivery of data. When examining the birth information she'd provided for herself, her husband and the husband's friend, it was blatantly clear that nothing would change. She and her husband would never have relations as man and wife. Instead he would continue living his life as, my mother would say, "a pathetic soul," "a deviate." The collective horoscope for these three confirmed that the "sickness" the husband lived with would not dissipate.

The way Mother saw it, the countless times we had prayed for poor Uncle Horatio in Winthrop, "the disease of homosexuality is not a mere affliction; it's a deeply rooted sickness of the mind." As a child, I'd never doubted her. Mother, I was certain, would have told me that it was far better for this unfortunate woman to know this information, so she'd be able to release herself from such an ill, misguided man and become open to encountering a normal and healthy one.

Whether I felt otherwise or not, the woman had forgotten to include the twenty dollar fee for the reading. As I did with all others that had done the same, I crumpled up the request and threw it into the trash.

# Sun @ 15° ARIES 35'26 (1913)

*I*n my business, people come and go. That's life.

"Miss, your dress will be ready soon," my secretary told me matter-of-factly yet still wearing a frown to show woe.

"Thank you, Sabine. And the flower?"

"Two of the girls here were finally able to find some. They're making a bouquet."

"Oh, no. A single stem. I'd like to place just one atop the casket. That's customary."

Black lilies, with pistols remaining natural in shades of undyed yellow, were my favorite flowers and my friend J.P. knew it. The moment I read the news, I knew I'd miss his impulsiveness the most. Those early days when he was so entirely skeptical, not wanting to believe a word I had to tell him. My, what a turnaround his stodginess had undergone.

Although I was able to spare his fate from the Titanic, J.P. departed only eleven months after the disaster. I'd never know if he died in fear, or if he'd somehow accepted what life, inevitably, had to offer. Never had I wanted to know beforehand the date and time J.P. would leave this world; never did I tell him. "Near your birthday," was the response any amateur could have made. Dying close to one's day of birth is common.

I couldn't stop thinking about him, about the phobia we'd shared about passing on. At the beginning of the century, I'd resorted to every trick in the book to keep J.P. coming back as a well-paying client. Baiting him with tasty tidbits linked to lucrative end results, teasing him record-breaking profits to come, forever feeding his ravenous anticipation with, "not until next time." Later on, it was his personality, his character I longed to grab hold of. Never did I have prior knowledge of his death. It was only after the fact, late in the night preceding the funeral, I chose to make my calculations. As plain as a day with no surprises, there it was. March 31, 1913. Exactly the same as it appeared in his obituary. The death of J.P. Morgan: two-and-a-half weeks prior to his birthday.

"Now, there is no one to flirt with me," my secretary said while attempting to lighten the mood.

I didn't respond because I was still trying to make sense of J.P.'s departure. Like King Edward, smoking a dozen or so cigars daily had given J.P.'s lungs no time to de-combust. Even in death, I saw my fiery Aries friend alive and well in the multitude of businesses he founded and ran. He had taught me much about life, about business and the reason we strived to make a success of both at the same time. All the papers were declaring him "the father of American finance," appropriate in more ways than one. J.P. junior had been ready and primed for years to take over. I didn't need to cast a chart to know he'd do well.

Only a handful of people knew how close J.P. and I had become, how much we relied on each other as friends. One or two condolence telegrams arrived for me personally. This quite surprised me, and it felt rather comforting. There was one that meant the most.

"I shall read this one to you. You continue dressing. *To be the confidante of such a fine and noble businessman and philanthropist makes you a very trusted soul. I am sorry for your loss, my friend, but I am happy for the cherished memories you two have created. As you and I have spoken about before',*" Sabine said clearly. Her recitation sounding deliberate, full of get-up-and-go. Yet slow. Comprehendible. With perfect diction. Not once did I have to ask her to repeat a single word. Now, placing her hand over her heart, Sabine continued by saying, *"'communication equals catharsis. Please, at any—'"*

"Who has written this message?"

"Miss, please. I was just about to say."

"Yes, go on."

*"'Please, at any time you'd wish to share your feelings, I'm here for you now and always. Your beloved, Emma'.*"

Sabine blushed as she read the last line, knowing that this had been a taboo subject between her and me. How utterly touching for Emma to have even thought of me now. I took the stylish Moss green envelope with its lavishly sophisticated Serif scroll from Sabine's hand, inhaled the hint of Cornubia Oriental Floral, Emma's signature fragrance, and brought it closer to my nose and then my eyes. Something about me already knew that a change had taken place. The return address showed New York, not Boston. I handed back the envelope. "That's lovely, Sabine."

Sabine placed her hand on my shoulder, left it there for a few seconds then told me, "That ship. Everything that happened, the way it did, was Schicksal. Or how is it you say...faith."

"Faith. Hope...during times of adversity."

"No, not this one. Faith, but without the *h*."

"Fate."

"Yes. No *h*."

"I'm not so sure I know what you mean."

"The way you see your friend, Emma, on the ship. By surprise. You meet her husband and son. And, you see me with—"

"We really need to finish getting ready. Our carriage will be here in the offing."

"I must finish, Miss. You saw me with her husband…and we've never discussed this."

"I don't wish to—"

"He told me many things. This man is not, how you say, a philanderer. Mr. Alfred explained to me that he and Mrs. Fry have no intimate, none."

"Sabine, this is none of my business. But did you happen to be intimate with Mr. Fry?"

"Oh, never. I flirt to get *attention*. I don't do that anymore. Miss, he has white flakes in his hair. Scratching, digging all the time."

Involuntarily my face contorted into a deflated beach ball after consuming this account. "How distasteful."

"His shoulders look like a fresh snow in the Alpen after he's done," Sabine said while shivering.

My secretary perhaps didn't have to be that descriptive, but it certainly did paint a colorful picture for those that fancy wintry backdrops. This matched the story Emma began telling me when I'd met with her in Boston.

New York, not Boston. Just as I'd seen earlier.

There were a few minutes left before I needed to leave for the funeral. I took the envelope back from Sabine and transferred Emma's address onto a fresh one. And fitting as it was on the day of J.P.'s funeral, I slipped out the letter I'd begun the day J.P. had visited me after the Titanic, and I began to write.

Before long Emma responded to my request that we meet up

in New York. I tried to temper my excitement, but Sabine could sense it, and she shared in my glee.

The day Emma was scheduled to arrive at my studio turned out to be a particularly hectic one. Whatever could go wrong did. Three clients in a row, this time men, had given me false information, forcing me to create replacement charts for them all over again. A headache was brewing inside me like tea with too many leaves left at the bottom of the cup. Residue was accumulating onto my disposition and I'd run out of lye cleanser.

A few minutes after my last client of the afternoon had departed, my assistant, Isabel, told me the news I had been eagerly awaiting, "Mrs. Fry is here to see you."

"Please do send her in."

Placed squarely before me was a sight to behold. "Evangeline," Emma said, offering a handshake.

Frozen with fear, my body didn't know how to react. It had become paralyzed. Immediately behind Emma's back my eyes observed an intruder to my office. "In Germany we hug," Sabine said without an invitation.

"Oh, of course," Emma replied as prompted.

Emma and I hugged each other right on cue and our embrace added to my feeling of warmth toward her. "It's wonderful to see you, my friend. You're a New Yorker now."

Emma beamed. "I was delighted to hear back." She glanced around my private office not like a detective, more an admirer of order and symmetry. "Your artwork is sublime."

Pointing to my favorites I said solemnly, "These two Gainsborough landscapes are from J.P. himself. Thank you again for your kind note."

"No one had to remind me about the special connection you two'd maintained. I'm sure he meant a lot to you, you to him."

In a rather forlorn way I replied, "He taught me a lot, too."

"He was *the* business leader."

My masked enthusiasm at seeing Emma again became muted momentarily upon discussing my father figure now departed. "No. About life. About..." I couldn't express what J.P. had actually taught me, because, all over again, I noticed how delicate, feminine and inviting Emma's hands looked. It's as if they were waiting to be held.

While I was not entirely clear as to why meddling Sabine was still in our presence, she said, "It's a good thing you're getting together now, otherwise you would have missed Miss Adams while she's in New Hampshire."

Doing my best to shush Sabine with my pursed lips, she then left the room wearing an obvious grin.

☉　☽　✭

On the late afternoon we two dined together at the new Oyster Bar on the lower level of Grand Central, it was as if no time had passed at all. Adding to the delight of our reunion, Emma and I had plenty of opportunities to get to know each other even better. Emma did not introduce any concepts that were foreign to me, but she, unlike anyone I'd known before, brought out my curiosity in between bites.

Towards the end of a somber tale about the sweet hereafter, Emma told me, "...that's when the soul leaves the body," while I continued prying crabmeat from the leg of a most stubborn and selfish shellfish. Not even amounting to a mouthful.

"And from there remains in heaven."

"Only for a time. It returns to life, you could say, once it's ready to learn more 'lessons'."

Immediately after hearing the word 'lesson,' the wedding song *Because* by Enrico Caruso began playing on an Edison Amberola or

Victrola in the background. I smiled at the thought of my impish Italian friend.

"I wonder if I have more lessons to learn."

In my mind I saw Sabine nodding her head as if she had a nervous disorder, while interjecting a rapid, "Natürlich."

I thought to myself, someday I'm going to fire her, but until then, I'm too afraid to do so.

"Your secretary had mentioned a trip to New Hampshire."

"Oh…it's nothing."

"You know, it's a shame we never got together sooner, on one of your trips to Boston."

"Well, I find myself more set in my ways as time goes by. My work, my obligations provide few occasions to socialize."

"My situation mirrors yours exactly. Sad."

"Quite sad, I reckon." Inside myself I knew it was profoundly sad. The debilitation that lived within me wanted so badly to be set free. I was afraid.

Returning to my initial dismissive response, Emma continued her query by saying, "It's so beautiful this time of year, New Hampshire. Which part?"

"A lake near Newport. A beautiful old lodge."

"How divine. Oh, how I wish—"

"I've been going up often lately, looking for a cabin to purchase."

Emma's dazed eyes seemed to be spellbound in wanderlust. Her longing to be transported to a different place, a new locale, was apparent to me in even the extended breath she'd just taken in. Could we two perhaps be thinking the same thing? As my heart pounded, I found Emma's being to be captivating, her expression confident yet she exuded vulnerability. Unequivocally, I knew that it was up to me to take charge.

"When exactly is it you're leaving?"

"Three days from now." One, two, three, four. Inhale. Four, three, two, one. Exhale. A momentarily lull in our conversation gave me the opportunity to practice balanced breathing, a technique Sabine taught me when we first met. "Would you...care to join me?"

After a pause or two Emma said, "Deliciously outlandish. I might just like to try that."

"You...enjoy the countryside? You...happen to be free then?"

Flapping her wings the way a firetail finch readies for flight, Emma said, "As free as a bird."

The precise moment Emma said that, just as my phobic nature next took a hiatus, a beautiful chirping sparrow positioned itself outside our window. It shook rainwater from its body and appeared to be dancing. How delightfully odd.

☉　☽　★

Emma and I did journey from New York to New Hampshire as if prescribed by destiny. Never ever did I do such things; traveling with someone who did not work for me. Our conversations on the train about childhood, siblings, family and peer pressure, expectations, growing older, goals and beyond were intoxicating, maybe even slightly curative. We even covered topics that were uniquely womanly: the morality of abortifacients, the end of monthlies, and "hitting the target." Those no-nonsense chats, quite rare for me, carried the two of us closer together. On occasion I was left awestruck by the unabashed candor of not only Emma's words, but my reactions to them.

Emma spoke so frankly of her somewhat pre-arranged marriage to her husband. In reality, she lived her life as a single woman, just as her husband lived as a bachelor. "Like I said earlier, Evangeline. As free as a bird."

"Well, then…so am I."

Something about Emma's confession left me feeling liberated. While my conscious mind began looking at her differently, my subconscious took over, now making me vulnerable, and together Emma and I acted on instinct alone.

Inching closer to me on a stylish, canary yellow Turkish divan, Emma reached out her hand and placed it on my right leg. "Caresses cure all, you know."

"Well, no…I—"

"Trust me," Emma said convincingly.

I did.

With diminishing fears, apprehension and guilt, Emma and I undressed each other in front of a roaring hearth that gave our parlor its only light. Few additional words were spoken over the crackling flames.

Clothing became unnecessary with the heat of our bodies, the inferno below generating warmth. Emma's lips touched mine first, softly on top of my head, then forehead, then onto my own lips. My reaction was volcanic. My hands, my lips went everywhere they could. Emma allowed herself to be touched, tasted and kissed simultaneously. "Oh, my. Salty." I couldn't stop myself. Decades overdue, my first time with anyone was well worth the wait.

From the sitting room to the bedroom, our intimate moments of titillation and rapture never stopped. It's almost as if they were foreordained.

After several hours, we paused. Our room became still as we wrapped ourselves up in a burgundy, fleecy wool, knitted double blanket together again in front of the fire. "So perfectly natural, my dear. Don't you think?"

"Emma…I'm speechless."

"You needn't utter a sound."

My nod back was all I offered as a reply. Conversation would only spoil the perfection of it all.

By the time I was ready to hear more words and absorb their meaning, Emma admitted that she'd never experienced closeness like that since the very early years of her marriage to Alfred.

Yes, on that trip Emma continued being my teacher, and perhaps I was hers as well. At the inn by the lake, the Almighty wasn't mentioned as much, or any subject that was discussed on the train ride there.

It was on this trip that Emma taught me without verbal expression whatsoever. She chose to teach me physically, in ways I'd never known or allowed myself to know. And at the end of our time together in New Hampshire, Emma whispered to me, "I'm the principal lesson you're meant to learn."

# Sun @ 23° TAURUS 18'55 (1914)

The New York Times

May 15, 1914

## FORTUNE TELLERS
## TRAPPED BY WOMEN

———

One Seer Was Taken from Expensive Suite in Carnegie
Hall Building.

———

## HER CLIENTS IN SOCIETY

———

Miss Bessie Block of West Tenth
Street Advised Detective
Isabella Goodwin.

———

Two alleged fortune tellers, Mrs. Evangeline S. Adams, who said she was a descendant of President John Quincy Adams, and Miss Bessie Block, were in Magistrates' courts yesterday as a result of the activity of women detectives attached to Police Commissioner Woods's staff. Much interest was shown in the case of Mrs. Adams, who appeared before Magistrate Campbell in the West Side Court.

The evidence against her was obtained by Detective Adelie Priess, and the warrant for her arrest was issued by Chief Magistrate McAdoo. Detective Roos of Headquarters, who made the arrest, said that Mrs. Adams had an expensive suite of rooms in the Carnegie Hall Building, at Seventh Avenue and Fifty-seventh Street, and that she was consulted by many women prominent in society. Her reception room was crowded with fashionably dressed women when he interrupted her work, he said. Mrs. Adams was held under $500 bail for examination next Wednesday. Mrs. Priess did not disclose the nature of the evidence she obtained. . .

⊙　☽　✫

*My* red, strained eyes were too tired to read about the misfortunes of Miss Bessie Block of West 10th Street, whoever she may be. Part of me felt demoralized, but not for long. The ire that inhabited me had come and gone. My blood, no longer boiling returned to a steady flow, just like the waters passing at methodically prescribed intervals through the new Panama Canal. This had happened too many times and my emotions had been numbed by such numerous assaults. I stopped counting the instances I felt insignificant and invalidated somewhere around the time of my eighteenth birthday. My brain grew tired of trying to beat life into my feelings of worthlessness. In my adolescence I somehow lost hope and chose to internally pass on. While I became absent, I concluded that the concerns and desires of my mother were more important than my own.

Out of habit, I continued to do as I did every morning; I proceeded to thumb through the remainder of *The New York Times* to look for antiques. In order to inevitably capture my finds of the day though meant that I'd first need to get out of "jail." Once again I was reminded of my dearest J.P., how he'd taken full and immediate responsibility for my legal predicament. Not this time. I knew I must do this on my own, for my personal satisfaction. If indeed a lesson, I knew it was up to me to be fully accountable for my fate and not be afraid to plow my own path to justice.

The voice living inside me was growing beyond the capacity to contain it, talking to me, screaming, infinitely louder than normal. "This is your chance. The moment you've been waiting for. Damn Adele Priess and her trickery. Setting me up like that. I'll show her. I'll show them all." I vowed to feel worthless no more. Mother had her time. My insides were set afire, igniting my soul. Raging. I knew I must soothe it, before it did me in. The time finally came for me to, once and for all, exercise defiance. For my past, present and future. Without hesitation, I began to pen the script I'd been longing a lifetime to deliver. Validation will soon be mine, I believed.

$$\odot \quad \math双 \quad \star$$

"Today, this defendant raises astrology to the dignity of an exact science." Judge Freschi's words to me would forever remain music to my ears. This pronouncement, the declaration of the judge, not only authenticated me and my life's work, but it gave credence to my beloved calling, astrology. The word Judge Freschi used was my favorite, a word I'd never heard prior associated with my work, "dignity." I shook my head that what I'd never believed to become had turned true. Like a flash of light, I briefly saw my mother's eyes in the face of the prosecutrix, and even she was smiling. Inside the courtroom I volunteered no display of emotion; I was blasé, making them *think* that I'd expected the outcome to be nothing but victorious. While my body oozed exultation, my relaxed crossed fingers in my lap displayed the expectation of a foregone conclusion.

When *The New York Times* had said, 'Much interest was shown in the case of Mrs. Adams,' they weren't just whistling Dixie. I knew that this public relations prospect could deliver unto me a veritable goldmine. Huge. If J.P. had lived a bit longer, he would have called this, "A once-in-a-lifetime chance. A legacy-maker." Although not physically there, his gale-force presence was felt often inside the courtroom by me. Especially when I'd noticed the French Comtoise grandfather clock in the back, nearly identical to the one I'd seen in J.P.'s office. J.P. remained faithful to me even in death; so generous to have provided, upon his departure, my legal counsel.

As I left the courthouse, I actually took pleasure in being interviewed again.

"Miss Adams, now that this litigation has concluded, would you like to re-consider your previous answer?" asked Mr. Slocum.

"To which question, sir?"

"J.P. Morgan. Other notables. Your expensive suites at Carnegie Hall? The real reasons the judge came to his decision?"

While beaming with pride, and oozing confidence, I said, "The judge's statements, I do not feel, reflected anything to do with those that have selected my services. I am a woman who conducts business. 200 Carnegie Hall has been a more than suitable locale to render what I do; it does not make me more credible, less credible, than the next person."

"These lofty goals of which you speak. Why again by the tenth of November, 1932? What's happeni—"

From out of nowhere it seemed, came both my attorneys. With the rudest of interruptions, the mostly silent, dowdier one exclaimed, "Miss Adams is needed forthrightly to again speak with the judge in his chambers. I'm sorry, she will only be able to grant one more response to what will be your final question."

"Why is the fee you charge so much higher than others doing the same type of work as you?"

I didn't have to laugh at that question, because Sabine already did. Although Scorpios gave me great cause for concern, the honesty they possess and their fearlessness while demonstrating it left me with envy. I did answer the reporter's question without a snicker and happily that was the last one. It left another, permanent-on-the-inside grin to my face. I felt so dignified, distinguished at my accomplishments; I next chose to hug myself with my stretched-to-the-limit fingers, squeezing the backs of my shoulders, until they hurt.

The truth be told, I wasn't needed in the judge's chambers at all. Yes, lawyers do make the most convincing liars, and at the same time, are the best at averting disaster as a result of their client divulging too many facts of their own volition. Mine were experts at playing the game.

The outcome of my court experience, I knew, would change the course of my destiny. It was the free will I'd elected to impose. I could have easily paid the trivial two-hundred dollar fine, but I'd chosen to defend myself and what I do for a living. As I had mentioned previously to the reporter, the judge may not have been impressed by the location of my office, nor the caliber of my clientele, but the judge just may have made positive note about the stature of the two attorneys seated near me. If so, I'd gladly accept the end result with prejudice. They were symbols of what I had meant to J.P., what he had meant to me.

"What now, Miss?" Sabine asked as we skirted past the reporter.

"We must wait for Emma. Will she be coming shortly?"

"Ma'am, Miss Emma walked out a while ago. She waved to you at the end. So happy. Tears coming from her eyes."

"Really?"

"You turned away so quickly. Then, you ran right up to this man."

"Oh, my. I hadn't even noticed she was there."

☉  ☽  ✭

Looking back now, it's silly that fear of appearances hold sway in a person's life. Emma was worried about her husband, her son, seldom about herself. And I was too focused on my own spotlight. It was as though our moments creating ecstasy and unrestraint in New Hampshire had taken place in a dream world that disappeared upon waking.

As Sabine and I celebrated the outcome of the hearing, oh, how I wished Emma were with us. I missed her presence deeply, wanted her to be included more than anyone else, in this intimate celebration of mine. How could she not take part in this victory? She'd, of course, say, in that most eloquent way of hers, that I was brilliant. And yet my pragmatic side had gotten its hooks in, keeping my emotions in check at all times. In short order, I ended up burying those moments Emma and I had shared in New Hampshire as though they'd never happened.

"More champagne for you, Miss?"

I shook my head. "The interview tomorrow. Will it be syndicated?"

"This man is from a Boston paper. But, yes, the interview will be reaching."

"Perfect. From now on, they all must be." The excitement I was feeling over the next interview grew larger by the minute. I want every interview to be better, with stakes raised higher than they were in any previous. "I'd love it if you'd glamourize me again, Sabine. Powder, blush. Vaseline and coal dust to my eyelashes. Just like before."

☉ ☽ ✦

"How fascinating. Your lineage to the Presidents. At what point in your life did you learn of this?"

"It must have been during my earliest years. I've always been aware. My mother must have told me as soon as I'd be able to comprehend such a thing."

"And your father died when you were in childhood."

"At fifteen months, yes."

With his cockeyed mushroom bowtie and half his morning meal encrusted on it, this seemingly innocent correspondent said, "It's quite paradoxical. I don't usually associate Jersey City with the Adams family."

How I wished these interviewers would come up with something novel. Their approach to what's already been divulged so many times over lacked all imagination. This particular man to whom I was speaking was a newcomer to *The Boston Herald*, and perhaps that's what made him more enamored of me than the typical horrid skeptic and jaded cynic. He was quite genial *and* he gave the impression the he was in awe of me. I love this quality in a man.

"We, my mother, my siblings and I moved back to Massachusetts shortly after my birth."

"That's the cornerstone of your prophecy, isn't it? Birth."

"Unquestionably."

"My birthdate is July sixth. What can you tell me from that?"

"I must also know one's time and place of birth. In addition to the year, to create a chart."

Knowing that casting a horoscope for this man may not make it to print, I decided to dazzle his naïveté with the obvious on the spot.

"Offhandedly, being born under the sun sign of Cancer, I can tell you that you enjoy home life, you feel things deeply, sensitive, you are prone to shed tears more readily than others and you are susceptible to bouts of moodiness."

"Uncanny. And you learned this, astrology, while under the tutelage of a medical doctor when you were in your…?"

"Teens." Twenties in fact, but who's counting?

The interview and accompanying article was syndicated to a huge variety of newspapers throughout the country. Not only did I receive many requests for chart casting, I was also asked to lecture at numerous clubs and functions. One of the most prestigious invitations came from J.P.'s utmost exclusive gentleman's group, the Metropolitan Club, at 60th and Fifth Avenue. I broke barriers by being the first woman to speak inside the male-only Clubhouse there.

These lucky new breaks more than made up for my drop in business by some of my most regular society ladies. Cavorting, on a weekly basis, with someone who's been arrested seemed to not be in their best interest.

Speaking engagements took me to wondrous places nearby and not. During the period when I addressed questions from the gallery, one nagging query came up time after time. Hearing it aloud any time made my stomach nauseous.

A woman asked, "Why haven't you yet written a book about astrology?" My mind instantaneously took me back to an afternoon tea with Mother in our drawing room when she said, "Procrastination dwells in only the weakest of individuals."

I had no satisfactory answer. Instead I offered the most predictable: "I haven't had the time."

So Sabine and I added it to my list of tasks to accomplish, someday when the stars were most favorable. And when not thinking about scribing astrologic methodology, my list of celebrity clientele grew, exponentially.

☉ ☽ ✴

"You will be most successful by making use of your exuberance, your comedic skills. This is your forte."

Screen actress Mary Pickford fashioned a lovely, innocent smile when I mentioned this. Her high spirits were contagious, and I found myself mimicking her flailing arms and squirming torso without realizing. Together, we must have appeared like two contortionists in a traveling circus troupe. "I'd always known dramas weren't made for me."

"The public loves, and is going to love, anything you do. It is in this next year, 1915, that you reach the pinnacle of your career. You'll have no competition from your peers, the women. Only one man will match your popularity, Charlie Chaplin."

"What a doll. He told me he'd been here to see you. Charlie's the reason I came."

"Oh, well, as you know, I can't deny, nor confirm. Confidentiality. Shall we move on to love life?"

"Should I cover my ears? I may be too afraid to hear."

"Why don't you cover just one. Your marriage, you will find at the close of this decade, is perhaps holding you back. Stifling you. I also see jealousy in his chart. Does this not surprise you?"

"No, it doesn't."

"Good. Immediately after this man you'll meet another and marry him. The marriage to your current husband will end in divorce. The next man will too be an actor. Also good for your career."

"Will he have dark or light hair?"

"I'm afraid I wouldn't know such a thing, dear."

"Good for my screen career. I like that."

"In all aspects of business. You two will complement each other well. Forging a union of some sort with other motion picture actors."

Miss Pickford's squeaky clean ears perked up. I could tell she was hungry for more, so I did indeed admit to her what I was at first apprehensive to divulge.

"There may also be yet a third husband. The second marriage could end in divorce as well. You will go as far as you can go with this particular man. I see that the third will keep you young. Lively. He is several years younger than you."

"Well-known? Benefit me in business, too?"

"Not necessarily."

"Well, at least he'll be good for something," Miss Pickford said while gazing at my left hand. Then she began tapping her index-fingernail onto my ring finger. "And...why aren't you married, Miss?"

"I beg your pardon?" I responded with shock. Although I knew I could have expected nothing less blunt from the spontaneous mouth of an Aries woman.

"You're a single lady of what? Fifty? Sixty?"

"Why, I'm f—, thirty-nine."

"Sorry to pry, Miss. Girl talk. Don't worry a bit, I've several friends in Hollywood who are…the same. It'll be our little secret."

What was she inferring? My goodness, the frankness of her speech. I wasn't the only spinster on the planet. Miss Pickford's words, whatever they meant, and the blatancy with which they were delivered, made me extremely concerned. Worried. For the first time I began to realize that it wasn't an arrest or judicial punishment that would be the demise of my treasured career, it may be the fact that I was so noticeably, so obviously unmarried, never-married, at my age. I'd worked too hard to allow this blemish to become a career-ceasing scandal.

For the next several days I looked both inward and out for a solution to, what I believed to be, my chronic impending public relations dilemma. Examining my own chart was the first order of business. I could see many men, an entire variety. Chubby financiers, down in the dumps physicians, double dealing lawyers, bigheaded actors, thrill-seeking aerialists, happy-go-lucky upper crusters, even shoemakers and cobblestone layers. My chart alluded that they were all business though, nothing coming close to a personal relationship.

I thought to myself, someone living far away might be suitable. We'd be married in name, but he'd be unable to interfere with my career. Or perhaps I would find the love of a man that is genuine.

But my heart belonged to my work. Never would my emotions be consumed by another. It was out of the question. Success comes from nothing but devotion and endless commitment, wasn't that what J.P. had always said?

Nevertheless, during a free afternoon, with shoe brush in hand and an eagle eye, I took myself to nearby Central Park once more. Wearing my figure-slimming black suit with my black Tahitian cultured-pearl necklace, to display my culture of course, I chose to commune with nature by not strolling, but by studying. Not considering passersby as prospective clients, but as romantic interests.

Demurely I crossed my legs after being seated on a park bench as one of the middle wooden slats split. It mattered not; "a proper lady displays no discomfort," according to my mother. Onto my scrutinizing. Hygiene and fashion were at the top of my list. Men with the crispest of creases to their trousers caught my attention above anyone else. Noticeably present on each and every one of these finely dressed men was a gold wedding band. Sometimes there was a woman attached to the other hand, sometimes not. Only men and women of a certain young age join appendages in public these days, I thought. A few pranced like peafowl, with the cock of the species parading its plumage so wide that it casts a shadow on the hapless hen that follows behind. The airs men bare, with relation to size, merely point out their hidden shortcomings, I was once told by a brothel madam visiting my office who forever went nameless.

It occurred to me rather quickly that it's not black hair or blue eyes or even manicured fingernails that would be the deciding factor; it would, of course, be the man's birth data. The most important variable of all.

At this stage in my life, less than eighteen years lingered in my calendar, I presumed.

# Sun @ 22° SAGITTARIUS 10'33 (1914)

*A*s if exiting onto La Scala's backstage after portraying playboy *Don Giovanni*, the world's most famous tenor asked with a straight face, "You like the Italian men, Signora?"

"Signorina."

"The best, eh?" opera star Enrico Caruso boasted, while arching both freshly and perfectly plucked eyebrows in dramatic fashion. Only for Enrico did I cast charts after hours. He insisted that the glowing golden flicker of the crystal candelabra in my office would bring him better luck, good fortune. One of his many superstitions.

I never responded to Enrico, or any other Italian man who demonstrated exaggerated machismo in my presence, because I always figured they were doing so to get a laugh. "You've conquered just about everything, but I do see you raising the bar within the next two years. Even *Otello*."

"This one is my dream. It will be big success, si?"

For whatever reason I couldn't see a positive or negative

validation of this role. "Many interesting things coming. Travel. Travel related to business, this time to a new and different place for you."

"This is why I come to see you, Signora. And your beautiful face. Singing for new people say my agent is what I do next."

"The direction I see is south, the Southern Hemisphere. South America. You will charm them all. Thousands of new fans will be yours, they'll be captivated by your performances, by your presence."

"Mamma mia."

"For you the voyage is never-ending, Enrico. But it's taxing."

"I pay to the government too much of these already. Here. In Italia. Too much of the taxes."

"I meant the travel and the lifestyle that goes with, with being you, is wearing, exhausting for the body."

More and more obvious to me was the ever-present fact that Enrico's poor habits of maintenance, not to mention his overindulgences, would lead to ill health in a very short period of time. "Now I have no good woman to take care of me. I love the food of my country. I love the women."

"I have seen this as well. Shall I tell you?"

While applying dark cocoa theatrical powder to the sheen of his receding hairline, debonair Enrico crowed, "About the women. You don't need to ask this question. It is always yes with the women."

Oh, brother. "We have spoken about Ada before. You will not—"

"Una stronza!"

"Well, as you know, it is over with her. I see you *shopping* around. You will do things differently for the next few years. I next see you with an American woman, a few years older than you. You may marry her. There will be opposition to this marriage, but it will nonetheless be prosperous."

My dear Enrico, whom I'd known for several years, let his eyes ever so subtly stray south from my face to my bosom. He didn't appear to be joking. His actions confirmed everything I'd ever thought about the Pisces male; they're as sweet as honey, but relish in indiscretions of the flesh at the drop of a hat. Sometimes while still wearing the hat. A good variety of the torrid tales that had made the rounds about Enrico would make my beloved and "adventurous" Sabine look like a pure maiden, draped in white-laced veil.

Was the new opaque peg-top silhouette I was wearing revealing too many of my womanly curves? If so, my psyche didn't appear to mind. As Enrico stooped downward to loosen his snug shoe bindings, I stopped snickering inside. Mediterranean swagger or not, I liked the attention.

"Signorina …you are beautiful woman and you know how to make money."

The latter was the compliment that flattered me most. It caught my attention so much that I excused Enrico's inappropriateness and looked more deeply into his chart. An American woman. Older than him. With money. Sounds very familiar to me. Not so outlandish at all. Just as I'd discussed with sweet, coquettish-only-on-the-outside Mary Pickford; a man who can aid one's career is the only type of man worth having. My imagination, for a mere second or so, took me to the matrimonial altar of the Trinity Church on Broadway where only Enrico and I stood. "This is meaningful to you, is it not, Enrico? A woman able to bring money to her union with you?"

"We are all the same, Signora, Signorina. I am no different from anyone else. When I look at a woman she may be pretty, but when I know she has money, she is that much more desirable to me. The same it has always been."

Enrico's right. To so many that are already rich and successful, they tend most to be drawn to similar, almost mirror-images of themselves, those that add to their publicity and bank accounts.

"I know you well, Enrico, and I appreciate honesty. I also have thick skin."

"I use the olive oil at night. In the morning I look like a bambino," Enrico said, as I instinctively began touching the rapidly increasing number of wrinkles to my forehead.

For a moment, or fraction thereof, my mind flirted with the notion. Becoming Mrs. Enrico Caruso would catapult me to new heights. But I came back down to earth the moment I realized that Enrico would never settle for being Mr. Evangeline Adams. If it's not 50/50, I'm out. At the end of our session it was back to business and Enrico was happy to hear of the future success he'd soon be realizing. In addition to his inherent superstitions he'd brought over from Italy, I also eased his fears about international travel. All appeared calm on the high seas.

"Ciao, Cara, Bellissima."

"Until I see you again, Enrico. Happy travels."

$$\odot \quad \pmb{\mathbb{D}} \quad \star$$

As the year 1915 began to approach, it was all work and no play for me. Very few antiquing trips to New England, no house hunting for the perfect investment find. I was content seeing my levels of satisfaction and fulfillment rise as a result of my public relations efforts. Accurate readings seemed insignificant to my ascendancy, the vast exposure I had created for myself. Daily deliveries to my office by post now reached an average of five thousand requests. Hardly ever less.

I'd hired an additional ten people, nine women and the first man with a keen intuition, to my staff. Some of whom I knew and some not. Sabine took care of everything, and for one of the few times, I was grateful for her Scorpio leadership abilities. A most awkward moment arose, though, when I overheard her speaking to a staff member about my wealth. In the direction of someone I wasn't so familiar with, an apprentice astrologist, vis-à-vis something quite confidential. Sabine's honesty had always been her strong suit, but not when it involved me and my life.

"Miss, many letters arrived for you today marked 'personal'."

"Similar to every day. And...?"

"You tell us to open them, but this one I did not. I respect your privacy so I give it to you now myself, unopened."

"I appreciate that, Sabine," I said, expecting some sort of bad news. I glanced at the name of the sender and shivers ran up my spine.

Sabine closed the door to my office behind her as she exited. My heart began to do something it hadn't done in months; it beat wildly with anticipation *and* anxiety. How wonderful it was, I recalled, having my hair stroked so sweetly. I placed the sealed envelope on my desk as I searched for my letter opener underneath. As always each drawer was in disarray, too-filled with papers, Goo Goo clusters, clasps, even one of J.P.'s leftover half-smoked cigars and I became blinded by the clutter. Being visibly unable to know what was under one layer beneath another; I accidentally stabbed myself with the very object I'd been seeking, the opener.

Not just a prick, but a conspicuous gash, leaving a wound on the top of my hand that needed quick attention. If only Mrs. Brush had been here; Virgo, nature's nursemaid. Instead, I summoned a substitute by shouting out, "Sabine, please come in here immediately."

"What is it, Ma'am?"

I showed her my right hand and she took expedient action.

Racing back to her desk, she retrieved liniment, a bandage and scissors. Sabine proceeded to wrap my hand tighter than a skinflint's during the holiday gift-giving season. In what seemed less than a minute, all was well again.

Was this an omen of danger to come? Or was it my punishment for not having responded to the last few letters Emma had written. As Sabine exited for the second time, I took a seat behind my desk, inhaled deeply, opened the envelope and began reading words I felt I'd have trouble digesting. Again, distracted a bit by the faintest aroma of Cornubia Oriental Floral coming from the unfolded page, it took no more than the initial salutation for me to know the contents were written with sincerity and the deepest of emotions.

*My Dearest Evangeline,*

*I hope you are healthy and content. My well wishes for you remain, although I'd love to be able to convey the same to you personally sometime. I'm doing just fine. Have you read my previous letters? Are you enjoying your ever-growing fame?*

*I must be frank. Watching you, now such a recognizable public figure, overlook the elation I displayed in my wave to you as you rushed over to that reporter, made reality set in.*

But I didn't ignore Emma outside the courtroom. There's no one I wanted to see more than her after the judge made his decision.

*My husband and son will always come first. You have your reputation at stake. And, now, you offer no reply to my correspondence. I feel sad that our time together, our closeness, lasted but one weekend. Your heart is an active and vital one, and I feel privileged to have been touched by it. Being with you for that brief time allowed me to, once again, feel love for a woman without experiencing guilt or shame.*

*Love? Love for a woman? Again?* Without realizing it I'd picked at my dry, brittle and cracked fingernails until they'd split apart at the quick; a single drop of blood now trickling onto the white pages I was reading. I sopped up what I could with the leftover bandages Sabine had delivered to me. My mental state was about to explode with confusion. Why was Emma doing this to me? How disturbed she must be, I thought.

*You will always hold a special place in my heart. Because of the commitment I have to my family, I must now be steadfast in my loyalty to them. As you can surmise, sadly, I've chosen to move on. It's my sincere hope that, in addition to the fame you've earned, you will also welcome, and feel free to express your deepest feelings, to someone new. If the stars are indeed infallible, your most authentic identity will be your guide.*

My eyes could read nothing further.

After gazing upon Emma's words, I searched my office high and low for a hiding place. My heart, mind and conscience could take no more. If anyone else were to discover this note so revealing, it would mean out-and-out jeopardy to me, to my career. Imprisoned for having had such a lapse in sensible judgment, engaging in such a lascivious act, a crime. Behind me stood row upon row of books I'd never read, never will, I imagined. Within the pages of the least obvious, was the most proper hiding place. *The Purloined Letter* by Edgar Allan Poe, perfect.

☉  ☽  ✷

"But, Miss. Why in such a hurry?" Sabine asked, while I attempted to prettify myself in between garment-folding. At midday, three days after having received Emma's letter, my frazzled nerves needed asylum.

As tremors became visible on my forearms and neck, Sabine just stood there gawking. "Help me, please. No time for questions."

Like a caged animal, I could think of nothing more than running away, escaping. Emma's words troubled me so. Causing nothing but sleepless nights, panic, seeing her in my dreams, conflicted in both my desires and actions. With my mind racing, I could no longer face reality. I had no choice but to flee. It had been several months since my last European trip, so I once again prepared for a trans-Atlantic getaway, but this time the way an Aries would, last minute. My carriage to the harbor would be arriving in a matter of moments and I still hadn't finished bundling my clothes and accessories.

"There are three women I could not reach to cancel."

"Well, then they'll just realize I've gone once they arrive in my office."

"And *that's* professional?"

"I told you, Sabine, I've no time for questions."

"Miss, you must calm yourself."

"Yes, you're right. The first thing you've said that didn't irritate me."

Sabine looked over at me as if she was meeting me anew. I must admit that my emotions had gotten the best of me. Too many clients, too many obligations. A person can handle only so much. The demands of others, their requests. Placing their needs above my own. How could I have been so blind? The charts they needed ever so expeditiously. Each and every one had made this happen to me. I held them all responsible for my un-wellness.

"Here are your pearls, Ma'am. The fancy ones. Now can you tell me why?"

"I already did. Weren't you listening? Count Kasimir is smitten with me. He insisted I come at once."

"When did you mee—"

"A while back. I don't— He's going to propose marriage." Sabine looked confused. Before she could ask another irritating question, I said, "Where are those bottles? The wine we kept for J.P. when he'd visit?"

"What do you—"

"Sabine! If you question me once more I must let you go."

"I beg your pardon, Miss. I'll fetch them."

So many things I couldn't find. All these people had affected my memory as well. Damn them. I'd worked so hard. Giving them the finest in the most cordial manner. This, that and the other—all about them—them, their needs coming first. Just like... This is what I'd gotten in return. Insolence. I regretted that I'd ever gotten into this business. These people were the crackpots, not I. Being so ridiculously dependent on someone else for the actions they must carry out themselves. How sad I feel for them. Their lack of power, especially the women; pining over men that shall never care less about them. Pitiful.

"Sabine!"

"I'm right here, Miss. I have found Mr. J.P.'s wine. What shall I do with it?"

"Pour me a glass. To the top."

Because of being so cautioned before, afraid to utter a single sound, I still heard Sabine's voice inside my head, saying, "But you nearly never drink, Mizz. It's only the morning. Much too early for—"

Drivel.

☉　☽　✶

At sea, aboard ship the next morning, too early to have wine at my disposal, sobering truth was my breakfast companion. My clients and/or over-loaded schedule hadn't prompted my abrupt departure, nor was it Count Whatever-his-name-was.

I left for Europe for no reason other than to seek a passing, fleeting substitute for what I had let slip from between my fingers: warmth, affection, tenderness, physical satisfaction, love, Emma.

# Sun @ 3° ARIES 16'15 (1915)

*"M*iss Adams, it's an honor to meet you, ma'am."

"Oh, how kind you are. And, you speak English."

"Yes, a fellow American. From Boston."

"A lovely place."

"Allow me to introduce myself. I am Miss Penelope Johnston. Pardon me, but I noticed you straightaway."

I was nearly desperate to be spotted and singled out by someone, anyone special in the City of Love's IIe arrondissement, and fate delivered unto me the most charming and alluring maiden lady inside the Palais Brongniart on the Place de la Bourse. Feeling the presence of J.P. and his everlasting influence upon me, I'd chosen to mingle with Parisian culture in a building that, during working hours, housed the Paris stock exchange. In this magnificent neoclassical Roman temple, with its sky-high Corinthian colonnade, I'd let my hair down and became open and available.

Underneath the vaulted, gold-embossed central chamber, there she stood. As delicate as dew on a field of wildflowers at dawn. I must admit that I'd noticed her as well, especially her innocence.

Secretly wishing to have Miss Johnston's attention and youthfulness all to myself, I asked, "And you are with…?"

The slight chill emanating from the ice statue of Michelangelo's *David* we were both standing before, left Penelope and I shivering in unison. Together, we took two steps back to warmer climes. "Stand tall and suck in your gut," I commanded to my body inaudibly.

"I came with my parents; they're in one of the conference halls. My father is in the stock-trading business. We've been coming to France for years and years, since I was a child."

"To me you're still a child." I guessed her to be no more than twenty. Up close, Miss Johnston's complexion was silky-smooth and I couldn't help but gaze at her absence of deep pores.

"Oh, but miss. It's miss, correct?"

"Précisément," I answered, while subtly removing a clump of charcoal from the corner of my eye.

"Miss, I'm nearly twenty-two. I'm studying to be an actress on the stage."

"You know…I can see that about you. Upon casual observance, you seem to possess a unique style. Savoir-faire. Mystery."

While my inner voice silently summoned up words never spoken; "A woman with whom I would feel a soul-connectedness, a dramatic woman…a profound and quite intimate union of sorts…a most definite closeness, attachment with a woman, not a man," the young lady before me began to blush. Coyly she kept covering her right eye with a thick lock of her raven hair. How appealing it was, being in the company of someone so innocent, rather shy, unassuming.

"I must say, miss. I truly admire you and the work you do,"

Penelope said while touching my shoulder.

Although it lasted but a mere millisecond, the tap I felt fostered gooseflesh, stimulation, excitement and left me tongue tied. "Asss…trolllogy?"

"Oh, I'm enamored with it. I'm a Scorpio, with an ascendant in Aquarius. Moon, Leo."

No wonder I found her so enticing, eye-catching.

"Born to be in control. Maybe one day you'll be a director."

"Maybe. I know you do your work in Manhattan. If it's not too much to ask, I'd love to have you create a chart for me there, in your studio."

"Why not here. In Paris. If you've the time," I said, attempting to convey spontaneity. My lips quivered to say these words minutes earlier, yet were somehow able to maintain placidity so not to appear deliberate.

"My goodness. I shall make the time, miss. Thank you. Thank you so much."

"I'm staying at the Ritz. On the Place Vendôme. What about tomorrow? In the afternoon."

"Perfect. I'll be there. Three-ish?"

"Excellent."

"You know, astrology fascinates me, and to be able to help others the way you do. What a blessing you must be to them."

"As they are to me. I cherish my clients, each one that steps upon my premises. They're the dearest. I recall every one by name and ask them to remain in touch. My regulars are like my children."

"My, how devoted you are. And who are you here with? Tonight."

Not knowing exactly why, after having felt decades younger for the past several minutes, I started to feel slightly suspicious of this young woman. Call it a premonition. I recalled having been conned so many times before now. Who exactly was this Penelope? And why precisely did she, someone, a stranger so many eons my junior, want to know so much about me?

"I was invited by my friends, the Tanners. But now it's my turn to know more about you. How long have you been acting?"

"Oh, dear. Since I was a youngster. I was encouraged by a very fine teacher. She used to be an actress, was quite well known. Maybe you've heard of—"

"And she's from Boston? Just like the two of us?"

I stood there motionless, just like the frozen *David* we'd both encountered, anticipating the mention of Emma's name. It was a mystery as to which emotion would take over my being first. Shock at this colossal twist of fate? Terror? Paranoia? Neither of these actually. It was as if I had just been pricked by a needle carrying cholera. Despite the frank-yet-sensitive words Emma had written to me, my heart began aching. Why? Like a ticking time bomb, my pounding core awaited the girl's next words.

"Why, yes. From Boston. Blanche Ring."

As if Emma's face was placed before me, when the time came to react to this young woman, I knew not what to say but, "...Mrs...Ring. I can't say...that I'm familiar with her work." While remaining a bit unfocused, my blurry eyes watched Penelope reach for a pen and a sheet of paper that were placed on a desk nearby. There she scribbled no more than one line and handed me the paper.

*4:20pm. 10 November, 1893. Cambridge, Mass.*

I'd received thousands of statistical mixes in print by this point; referencing birthdate, place and time for the purpose of casting an astrological chart, but this one left me aghast. Breathless. While it landed upon the floor face-up after slipping through my fingers, Penelope said, "I thought you might like to know my natal details—if that's how they're called—in advance of our meeting."

The tenth of November at four-twenty in the afternoon was

the precise day and time that's lodged indelibly in my mind. The looming date of my all-too-imminent departure. Was this another case of a cosmic coincidence that flaunts itself shamelessly in order to be taken seriously?

Only a few minutes passed before I could no longer tolerate being near people, any sort of people. I excused myself to the balcony and, for the first time in what seemed like a decade, not knowing how I was supposed to act or how I should feel, I wept. Yes, I wept. In public. No one was actually near to witness my vulnerable manner though. Thank the stars for that.

Emma was now gone from my life. With a full moon at twenty-eight degrees Capricorn hovering above a meticulously-sown rose garden, solitude was mine.

When my tears stopped, my hands embraced the handrail, sternly, separating me from the grove of recessed and perfectly-aligned Italian cypress trees below. In that moment, I didn't want to let go. The rail kept me upright. Melancholia, not cholera, had instantly and viciously embraced me with its might.

On such a clear night filled with innumerous visions, I, without warning, felt a palpable sensation on my left calf. At first I thought it may have been a leg cramp, but no, a beautiful light- and dark-colored, Calico housecat craving my attention. This simple furry creature filled my heart in a second. I petted it and spoke softly. The more I petted its mane, the louder it purred. What great pleasure I was feeling. Something so natural and spontaneous.

Being so enraptured with sentiment, I proceeded to take it one step further. I next did something I'd never done before in my life. I bent down and lifted the kitty up, took her into my arms, both realizing that our mutual touch would, most assuredly, not lead to the culmination of my career due to distorted tittle-tattle. Her purring grew even louder. Both of us, simultaneously, giving and receiving what I can only imagine to be love unconditional.

Kitty, wearing a regal-looking bejeweled collar, seemed to want to know all about me and my life. Still in my arms, I told her, in English of course, about my plethora of friends that happened to be above us shining so brightly; the moon, Jupiter, Neptune, Uranus, Pluto and the rest. Kitty was beyond captivated. Just as my story reached its climax, Kitty fled my embrace to chase after some scurrying beast on the illumined pristine lawn before us. Maybe she already knew more about astrology than even I did.

Shortly after the precocious feline left my presence, the warmth in my heart began to fade away. The stars certainly are up to something, I thought—how else to explain the singular sign of a girl bearing the date and time of my death in her birthday? Immediately, I knew what filled my heart most was waiting for me back in New York, my astrology practice. I ended my European trip nearly a week before it was scheduled to be over.

Wanting to yield at least some productivity from this impetuous journey of mine, aboard ship on the return to America with no charts to create, I did my best to summon my writing ability. For years and years and years I felt compelled to write a book about astrology, but had not found the fortitude to get it going. My primary mission in life remained constant; become and remain known as the utmost authority on astrology until the end of time, before it's too late. All experts have written books, so I'm obliged to do the same, I figured. Writing will lend credibility to my cause, bestow virtuous repute to the name Adams once again, I felt for certain.

One day, I spent ten consecutive hours sitting at my desk while accomplishing nothing. I just couldn't do it. Some people are meant to compose their words on paper, but I wasn't one of them. The very next day I attempted the same, but was met with an identically unproductive result. On this journey home, I realized that I needed an assist in writing. No doubt about it.

☉  ☽  ✶

Business as usual met me in New York yet again. Just as I had done every day for so many years, I stroked my clients, they purred back, still I felt nothing in return. If only they'd been born house pets. The truth be told, they'd stopped stimulating me long ago. Business as usual. Money to be made. More promotional strategies to put into practice.

"Miss, you didn't answer this dinner request."

"I'm mulling it over, Sabine."

"Mr. Carlisle wrote a personal message to you. Shiny ink. Aluminum, I think. He says it will be *most* worth your while." My curiosity was piqued by this invitation sent by one of New York's most innovative hoteliers. He makes sure a single red rose is placed at the base of every bedstead one half hour preceding slumbertime.

"Let me see it, please."

Not necessarily needing to inspect the invitation, my Pisces instinct made up my mind for me. I just wanted to hold onto it, feel the smooth fiber of the envelope, and to see if the gold flecks came off after flicking the embossed lettering with my fingernail. Something told me to go; it would be prosperous, good for business. I told Sabine to answer affirmatively.

☉  ☽  ✶

As soon as I was greeted by vintage mauve tuxedoed-Mr. Walter Carlisle and his pet capuchin monkey, Hyrum, he insisted on taking me to meet the man he described as "radiant."

I'd heard of the Englishman, Aleister Crowley, many times when in Europe. They'd raved about him. Soon I'd be finding out what all the fuss was about.

"He's a famous astrologer, Miss Adams."

"Really? I hadn't known that. I thought he was known for, well, a host of other things."

"Oh, there he is," Mr. Carlisle said, pointing to an insufferable sight of a man, wearing a fur cape indoors and a smirk that was nothing short of maniacal.

Upon seeing me, this man, and his apparently waxed eyelashes, hopped up into the air, leading with his outstretched right arm and continuously wiggled his fingers at me, a copper ring on each. I wasn't sure what I was supposed to do in return.

"You're Evangeline Adams."

"Yes, I am," I responded.

"You two are meant to be together. I can just feel it," Mr. Carlisle said.

"Trust me. I'd love to feel it," Mr. Crowley said while looking straight at me.

"It's a pleasure to meet you, Mr. Crowley."

"Out of the question. Not Mr. Crowley. Your Highness."

"Oh, I beg your pardon, sir."

"Aleister is joking, Evangeline. You are joking. Aren't you, Aleister?"

Mr. Crowley sneered and hissed an incomprehensible response to Mr. Carlisle. At the same time I felt like I wanted to purge the undercooked crab cake I'd just devoured. This man had instantly repulsed me.

He must be a Leo with his overt theatrics. "I hadn't known you were too an astrologer, Mr. Crowley."

"Simply Aleister. I do all, ma'am."

"I'd imagine you to be a Leo. Or your rising."

"On the nose. My ascendant is most assuredly in Leo. Sun in Libra."

"Makes perfect sense."

"If you'll excuse me, I'll let you two talk shop by yourselves."

Mr. Carlisle left me alone with Aleister. In a short time my repulsion was replaced with forthright curiosity. This man was in fact captivating, in a convoluted way that was hard for me to articulate.

"We must perform a ritual someday."

"I beg your...a ritual?"

"You do know why I'm most famous, don't you?"

"I've heard of many things you've done. You've founded a new religion of sorts."

"If I could plunge a dagger into my heart at this very moment, I'd do so in front of you so you can witness the carnage."

"I didn't mean to—"

"Assassin! That's what you do to men. I can tell from your demeanor, you trivialize each one of us."

"Once again, you're toying with me."

"Once again, I'd love to."

"I have to admit, I've also read some of your poetry. You possess quite a talent."

"Finally, you see merit. To be most clear, I'm the world's greatest poet. Living or dead."

"That certainly makes a statement. I'm trying to write a book myself. I'd like it to be part of my legacy, so that others may later on reference much of what I've learned, accomplished after I've...departed."

"I live to make statements. This is the assignment I've been granted from the cosmos." It was as if Aleister's hearing was fitted with a mesh filter, forcing out anything that didn't pertain directly to him.

"Mine is to cast charts."

"Your 'destiny,' as you'd say. And you profit greatly from it, I presume," he said with protruding, pinkish eyes.

"It's my living. I'm a professional. Without—"

"Never would I allow myself to be recompensed monetarily for sharing the gifts of my soul. Karma would cast a dark shadow on my being and wreak havoc on my every action undertaken."

"You and I think differently, Sir."

"Opposites attract, Madam."

"I'd prefer talking astrology with you, Aleister," I said, dodging his flirtations, if that's what they indeed were. I'd heard he did this with all women—and men. "It's the common thread which connects us," I added.

"More trivia. To get to know each other better I must create a unique and star-ordained ritual for the two of us to carry out together."

"I must tell you now, I have minimal interest in such a thing."

"Give it time, Miss. It is Miss, isn't it?"

Not in my wildest imagination would I have believed that this man and I would talk well into the next morning after the majority of guests had departed. Alone in a remote parlor, staring at Aleister's face backlit with a roaring fire, I flinched not as he found himself comfortable enough to stretch his exposed limbs and bare feet while lounging atop a white Polar-bearskin rug. Aleister's knowledge of astrology astounded me. It happened so seldom that I could converse with anyone about the intricacies of my beloved horoscopes. Although a most bizarre figure, I commended Aleister's devotion to the many things he held dear, including his religion, Thelema. He could speak hours on that topic, but he had such a volume of others: President Wilson, the English monarchy, the American way of life and so much more. Some of which held my interest as well, but nothing came close to our parallel-yet-slightly divergent points of view regarding fate, destiny and the infallibility of the stars.

We set an informal dinner date for later that same week, just the two of us. I was eagerly anticipating what Aleister would share with me next.

☉   ☽   ★

"No secret at all. I've engaged in sexual intercourse with numerous men," Aleister admitted.

Sitting inside an establishment to which I was tremendously unaccustomed and already squeamish, I looked around sheepishly to see if anyone had overheard Aleister's bold confession. It was my first time at the White Horse Tavern on Hudson Street, a place I'd only heard about from the many musicians that come and go inside Carnegie Hall. They don't even serve Postum there. And the soggy seats smell of ale. Never did I think I'd actually set foot in the place, but Aleister insisted.

In a near whisper, I asked, "But why do you speak of this? Publicly, for all to be made aware? Most associate such a thing with heathenry." My brain couldn't fathom confessing anything regarded as being so deviant.

"Who or what is 'most'?"

"Society. The church. It violates the law."

"Madam, haven't you realized by now? I create my own laws. I am the master of my own world. Everything I do is in violation of nothing." I began looking to Aleister with awe; rather than being imprisoned for his actions, he was celebrated; a rather miraculous feat.

Not wanting to discuss this topic any longer out of fear, I changed the subject by saying, "I certainly would like to read more of your writings. Your poetry."

"Your wish is my command," Aleister said, unleashing a volume of compositions from his petite black portmanteau. The Sapphire-blue crescent moon stenciled on it, possessing the glow of neon, captured my curiosity most.

"Something that depicts the real you. I'm in the mood for something uplifting, words that will make me feel deeply."

"I know what will make you feel deeply, miss."

"Please carry on."

"I shall recite for your arousal *A Ballad of Passive Paederasty*. An homage to those lusty young men with whom I've made…an acquaintance."

☉　☽　★

"And…this was published?"

"Yes, indeed. 1898, Amsterdam. Under my nom de plume, George Archibald Bishop. An anthology entitled, 'White Stains'."

# Sun @ 22° CANCER 9'16 (1916)

*A*leister's time spent in and around New York proved to be more than auspicious for both he and, I can only imagine, his conjoined ego. Everyone wanted to be near him, close enough to touch, clamoring for his autograph even while he was chewing his fingernails before swallowing them. Manhattan's avant-garde found Aleister to be enlightened, mysterious and charming. To common folk, nothing more than a self-proclaimed English wizard with five-o'clock shadow. But the élite couldn't get enough. Every guest list composed by every A-list socialite residing on the Upper East Side—Rosalie Edge, Cettie Rockefeller, Almina Herbert and countless others—included the name Aleister Crowley, a Libran, the zodiac's quintessential party-goer. Only weeks in the United States and he'd become an instant celebrity of enormous measure.

Me, I saw Aleister as a means to unite common forces. The majority of what he represented I wanted no part of, yet he'd proven himself to be a gifted and acclaimed writer. Having attempted and failed time and time again, I knew that I didn't possess the discipline, or perhaps the confidence, to write a book myself. I saw Aleister as the perfect person to author a book or two for me about astrology.

Considering his vast following and scripting savvy, I felt I could withstand his innumerous idiosyncrasies for the purpose of turning my life's work into a literary legacy. Reluctant at first, Aleister agreed to collaborate with me only after I told him I possessed no more than 5,840 days alive. Just like J.P., Aleister's bravado grew into vulnerability whenever the topic of mortality came up. As it turned out, Aleister wanted his name to appear on as many books as possible, so he, too, would be remembered and talked about long after his demise.

Our working relationship was something Aleister and I genuinely became enthusiastic about, as long as I didn't have to call him "Your Highness."

$$\odot \quad \pmb{)} \quad \star$$

Aleister and I had gotten together more than a few times in the city—flashy uptown restaurants where reservations are required, delicate midtown tearooms ideal for eavesdroppers, eccentric downtown cafes, pretentious social functions in the company of interfering wannabes—but it was the woodland he most wanted to explore. Away from an audience of any sort, I invited him to spend the entire summer of 1916 at the country home I'd ended up purchasing in Hebron, New Hampshire a few years earlier. He called it primal. I cared not what he chose to do in his free time there, but I made it quite clear that his principal duty was to commence writing. Although Aleister'd mentioned prior that Karma would not allow him to be compensated, his mind changed once he realized that he was creating a tangible commodity. We haggled about living expenses, but when I convinced him that an increase in P.R. would gain him even more followers, payment to his ego was all he required from me.

☉  ☽  ★

On a rare occasion when my weekend was clear from commitment, I traveled up to Hebron on the first train early in the morning by myself. I'd not heard from Aleister for weeks and I wanted to see how the book was progressing. When I arrived, I discovered an abundance of green moss growing atop the roof and all the firewood missing.

Even before opening the front door at 14 Church Road, I knew that I wouldn't necessarily feel relaxed in my own home. Upon entry, my eyes must have broadened wider than the span of the Brooklyn Bridge.

"Aleister…why are you wearing my gown? And why is it so cold in here?"

"You don't like it? I think the gray matches the mood of the outdoors. From now on, please refer to me as 'Father Nature'."

"And that foul odor?"

"Best not to ask."

With a sigh I turned my back to Aleister and attempted to light a fire with the red oak branches resting in the hearth. "The book?" I asked.

Aleister said with pride, the manner in which he says everything, "I'm nearly finished. Sometimes I went days without sleep because the vibration struck me so strongly to continue without stopping. Come."

"I'm impressed," I said, following him and his drawn-out strides. "Most of the time it takes me days to complete a single letter to a friend."

Before me in my office nook stood stacks upon stacks of

manuscript pages. Exhale. My anxiety vanished; I stopped sweating. Towering high like a skyscraper. I'd never seen anything like it. I attempted to grasp onto the one at the top.

"No, you mustn't!"

"Oh, Aleister. I'm sorry. Can you please retrieve it for me? I'd like to take a look."

"You can't view it yet, miss. Under no circumstances."

I couldn't understand his apprehension. What was he being so secretive about? The vision inside my head was a burning building ready for ruin, much like the Windsor Hotel, a monumental disaster.

"Let's sit down and discuss this, shall we. Perhaps outside. It's such a sunny and delightful day."

"I've never noticed anything delightful about the sun. It bores me."

"Aleister, you're being obstinate. I'll make tea, we'll sit at the table under the pines and we can reflect upon your progress."

In a sulking manner, still sporting a lavender sash around his neck, Aleister put on his boots but hadn't re-dressed into more masculine attire. "You're worried what people will think of you should I go out like this."

"There may be children in the schoolyard, Aleister."

"It's for those children I shall make a wardrobe change. Not for the likes of biddies."

I ignored Aleister and his caustic remarks. Instead I set my Japanese iron tea kettle on the stove to boil and I waited inside the kitchen to prepare our outdoor snack. Postum, Darjeeling Tea and cranberry and orange fruit tartlets were on the late-afternoon menu. Aleister, once properly clad in baggy denim overalls but missing brass buttons, excused himself to my cottage's back porch. Through the looking glass I could see him sitting on a chair, away from the sunlight, chatting to himself as if performing a

Shakespeare soliloquy on stage. Before the water on the stove reached its boiling point, I decided to peek further into the business at hand. From the desk I picked up a few pages of script and began reading something titled *The Pasquaney Puzzle.*

Rather than read the piece in its entirety, my eyes merely scanned the first page for proper nouns. Lake Pasquaney, New Hampshire, Bristol, Boston, Europeans, Scotland, Switzerland. Taking the time to splice them all together, modifiers and dangling participles included, didn't interest me.

What in the world do any of these have to do with astrology? This was the only reason I'd invited this man to stay at my cottage, yet he'd found occasions to write entire travelogues here! This was complete gibberish as far as I was concerned. His time here had been nothing but leisure, while I slaved away at my studio in Manhattan.

As the tea finished steeping, the Postum finished brewing, I positioned a few stale, ready-to-disintegrate currant cakes on a chipped plate because my agitation had forced me to devour the pre-planned tartlets as medicine, and then I carried them all into the next room. I set everything down for a moment so I could retrieve an article I'd read in New York a short time ago, one I originally intended to be silent about. But not now. With a heavy foot I marched into my room, reached inside my valise and pulled out a newspaper from a few days prior.

Placing it on the tray with shaky hands alongside the tea, the Postum and a few long forgotten cakes about to breed mold, I entered the porch with a scowl.

"How decadently American. Service without a smile."

"Aleister, I want so much for this to work out between us. I've waited a very long time to find the right gho—, collaborator."

"All will be brought into being, ma'am. When the moment strikes, the words will flow like…"

Aleister did not finish his sentence and I was glad he didn't. To me, the indication was clear that he had not devoted himself to my astrology books as he'd previously said he would.

As I handed my English houseguest the article, I asked him to orate. "Your recitations are memorable, my dear sir. Please commence."

Aleister smiled brightly upon seeing his name. With dramatic verve, complete with gyratory outward-thrashing hand gestures, he began.

☉  ☽  ★

---

## The New York Times
### July 16, 1916

### A Curious Kind of Lightning.

*To the Editor of The New York Times:*
I do not know whether globular lightning is a sufficiently rare phenomenon in this country to merit remark. Yesterday a globe of fire with an apparent diameter of about a foot burst on the floor of the middle room of a cottage here and within a few inches of my right foot. Curiously enough, no damage of any kind was done.
ALEISTER CROWLEY,
New Bristol, N.H., July 13, 1916.

---

☉  ☽  ★

"Usually the only way I make it into *The New York Times* is when I'm arrested. You've done it with this."

"I do have a way with words."

Upon hearing that, I did all I could to keep my tangy teacake down. "I'm making a point, Aleister."

"You needn't spend a moment concerning yourself with the welfare of your precious cottage, miss. I kept my word, I've cared for it as if it were my own."

My glare made him bolt from his seat. He then took me by the hand and dragged me into my pintsized sitting room, while pointing to a spot invisible to me on my yellow pinewood floor. Was this a case of an overactive imagination? Or delusional psychosis?

"No damage was done. Just as I said. Your precious cottage…perfectly intact."

"I can see that. I know you well enough to realize there was no lightning. My concern has to do with my books, the way you're spending your time."

Without a verbal reaction to me, Aleister proceeded to depart from the interior of my cottage, walk through the white, faded French doors to the porch and onward in the direction of the lake. Apparently to the black and baby blue spruce trees above him, he said, "Obviously you're no artiste. You haven't the foggiest how it all comes about."

I stood there, dumbstruck, with only the stack of papers to look at. I proceeded to examine more. Every single page appeared to be previously written work, all sorts of scribbles existing in the margins, more than likely draught to be edited and reworked. Not a one had to do with my astrology. What a colossal error in judgment I'd made. I shook my head and then wondered how I could get myself out of this predicament.

Needing time to ponder, I found myself walking into town on Slippery elm-lined North Shore Road to gather food for dinner at the town's general store that always smells of sweet maple syrup. The clerk there, who moonlights as the local Postmistress, someone I'd spoken to every time I happened to be in Hebron although always crossing her arms the minute she sees me, was in a particularly cheery mood. After greeting Mrs. Hopkins and Rusty, the beige and blind twenty-year-old tomcat at her feet, I handed her my list of items to purchase. Butter, lamb, onions, carrots, potatoes, garden peas, Worcestershire sauce and white Cheddar cheese.

"Oh, Miss Adams. You preparing Shepherd's Pie?" Mrs. Hopkins asked while collecting miscellaneous ingredients to fill my cupboards.

"A Shep—, I hadn't thought about it. Wh—?"

As I stared at the top of Mrs. Hopkin's rather small head, wondering why she was wearing her Sunday bonnet on a Saturday, she said, "I'll write it down for you step by step if you like," while sounding like a student vying for the sought-after position of teacher's pet.

"I've never made one. Wh—?"

"Your English gentleman's the talk of the town. He's been coming in nearly every day. Goes on and on about you, how he'd like nothing more than for you to personally bake him a Shepherd's Pie."

"Bake? He'll be leaving after a few months."

"What a shame. Well, it's lovely to see you two together."

"I'm just here for the weekend. He's not—"

"He's not returning with you? Ahh, that means you'll have to come back again real soon. Spend more time together before summer's end."

What a nauseating thought. I didn't let on because I wanted to see what else this woman would let slip out. Nods were the best answers I could come up with, knowing that she'd probably keep talking until she was forced to stop.

"We're all so pleased to see you with someone."

Nod.

"Ebenezer and I worry about you, coming up here alone all the time. No one to protect you, keep you company. And, he's so famous."

Sideways waggle.

"That's always the way, isn't it? Famous folks usually end up with other famous folk."

Up-and-down nod.

"I bet before you know it, we'll all be calling you Mrs. Aleister Crowley."

That was all my already queasy innards could handle. Not once did I correct Mrs. Hopkins, because this manufactured gossip was all so ludicrously entertaining. What harm, in fact, would it do for New Englanders, and perhaps others even more far-reaching, to think that Aleister and I were romantically attached? This was the kind of public relations money couldn't buy. By this point I'd given up trying to understand Aleister's universal appeal. He was somewhat like that strange high-pitched whistle only dogs in the distance can hear. Everyone else being the dogs, me being deaf to its frequency.

The illusion wouldn't be maintained if I continued to be irate with this man though. A nicer, more accommodating and patient hostess was my role for the next month or so, I figured. Sabine would be so pleased if she knew that I'd, even for a fleeting instant, contemplated making use of her breast-heaving guidance to entice a suitor. Or would she just be having a hearty laugh at my feeble attempt to implement it?

"I'm off for a bathe," Aleister said as soon as I returned to my country home, satchels in tow.

"I'll join you."

"Splendid. I'll be to the right of the costume house."

"No! Allow me to walk with you there. In just a moment I'll

have these goods in their place."

In no time whatsoever, my ingredients for Shepherd's Pie were put away in proper order, minus the garlic and beef stock I forgot to buy after re-examining the list provided by doting Mrs. Hopkins. It would remain a mystery if I'd be able to actually concoct authentic British food, but my fingers stayed crossed. "You do like Shepherd's Pie, don't you, Aleister?"

"Oh, heavens yes. A staple back home."

"Done. Let's be off, shall we."

As Aleister and I stepped off the back porch I grabbed onto his left elbow and slipped my right arm through his bent left. Arm in arm is the way it's done. A true gentleman would have offered first, while someone like Aleister must be coerced, I meant to say, coached.

"Turning out so lovely. This trip."

"It makes me so happy knowing that you're enjoying your time here."

"America is a wondrous place, Evangeline."

"Please call me 'Evvy.' That was J.P. Morgan's pet name for me."

"The Master of Finance. Although I despise greed, I applaud his convictions."

"He treated me so well. A fine man. He was afraid of d— dandelions, you know. Yet...so virile. Not as brawny as you though."

"Some consider me primitive. Mr. Morgan should have practiced Thelema along with me."

"Perhaps you could tell me more."

"I'll accomplish even more than that. I'll speak...as I gather," Aleister said as we made our way through the thickest and darkest part of the forest. Not letting a single bush, shrub, plant or tree go untouched, he picked at bark, herbs, leaves, branches, droppings in the dirt, berries, weeds, ferns, everything imaginable that's living in nature, with his bare hands. All for the purpose of later chopping it up, mixing it with lake water and drinking it as a vitality tonic, "guaranteed" he'd said, to make me live as long as I wished. "I shall create for you a refreshment ordained by the Gods Nuit, Hadit and Ra-Hoor-Kuit."

As the burlap satchel carrying his black-and-white-striped swimming costume filled with ingredients, I said, "Thelema sounds so intriguing. And its main premise?"

Aleister chose to ignore my comment. His overtly loud inhale through his teeth and exaggerated exhale, sounding more like an asthmatic wheeze, told me that I'd offended him. I'd grown used to this. "Excuse me. 'Premise' was the wrong word choice. How about 'tenet'?"

"Infinitely better, madam. 'Do what thou wilt shall be the whole of the law,' Thelemic law. Seek out and follow your own true path. Your true will, not your egoic desires."

"I can see merit in that. And participating in it lengthens one's life?"

"Wrong again, Evvy. That's what the pick-me-up will do."

"Well, I must say you've seemed very shrewd while collecting. Not once did I see you go near the poison ivy. You knew to avoid it."

"Naturally. The same cannot be said about the hemlock though."

"You picked hemlock?"

"Perchance yes, perchance no. I know not what it looks like."

"Neither do I. I must say that I'm rather reluctant to drink it. Not knowing."

"Miss, the 'not knowing' is the most crucial ingredient of all. Nothing's more intoxicating than gambling with life itself," Aleister said, before licking his lips.

☉  ☽  ★

Between my cottage and the lake, in front of the unpretentious schoolyard with several rails missing from its faded while picket fence, a congregation of children and parents were gathered. The squealing youngsters appeared to be recreating freely, perhaps playing foot hockey or dodge ball on the dry, sunburnt lawn. I persuaded Aleister to veer off course a bit so we could spectate up close for ourselves.

"No, keep your arm where it is. Such a warm, titillating feeling."

Aleister liked what I'd just said as he began staring into my bosom. I blushed on purpose. Although we had never been introduced directly, I began motioning to the group of townspeople in a rather affectionate manner.

"Wave to them, Aleister."

"But I don't know them."

"In America, it's customary. A friendly gesture."

Somehow he and I unhurriedly wandered all the way through town before making our way to the shores of the lake. Everyone seemed to notice us, Aleister and I, together. Occasionally, a few of the most curious onlookers, wearing beach cover ups and carrying sunbathing blankets, came up to us and offered a greeting. This time, I encouraged questions. "How long will you be up here, Miss?"

"Oh, we're having a gay holiday. Aren't we, Aleister? The longer, the better," I replied while tweaking Aleister's cheek hard enough to leave a mark.

Aleister's wry grin to me expressed pleasure in my masochistic display. Being brutally sarcastic, Aleister, and his counterfeit American accent, interjected, "My honey bunny and I are having the time of our lives."

Back on track we headed. To the lake, then back to the cottage for us. Now, with no one else around to evidence our union, my stride grew brisker. Aleister selected a more isolated bathing place behind a jetty made of boulders, bog birch and abandoned rowboats.

"I choose to wear no costume. And, so shall it be."

"I'm returning back. Dinner won't prepare itself," I said with my back to my undressing boarder.

My Shepherd's Pie ended up being barely stomach-able that night. The cheese atop the pie was charred black and the mashed potatoes underneath resembled a paste I'd once used to plug holes in my furniture, but I cared not. Aleister and I strolled through town twice more before it was my time to go, giving the townsfolk more news to invent and discuss. He promised me he'd devote the rest of his stay to the "completion" of my book and I acknowledged his assurance. With much satisfaction I headed to the train station in Bristol knowing that I'd accomplished much for my career while in Hebron.

$$\odot \quad \rD \quad \star$$

As I waited for the departure of the overdue train, I noticed a woman from behind wearing thrice-braided hair, much like Emma. Emma'd been the last person, non-employed companion, with whom I traveled to New Hampshire and had been on my mind ever since my arrival; a bit of self-torture, one might say. This time for business, last time nothing but pleasure…the way Mother Nature intended.

And, the grocer, the townspeople. How impressed, bowled over they were to see me arm in arm with Aleister. What would their reaction have been had they seen me walking with Emma on my arm instead? The sight of her hand gently touching mine? Oh, the scowls, perhaps jeers, the condemnation. Instead, they were most impressed by the fraud I've perpetuated. "If the stars are indeed infallible, your most authentic identity will be your guide," I remembered Emma telling me in a letter.

When the somewhat plain-faced woman with no sparkle in her eye turned around, she looked nothing like Emma. No one was more beautiful than she.

# Sun @ 1° LIBRA 34'58 (1916)

*I* don't know if it was the hemlock or Aleister's pitiable hygiene habits that turned my stomach ill, but on-and-off delirium accompanied me on my train trip back to Manhattan. Still, by the time the train reached Grand Central Terminal and its imposing forty-eight foot high ceilings, I felt more or less myself. Noticing my uneasiness along the journey, a charitable tall Dutch gentleman of about fifty seated inside my cabin, looking like he possessed the strength of the Greek god Kratos, offered to carry my bags. This simple act of kindness lifted my spirits immeasurably and even brought a smile to my face. I was counting the seconds 'til my arrival back to civilization.

Exiting the rail terminal was to be a cautionary experience this time around. All passengers disembarking the railroad cars had been forewarned that a protest involving suffragettes was taking place on the Park Avenue Viaduct motor crossing, one floor above the E. 42nd Street exit. The ostensible intent was to make known their cause at each and every accessible outlet available to the public. By means of strategically placed megaphones, parents were told to leash their children until having departed the station, completely clearing the two-block radius that surrounds it. A horseless carriage to take me from hectic and overfilled Grand Central to midtown would be hard to find, I imagined. Traffic was likely to be at a standstill. But the demonstration was scheduled to conclude only thirty minutes after my arrival. I figured I could tolerate a temporary inconvenience, barely.

Many of the wooden signs, paperboard placards, lithographed posters and linen pennant banners visible to me just outside the street-level exit at E. 42nd and Vanderbilt Avenue displayed the same catchphrases as the many leaflets falling from the outside floor above. Agitated but obedient female protestors; young women, mademoiselles, matrons, dowagers, and everyone in between were to be found everywhere.

☉ ☽ ✫

> **WE WERE VOTERS OUT WEST!**
> **WHY DENY OUR RIGHTS IN THE EAST?**

> **DEEDS**
> **NOT**
> **WORDS**

☉ ☽ ✫

The energy encompassing a national right to vote was becoming frenzied. Although I'd appreciate having this privilege granted, it wasn't imperative for me that I had it. As always, I did my best to steer clear from controversy.

Standing on the curb of 42nd Street, noticing an even larger amount of very vocal and conspicuous protestors than above, possibly thousands, I observed my frank, mostly youthful, female colleagues marching, chanting in unison. All with similar, solemn styles of black dress. All women, all carrying virtually the same white placards with large black text, waving them up and down in the air. It felt as if they'd been preparing all their lives for this singular demonstration. Every one of them, presumably new recruits as well as lifelong members to the National Woman's Party, appeared proud to be taking part. That everlasting euphoric feeling of pride—following my court trial of 1914—made me reminisce about the joy, the exuberance of having attained justice, validity.

"Join in! There's power in numbers," a bold blond suffragette shouted in my direction after having approached me from behind. She wore no hat, and her hair was cut shockingly short. Her direct address startled me, causing my brown and beige-striped parasol to become dislodged from my hands.

To my grand astonishment upon picking it up from the soot-laden gutter, I found a familiar face in the next person that approached me, appearing determined and full of life. Breath left my lungs and took a pause before re-entry.

"Emma," I gasped.

Her eyes widened in surprise and—I hesitated to admit it—dismay. "Evangeline. Care to accompany us?"

Purpose and passion showed on Emma's face. Dressed in formal business attire, she looked smart in shades of black and neck adornments of red. Her high-brimmed gray hat made her appear taller in stature. "Well, I don't—"

Before I could give my reply, Emma grabbed onto the first woman, fully embracing her at the waist; then she proceeded to kiss her on the lips.

Was this in jest? The first woman appeared to thoroughly enjoy this expression of, what I could only imagine to be, desire.

The woman began stroking Emma's hair, touching her in every way visible to me. "This is Roberta. She's a good friend of mine."

Forthright Roberta, clad in nothing but black and white, reached out her right hand for me to shake cordially. Now close enough for me to examine the details of her face, I could tell that she was significantly younger than Emma by about twenty to thirty years. No blemishes, few discernible creases to the forehead, no smeared-on beauty-adorning face paint.

"How do you do, Roberta," I said, just as Emma winked at her favorably. Noticing this gesture with one eye, my other began scanning the faces of the crowd surrounding us. Most resembled Roberta and the girlish vivacity she exhibited as I discovered other Suffragettes cheering and clapping upon kissing each other. An overt ritual I was unfamiliar with. The sight of so many women expressing such outright fondness with one another made me blush. Made me turn away from them; for a few seconds there, in every face thereafter, I saw Mother's squinted ebony eyes. Part of me never truly knew what that gaze from her meant. Confusion? Disapproval? Or both? Perhaps love among women, like the right to vote, is an equal right valued more by the younger generation, I thought to myself.

"Nice to know you…?" the young woman said.

"Evangeline."

Roberta froze in her stance, motionless. Seconds before, a face that was animated, now blank. Next, she looked at me with what appeared to be microscopic eyeballs. Analyzing my being up close and at length. From head to toe I felt inspected.

"*You're* Evangeline Adams?" the young woman said in a rather skeptical fashion.

I admitted to it, and that was pretty much the end of the

conversation. In every way imaginable I felt queasy. Sick to my stomach all over again. A silent belch not yet fully formed forced my lips to open fleetingly without anyone noticing. As Emma and her woman friend said goodbye and walked away from me, they appeared to be laughing. Why? The rally was disbanding and soon I'd be left there on the street corner by myself.

Hearing that next to no carriage drivers wanted to come anywhere near Grand Central during a protest, especially this one, I waited nearly an hour to find someone that was willing to take me uptown. A few women, Suffragettes, passed by me outside my carriage as we made our way up Madison Avenue. They appeared content; apparently still unified in the cause for women, even after the rally had long concluded. Seeing them—reflecting on my own indifference to their dedication—made me feel anything but feminine.

By the time I reached Carnegie Hall, the sun had gone down and everyone in my employ, including Sabine, had left for the day to go home to their loved ones. Not until now had I noticed that the clock inside my studio, actually any clock, ticks loudest in solitude. I placed my luggage onto the floor, slipped off my shoes and stockings. My gaze scanned the books in my library until it landed upon *The Purloined Letter* by Edgar Allan Poe.

The letters that had previously angered me so were now all I had left of my connection to Emma. How horribly sad and alone that made me. Indecision, induced by debilitating heavyheartedness, paralyzed me once more. Would my collective inabilities worsen should I open one of these letters? Or would it fill me with comfort reliving my dear friend's truest, now seemingly former feelings for me?

I ended up opening the one I'd first received. The once biting scent of Emma's citrus and jasmine Cornubia Oriental Floral perfume emanating from the envelopes and contents, now barely noticeable. The detail that stupefied me in these correspondences most was how matter of fact Emma was, not hesitant or embarrassed at all in sharing. Why was it that the most solitary moments I'd ever experienced were those in my own office? The very same place where, by now, thousands upon thousands of people have sat before me?

Rather than reading any more or opening any others, I instead chose to pen my own thoughts. The wish to expel my feelings overpowered my indifference towards writing. There was no way I could avoid the mistake I knew I'd made.

Perhaps my time with Emma was more than a mere experiment. Maybe there was credence in our actions. It could be that I did feel love, but couldn't necessarily accept it at the time. Ah, those warm and gentle moments just beyond Newport.

☉　☽　✶

*Dearest Emma,*

*Sadness overwhelms me now. I have no excuses whatsoever for the poor errors in judgment I've demonstrated to you within the past year. I apologize to you for not responding so very much earlier. Seeing you today, along with your friend, made me realize that I've disrespected you in ways you don't deserve. I'm so sorry. Your decision to part from me was warranted and I agree to it completely. I hope your family is doing well.*

*Yes, I can be consumed by my concern for being in the limelight. Again, no excuses. I was in New Hampshire this weekend and thought of you and the time we had there together. That burgundy double blanket. The afterglow of the hearth's last flickering flame. These were fine memories. Times I will never forget.*

*It's taken me this long, but thank you. Thank you for your true expressions. Every word you chose to share with me was appreciated. It took great courage to compose your thoughts the way you did. When you told me,*

*"Never had I felt more alive than when I am beside you," I felt the same. Yes, the intimate nature of our weekend was special—to be honest, something I've never experienced with anyone before. Only with you did I feel comfortable. I, most likely, didn't hide it very well, but you made me weep. Your tender touch awakened in me sentiments I'm just too cowardly to admit I possess. You made this Aquarian open up.*

*You have brought out the best in me and I applaud you for your infinite patience. My fears could have easily gotten the best of me, but*

⊙　☽　✭

Before being able to finish that last sentence, a rap came on my door. It was beyond dusk, yet still perfectly acceptable to receive evening guests. I inquired as to who was there. The voice replying was soft but excitable. "I'm your biggest admirer, ma'am," a young woman answered through the glass door.

"Well, thank you, dear. But my office is closed now."

"I'm, I'm so sorry to bother you, ma'am. I leave tonight on a trip and now I beg you for your autograph."

Noticing an aura of innocence and missing agenda about her, I said, "My autograph?"

"I'm rather keen on astrology and I couldn't leave New York without at least hearing your voice. I live by every word you deliver."

"Well, my heavens," I said while opening the door. There stood a petite, cherub-like adolescent with hair shimmering like curly rays of orange light at sunset; even her blood-red bow seemed to pulsate upon greeting me.

"Oh, it really is you. *The* Evangeline Adams, the Seer of Wall Street."

"Yes. And who might you be?"

"Wilhelmina, Wilhelmina Hearst. I'm visiting from San

Francisco and I'm about to return."

"A lovely city."

"Yes, but New York…My, I can't believe I'm talking to you now. I'm a Cancer with ascendant in Aries."

"Well, that does explain your desire to return home. Doesn't it?"

"Oh, I've followed your career since as far back as I can remember. And, keeping company with *the* Aleister Crowley. How exotically elegant." The girl waved her hands dramatically somehow in the same flailing, outward manner as Aleister. Fingertips on the left hand pointing up, fingertips on the right pointing down.

"And how did you come upon that information, dear?"

"It's the talk of the town. I just came from Greenwich Village and…I beg your pardon, ma'am. I hope you don't think me a gossiper."

After taking a moment or so for my mind to catch up, I asked, "Now, how did you say you were named?"

"Miss Wilhelmina Hearst."

"Do you happen to be related to Mr. William Randolph Hearst?"

"Yes, indeed, ma'am. He's my uncle. The newspaperman. He owns tw—"

"Twenty-eight newspapers across the country."

"Oh, you've heard of him. From S—"

"San Francisco."

"Miss Adams, you're reading my mind, aren't you?"

"Maybe yes. Maybe no. Either way, you must tell your uncle I said, 'hello.' The same from Aleister."

"It would be an honor."

After a bit more chit-chat, the enamored young woman lent me her paper on which to write. I issued my standard autograph and told her that I'd call upon her the next time I go out West. Made me recall the first time I was asked, taken by surprise, by a young woman similar in stature. What a charmer. Ah, the jubilation of being so admired. Miss Hearst's high regard for me provided an instant dose of confidence tonic, a homemade concoction my own doctor was never able to prescribe. Much more safe and effective than New Hampshire hemlock. And I could see that my strategy of using Aleister's association by name was paying off considerably. Doing this more often at every possible occasion will most certainly be in my best interest, I thought.

I prepared a light dinner and retired, secure in my fame.

$$\odot \quad \rightmoon \quad \star$$

Facing my letter to Emma caught me by surprise when I sat at my desk early the next morning. I hesitated at how twofaced my feelings appeared in the light of day. And yet what was a person without courage? I picked up my pen again. Healthy for the soul, I imagined, a show of respect for someone who's worthy of a response.

*You have brought out the best in me and I applaud you for your infinite patience. My fears could have easily gotten the best of me, but you erased them with conviction. Oh how I'll*

"Sabine!"

"Miss, I'm so sorry."

Gawking at Sabine's smudged lip rouge, I yelled, "You startled me. I wasn—"

"Oh, I should have knocked. Please forgive…You are here so early."

"I'm eager to get back to work. A full week ahead."

"But…your visit. How was it?"

"Perfectly fine. Nice to get away."

"And Mr. Aleister…what was he like? As crazy and wicked as

people say?"

"In some ways, yes."

"I told my friends in Germany that you know him well and now they are so jealous of me."

"Of *you?*"

"Yes, because I know you and you know him. He's a very famous man."

"I had no idea. He is who he is... I did notice that he does have a talent for writing though."

"You're so lucky to have him writing your astrology books. The most famous astrologer and one of the most famous writers. Together."

Yes, together. How fortuitous is that. Never would have I foreseen this extra attention I'd be receiving as a result of this oddball. It's a connection I must cherish and be grateful for, I assumed. I just knew that keeping my wits about me in Aleister's company will prove to be of paramount importance in the future. Not losing my temper would be challenging, but so worth the enduring effort.

"He still thinks that we're collabor— You know the word 'collaborating'?"

"No, Ma'am. You teach me."

"Aleister thinks he will be known as the author of these books, with my name adjoining his."

Sabine tilted her head in question.

"His name mustn't appear on the cover. Under no circumstances."

"Because of...money."

"Precisely."

"Miss, now you know exactly why I am the way I am, was. Men are not for play, for fun. Without a man, I'd never be in this country."

"You're saying you only use them? Then, what do they get out of you? Never mind…I can just imagine."

"The trick is to make them want even more the next time. Make them weak, venerable. I did this then, but I stopped. My life before." Then Sabine blushed.

"*Vul*nerable." A feeling about me instantly became reluctant to learn more; as a result, I didn't question what my ears didn't want to hear.

"Yes, Miss. I had to. The day before you met me, looking at Lady Liberty downtown."

"After I came back from Wall St. Seeing you on the pier. Crying."

"I was happy. So very happy. I waited all my life for this day…to be free. I told my husband that—"

"Husband?"

"Yes. I must tell you now. That was the day before I said, 'goodbye.' I married this man only to get to America. To start a new beginning."

"You're no longer married?"

"No. It was the only way. In Germany, it's hard for women. Always controlled by their men. For years it was my plan…to be free. I met this American man in München. We had an arrangement. We married. He brought me here. I don't see him again. He won't see me. You gave me the job. Now, I don't need to…do these things anymore." Sabine blushed a second time.

My imagination transported me to Sabine's previous life for a bit, then I came back. My heavens. What courage. The confidence Sabine possessed while confessing her independence to me took over my entire office, leaving me feeling a bit small. What an ordeal she'd gone through, just to create a better life, all the while I'd been taking my inalienable rights for granted. How appropriate that we'd met while gazing at the Statue of Liberty and all she stands for.

"I will remember this story. And, it will be our secret."

"Like the balanced breathing, Miss. And, the breast—yes, our secret."

Although one in a few may have been born with a heart of gold bestowed upon them, more and more I was grateful to have learned what I had from my Scorpion secretary. Thank God Sabine'd been loyal to me, most of the time. I cowered to think of the consequences if she hadn't.

# Sun @ 11° GEMINI 36'06 (1918)

*L*ove and finance. Love and finance. Women looking for love. Men seeking to strike it rich. Always the same, always will be.

In the mid-afternoon, close to three-forty-five, feeling fidgety and uneasy I finally completed my letter to Emma in what she would call pristine penwomanship. Seeing it lay there atop my desk brought my mind back to New Hampshire; the warmth we felt as we noticed that bowl of wildflowers on the walnut hutch, the closeness of not only our bodies but our minds, the honesty of our conversations afterwards. My fiftieth birthday had just passed this February; my sixty-fourth year, my projected last, coming up within 156 months. The truth of the matter: in maturity, timepieces tick more noticeably as each day passes. I folded my letter to Emma in thirds, placed it inside an envelope, addressed it, and for the first time scented it, exactly as Emma would. My nose grasped for the remaining aroma of Houbigant's Mon Boudoir wafting around me. I clutched onto both my upper arms with my hands, hugging myself briefly, tightly, feeling proud. I couldn't wait to mail my letter to Emma.

"Miss Addddams?" Without warning, emerging next into my office was a somewhat skittish man I'd seen two to three times prior.

Immediately I removed my hands from my arms. As my reflexes got the best of me, I grabbed onto the envelope on my desk, crumpled it up and threw it into the rubbish. "Mr. Mortimer, you gave me a fright. I wasn't expecting you."

"I'm sorry to have startled you, ma'am. It's four o'clock. No one was there to greet me, so I came right in."

It took me a while for my nerves to steady, but as soon as they did, it was back to business as usual.

Mr. Mortimer, like countless others had done before, seemed to be copying the method J.P. made use of so many times. Having a chart created for a proposed business venture by providing me with the birth data for those involved. When not given the birthdate of an individual I'd ask for the date when the company was formed. Either way, these particular clients were seeking out a financial match made in heaven.

My infrequent patron, looking skeptical and bewildered, as most men seem to appear before me, greeted me, once more hoping the information I gave him would increase the size of his wallet. James Mortimer firstly asked a question about his wife—as I could see, with my mind's eye, his bald spot growing bigger by the minute. A slight stammer to his speech delivered through chapped lips, he wanted to know if she had a hidden interest in another, much younger, more vital man. Mr. Mortimer gave me her birth information and I assured him that she was entirely devoted to her husband. It was his overwrought Pisces imagination playing tricks on him.

Next, the focus shifted to commerce.

"My goal is to expand my firm, to structure it in a more

professional manner. Add on another partner."

"Please, sir, tell me once more about your business. The way you make your living."

"Poultry. Supplying fresh hens to the finest restaurants of New York."

"And this other man is also a supplier?"

"No, ma'am. He's a—"

"No need. I'll tell you what I discover."

"Here is his birth information, Miss Adams."

While inspecting the soiled scrap of paper, making note of the inconsistent hen scratch; some 'I's dotted, while others contained two, I called out, "His name's missing."

"You need to know that as well?"

"It's sometimes helpful."

"Why don't you tell me what you find out, then I'll identify him if you still need to know."

How unnecessarily mysterious. Nothing new there either. Before me to ponder was information about a man born on the twentieth of June, 1890. Five-ten in the morning in Foxborough, Massachusetts.

The mystery began expanding in the twinkling of an eye as soon as I investigated this man's chart. I found myself examining it a second, third and even fourth time. It was uncanny, like a carbon blueprint of mine, yet matching my weaknesses with his strengths, exactly.

"Mr. Mortimer, although you hadn't stated it, I detected that this younger man has nothing to do with the poultry business. But his ability to promote, to make known, to not only capitalize on opportunity but to create it, is noteworthy," I said as my breath became short.

"You sound excited discussing him."

"Perhaps."

"You've portrayed him as he truly is, ma'am. And…?"

"He'd prove to be a superb manager or promoter of your hen-distribution enterprise, Mr. Mortimer. An excellent communicator that draws people into his endeavors somewhat unsuspectingly. You do trust him, don't you?" I noticed something rather disturbing in the configurations surrounding the prospective partner's seventh house, justice. Something criminal in his past—yet I was cautious about mentioning it.

"That's what I'd like you to tell me."

Of course, being in my position, I never offer anything subjective. My obligation is to divulge facts as I see them and scrutinize how they're fitted around timeframes. After volunteering the information I gather, my client can only speculate as to how this affects them, their future decisions and plans, then take actions accordingly.

"I see that this man learned his cunning conduct from a male figure in his immediate family. Together, they have experienced a legal tussle. Perhaps in this gentleman's youth."

"Anything serious?"

"I wouldn't know. I see that this man would go the extra mile to secure what he desires, regardless of the consequences. That may very well be a positive attribute. He comes from a rural, farming background, but acts as if he's a man of fine breeding, born into society."

"That's exactly what he'd like you to believe, ma'am." My client, Mr. Mortimer, looked at me differently. Not so altogether favorably this time. Perhaps solving the mystery to this puzzle himself. He was the sweetest and kindest man, from what I'd gathered, yet whenever he came to me he continued to see himself as a victim. He hadn't yet understood the way life works, that there are those that continuously refer to themselves as "poor me," are taken advantage of and the rest take advantage. The truth of the matter, plain and simple.

"He also fancies himself a lady's man. Quite a youthful form. Only older women. No children, but socially well-connected."

I continued. "This man is handsome, I take it. Charms people with not only his words, but his boyish appearance. Dark hair, hypnotic eyes, ta—"

"Miss, I'm still looking for an answer. Should I go into business with him? Or not?"

"I completely understand, Mr. Mortimer. Any questions posed to me with the word 'should' in it I never answer. Any decision made is entirely yours."

Everything about this man's chart seemed to beckon me. To shout for my attention. It was like a chart I'd never seen before. As I lifted up one of the pages of my analysis to show Mr. Mortimer, the tall stack of papers atop my desk teetered and fell downward onto the floor. A lesson for me to, once and for all, assemble shorter stacks.

Very gentlemanly of him, Mr. Mortimer stepped behind my desk, reached down and helped me restore the heap the way it had formerly been. Being keen on confidentiality I told him I'd re-place the papers myself as his eyes began to wander to the rubbish can below my desk, Emma's envelope contained therein. Because of his sweetness, his vulnerability, I posed an enquiry to him I'd never brought up to anyone else. "If at all possible, I think it best for me to meet this gentleman myself. It could be quite a prosperous union for you, or not."

"You...meeting him. I'm not so sure about that. He doesn't know that I...see you."

"Mr. Mortimer, you needn't tell him that you were asking about him. You could say that we'd met on the street, a church social, the interest was entirely mine. You'd be humoring me, my request, as a personal favor. Perhaps he's heard of me and my reputation. It wouldn't hurt for you to mention my previous clients, J.P. Morgan, Charles Schwab or Seymour Cromwell, President of the New York Stock Exchange. I've made many men millionaires."

"Well, Miss. All I can do is ask. If you feel it will help me make up my mind regarding a future association with him."

"Absolutely, Mr. Mortimer. I have only your best interest at heart. This will allow me to give you more definitive options from which to choose."

"I assume there's no harm in it, miss. That's all you have to tell me now?"

"Not another word comes to mind."

⊙　☽　★

With my usual collection of clients before me, most of them society matrons from both sides of Fifth Avenue, not one of which a spinster, I conducted my mathematic calculations. Each and every morning before my days' work began I scanned my list of upcoming appointments. Whenever a man's name appeared I sometimes anticipated that it was Mr. Gemini from Foxborough. Curiosity had gotten the best of me and I longed to finally match that most attention-grabbing horoscopic chart with a handsome face.

I hadn't heard back from Mr. Mortimer for a while, yet somehow I felt for certain that his anonymous-to-me partner would arrive at my doorstep, maybe when I least expected him to do so. Nearing the bottom of my list during a most tiring day, I spoke impassively to a relatively precarious client who showed up in front of me every week, always at the end of the day when my energy was at its lowest threshold. Her questions, similar to my answers, were always the same.

"But is it my diamond necklace or my jade that will be more

breathtaking? After all, first impressions are what matter most."

"You're entirely right, Sylvia. Def—"

"Sylvie."

God, in Your infinite wisdom, please spare me. "Bien sûr...Sylveee. Most definitely the jade. The stars favor green on the night of your par— soirée. Any other night I'd have to say diamond."

"Oh, Evangeline. I don't know what I'd do without you."

This was what Sylvia Bernbaum, now afflicted with a poor man's French accent, wanted to know most and I still had twenty-five more minutes to kill. I prayed she had questions for me that were infinitely more stimulating than selecting the color of jewelry to wear. My patience was wearing thin; I was developing a headache and felt that a head cold was coming upon me. More than all else, Mrs. Bernbaum's trivial, inconsequential concerns were taking light-years away from the legacy I'd planned on leaving. Time was of the essence and this woman was robbing me of it. "You want to know about the scheduling of classes to take? Goals to set? Charities to support?"

While rather overtly re-clasping the ruby and sapphire brooch atop her black velvet hat, perhaps for me to make note of, Mrs. Bernbaum said, "Why, my heavens no. Classes, goals...preparing the chicest of soirées is what keeps me most content. Why on earth would I bother putting my attention elsewhere?"

The next twenty-or-so minutes passed at a snail's pace. "We're just about out of time, Sylvia. It's been a pleas—"

"But you haven't yet told me which shade of sash suits me best when I take my morning constitutionals."

"Violet. Most definitely."

"You hadn't looked into my chart. How do you—"

"I saw it earlier. Violet."

With no more color-schemed questions in front of me, my last client of the day entered my office appearing supremely confident.

There was an air about him that invited stares, not to mention upturned noses. Every sense of mine, except for smell, became seduced. This man, and his unusual fragrance, made me curious on a host of levels.

"I am Mr. George Edwin Jordan, Jr. I'd like to know my future," he said, as he removed the spectacles from his perfectly proportioned face, framed in the middle by high cheekbones.

"I'd be happy to help you, Mr. Jordan. The way I conduct my business is to tell you which aspects of the stars work in your favor at a given time. Is that to your liking?"

"Sounds fair enough."

"May I have your birthday, time and place, please."

Before he made me aware of this information I innately knew this was the gentleman Mr. Mortimer had referred to. The most challenging issue for me was to either play the game of telling him I already knew much about him and his personality *or* act surprised by it all.

Mr. Jordan reiterated the data I'd already known, and since the information was now coming from the gentleman himself, I proceeded to cast the very same chart all over again. Nothing about its outcome was the least bit different. Instead I was reminded about how much in sublime synchronization it was to mine.

"All planets favor the continued use of your persuasive skills. Your ability to gain someone's trust and convince them of 'doing things your way,' will always be your strong suit."

"My head's full of business ideas, ma'am. I'm a man who knows how to get things done."

The cockiness of his comment, and his unapologetic use of the word 'get,' would have made others blanch. Not me. For the very longest time I'd had to fight my way through a man's world. To so many, astrology has been perceived as a novelty, and I've had to brawl my way through the minds of skeptics. His overconfident attitude was what was needed in business, promotion, to cut to the chase, I was certain of it—a gentleman's touch.

"I must tell you now, Mr. Jordan, than I know it was Mr. Mortimer who first introduced you to me, via your birth data. He—"

"I told him not to—"

"He didn't say a word about your identity. Mr. Mortimer remained a true squire. But, if I can be brutally frank, in the long run your efforts with him, his with yours, will not be entirely beneficial."

While flapping his illusory wings, Mr. Jordan said with embarrassment oozing from his pride, "It's the chickens, ain't it? I mean, isn't it?"

"Yes, that's part of it. I see you having the most success with an esoteric partner. Someone purveying a product more cryptic, more alluring than fowl. I see positivity around you and your ability to make this product known to the masses here and abroad. What is it you now do?"

The attractive young man in his late-twenties paused for more than a few seconds. This gave me time to inspect his immaculate dark grey three-piece pinstriped suit, black leather soled shoes, pale grey silk ascot and charcoal grey Borsalino Trilby hat he still carried in his right hand. The moment I was scrutinizing, he pursed his lips, and said, "I peddle manure."

"Oh...well that explains that od—"

"In the farmlands of Massachusetts. I'm getting out of it though. Moving here permanently. I've got big plans."

Mr. Jordan gazed into my eyes intently. Within his I could see my same passion for aiming high. Just as he did, I was unafraid to stick my toe out beyond where it's never before gone. I examined his chart more deeply and while looking at one of the most interesting aspects, Mr. Jordan interrupted my concentration by asking, "How do you find yourself in the business world, ma'am?"

"I love it, sir. It fascinates me as much as my astrology practice does. It's invigorating."

"That's the perfect description. I see it exactly the same."

"Turning a non-believer into a believer."

"Conquering new territory."

"Providing my clients with more than they'd expected."

"Reaching new ones. Expanding the marketplace."

"Adding a new depth to my presentations."

"Leaving audiences satiated yet hungering for more."

"Mr. Jordan, I feel myself becoming lightheaded," I told my much younger, captivated client in a jesting manner.

His husky and extended laugh exuded self-assurance, coolness. While I felt myself becoming intoxicated, Mr. Jordan gave the impression of being serene. I could tell that the passion he felt for what he did was routine and commonplace in his daily life. Nothing new whatsoever. "Tell me more, Miss Adams. It is Miss, isn't it?"

"Yes, it certainly is. Well, Neptune in your twelfth house indicates that everything—"

"No, tell me more about you, your aspirations."

"But, sir, this session is about you and your affairs."

"Where do you see yourself in twelve months? Three years from now?"

"Well, my chart indicates—"

"No, no charts. Put them out of your head for the moment. What are your future goals? Dreams?"

For the very first time, going far, far back I had become the skeptical one sitting inside my office. Looking over at this man who seemed too good to be true made me disbelieve what fate had brought to me: the man who could help me turn the rest of my dreams into reality.

"I want to be known as the world's most famous, most successful astrologist, man or woman. Not only now, but forever in history. I would like to die feeling confident that I'd accomplished this feat."

As I spoke, Mr. Jordan borrowed the pen from my hand and took a piece of paper from the stack. He began writing profusely as I dictated nothing, while still taking the time to dot every 'I.' Was he even paying attention to me at that point? It was difficult to find logic in his actions. *I* was always the one jotting down data and making notations.

"I hope I'm not disturbing you with my presence," I said to Mr. Jordan acerbically. At the same time he looked up to me, I squinted over my desktop to catch a glimpse of, upside down of course, his compositions. It appeared as if one word, the same word beginning with "B" was written down repeatedly. Boat? Book? Boot? All other letters were unintelligible to me.

"Forgive me, ma'am. These notes are all in your favor. Success is invalid if it's not preceded by an intelligent business strategy and promotional plan. You have done me a great service by moving me away from...fowl. In addition to your compensation I'd like you to take these thoughts, professionally speaking, and contemplate their execution."

"Of course, sir. I will. Thank you."

"The pleasure has been entirely mine, Miss Adams," Mr. Jordan told me while reaching for my left hand with his left. Electricity charged through my being the moment our flesh touched. His kiss on my hand was warm, stimulating, like one I'd never experienced before.

Perhaps Mr. Jordan was the just man I'd been waiting so long to place into my life, I thought. How impressive it would be to show him off. A male figure, statuesque-like, that would attract attention in my company, in public, for all the right reasons.

Young, fearless, self-assured; eager to make a name for himself while focusing on nothing but me, my success and the grand legacy I intended to pass on. Mr. Jordan could certainly solve a multitude of dilemmas in my life; personal, professional and public relations, all rolled into one.

After he left my office, the enchanted feeling I had remained for several days to come.

# Sun @ 3° SCORPIO 16'24 (1920)

*M*y calculations once again proved to be correct; not once did I have to strain my psyche to ascertain much. Every time Mr. Jordan and I got together to discuss strategies, a restored verve entered my physiology. A sensation akin to when I once drank Kola Compound elixir by mistake, not knowing it contained the stimulant cocaine. Newfound dreams came to me by day and night and, with the help of Mr. Jordan, G.E., I could witness their actual transformation before my very eyes. Being so near his youth gave me back some of mine. I even started using the word 'get,' but *'ain't,'* never. G.E. had just reached his thirtieth year, a time when most people lose the air of invincibility they were born with; this is when most people let fear begin to dominate their lives. I wanted so much to make the most of him before it was too late.

Into the late hours of the night, G.E. and I would talk about reaching higher. Before the roaring fire we sipped a champagne toast, over and over and over again, to our new professional union. The key ingredient to my hiring him was a natural trust that I felt.

He'd admitted that, in 1910, he had been found guilty of crashing into a young woman's horse and carriage with his automobile and was ordered to pay $2,250 by the court. "Not at all my fault," G.E. claimed. Accidents will happen. This was what I must have seen when examining his chart in the company of Mr. Mortimer. Any sort of skepticism I'd sensed previous had vanished. As I'd assured each client of mine, G.E. promised me that all strategies expressed between us, such as courting the media, delivering grandiose predictions for the masses and concocting a compassionate, mother-like brand image for myself, would remain confidential. This was G.E.'s idea and it meant a lot to me that he initiated it.

While glancing at the books contained in my office bookcase, G.E. perused several before hand-selecting *The Purloined Letter*.

"Oh, not that one! It's...a women's book."

"Edgar Allan Poe, Evangeline. Women's?"

"Here...take this instead. *The Hound of the Baskervilles*. You'll appreciate this one most."

G.E. accepted my choice and changed the subject back to me. "A book is a necessity for you. For anyone of your stature. In all honesty, you should already have one, at least one, out by now."

"You've mentioned this before. I've known this for ages, G.E."

"And, that Elister won't complete the task. He's too provocative. Too few readers will be able to absorb his *madness*."

"It's Aleister."

"A book, simply written. About your clients perhaps. An attention grabber. Exposing the secret comings and goings of the la-di-da."

But this was my core audience! The artists, the avant-garde, the financiers of the world had made me a celebrity, but it was the society matrons who had kept my wallet consistently fat for decades. "I could never...not my clients."

"Disguise their names. Put in a few real ones. With their

permission, of course."

"But who would write it?"

"You! It must be written by you. To lend authenticity. No one knows this business better than yourself."

"I certainly have collected enough stories. Nearly every one of my predictions has come to fruition. After all, the stars are infallible. Why, I must have—"

"What a title! *The Stars Are Infallible*. Transcendent *and* highly commercial."

"G.E., you're making me excited again."

"Then we've gotta do something about that."

As I poured more champagne into G.E.'s black Waterford flute, he reached for more paper and a pen. Designs and ideas appeared to be spewing from his brain faster than he could translate them into business English. "More caviar?"

"No time for that. Success stories. That'll be your book. An exposé of your success stories. Nothing will make people want to know you more than the triumphs you've created."

"I've helped them along. Let's be honest, I haven't necessarily created them."

"In the book…you *have*."

☉　☽　★

G.E. was a genius when it came to promotion. On what seemed to be a daily basis, we went on to spend many strategizing sessions together. Cobb salad luncheons at the Waldorf. Beef bourguignon dinners at Delmonico's. The first few at his expense. My mind had never been as compatible with anyone else's. Selecting him as my business partner was one of the best decisions I'd ever made. I could just tell that our union would be more than prosperous for us both. With G.E.'s help, I knew that I would be immortalized as 'the world's greatest astrologer.'

A minimum of twenty to twenty-five lectures and public appearances were placed on my agenda on a monthly basis and, as G.E. predicted himself, they, indeed, raised my level of exposure in ways I'd never experienced before. They took me to places beyond the periphery of the New York City area, but one or two happened to be quite close to me in Manhattan or Brooklyn. Metaphysical groups kept springing up and interest in astrology and forecasting was continuing to become more and more popular.

On a blustery evening, I found myself booked at an all-women's astro group, Heavenly Dames in midtown Manhattan close to Central Park West, where G.E. was welcomed as a guest. He accompanied me on every one of my lectures and always offered critiques of my delivery afterwards.

Stepping onto crunchy autumn leaves as we walked briskly, G.E. raised his coach's voice as he told me, "You want to go for the women's angle at this one. Use your emotions. Make them feel like they need to buy your services. Like they need *you*."

"I always like to give a thought-provoking presentation. Without pushing though."

"By the end of the evening, they should be thinking that their lives can't go on without buying a reading from you. If they think that meeting with you will bring a man into their world, let them."

"G.E., you're not giving them credit. You make it sound as if all women are desperate to meet men."

G.E. said nothing back. He was too busy using his fingers to count the number of sales tactics he insisted I make use of. Evidently after reaching ten and running out of appendages, G.E. looked me up and down and frowned. "What?"

"Is there anything else you can do with your hair?"

"I had it set only last Tuesday. At a Park Avenue salon. Yvette's House of Beauty. By Madame Yvette herself. It looks fine."

"Maybe put a bow in it."

"I'm not a child, G.E. I don't adorn myself with bows and ribbons."

Like the book G.E. wanted me to write, my plan was to speak about some of the more interesting readings I'd done, along with the many predictions that have come to pass. Without revealing any true identities, of course. As always, I kept my private life out of the program.

"I never noticed this before. Do you always walk this way?'

"Which way?"

As if his nose had taken too big an inhale of Limburger cheese, G.E. said to me, "You're rather hunched over. You never want your face to be pointed to the ground. You must directly address your audience at *all* times. Never look down at your papers while you're at the podium. Always raise the papers up to you, but never block your face from the spectators."

"I don't think I ever would have imagined that these little things make a difference."

"It ain't so little when they cost you sales."

"That's another thing. I never think of this as selling. I'm providing enlightenment to a group of people that are perhaps curious. To some, it may even be considered entertainment."

"That's *excellent*, Evangeline. Keep up that pretense."

How odd. A "pretense" he calls it. I must appreciate the way G.E. sees my business, I told myself. Life was all about selling. If one doesn't make known their worth, their value, how in the world would anyone else recognize it?

After being greeted by the event hostess for the evening, dressed entirely in shimmering silver, hair included, I took my place on a raised platform directly below a thirty-foot high, pewter-framed proscenium arch. It was a wondrously restored timeworn venue, previously used by Shriners that held about two hundred or so female astrology aficionados. The acoustics were perfect and not once did I have to raise my voice artificially to be heard by all.

"As I've mentioned once or twice before, the planet Mercury rules travel, communication and contracts. This planet moves in what we refer to as a retrograde manner about three times during the year, for a duration of approximately three weeks. Throughout this inauspicious time in our lives we are prone to bouts of forgetfulness, we miss appointments, our travel plans are met with delays and cancelations that are, for the most part, out of our control."

As my eyes scanned the room I could tell that questions would follow my presentation. To prevent some, I explained words that don't come about in everyday use.

"A planet in retrograde means that it, for a brief time, appears to be traveling in a backward direction in the night sky. Of course this is merely an illusion, but its effects do seem to be quite real."

I proceeded to point out that, for exceedingly important ventures, one would be wise to wait until these tumultuous weeks have passed. At this event in particular the questions raised were unusually profound, relevant.

"Does everyone experience this Saturn Return you spoke of earlier?"

"Oh, absolutely. It's entirely assured in the stars that each and every person undergoes radical change every twenty-eight years of their life."

"It would be a delight if you could share with us now how you were affected during your Saturn Return, Miss Adams," the same woman said intelligently. In the back of my head, the voice I'd come to know so well, G.E.'s said, "Steer away from anything personal. Make it about them, not you."

Wanting validation of some sort, I ignored what I'd been told and graciously answered on my own behalf when saying, "I'd be happy to. When I was about twenty-eight I was preparing to move to New York, permanently, from Boston. This changed my life immeasurably. As you all know, that was when I'd predicted the now-historic burning of the Windsor Hotel. From that point on, my life would never be the same."

That incident actually happened a year-and-so later than my twenty-eighth year, but now being a woman of society, I was obliged under unspoken oath to never reveal my true age. In reality, my second Saturn Return, my second twenty-eighth year at age fifty-six, was fast approaching. My point was made emphatically that dramatic changes are charted to take place every twenty-eight years and that's what's most important.

"And what do you anticipate for your next Saturn Return?" a voice from the back of the room asked.

"What I *anticipate*? Have I already charted it? Is that what you'd like to know?"

"Precisely," the woman answered while gradually making her way into the light of the hall so she could then be visible to me.

The voice and the face put together, both of which I had not heard or seen in nearly five-or-so years, left my consciousness in utter shock. My blurry, overtaxed and aging eyes, now having turned a muddled shade of blue, first processed the changes created by time: the grey head, the wider hips, the outlined features to the face. After a second or two to catch my breath and compose myself, a bolt from the blue became glee and I continued on by saying, "Emma. How wonderful…to see you."

"You don't need to answer now."

"Oh, I have indeed foreseen my second. It's work, work and more work."

In front of two hundred strangers I wasn't about to disclose what I had really seen and Emma realized that, because she knew exactly what the future had intended for me. The truth of that long-ago cast would remain private to strangers.

With only a few minutes more remaining to my event, a small number of routine questions followed. After that, a bevy of fidgety, nervous women, preoccupied with the adjustment of their corsets, chose to speak to me while the others made appointments from the back of the room to meet with me privately at my studio. G.E. was there, overseeing my staff recording appointments and finishing up the business at hand. Collecting the money was what he seemed to enjoy best, especially when it meant that future funds would be arriving in addition—for him, a drug.

Seeing Emma there, waiting to speak with me, left my heart palpitating while my face felt flushed, hot; ready to explode. Extraordinary that one hundred and ninety-nine women there left me as comfortable as a worn-in quilt, while one lone female made me weak at the knees. Several of these women chose to talk and talk and talk to the point that two of my assistants had to come over and kindly remind them that I must move on.

Emma was one of the very last few to speak with me. As I was able to focus upon her uninterrupted, she looked so perfectly natural, unadorned and pure. My rubbery knees began to wobble by the time she approached me. Emma appeared as calm as a cucumber. My hands turned clammy and every hair on the back of my neck stood up to be recognized.

"It's been an incredibly long time, Evangeline," Emma said, now a bit deeper in the voice.

Recognizing the white Victorian lovers shell cameo surrounded by seed pearls on a gold chain I'd seen around her neck so many times prior, made me smile inside. "It most assuredly has. I almost don't know what to say."

"I do…but maybe not here. I thought about—"

"You needn't say anymore. Emma." My next words stopped

dead in their tracks as I looked not once but twice at the beautiful younger woman standing shoulder-to-shoulder with Emma. Hers was a face that appeared somewhat familiar to me.

"Oh, please allow me to present Miss Penelope John—Well actually…"

"Actually, we met in Paris several years ago. Miss Penelope Johnston, ma'am. You created my chart. We met at that party given by the Tanners. I'm a Scorpio with Aquarius rising."

Something about my internal workings couldn't piece together why Emma and this Miss Johnston were together. It took me what must have seemed like forever to come up with a reply. "The actress. From Boston."

"Yes, indeed," Miss Johnston acknowledged.

"It was Penny's suggestion that we come to see you tonight. A huge fan," Emma said.

"Oh…Penny's. I see. Well, how wonderful…Thanks to you both for coming. What a small world."

"Isn't that uncanny? I'm about to enter my first Saturn Return in a few months. I can hardly wait," the young woman said with a demeanor so different from when we'd first met over six years earlier. The way she introduced herself, confidently, outstretching her hand to shake before even I did. Not at all meek or naïve this time. A blossom gone full bloom. A grown woman.

Emma and I just looked at each other after hearing those words. "To be twenty-eight again. Wouldn't that be nice?"

I nodded to Emma, while Penelope chimed in, "Miss Adams, you never told me that you were related to Abigail Adams. Her 'Don't Forget the Ladies' campaign started it all for us women. Right, Emmy?"

"Yes, she certainly got the ball rolling alright."

Still feeling a bit too confused about things, and knowing that our time inside the hall had long expired, I said to Emma, "I would be honored if you join me for lunch someday soon."

"We'd love to," Penelope answered, looking comfortable and cozy with her hands inside the pockets of her hip-length carnelian cardigan.

I had no idea where my courage came from—perhaps the fearless spirit of J.P. Morgan had prompted my invitation.

With Emma's raised eyebrows and teeth showing, I could only presume that her calmness next turned to joy. I'd be a fool not to notice it. My nervousness returned. When things are meant to come together, maybe it just takes one person's courage to forge action between two, or three. Whomever or whatever's responsible, I was thankful for this rare second chance.

$$\odot \quad ) \quad \star$$

"It's over, Evangeline. Something we'd been waiting years for. Now ratified. As of August Eighteenth, 1920, every woman across this country has the right to vote."

"I'm proud of your diligence, Emma. While I've done nothing, you, and people like Penelope, have helped this victory come to pass."

"Ah…not I. Me and thousands upon thousands of others."

"Here *and* in England, I mean, now Great Britain."

"Maybe we could go there together sometime. It would be nice. Another trip. A chance to get to know each other all over again. Or…maybe back to New Hampshire."

"I wonder what could be keeping Penny," Emma replied, after she took another slice of warm rye bread from the basket. Her change of subject was deliberate, obvious and noticeable by anyone. "It wouldn't be right. I'm with her now, Evangeline."

My stomach ached as I forced the rest of my lunch down. Without really understanding why, I'd become heartsick.

The words that I'd longed to say so many times before in my dreams now existed in reality. I actually pinched my left thigh to demonstrate that I wasn't imagining any of it. Yet, the time to take action that may have elicited a response had expired. Now, it's too late.

And yet, somehow, despite my mistakes, I'd recaptured an old friend and made a new one. Over the next several weeks, Emma and I and Penelope became, as Sabine would say, "bosom buddies." Whether Mercury had gone retrograde, or was direct, the timing was right for Emma and I to resume the soul-destined voyage that my stars had predicted long ago.

☉　☽　✫

On an early evening during a summer Sunday, Emma, Penelope and I prepared a sumptuous Mediterranean dinner for three, in honor of my beloved Enrico Caruso, who had passed away at age forty-eight the week prior. Veal Neapolitan, Enrico Caruso-style, was on the menu for the night, reminding the mature members of the group, Emma and I, about the shortness, the delicateness of life.

Enrico's celebrated La Scala recording of *Vesti la Giubbia* from *Pagliacci* was playing in the parlor. Emma and I both seemed to be mesmerized by the gut-wrenching passion of Enrico's delivery, the throaty gasps he takes between lyrics. "I think I've heard of this guy, but I don't really know this song," Penelope said.

"Penny, this recording of his was the first in history to sell over a million copies. Mr. Caruso's probably the most famous opera singer who's ever lived." What an understatement. I concurred by meeting Emma's eyes.

As Emma held my hand above the oregano and sage waiting to be dissected, I said, "This is one of the most sacred times of my life. I'm so grateful."

Penelope didn't utter a word.

Emma, seeming nonplussed by my use of that particular word, said, "Have you become closer to God since we last met?"

"Not at all, my dear. When I say sacred, I mean ordained by the stars. Perhaps *they* are my God."

"I know they are, Evangeline. Regardless of the vernacular, I appreciate the thought behind your word choice." She then left me to my slicing and dicing while moving her hands onto my shoulders, and squeezing. "This time I'm not letting go," she said with warmth before noticing Penelope's piercing stare that would make even Beelzebub tremble. "I'm so lucky to have my good friend back."

My smile expressed my feelings without having to speak. Emma, in turn, looked away from me to Penelope, and said, "Life's short, Evangeline."

In a show of equal rights within my kitchen, Emma stepped aside, walked back over to Penelope, removed the soup ladle hovering above the boiling pot of Minestrone from her hand and placed it on the countertop. Her reach for Penelope appeared lust-filled and genuine, not for show. Emma next began to kiss Penelope on her mouth forcefully with passion. Penelope reciprocated. Theirs was not a demonstration of mere affection; it was one of love, perhaps deep love. This display seemed to last minutes, not seconds. So noticeable to me, the only observer in the room. Since I didn't know what to say or do, I fainted.

☉  ☽  ✴

### 𝔉𝔦𝔱𝔠𝔥𝔟𝔲𝔯𝔤 𝔇𝔞𝔦𝔩𝔶 𝔖𝔢𝔫𝔱𝔦𝔫𝔢𝔩
FITCHBURG, MASSACHUSETTS
SATURDAY, DECEMBER 31, 1921

# Watch Your Step in 1922!
## That's Message of Stars

### BY EVANGELINE ADAMS
**World's Most Famous Astrologer**
(Written Especially for NEA Service)

The fact that the sun and Venus will travel side by side during January, indicates more harmony may exist in the world and more will be accomplished along constructive lines.

In fact everything should be done to establish confidence and optimism, for unless there is a very material advance forward before the 3d of February, when Jupiter turns retrograde, I fear we can look for little real activity before the 6th of June, when Jupiter turns direct.

When Jupiter turns retrograde, as it will on the 3d of February to remain so until the 6th of June, a very restricting and depressing influence becomes evident in business.

During this period it will be well to try to bring to a successful termination matters already under way rather than to initiate any new ventures.

On the 8th of October Saturn will enter the sign of Libra and will remain therein through 1922.

This sign rules Japan, China, Austria, parts of India, upper Egypt, and the city of Denver in this country.

It is to be feared that these parts of the world will be in a most afflicted or war-like condition.

People born from March 20 to April 20; from June 22 to July 22; from September 24 to October 24, and from December 22 to January 21 should avoid overloading of the system.

During some part of the Libra period people born at these times are in danger of suffering from poor health and depressed business.

The world will be fortunate if there is not an epidemic which will attack the nervous system.

Surgeons will be unusually busy.

If your birth date is between the 7th and 8th of February, the 8th and 30th of June, the 12th and 31st of October there will be a period during 1922 in which you will come under the influence of Jupiter, and experience an increase in influence.

There will be an auspicious period for the pressing of new undertakings and establishing of family ties.

If you were born during the last few days of February, the first few days of March, the last few days of June, the first few days of July, the last few days of October or the first few days of November you will come under the influence of Uranus.

During the coming year you will find success will come easier.

If you were born during the last few days of May, the first few days of June, during the first week of September or the first week in December you will come under the perverse influence of Uranus and will find that you must continually exert your will to keep from disastrous impulses or undertakings.

If you were born during the first 10 days of January, the last few days of March, the first 10 days of April, the first 12 days of July, the first 12 days of October or the last few days of December, you will be influenced by the evil aspects of the planet Saturn. You will find it necessary to guard your health.

# Sun @ 19° SAGITTARIUS 57'14 (1922)

"**Y**ou certainly are spending a lot of time with those lady friends of yours," G.E. told me during one of our many private, weekly board meetings at his English Mahogany Partners desk with burgundy leather top, after everyone else had gone home.

"Emma's a fine person. Penelope's more a loyal fan. I cherish any time I'm able to spend in their company. Wonderful friends indeed."

"What a cozy connection."

My brain wasn't yet able to splice together the insinuations G.E. had placed before my face. To me, it mattered not to him which friends I kept. Maintaining our agreed-upon professional commitments should have been all he expected from me. My life had never been busier and I never could have been happier. The sun, the moon, Earth, Mercury, Venus, Mars, Jupiter, Saturn, Uranus, Neptune and Pluto had become mine and I relished every moment of the monopoly I'd created upon each and every celestial dweller. Next: Ceres, Pallas, Juno, Vesta and Chiron.

"I guess you could call it 'cozy.' Thinking about my dear friend Emma leaves me with a warm feeling that I long to keep hold of."

Before G.E. responded, he rose from his desk to adjust the copy of *Gabrielle d'Estrées et une de ses soeurs* given to me by J.P. that was hanging on the wall nearby. Looking at me, then ogling the two nude women. Looking at me, looking at the two nude women. Looking at me, looking at the two nude women, G.E. said, with no hint of subtlety, "As long as you don't let others see you two 'warming up to each other'."

I proceeded to ignore G.E.'s comment. Rather uncalled for and most likely created out of speculation. What was it exactly that he was implying? As a public figure, I could see how others may feel as if they're owed information about my interests, hobbies, my background, my private life. With their investment in me, it's as if they feel they *deserve* to know. All part of the trade-off. An agreement of mutual trust, I can only assume.

For decades I'd been an independent and self-sufficient woman. As long as I kept up my business obligations, I didn't see why G.E. needed to know who I spent time with, where I did my shopping, who I voted for in the election, nor my real and true age. Maintaining mystery is something G.E. apparently never mastered in business school, had he ever attended one. As far as I was concerned, inscrutability was the secret component to life's most alluring and noteworthy successes.

With Sabine's energies now primarily focused on her newest, and this time, legitimate husband-to-be, a childhood sweetheart from Bavaria, and less on her work, weeks passed slowly for me. G.E. went about his dealings, I went about mine, while the two of us combined thoughts and strategies when it became necessary.

Walking into my kitchen, a miniature replica of the "Don't Let this Happen to You" chambre at Le Cordon Bleu—noticing Emma and Penelope pawing each other as their hands sliced a loaf of French bread together—G.E. and his nose said, "Something stinks in here."

"Could it be the lingering smell of victory, sir?" Penelope asked with an upturned nose, yet in a most apropos tone.

"Equality...here we go again," G.E. whispered to himself. "Now that women have the right to vote these last two years, what's next?"

"Mr. Jordan, this was a huge triumph. I'm perfectly willing to celebrate by living in this very moment. We'll all find out 'what's next' in perfect order," Emma replied, while watching the sand drift downward in the antique hourglass she grabbed onto with an open palm.

In a rather bold move, Emma, Penelope and I were making a valiant attempt to prepare dinner for G.E. as a sort of icebreaker. Introducing him, properly, to my longtime comrade Emma and her good friend had been long in coming, but was most called for.

During his first visit into my kitchen, G.E. said, "I never eat potatoes. Red ones. They make my nose run."

Emma rolled her left eye like a pinwheel. "Perhaps not your nose, but your mouth is surely to water, Mr. Jordan. These clawed lobsters come directly from my uncle in Bar Harbor."

"Caught fresh this morning. Isn't that right, Emmy?" This time it was G.E.'s bloodshot left eye that made a counter-clockwise revolution.

Wearing what appeared to be purple floral print mother-daughter matching aprons, Emma assured Penelope that she was correct, while my own mouth proceeded to salivate noticeably enough for me to reach for a napkin long before the water in the vat began to simmer.

"You know, many folks still believe that a woman's place is the kitchen, slaving over pots, pans and a passel of youngsters."

"Those folks can think anything they like, sir. My husband believes the opposite. He gives me free reign and I allow him the same."

Nearly choking on his full tumbler of bathtub gin, G.E. said, "You're *married?* I had no idea."

"Alfred travels often for his career. Just as I oftentimes do for mine."

"Me, too. I'm also a career woman. Destined to be a screen star. Miss Adams told me so," Penelope said as she raised her shiny chef's knife in the air, resembling the "statue-ized" version of Joan of Arc riding a stallion, thrusting her trusty sword above her in Riverside Park.

With nothing but disbelief in his blank expression, G.E. looked at me and said, "Nice."

Feeling the need to spell out the capabilities of my closest confidante, I responded by saying, "Now, GE. Emma is a fine instructor. She teaches adults the art of dramatics as a cathartic means of expression."

"And why did you stop acting yourself?" he asked her.

Emma first glanced at me, looking confused, but without further hesitation replied, "My husband and I thought it best."

G.E. nodded, apparently having expected that answer. "So, although you are now equal in the voting booth you still defer to a man with regard to important decisions being made."

Penelope, quick on the draw, shouted out, "Now, wait just one damn—"

"G.E., that's not your place. Emma, I apologize."

"You needn't apologize for me, Evangeline. I can do it on my own. Pardon me, Mrs. Fry. I didn't mean to appear improper."

"To be honest, I'm glad you *pried* the way you did. Yes, in the early days of my marriage I did expect a man to guide me. That was nearly three decades ago, sir. For the last two, I am my own woman."

G.E. began applauding with his hands raised above his head as if anticipating an encore performance. At the same time I didn't know quite how to react. As a result, I did, and said, nothing.

"Thank you, Mr. Jordan. It's an attribute I'm rather pleased with myself. That's one of the lessons I was born to learn. To be independent, to rely on only myself to make decisions, to be proud of a life that I've made mine…not for one that's under the control of another. It took me some years, but I did it."

Hot-under-the-collar Penelope next uncrossed her arms, and let them fall by the wayside, as she exhaled and smiled.

This is why I cared about Emma the way I did. When she spoke of lessons to learn, at first I'd been repelled by such talk, but now I was beginning to see the relevance. Emma had accomplished much in her life. Learning to be free, independent and self-sufficient was a tremendous task. Most of my female clientele were held captive by the motives of the men in their lives. The vast majority were far removed from being self-sufficient.

"I'm proud of you, Emma," I told her.

"Me, too, Emmy darling."

G.E., now seated at the breakfast table, grasped his jaw with his right hand and looked straight at me after I'd said that. His demeanor changed oh so subtly from that point on. The four of us went on to dine on a meal fit for a king. Every one of my senses was satiated. The pineapple upside-down cake, of which I ate too much, stole the show. And the after-dinner Mint Juleps weren't so bad either. Thanks to the culinary skills of Emma, and Penelope, the Maine lobster Pochée au Beurre Doux was prepared to perfection. For a communicative Gemini, G.E. exchanged few words until the time he readied to depart.

Placing his glass on the table for the first time in approximately five minutes, G.E. said, "Thank you for the loveliest of meals, Madame et Mademoiselle. Mademoiselle-zzz, plural."

"I'm glad you enjoyed it, Mr. Jordan." As always, Emma's sincerity and eloquence shines through every time she speaks.

"I'll see you at the studio tomorrow afternoon, yes?" G.E. asked, with his raised eyebrows and furrowed forehead expecting an affirmative head bob.

No contest between work and pleasure. None whatsoever. "Most assuredly. For me, business comes first every time."

And, that's what I liked about G.E. His ability to concentrate on career pursuits before all others is what drew me into his world without effort. How lucky I was to have met a man, a business manager that knew how to produce end results and desired outcomes so simply, straightforwardly. Quick on the uptake G.E. orchestrated my every action, no matter how trivial or ordinary, as if it were a part of a massive advertising campaign. In less than one year he was able to raise the number of my newsletter recipients from a mere few hundred to well over one hundred thousand. Ever since having met G.E., he has turned my every move into increased exposure on a grand scale.

Penelope left shortly after G.E. did. Emma remained for a few minutes longer while we chatted before a warming fire, situated on the plush cushions of my camel back settee. Everything about my being felt snug. After a lengthy pause had passed, Emma, with now her third Julep in hand, told me, "G.E. is a rather strong man."

"Is that how you see him?"

"Strong in the sense of doing whatever it takes to get what he wants, the way he wants something done."

"That's exactly how I see him as well," I replied to Emma while smiling.

"And you like that about him? Your trust in him is genuine?"

"Oh, my. I can't imagine going into a business partnership with anyone I didn't trust. He's suave, debonair, maybe even a bit flashy on the outside, but on the inside G.E.'s morals are properly intact."

☉ ☽ ✲

"And you trust her?"

"Emma and I have known each other for years and years now. She's a truly good soul."

"I'd advise you not to invite her to any of your public functions, places where you'll meet prospective clients, mingle."

"But Emma's of such beneficial support to me. I also feel she's been given a remarkable literary talent. She could inevitably help me with my book endeavors."

"Oh, no. Absolutely not. She doesn't have the clout that that Elister carries."

"Aleister. I'm just saying, if he doesn't work out—and he hasn't so far—Emma could fit the bill quite satisfactorily."

"But, that Aleister, is it? Has already written them."

"Yes, I imagine. It seems though that he's now devoted to running his commune. His Abbey of Thelema. In Sicily."

"And he can't do two things at once?"

"Times have changed, G.E. His reputation. Denunciated in the British press. They now call him the 'wickedest man in the world.' Emma's a better choice, trust me."

"There's my point exactly. You do know that bad P.R. can ruin my career overnight, don't you? Every one of us is susceptible to it. Not even the God-fearing are immune."

"Yes, I'm well aware of negative publicity, G.E. I've been at this game a long while. Emma is my dearest friend and always will be. Whether people assume to see the two of us any differently than we truly are is their own misconception."

The reasoning behind G.E.'s sermon about the evils of negative publicity fell upon my deaf ears. The success of my trial in 1914 proved that the truth wins out every time…if you're willing to fight for it. Emma and my loyalty to her would forever stand the test of time. She had been there for me then, encouraging me to be brave and fight for the justice I deserved to behold. It was no one's business whatsoever why I continued to remain an unmarried woman.

"Oftentimes misconceptions prove fatal, Evangeline."

"Nonsense."

"Just don't expect me to bail you out when your star has fallen."

⊙　☽　☆

"How could you?" G.E. screamed at me, nostrils flared. Blaming me. Chastising me for doing my job. The way I always imagined my father would have, had he been alive to see the way in which I attained my success.

"It's what I do, G.E. Part of my business."

"Didn't you learn anything from that Edward fiasco? What an idiot."

I couldn't take anymore of G.E.'s yelling. Instead I placed my fingertips to my temples and attempted to massage the stress away. G.E. continued pacing back and forth like a prisoner caged in his cell. Yet, sometimes when alone with G.E., I was the one made to feel imprisoned.

"People are going to forget all about it. Just as they did before."

"How many times have I told you? 'Tell them what they *want* to hear, not the truth'."

All I had done was answer a reporter's simple question. I'd presented nothing more than a demonstration of my abilities, that's all. He'd slipped it in so nonchalantly. *"How much longer will Rudolph Valentino be America's heartthrob?"* I thought the reporter was referring to the length of Valentino's life. So I showed him, astrologically. I had no idea the hysteria it would cause. Hundreds upon hundreds of hate letters accumulated in the post that first week, all stemming from the date I provided, August 23, 1926, less than four years away.

Although I'd also seen everlasting iconic status for the world's Latin Lover upon his death at thirty-one, no one, especially Sabine, who worships Valentino as if he's God, wanted to see him leave so soon.

"This job's not an easy one, G.E."

"Great. Retract. Say you were wrong. Say you made a mistake. Tell them that the stars *are* fallible."

"Never."

During that first week following my prognostication's publication in the worldwide press, both G.E. and Sabine stopped speaking to me.

☉  ☽  ✶

---

### The New York Times

January 25, 1923

### FORTUNE TELLER IS HELD.

---

**Woman Says She Is a Lineal Descendant of President John Adams.**

When Miss Evangeline Adams, 50 years old, who asserted she was a lineal descendant of President John Adams, was arraigned on a fortune-telling charge in the Tombs Court yesterday, Magistrate Max. S.

---

> Levine said he would take a motion for the dismissal of the charge under advisement. She was accused of having accepted $10 from Mrs. Helen B. Osnato, a policewoman, for telling Mrs. Osnato's fortune in a studio occupied by the prisoner in Carnegie Hall.
>
> Mrs. Osnato alleged that she visited the studio on June 6, told Miss Adams she had quarreled with a man to whom she was engaged and suggested that the policewoman patch up the quarrel with her fiancé and marry him immediately.
>
> "She charged me the $10 after she had written the date of my birth on a horoscope chart," Mrs. Osnato alleged.
>
> The Magistrate continued Miss Adams's bail of $500 until she is arraigned again on Jan. 21.

☉   ☽   ★

"But it was dismissed, G.E."

"Doesn't matter one iota."

Even during the aftermath of the Valentino prediction, I'd never before seen G.E. angry like this. Not even after he caught me eating that third Eskimo Pie. Clenching his teeth made even his eyes turn red. And, to be offered no sympathy whatever. Although I wanted to do nothing more than sulk, G.E. wouldn't stand for it. My body never hungered more for a parental-type embrace. All about G.E. It was as if he was the one placed in jail.

Although my court victory in 1914 had made me an astrological superstar following the judge's "exact science" declaration then, nothing about the City's Penal Code had ever been amended. For the third time I, according to the law, had violated the "fortunetelling" ordinance and, as a result, was obliged to pay the penalty.

"I see it as a mere nuisance. This has happened to me twice before...I suffered no consequences as a result."

"*The New York Times,* Evangeline! My career is ruined. How will I be able to show my face in town again? For you to be called a fortuneteller in the newspaper, an unknown fortuneteller. Charging only *ten* dollars. Amateurish," G.E. yelled out while his face became plastered in self-agenda.

"It's *my* career that will presumably suffer, G.E. Not yours."

"But I manage you, promote you. If you are my star client and this is the way you're being perceived, I have failed miserably. It's utter humiliation. Years to undo now."

G.E. paced back and forth inside my studio while he smoked a Chesterfield and sucked on a Sen-Sen simultaneously. Emma was nowhere to be found and Sabine was still on her honeymoon in Germany. The dismissal of my case seemed to have alleviated none of the persecution I was now facing from the very person that's supposed to build me up.

Although I'd spent only a negligible amount of time inside jail, my first night out brought on bleakness and misery instantaneously. Not to mention a headache that could crush atoms. All I could think of was the damage I'd caused. G.E. was entirely correct: every action that's taken by a public figure is seen through the eyes of public relations. Why hadn't I noticed this woman's false motives?

☉　☽　★

"You haven't yet signed it, Miss Adams."

Glancing at the greeting card that was the size of The New

World Atlas, I said, "Oh, it must have slipped my mind, Rosemary. Leave it here and I'll get right to it," to one of my attentive Virgo stenographers.

"Please do hurry. Sabine will be here soon."

By taking only a quick assessment of the handwriting styles, I was able to easily identify the signs of the authors immediately. Curly Qs belonged to the Geminis, unfinished sentences, Aries, the cursive sketching out of anything heart-shaped, Cancer, and the use of any daringly risky or foreign phraseology, Sagittarius.

This was the day thirty of my thirty-one employees had been eagerly awaiting, Sabine's return from her European marriage and honeymoon. Except for the latest royal nuptials, Prince Albert, King Edward's grandson to Lady Elizabeth, I'd never seen so much hoopla, excitement and anticipation over anyone's matrimonial aftermath.

The waiting area of my studio was "leading lady" theme-decorated as if expecting the arrival of Clara Bow herself. Half my staff dressed as flappers wearing high headbands and glitzy jewelry, all set to dance the Charleston on cue. The Victrola in the background was ready and primed to play nothing but red hot jazz. If I'd ever doubted it, now was the time for me to notice how truly popular Sabine was amongst her office peers. To have finally found a man worth marrying, one truly deserving of her affections, after having experimented with so many prior, was quite an achievement. I must say that I'd missed Sabine and her attributes terribly—mostly the way her much-too-honest face under no circumstances expressed shame—although I'd never let her know that.

I did write a brief inscription where I could find room on the filled-up greeting card and, for one of the few times in my life, I signed it with love, because I truly felt it. I couldn't have been happier for my very good friend.

A few minutes before the stroke of eight, each one of us was in our assigned spot. If Sabine had decided to be late, my poor back would never be able to recover since I was scrunched up and hidden under her desk like a concealed, ready-to-emerge Jack-in-the-box. Five to ten minutes was my back's maximum before going into spasm. Finally, the doorknob turned.

"Surprise!" we all exclaimed.

Possibly not being familiar with this American custom, Sabine shrieked with fright and began running in the opposite direction. No one knew what to do. Perhaps she was embarrassed.

"What should we do, Miss Adams?"

"I'll go get her."

My dress shoes weren't meant for speed, but I knew my voice would get her attention. "Sabine! Komm hier! Jetzt! Wir haben ein Fest für dich." After all my years of teaching the poor girl English, it was only natural that I'd pick up a few words of German.

She timidly showed her face to me from around the corner. "A party? For me?" Sabine asked from the corner of her mouth.

Like the fairy godmother leading Cinderella to the ball, I said, "Yes, of course, dear. Come."

"And this is why everyone yells? I have done nothing wrong?"

"Everyone wants to celebrate with you. We're all so happy for you, dear."

"You do this for me?"

Before I could say "yes" once more, Sabine began crying into the folded-up *New York Times* she'd been carrying. Knowing how private-Scorpios never let anyone see them shed tears, the two of us remained in the hallway and I held her tightly. It was a wonderful feeling. I truly cared for Sabine and all she'd been through, as a friend, as a sister, as a daughter, as a guide and as my beloved workmate. Somehow Sabine's emotions spilled over onto me and I began doing the same as she. Weeping. I felt everything coming from her; the host of dubious partners she's been with to the authentic one she had the courage to actually let into her life. How noble, admirable to be strong enough to select an equal partner, a man she felt certain would force no control over her. What an honor it was for me to hold her in that moment and share the joyfulness, the pride, of this august, no, *most dignified* occasion.

With tears still flowing from her eyes Sabine said, "Schönen Dank, Miss. You know...I love you."

After recovering my ability to speak without choking I was able to say, "I love you too, Sabine."

# Sun @ 5° ARIES 18'30 (1923)

"*T*he Lindstroms, the Vanderbilts, Miss Duncan. I think I have invited everyone," Sabine told me, after examining the totality of G.E.'s 'Who's Who' list.

Contemplating that the parlor in which we were seated would now become *our* home, no longer just mine, I kept and eagle eye on G.E. before replying. "And that makes an even hundred?" As G.E. gazed out the window facing West 57th Street, I could tell his focus was elsewhere.

"No, there are spaces for perhaps one or two more."

"I've got a rich cousin in the Hamptons. He doesn't really speak to me anymore, but it couldn't hurt," my intended said while entering the room with a lit cigar in his right hand, knowing too well that his selections were far outnumbering mine.

"Well, why don't we just save those for later?"

With a bit of hesitation, and just after picking an unhealed scab off her left cheek exactly the way Mrs. Brush used to do, Sabine asked, "What about Miss Emma?"

"Sabine, Mrs. Fry wasn't here for us when Evangeline was incarcerated a few months ago. Certainly not. I don't believe she's earned the right to be invited to our ceremony. She obviously doesn't care."

"That's rather harsh, G.E. Emma was in California, coaching Penelope for her screen acting."

"Face facts, m'dear, theatre people are flighty. She comes and goes from your life on a whim."

"What is 'wim,' Miss?"

"It's not important, Sabine. I wouldn't know where to have the invitation sent. I tried reaching her again, recently, but no—"

"I hadn't known you were in touch," G.E. said.

"Well...no. I said I *tried* to."

With an authoritative, partisan glare coming from but one eye, G.E. said directly into both of mine, "You should refresh your memory as to the discussion...I take it back, the *many* discussions we've had about that woman. About you and she. Not to mention that other—"

"*Her*," Sabine said.

"What?"

"It's 'her,' not 'she.' Subject versus object, Mr. Jordan. I learned that in English class."

"You can leave now, Heidi. That'll be all."

Sabine gave G.E. her now-famous Scorpio leer, the ones that last a good five seconds from start to finish, as she left my drawing room in a huff. Something about her red-faced ire seemed deep-seeded to me. Only did I notice it whenever she was in G.E.'s presence.

"G.E., you know she doesn't like it when you call her that."

"Her, not she. I think that bitch's dirndl's on too tight."

"There's no reason to speak ill. I won't stand for it. Sabine's been with me for over tw—"

"I'm sorry, Ma'am. I apologize," G.E. said as he took both my hands in his. G.E. never did mean what he said once he was able to take a moment to breathe and reflect peacefully. That was what his doctor told him to do time and time again when becoming unsettled and twitchy. G.E. also possessed the diplomacy to offer an apology at nearly each occasion after unleashing irritability in public. Except when he refuses to pay the fare on the Interborough Rapid Transit; he says they don't deserve payment when the trains run more than five minutes behind schedule.

Moving me over to the window, G.E. next held me in his arms after letting go of my hands as we stood there quietly with the moon, the stars and the nights' sky peering onto us both. I couldn't believe it would now only be a matter of weeks until I'd be Mrs. G.E. Jordan, Jr. Statistics reveal that married people live much, much longer than those remaining unattached.

As I mentally crossed off "find a mate," with an imaginary fountain pen from the decades-old To Do list inside my head, I knew I'd be killing two birds with the same stone. Longevity *and* career enhancement; the perfect match for me, a complementary union I'd been waiting my whole life for.

"Now, why again shouldn't I invite Emma?"

No more than a second was needed for sugary sweetness to turn sour again. After having portrayed Dr. Jekyll in so many acts prior, now with the steely sinister stare of Mr. Hyde, G.E. let me go and said, "People will talk. You don't want that to happen, do you?"

"Pardon me. I'm not exactly sure I know what you're implying."

"That's probably best."

"Let's move on then, shall we?"

"Remember one thing, Evangeline. When given the chance to talk, those same *people* will simultaneously end your career."

☉ ☽ ✶

With dark clouds forming in the sky, the day of my stroll down the aisle had arrived. Just an hour before the service at the Church of the Transfiguration on E. 29th began, I waited nervously with only my secretary by my side. Breathing softly and in full control as if she'd be the steady one bringing me to the altar, Sabine reached over while we both were on the divan in a back room with no windows, and deliberately unfolded my crossed arms with her soft hands, placing them both on either side of me. The master of body language began our private conversation by saying, "Miss, you tell me that Scorpions were born to ask why."

"That's entirely correct, Sabine. Scorpio, the detective."

"Then now I must ask you…why you do this." The look on Sabine's face was one of guilt, responsibility, maybe even shame. Incognito, of course. Every time in the past I'd witnessed her wearing it I saw her maternal nature. One eye scrunched close, with the head tilted downward. It's almost as if, the way our relationship had evolved, she cared for me the way a lioness looks after her cub. "I…wish I'd been here for you then. But now, at this time before your wedding, I am here for you."

By the way she was talking to me I could tell that somehow she felt personally accountable for me choosing to marry G.E.

"You know I don't do this often," I said. "It's—"

"Your Aquarius sun."

"Exactly. Well, if we're being completely honest. My fears became insurmountable the night I was released from jail. Emma had left. You were in Europe. And G.E. was…" The tightness of the knots inside my stomach prevented me from saying a single word more.

Sabine next touched my hand and I shied away. "Again to you, so sorry. I know how Mr. Jordan is. A tyrant...sometimes. Finish what you were going to tell me, please."

"He left too. He told me I'd ruined his career. People would now see him unfavorably because of my misfortune. A 'laughing stock,' he'd said."

Sabine shook her head vehemently. "My Holger would never care about such a thing. He is his own man. I am my own woman. I am not responsible for his career, he's not responsible for mine. We're equals."

I sighed. "Truthfully, I must say, I wanted to die. That's all I could think about...after he left me. I'd ruined his career, I had been arrested now for the third time. It was in the newspapers. They referred to me as a fortuneteller. I've never felt such humiliation and remorse."

"But, Miss. Humiliation only comes from the fear of what other people think that they really don't."

"Fear...I don't know what you mean."

Sabine didn't explain. Instead, she reached around her neck and unclasped her necklace after four or so attempts. And then, when the moment came for my wedding ceremony to take place, in my brassiere, as a promise to my devoted secretary, I tucked away the silver Hamish hand with a now-tarnished chain, she'd given me. Hanging from my own neck was the gold Chai medallion on a chain that Sabine had placed there herself. "The hand is for protection, the other symbolizes life," she'd told me. Sabine was not trying to convert me to Judaism; she merely wanted to assure me that a piece of her would forever be close by the next time I should ever feel fear.

Nothing about the ceremony was eventful. Even the minister we hired, clammy-complected Reverend Moynihan, yawned during the marriage vows. G.E. made sure the somewhat modest happening was projected in grand style to media everywhere. His objective was simple: Make sure the coverage was bigger, wider-reaching and more extensive than the news of my third arrest. Considering the fact that half the wedding invitees were either journalists or photographers, reaching his goal was virtually guaranteed.

The "real" guests left the ceremony, and the brief reception that followed, only a mere few minutes after completion. But it was G.E. who made certain that the assemblage of press accompanied the two of us to the ship, where we were to depart on our nearly three-month honeymoon. On that particular afternoon, I must have been photographed more times than Rudolph Valentino himself.

☉   ☽   ★

Unpacking my luggage in our Honeymoon Suite aboard ship, three enormous-sized trunks in total, was a challenging task. Naturally, I brought some work along with me; chart casting that couldn't wait. I placed my astrological and de rigueur writing paraphernalia next to the bouquet of red roses and Champagne Krug the cruise line so kindly provided to G.E. and I, the happy couple. For the hundredth time, G.E. begged me to proceed with the composition of my book. "The clime of the open sea will inspire you," he'd told me.

Before the liner had even reached the Atlantic, G.E. entered our stateroom to announce, "With the extensive work you'll be doing I arranged to procure a second cabin."

"As an onboard studio."

"Not necessarily. That's just what I told them...so I could get a second."

"I've already set up this suite as my workspace, G.E. I'm perfectly fine writing right here. My papers are all laid out."

"Your work ethic is truly admirable, dear. My guess is that you'd like to start on your book as soon as possible, undisturbed."

"No. I'd equally like to spend time with you now. The ceremony was a smash, wasn't it?"

"That's exactly what it was, m'dear. You hit the nail on the head."

Feeling a tingling on the inside of my thighs, I was eager to get the ball rolling. "I must say, I'm a tad uneasy. I've never taken part in a wedding night before. Inside my bag I packed my finest—"

"Oh, we can always talk about that later. Dinner is promptly at six. Sitting at the Captain's Table...in front of...everyone. What a grand opportunity."

"I suppose so. Maybe you'd like a glass of sherry first. As an aperitif."

"Since we're going to Russia, how about straight-up vodka?"

"You may. That's a bit too robust for me."

G.E. poured himself a glass half-full and I began to sip my sherry, before we both sat down. Relaxing on the heart-shaped burgundy divan together was something I'd looked forward to for days now. Time to unwind and get to know G.E. on a deeper level. As soon as I crossed my legs in front of him, exposing my flesh for him to see, G.E. placed his vodka on the table, bolted forward like a jackrabbit and began positioning his unopened bags nearest the door. One after the other.

"Well, that's the lot of them. I'll carry them myself...two trips, maybe three, should do it. Ain't no need to call a porter."

"But why the need to store them? There's plenty of room here."

"Store them? The second cabin. Like I said, they gave me a second based on the fact you'll be using it for your working studio. Now that you've decided to write here, I'll be moving into the other."

"We're married now, G.E."

"I must hurry. Dinner in less than an hour. Yes, two trips should do just fine."

As I watched G.E. exit the door to our, my cabin, the now-single occupancy Honeymoon Suite, I could see my personal power slither out with his. Already the illusions I'd had about marriage were beginning to disintegrate. The wedding night I'd anticipated for decades became nonexistent. G.E., instead, chose to spend the night with his closest and dearest companion, P.A. Smirnoff.

It took less than one whole day for me to remind myself, once again, that my purpose on earth was to promote astrology and have no distractions, no emotional or physical fulfillment, while doing so. Emma had always argued that my true purpose had nothing to do with astrology. "There will come a time for you, Evangeline, when you are given a choice. To learn your lesson or not. Should you do so, you'll then discover what your true purpose is," she'd told me.

Until that day came, when I chose or didn't choose to learn whatever she'd been talking about, I'd go on with my life as I knew it. Showing the world that astrology is an accurate, and has always been, revered science through the ages.

Onto book writing it was. Aleister always told me that outlines are essential; one can't contemplate writing without some sort of structure being established ahead of time. Perhaps my connection to him was, in some odd way, valuable after all. The way he told of his unsuccessful attempt to climb Kanchenjunga entertained me so. As my own years had passed, I'd reflected on Aleister's credo, 'Do what thou wilt,' and I agreed with it to a certain extent. Whatever it is that makes one feel good…within reason. Aleister was on our itinerary of European business appointments and, somehow, I began looking forward to seeing him again.

☉  ☽  ✶

"My blessed Thelema will live on, I tell you."

"I'm sure it will, Aleister. I read about your adventures. The stars tell me it was best you returned."

Speaking from our three-room suite at Claridge's adjacent to Grosvenor Square, our visitor told me while wearing an oxford white linen shirt and wool Viking tunic, "It was my haven and hell. Communal living at its finest. And those Italians had no appreciation. Savages."

"I've been to Sicily. Southern Italy *is* rather provincial."

"The locals caused the least of the hubbub. It was Il Duce himself, the chief fascist and his sorry excuse of a government that banished me from the country."

"Mussolini's letting his Leo-ness go to his head."

"That's precisely it. Along with his other zodiacal flaws."

"Well, I must say that it's good seeing you here in England. Did you know people still talk about your time in the Hudson Valley? In America? You've become somewhat of a legend."

"Miss, I've always been."

"Mrs."

"Correct you are. And decades younger than you. You're taking after me. I'm flattered."

Although expelled from Italy for life, Aleister and his ego remained fully intact. Wherever he may go, his ego would follow and continue to thrive, I felt. Aleister certainly did possess the capacity to amuse.

"G.E. will be joining us as soon as he's finished his previous appointment."

"I'm licking my chops already. Perhaps we three can perform a ritual together."

"No. That won't be happening."

"How about borrowing you alone? The world's most famous occultist fusing with the world's most well-known astrologer. Lusciously sinful."

"Fusing, no. But I am curious to know what you plan to do with your Thelema next."

"Keep spreading the word."

"'Do what thou wilt.' I remembered that from when you first mentioned it, nearly ten years ago now."

"You appreciate it to a greater degree now that you're older, don't you? We no longer have time to worry what others may think. Damn them to hell."

Aleister spoke the truth, but it was more complicated than that. The tension I'd been wearing daily must have spread to my outlook without my knowledge. As I began massaging my forehead, he said, "Close your eyes. And do not open them for any reason."

Giggles took over my temperament immediately as I began to recall Aleister's craziness. "Silence!" he exclaimed.

"Yes, your majesty."

My ears heard rustling of some sort. Drawers being opened and closed. Papers being shuffled. With eyes still tightly shut, I imagined to find Aleister dressed in a floor-length evening frock by the time they reopened.

"Extend your left palm unto me," Aleister said.

Fright kept my hand nearest my body. I didn't ask, because I didn't want to know. After a deep breath, I gave my left hand, palm upward, to Aleister. He, in turn, placed one of his hands underneath mine. I could feel his warmth.

"The words you chose to recollect were incomplete. Listen, listen closely and never forget. Put them into practice the moment they become a fiber of your being."

I nodded and did nothing else.

"*Do what thou wilt* shall be the whole of Thelemic law. Seek out and follow your own true path. Your true will, not your egoic desires." Eyes still closed, I felt comforted hearing those words again, a magnanimous reminder about the choices I make. Instantly, upon exhaling tension, I experienced a sharp stab to my middle finger.

"Ouch!" I yelled out with eyes wide open. I could sense a small droplet of blood oozing from the tip of my thumb. My next sight was Aleister, appearing calm, peaceful, with white cloths already bandaging up my fresh wound. "Aleister, what's the matter with you? Why did—"

"Pierced by the claw of a rooster. So you'd never again forget these precise words, this memorable prick, the price one pays for living out a false destiny."

☉ ☽ ✲

"Dear, Aleister tells me he has finished both books."

"Effortless. I could have written them blindfolded. Maybe I should have," Aleister said, while removing some sort of pointed cone from his head.

"Mr. Crowley, you surely do enjoy unique talents. When can we have those manuscripts?"

"As soon as you pay me."

G.E. looked at Aleister as if in disbelief and abruptly stopped pouring gin into his glass. With a wry grin he said, "You mean, as soon as *the publisher* pays you. We have to get a deal first."

"But we'd agreed th—"

"Every manuscript needs to be edited, revised and proofread before it can be delivered to a pu—"

"Young man, telling me how books become published is beyond fruitless. My first writings appeared in print before you were ever born."

Quasi-apologetically G.E. rephrased his statement, while I remained silent and embarrassed. "I've already spoken with them, the publisher, and they are going to pay you handsomely."

I glanced over to G.E. quizzically, and before I could get a word out, he continued saying, "Isn't that right, Evangeline? They were most generous with their offer, thrilled to be publishing your work." Instead of answering, I just let my heart sink about an inch or more.

At that point I could no longer make eye contact with Aleister, because I knew he was being lied to by my husband. There was no publisher, no offer, no agreement, nothing. What had I gotten myself into?

# Sun @ 17° LEO 4'10 (1924)

"*G.*E., it's your lucky day. I heard from Sabine that Deirdre's leaving, taking a job upstairs. Her corner office will be vacant soon."

"Yes, dear," my husband responded with his eyes still fixated on our accounting ledgers. "I already know that. I'm the one who hired her."

"Well, we both hired—"

"I'll no longer need office space here. With you. Didn't I— Deirdre told me that, for legal reasons, I need to have a separate address from yours."

I didn't have a clue what G.E. was muttering on about. For months, he'd been nagging at me to provide a suitable office with a view of Seventh Avenue and a hinged-window for his cigar-smoking habit, and finally, space opened up. We'd taken on Deirdre a few months earlier, a legal assistant, to help with all matters pertaining directly to New York law, so I could prevent arrests, citations, violations and such from ever happening again.

She'd also composed a blanket confidentiality and consent agreement for all clients to sign.

"A separate address?" I asked G.E., not at all understanding, as my back seized up.

"Yes. G.E. Jordan Enterprises, LLC. My company. I just ordered my nameplate today. Teakwood with brass lettering."

Too much was going on too quickly and my patience was beginning to wear thin. As I sensed control slowly slipping through my fingers, I said, "*Your* company?"

"My dear, I'm so sorry I confused you. I should have told you. A thousand pardons. Please let me clarify."

"Yes, please. Let's."

"I'm still your partner wholeheartedly, no question about it. But Deirdre said that if I were to be sued, as your partner, my own assets would be at risk. I formed G.E.J.E. to protect myself."

"G.E.J.— I didn't know you *had* any assets."

"Well of course, sweetness. That inheritance I'm expecting. Land. Real property. It'll be worth a pretty penny by the time I get it."

"Is this company, this separate address of yours, nearby?"

Looking at me completely baffled as if I'd missed a step in this convoluted rundown, G.E. told me, "Upstairs. With Deirdre. My new office."

"Up—"

"She'll still be *your* legal assistant, but she'll now be working directly above you, your office. As will I, darling."

"This entire scenario upsets me greatly," I said to my two-faced husband while pacing back and forth. "I'm quite disappointed in you."

"You're disappointed in the three-book deal I'm cooking up? The syndicated columns I've put together? Innumerable speaking engagements? The increase in exposure? The business strategies?

The marketing schemes? The money? The celebrity? Well, you told me that it's my job to make you forever known as the 'world's most famous, successful astrologer'."

"Yes, I know, G.E. I appreciate all that, everything."

Reaching out my right hand to now make *G.E.* feel better, made him turn away from me, leaving him to focus once again on nothing but his ledgers. "Evangeline, what is it you have left now? Seven-and-a-half years? Eight, tops?"

G.E.'s blunt insensitivity nearly killed me on the spot. Almost unable to utter a reply, my desire to be most precise forced my mouth to declare, "Eight years, three months and two days."

"Well then, I'd better get on with it…hadn't I?"

⊙  ☽  ✮

Only days after our return from our so-called honeymoon, G.E. had been able to negotiate and, of course, procure a three-book contract with Dodd, Mead & Company. I was ecstatic that a book, albeit an elementary one having to do with astrology, was about to be published with my name on it. Now that G.E. was my business manager it became his responsibility to tell Aleister that his name shall appear nowhere on the contracts, nor on the book cover.

G.E. felt certain that the book I was supposed to be writing about my astrological practice should come first, precede the books about astrology itself, as a seductive tidbit. Along with my usual business and my steady stream of clients pouring in, I still somehow found time to begin fleshing out my pseudo-autobiography. Full of anecdotes, disguised of course, having to do with the host of prophesies that had been fulfilled. Whenever I did choose to write about a celebrity client or acquaintance, I sought out their permission to use their real name. H.G. Wells, Charlotte

Potter and Rabbi Charles Fleischer obliged, while others did not. Although I'd stated many times that J.P. Morgan was a regular visitor of mine, since his departure I'd chosen not to make mention of him so directly.

On many occasions sitting at my antique cherry Knob Hill Flip writing desk during the evening hours I was able to produce nothing. In short order I concluded that I was not born to write, but instead I was born with writer's block. Reflecting on the process itself, I began to ponder how and why writers were able to produce so many words with meaning consistently. These reflections made me remember Emma, the most gifted literary craftsperson I'd ever met. My skirmish with G.E. left me hurt, sad and feeling more alone than I'd ever felt in my adult life. Oh I missed my confidante so.

☉ ☽ ✶

*Dearest Emma,*

*I hope this letter finds you and Penelope well and in the finest of spirits. Every time I read about you two in the newspapers I smile. I think about how lucky the people are who become the recipients of your enthusiasm for drama. And, I'd seen that they're calling Penelope "the next Theda Bara." My heavens. It seems you've both been traveling to many locations. How I envy the variety of freedoms you enjoy. In all honesty, I have no idea if this letter will reach you or not. In my imagination I see you reading it here in New York and I can only hope that you'll be able to smile when doing so.*

*More than any other news I can share, I want you to know that I'm composing a book now. It's nearly as difficult as anything I've ever attempted to master in my lifetime. Oh, the respect I have for you and your craft. I so admire the way you are able to construct those eloquent, descriptive and rhythmic paragraphs of prose that seem to effortlessly speak to everyman. You might recall that Aleister Crowley was ghostwriting two books of mine about astrology. His words need amending though. They're rather highbrow, unintelligible to the average reader.*

*I'm finding myself veering off topic at your expense right now. So sorry for that. Primarily, the process of my writing made me think of you. Many things make me think of you. I'd so like to see you again. I want to know how you're getting on in life. The both of you. How are things progressing between you and Penelope? As you've told me so many times, sharing of the soul is one of the reasons I'm here, what I'm meant to learn, experience. My "lesson," as you'd call it.*

☉　☽　✳

Strangely, I found myself scribing all night long. Writing pages upon plain, unscented, unadulterated pages of my letter to Emma was effortless, somehow fulfilling me more than any book ever could. One way or another I was able to incorporate more of my feelings with less surface chit chat. With no expectations, I completed this composition to a friend, a dear friend and as I folded it, sealed the envelope and stamped it, I felt inside like I was satisfying a part of my destiny. Sent the composition off by post; my work was done.

☉　☽　✳

Almost identically as when we were aboard ship on our honeymoon, G.E. did end up re-locating himself away from me, this time to a separate studio in Carnegie Hall directly above mine. As I'd now found a man to look after me, Mother, God rest her soul, ultimately got her final wish. G.E.'s guidance over me felt comforting on occasion, yet too calculating, like a puppet master pulling the strings of a marionette, at others. Regardless of what my feelings were, it was obvious that he controlled my career, my professional life, beautifully. Daily he would check in on me to gauge my progress as an author.

"*My Life In The Stars* leaves me empty, G.E.," I said to my husband/business manager while seeking nuances in the titles we'd been coming up with.

"The word 'star' has to be there, for sure. Star, stars…something like that. We'll have to conduct some market research to see which the public favors most."

"I'm also not keen on anything beginning with 'My Life.' After all, this isn't necessarily an autobiography. No one would have the slightest interest in my personal life. It's my business, my clients that will catch their attention."

G.E. lit up another cigar and together we batted ideas around for the next two to three hours. Although I was in *his* office, I found it necessary to open his window so I wouldn't suffocate. Still, whatever titles we had a preference for needed the approval of the editorial department at the publishing house. They had the final say.

"How about *Astrologically Speaking?*"

"Nope. Can't have 'astrology' in it. You've gotta fool them. Make them believe it's about more than astrology, which it is. A catchy title that'll make them think twice, leave them wondering, curious."

G.E. and I had reached the end of our time allotted to title discovery and he went back to counting the cash in his wallet. Next, for me, revisiting the writing itself. I loved this diversion, but it was perhaps a bit premature considering I'd only completed ten pages total when I'd need close to three hundred. It was my well-kept secret that I was so far behind schedule. I'd always assumed that I'd eventually catch up once I'd become inspired enough to actually write. Looking up to the sky as I did by day and night, I sought hope from my oldest and dearest friends who inhabit it; the sun, the moon and the stars.

☉　☽　✳

"Maybe if you drink more sherry."

"I still have a few more readings to do today, don't I?"

"Yes. Two more. Mrs. Peabody and Mrs. Higgins."

"They wouldn't care if I'm half-sauced. I basically tell them the exact same thing every week. Never makes one bit of difference."

"This can be in your book, Miss. The people who never change. Their problems with dinner parties, troubles in the office, shortcomings in bed," Sabine said, caressing the curves of her posterior through her much-too-sheer peach chiffon dress.

"Oh, my Lord in Heaven. I could never divulge such a thing."

"Think about it. People read books because they are bored. They don't have anything happening in the boudoir…this is why they read."

"Sabine, marriage hasn't changed you at all."

"Thank God in Himmel for that."

"But you are faithful to your husband now that you're married, aren't you?"

"You tell to me yourself, 'Fixed-sign people are the most loyal.' Just because I may seem like a nymphenmaniac doesn—"

"Nymph*o*maniac."

"Yes, this one. I love my man and I am only with him. Many times I leave him tired and sore. He thinks someday I will break his back."

Hearing about Sabine's continuing and much too frank sexual exploits made me shake my head. It also compelled me to think about my own intimacy, minus the crudeness of Sabine's, of course. I wasn't left to ponder this hot topic by myself much longer though.

"Ma'am, you are a married woman now yourself. Have you learned anything new?"

"Sabine, if I didn't know any better…sometimes you still amaze me. The words coming from your mouth."

"But you didn't answer my question. I'm still waiting for the answer."

"I'm going to leave it entirely to your imagination."

"Never mind. I just did…inside my head I am bored stiff."

My ears didn't need to hear that, although I was not the least bit surprised.

"Oh, Miss. I forgot to tell you. I saw your friend Miss Emma the other day outside. I told her 'hello' from you."

"Emma?"

"She was leading a group of younger women, with their movement. 'Like the wind,' she called it. Dancing with their arms."

"Her dramatics. Where?"

"In Battery Park. With many other people watching. Wearing veils, too. Like maybe they're crazy but they're not."

"Battery Park. You spoke with her?"

"I just told you. Emma says 'hello.' She wishes you good fortune on your marriage."

"You told her I was married or she already knew?"

"Why don't you ask her yourself these questions? She said she got a letter from you. I invite her to meet with you. To the luncheon reception you have for those museum-goers, the society ladies."

"*What?*" I said, nearly spitting out the mouthful of decaffeinated Tummy Tea I was sipping. "When?"

"This Friday. It's good?"

"Yes, Sabine. Excellent."

It amazes me sometimes the ways in which fate deals its cards. You never know what card's going to come up at any given time, but eventually, the card you've been waiting for was right there atop the deck all along, just waiting to be drawn. Emma had told me time and time again about cause and effect. With her line of reasoning, she'd say that if I hadn't written that letter to her, without having made that effort, having taken that initiative, she and Sabine never would have manifested their chance encounter. Whether the world turns as Emma suggests or the way I believed it did, I felt fortunate for the many lucky chances I'd been given in life to re-connect with her. Despite the fact that our paths in life had become radically different, now joined with other partners, I didn't see why we couldn't remain friends, close friends.

⊙ ☽ ★

When she entered the room my breath left my body. A feeling no one else had ever fostered within me. Emma was dressed in light hues, blues and violets, an assortment that complemented everything about her multi-colored spirit. She appeared lighthearted as her two-tone T-straps tripped slightly on the carpet the same second our eyes met. I, dressed in nothing but old-school, established shades of grey, knew for sure that I was far more nervous than Emma though.

Without even realizing, I'd stepped right away from the conversation I'd been having with a Fifth Avenue matriarch in my foyer at mid-sentence. The needy words flowing from her mouth became a blur. Emma, looking poised and assured, approached me. Having forgotten the proper anti-anxiety breathing techniques I'd learned from one of my clients, I instead called upon another I'd learned from Sabine long ago, the standard four-count in, four-count out method.

As I ushered Emma into my office, she said, "Evangeline, you look marvelous." She squeezed both hands in hers. Passively at first, then tightly. "Your letter moved me so, thank you so much for that."

Her warm touch gave me my breath back. "Writing that letter to you made me so happy, Emma. I wasn't sure I'd ever hear back. Somehow still I knew we'd meet again. How are you?"

"I'm so well, but indeed, so busy. Sheridan is fine. He's an aviator now, that's been his dream always. Alfred travels with his job, enjoys it. Penny's coming home in a few days and that thrills me to no end. And I'm living my own dream…people teach my book in schools now."

Hearing Emma mention Penelope took away my enthusiasm in short order. "You know, I re-read it all the time."

"I'm in the middle of writing another right now as a matter of fact."

"Congratulations. I am too."

"Yes, you'd mentioned that in your letter. Aleister Crowley. About astrology."

"Of course. Not about astrology exactly, about my astrological practice. My husband, you know I'm married now, do—"

"Yes, I surely do. I'd read about it in the paper, actually a host of them," Emma said like she'd just recognized a fib. "My hat's off."

"He's a fine man, excellent with my business. G.E. now manages my entire career. Quite gifted at doing so."

"I see."

"He's an air sign, like you."

"How very compatible. Well, as long as he makes you happy."

"Does Penelope make you happy?" I asked.

"Incredibly so. Her zest for life, trying new things, stimulates me. Also, sly beyond her years. On a daily basis she and I learn so much from one another. Perhaps Penny and I are soul mates."

I smiled at Emma, because she was doing the same when she

spoke about Penelope. She appeared happy. Somehow, when looking at and listening to Emma, she seemed so much more mature, evolved than myself. Like she deserved true love more than I did; she'd earned it.

That elegant lady's luncheon at Café Des Artistes on West 67th proved to be most fruitful for Emma and I. It re-united the both of us and filled me with joy to have such a wonderful confidante, companion and friend in my life. We spent the next several weeks together and Emma was more than happy to share her writing strategies with me. When time permitted we took walks through Central Park while stopping occasionally to jot down notes about my experiences, "personal reflections" and "private musings" Emma called them, for my book. By some means, with Emma next to me, words flowed like water from the eight-foot bronze Bethesda Fountain in Central Park.

In between scripting my stories, Emma and I would partake in private banquets, picnic-style, put together for just us two while Penelope was out West, at our favorite spot, Inwood Hill Park, uptown. My chef, Madeline, would pack up the most delicate array of finger sandwiches, cold and warm salads and imported cheeses. Not so much to my surprise, Emma left hearty portions uneaten on her plate, while I left mine squeaky clean. Our custom meals provided us with the nourishment to enjoy many productive and engaging exchanges. When I thought about all I'd gotten from Emma, the help with my writing, along with the insightful spiritual lessons about life's true objective she'd taught me, I wondered yet again what in the world I would be able to give her back.

"I enjoy helping people, Evangeline. To see you think more deeply about the purpose of life. Recognizing now that you are the one that holds the key to your destiny, astounds me."

"Emma, it's a rich experience knowing you, learning from you. Whatever in the world can I do for you to make it all equal?"

"Evangeline, I'd be honored if you'd be the witness at our promise service."

Although irrational, I felt as if I'd been punched in the gut. I had no right to feel jealous, betrayed, nor disappointed for having missed a multitude of opportunities, so instead my body and mind chose to feel empty once again. My sober head knew that matrimony, or any version thereof, between two women was impossible, but not for Emma. The way she viewed and lived life was at least a century ahead of the times. As one friend being there for another, I graciously said, "Of course," before admitting, "You know, today I was going to tell you I, that I… Oh, never mind."

☉　☽　★

"This is perfect. Over two hundred pages. And we're right on schedule," G.E. said to me at our weekly business meeting while hovering over my desk.

As I brushed cigar ashes off my manuscript pages, I told G.E., "Emma has taught me so much. Sometimes she meditates before she writes. It calms the creative process."

"I guess writing agrees with her. Maybe she should have given up acting long ago."

Dreamlike in my response, I imagined what those days must have been like. "I wish I could have seen her then. I bet she was something."

G.E. just stared at me. "I feel the need to remind you once more. If you two resume this thing you have going on, it'll be the ruin of your career." He stood, our meeting abruptly over. "I'll make sure of that."

# Sun @ 0° CAPRICORN 39'12 (1925)

"*P*ersonalize. Do your best to bring in more specific sensations, perceptions; those should be much more evident in your next draft."

"There really aren't that many though. I'm not writing a novel," I said, while glancing over to the blue and red tubular Qianlong flambé vase in the corner of my studio, noticing how much it needed a polish.

"Even when presenting facts you have to make it all story-like. Recall the feelings associated with those that come to you when creating a chart, *your* feelings. I know you're rather passionate about *some* of your clients."

"So, you're saying this draft isn't satisfactory?"

I'd just answered my own question seconds after having asked it. This is why being an innate writer was not me, so far removed from my calling. Making a manuscript *better* didn't interest me that much, not within my scope of desire. Writing it the first time was perfectly fine, no need to do more. More than my lassitude to rewrite, I respected Emma's intrinsic ability, her longing, to make "it," better.

Clutching her hands to her bosom, Emma told me as if on stage at the Old Globe along the south bank of the River Thames, "The more feelings, sensations you input, the more your reader will see it all as being real. Don't expect your reader to feel anything if you've felt nothing writing."

"I'm going to have to check your chart to see if I neglected the detection of additional water."

I could tell Emma didn't quite comprehend what I was getting at, and most likely knew that my mind was on my work, not at all on writing, not even on her, but at least I got a chuckle out of it. It's the artist in Emma that does *everything* with feeling. How I admired this so. How often I'd been mistaken for an unfeeling, unemotional airy Aquarian, when it was merely the outward display of it all that I avoided. Because of G.E.'s threat, and Emma's plans to create a binding commitment with Penelope, I knew it best to stifle any residual sentiment I had bottled up inside me. Working with Emma as my editor was fine with me.

"I'll be teaching outside of New York next year. Far outside," Emma said coyly.

I hadn't expected the change of subject to be so dramatic. For the first time I recognized the pattern that had been evident for decades now. Whenever emotions, or to be most precise my deficient display of them became conversation, Emma declared somehow that she was moving on. In the past my response had always been the same: I had none. Too difficult. The scenario of openly expressing face-to-face what I was feeling inside, after so many years, still made my nerves tremble, my palms sweat and my stomach roar.

Again, similar to times past, Emma provoked me. "I won't pretend that you didn't hear me. You're not deaf and I'm not dumb," Emma shouted, covering her own ears.

Acting coolly as I adjusted my wristwatch, I asked, "Where will you be going?"

"Back to California. Penny's there, achieving more and more success, garnering attention, making additional contacts by the day. I was also hired to be the dramatic director at Oakland's Mills College for adult education."

"I've heard of it. A college for women."

"Yes, me with young women. Oodles of them. Curious. Uninhibited. Young women hungry for...someone to guide them toward dramatic expression. Budding young women, yearning to emote, unafraid."

Realizing that I'd soon, once again, be feeling abandoned, isolated and alone as a consequence of Emma's absence, I was only able to say, "How lucky they will be."

"Some of them won't be successful though. Some women cast their hearts aside...imagining that if they only had a man in their lives, they'd be taken care of, provided for, no longer in search of their true needs. Subservient, unequal, bound."

I turned away from her. Why was Emma becoming so callous regarding the manner with which I chose to live my life? Why did it now matter to her if I was emotionally present or not? My mind, still focused on my book and its completion, couldn't process this disparaging jibber-jabber. Emma had once again tried, in vain, to make a point I wasn't receptive to comprehending. Besides, I was stuck. If G.E. made good on his warning, my life would end up in catastrophe.

"*The Bowl of Heaven*...they selected that as the title for my book. Did I tell you?"

---

## 𝕿𝖍𝖊 𝕳𝖊𝖑𝖊𝖓𝖆 𝕯𝖆𝖎𝖑𝖞 𝕴𝖓𝖉𝖊𝖕𝖊𝖓𝖉𝖊𝖓𝖙

Helena, Montana

SUNDAY MORNING, DECEMBER 12, 1926

### THE BOWL OF HEAVEN

There is an archaic law in the state of New York framed to protect the community against "acrobatic performers, circus riders, men who desert their wives and people who pretend to tell fortunes." All such, according to the statute, were "disorderly persons." The statute long since ceased to be invoked in the interest of order except in the case of necromancers. On the strength of it a discontented client of Evangeline Adams, now the best known practitioner in which she calls "horary astrology," caused her to be haled into court, where her counsel so ably defended her that Judge Freschi, before whom it was tried, handed down the decision that the defendant had "raised astrology to the dignity of an exact science."

The decision was rendered in 1914 and since then Miss Adams profession enjoys in that state legal par with law and science, as she proudly informs her readers in her volume of autobiographical reminiscence. This was the grand turn in Miss Adams fortunes as a predictive astronomer—she had already attracted consider-

---

☉  ☽  ✶

"So far, so good," I said in the midst of the haze inside G.E.'s tobacco-stuffed office.

"Blah, blah, blah…mentions archaic law, good. 'Ceased to be invoked,' good. 'Best known,' very good. 'Horary astrology,' OK. 'Raised astrology to the dignity of an exact science,' excellent."

G.E. sucked long and hard on his lit cigar, the way Sabine would if she were a smoker.

"I'm thrilled by it. I think it makes me look rather accomplished."

"Shh, I'm still reading."

☉  ☽  ✶

able attention by foretelling the Windsor Hotel fire—and now distinguished persons in all walks of life seek out the lady at her offices in the Carnegie building without feeling they must need disguise their identity. Such is the advance present status—at least in the state of New York—of a vocation whereof Voltaire remarked that credulity made half the science.

Miss Adams does not attempt to defend this vocation of hers, though she explains how she casts a horoscope. She merely submits the evidence of her predictive successes. They cover hundreds of cases of which the clients themselves supply the authenticity. And her clients have numbered John Burroughs, J. Pierpont Morgan, and many others accredited with more than the ordinary amount of good sense. They have

☉  ☽  ✶

"People aren't going to have a clue. Celebrity names are all they'll care about. Finally...'John Burroughs, J. Pierpont Morgan.' They're should have been more. What's *credulity*?"

"I did my best to make the passages simple. It's an excellent review, G.E. You should be proud."

"Let me finish. So far though, it's *not* making me want to run out and buy the book."

G.E. refused to believe that no one knew my prospective clients better than me. To him, they were nothing more than dollar signs.

> believed in her and her forecasts and Miss Adams says that, conscientiously searching her records, she knows of no instance where her predictions have failed. It is a splendid advertisement, and one can hardly blame her for making the most of it in her book; which, in some ways is more interesting to those who disbelieve in her stellar science than to those who believe in it. "The Bowl of Heaven." By Evangeline Adams. New York: Dodd, Mead & company; $3.00.

"Now we're talkin'." Looking like the proud pupil who'd just received the highest marks in class just before he pokes fun at the boy wearing the dunce cap, G.E. said with a swagger, "I told them to put in that last part. At the very end; the clincher. That'll bring in even more business; consultations *in addition to* book sales. They'll work in tandem."

"I wonder how many people subscribe to *The Helena Daily Independent*."

"Not enough, I'm sure. I'm still furious with them for putting this in so late. The book came out on the tenth of last month, and they don't print this until December."

Shivers next sprinted up my spine, but I didn't let on. "I hadn't thought about that. November 10th."

"Uncanny, ain't it? Six years left…on the dot."

"This book. My legacy."

"You said it yourself, hon. Now, in the papers. *'You can't beat the stars'.*"

"Sometimes I wish I'd never uttered those words."

As he scratched his privates underneath his beige woolen trousers before me, G.E. said, "There's no goin' back, Evangeline. Your head'll spin thinking about what we'll accomplish in these upcoming six. We've made astrology all the rage; next, *'The world's greatest…in history'*. I'll make certain of it."

$$\odot \quad \rangle \quad \star$$

Not having set my weary feet inside a church in decades, I made my late-in-life pilgrimage to St. Bartholomew's on East 50th Street on impulse. I must have paced up and down Park Avenue between 50th and 51st a dozen times before entering the bronze doors of this Byzantine goddess. She welcomed me with her Episcopalian arms and made me feel as if I hadn't missed one day of worship.

For years, I'd gone to church with my mother when I was a child; it was our private ritual. I didn't understand much then, but I could see in my mother's face that being there soothed her. If I was sick and unable to go, neither would she. It's what we'd done together most. I missed my mother. I still practiced astrology, something she told me was "unbecoming an Adams," but I *had* married, something she'd greatly approve of. Her many years of being a widow had jaded her, I'm fairly sure that's what it was. Always thinking that life would have turned out better with a man in the family.

On this afternoon in church, with the organist rehearsing above me, I began to pray. In a seated, upright position because of my bad knees, and with eyes fully closed, I silently did something my mother taught me to do above all else, I expressed gratitude. Hearing what sounded like Benedetto Marcello's haunting *Nineteenth Psalm* took me back to my childhood. With less than six years left in my life, I'd already been rewarded many full lifetimes over. I went through the list in my head of all the "miracles" I felt that I'd *made* happen. World's most famous astrologist, millionairess, accomplished antiquarian. Time prevented me from going over the majority.

Feeling as if it were an even trade after a half hour of venerating nonstop, I thought it an unselfish time to ask for more. Five years. Four. Three. Whatever seemed reasonable. Anything that took me beyond November 10th, 1932. In my head, I began every sentence with "Dearest Savior Almighty…" What a relief it was for me to have even asked. A colossal release of tension after I'd made my final plea.

Hopefully I didn't seem desperate. Synchronistically, just as I was about to rise from my seat and depart, the organist had come downstairs to tell me, "I'm afraid it's time to go. No one allowed inside during rehearsals. You're always welcome to come back though."

I never did.

$$\odot \quad \math{D} \quad \star$$

At our most recent business meeting that now always includes Sabine—so G.E. can more scrupulously "supervise her at all times"—my dedicated secretary said, "I've counted nearly one hundred speaking invitations, Miss."

"No, there's got to be more than that," G.E. said directly to Sabine's chest.

"This doesn't include today's post, sir."

In the most creative way Sabine managed her demeanor. Staying calm and serene, I noticed that she avoided all eye contact with G.E. Looking at the floor, at paperwork, at me, out the window, at her precision-sculpted and mauve-painted fingernails. A remedy that seemed to be most effective. There was no way I could do without either of them. A truce between them *must* be in their cards, I'd hoped.

"Anything else noteworthy, dear?"

"The…" they both answered at once.

"You were addressing me, weren't you, Evangeline?"

"Well, no. Sabine. Curious to know if any other invitations, letters would be of interest to me."

"To *us*."

Still looking at the ground, Sabine's eyes shifted to a colorful postcard of Hollywoodland she was holding in her hand. My eyes lit up like fireworks once they spotted that the stamp was postmarked in Los Angeles, California. But G.E. noticed. He grabbed onto the card and said, "Looks like good news. I'll read it. Aloud."

Not letting go, my strong-armed Bavarian with a death grip said, "No. It's for Miss."

"I'll take it, Sabine."

Sabine handed the card over to me and G.E. seemed to relinquish a bit of the hold he'd had upon me. He appeared rather resigned, like waving the white flag after one's fought a losing battle that had already lasted too long.

My book having been published, and having received rather positive reviews gave me confidence that I'd achieved much in my life, my career. Perhaps all I'd ever dreamt of.

"I need a cigar," G.E. said to us both as he exited my office.

"It's from—"

"I know who it's from."

Sabine, always in the know, smiled, happy for me. She respectfully left me to read the postcard in private as she retired to the front room.

As usual, the person that made me feel the best had written to congratulate me. Emma's was the most meaningful of all acknowledgments. This was a simple and brief note, no more than a paragraph in length, written with pride from one friend to another. How happy was I to share my feelings with my dearest well-wisher. Thinking about Emma made me reach for the rainbow-colored afghan she'd crocheted for me, the only one she ever finished. Placing it on my lap warmed me so.

Her analysis of the positive newspaper reviews had nothing to do with promotion or perception of me and my "beloved astrology." Emma praised my triumph as the work of a true wordsmith. *A million and one people say they're going to write a book…and never do. You did it. You edited it. You re-wrote it. And now it's published.* Not once did Emma bring to my attention that I'd ended sentences with prepositions on a few occasions. I'll always be indebted to her for that, I thought.

☉ ☽ ☆

Taking the familiar Old Put, the railway that connects Manhattan to Brewster along the Hudson River, to my new house in Yorktown Heights was a delight. My core felt solid and secure and was ready to expand its reach. I'd bought the house shortly before my marriage to G.E. Similar to my days spent antiquing, this was my chance to get away, even if it was only forty-five miles away from the City, where the only forecasting I had to do was at suppertime. Fish? Or fowl?

The aura of northern Westchester County was quite different from Midtown's 57th Street in more than the obvious ways. The townspeople there took the time to ask and answer questions that contained more than one sentence. It was a place where nature takes over and daily calendars become non-existent. Heading up there close to every weekend, was going to be my newest ritual, my weekly renewal of sorts. And this time I was doing it with Emma, as a sort of therapeutic retreat for her. A place for her to heal, a place for me to console. Somehow this was near enough the way I'd envisioned it in my mind. The two of us.

"Much better than Central Park, isn't it?"

"Divine. These towns we're passing through…like a fairy tale," Emma said, while appearing a little emotionally absent after we whizzed by a billboard displaying Buster Keaton's latest picture. Maybe made her think about Hollywood. Yet forever marveling at the rusticity of country life and its meandering native inhabitants as seen from a speeding locomotive, she decreed, "How can these people live up here?"

In an effort to sober her up I playfully shook Emma by the shoulders and said, "My darling dearest, you do need to get out more. Not to sound insensitive, but now that you're no longer attached, you have no excuse."

"Kitchawan, Amawalk, Mahopac. Pardon me, I'd neglected to pack my Hiawatha costume in my trunk."

"Consider this an education. I know how much you value learning. Absorb as much as you can as you set foot into the twentieth century."

⊙　☽　✷

As our train disembarked at the Yorktown Heights station, with its hanging white-wooden sign boasting, "Population: 37," some of which may even be fruit and fir trees not humans, Emma had little to say but, "Where's the rest of it?"

My companion and I, the only two to descend upon the train's platform, found no porters, no one to greet us upon arrival. "The rest of what?"

"Yorktown Heights."

Her sarcasm shouldn't have expected an answer. Considering what Emma'd been through, I allowed her to spew whatever she wanted without repercussions. Needless to say, the self-conceived pledge sacramental between her betrothed Penelope and she was off. Emma was devastated, now trying to put the pieces of her life back together.

For a change I was the calm, cool and collected one. Work was the furthest thing from my mind. All attention on Emma. Supporting her wholeheartedly. There she waited impatiently inside my humble abode, sitting, prematurely, on the tarp-guarded vintage divan with her legs crossed securely in a locked position, while saying very little. It wasn't until we settled in with tea, Postum, cookies and cakes on the spruce-surrounded loggia with its thin carpet of pine needles that she began to relax. It was strange, me being the teacher this time. Now, feeling so comfortable in my own skin, I felt like I not only wanted to have it all, but that I truly deserved it.

"As soon as I remove these dust covers, let's sit. Be comfortable. I want to hear more about…what happened."

"I'll help you," Emma said while taking control of one end of the covering. Together, one step at a time, we held and creased our respective ends until the dusty crème-colored canvas drop cloth was perfectly folded. "Who knew Hollywood was filled with so many actresses…that only fancy other actresses, not actors. Penny was like a kid in a candy store."

"The men there are the same, I'm sure. Except for Rudolph Valentino." Dryly I told Emma, "I detected heterosexuality in his chart."

"Can you believe those hysterical women? How empty their lives must be, throwing themselves upon his coffin."

"Those are the same women who chastised me earlier for my forecast."

"Were you right?"

"Naturally. August 23, 1926. After all, the stars are infallible."

"I wished you'd told me what the stars had in store for me out there. I could no longer compete for Penny's attention. I'm too old. She didn't say so, but I could tell."

"Emma, life will improve. You never seemed to like California anyway."

"You're right. Earthquakes scare the vinegar out of me."

"Well, that can't be good. And the same for your job."

"It was fine enough. But the blather about me. From the teachers. Evangeline, I was never, in the least bit, lascivious with *any* of those girls," Emma said, as her voice began to quiver.

I caressed her right hand warmly and didn't let go. "Perhaps your return to New York was predestined. For obvious reasons, and others unknown."

This was how it was meant to be, from a very long while ago. For the first time I could feel it all without fear, a very equal and balanced give and take between us. Akin to horoscopic polar opposites, the perfect marriage. What a new sensation for me, one that I favored greatly.

"This is good. Warm. You feel any better? Discussing it all with me?"

Emma, with a lock of hair camouflaging one eye, just the way she appeared when I first caught a glimpse of her twenty-four years earlier, peered up from the tea she'd gone back to sip and said, "I almost don't know how to react. You're so different now. Mature. Less jittery. Present."

"I'm not so sure these are compliments."

"Of course, dear. Yes, I'm feeling better already. You. Me. Here. I'm certainly set to make the most of this glorious weekend together. Strolling through the woods, cooking fine meals, reading good writing aloud."

"And more."

At the same time, we embraced each other tightly.

"Yes, certainly much more. Not only now. Many occasions to come."

# Sun @ 7° AQUARIUS 50'34 (1928)

*M*y time with Emma in the "wilderness," as she liked to call it, had become one of the true highlights of my personal life. Being able to comfort her with my words, my emotions, not to mention the warmth and affection of my hands, ended up soothing my own spirit. Somehow made me feel wiser, more learned deep down. Whole. The other passion in my life, astrology, kept me busier than I'd ever been. 1928 had come upon us and the country was virtually unified in its opposition to Prohibition. Speakeasies were all the rage and thrived everywhere. Although he'd never admit to it, this is where I'd found out from a few male clients that G.E. was spending the bulk of his nighttime hours. Chumley's on Bedford Street to the south and the Cotton Club in Harlem much to the north.

The subscription to my regular newsletter now numbered over three hundred thousand. As a nation, we were collectively headed in an extremely favorable direction in many aspects. Economically, socially and culturally. Aleister Crowley had come and gone from my life, but in the process, provided me with my next book. It took many years for us three to come to terms with copyright ownership. In between, there were failed attempts to sue G.E. and I, five court appearances and numerous private threats indicating fraud by Aleister. From the inception I'd always seen him as a ghostwriter. Aleister saw otherwise.

☉ ☽ ✫

---

### Oakland Tribune

OAKLAND, CALIFORNIA

SUNDAY, FEBRUARY 12, 1928

### Book Reviews *and* Literary Notes
### "Astrology"

---

The astrologer is usually considered to be a fatalist, one who believes in an appointed lot which is outlined by the stars and from which there is no escape.

It is, therefore, somewhat of a paradox to find Evangeline Adams, in her new book, "Astrology," championing the mastery of destiny by the intelligent use of the free will.

There is a fate, she argues, and that fate is interlocked with the movement of the heavenly bodies, for none can prevent the rays of the stars from reaching them.

However, it is within the province of man's free will to determine what he will do with those powers as they beat in upon him each second of his earth life. For instance, a Mars vibration is always charged with energy. One will give

---

expression to this influx of energy by a great outburst of temper, while another will use it to mentally conquer the difficulty which caused the first to lose his temper.

The author therefore gives the first 316 pages of her book to a description of the sun, moon and planets, and the manner of their expression in the various signs as they journey through the zodiacal belt. She devotes the final twenty-seven pages to a chapter entitled "Free Will Versus Destiny."

And in this final chapter she advises all to use the knowledge given through the science of astrology to discover "the pattern on which the life is built," and to employ an intelligent free will to live our lives faithful to that plan, thus gaining "happiness, efficiency and usefulness in the world."

"Fatalism only exists on the material plane. The soul is not shackled by fate," she says.

If the time of birth is known the ascendant of the horoscope can be obtained within one degree from a table contained in the work. This is a valuable feature because many students do not fancy the mathematical figuring necessary to obtain this information.

The author has given thirty years of her life to the study of astrology, and she writes of the sun, moon and planets as though she was discussing intimate friends, and the signs of the zodiac as though she were describing their beautiful mansions. The subject of astrology is not covered exhaustively. She contents herself with the high lights.

("Astrology, Your Place in the Sun," by Evangeline Adams. New York: Dodd, Mead & Co., Inc.; $3.50.)

☉  ☽  ✴

A bit blander than the review in *The New York Times,* but certainly more accurate in its delivery than the latter. In *The Times* I was once again misquoted. How in the world can anyone be born under Venus? Scorpio is the eighth sign of the zodiac. Venus is a planet. The author, although he'd apparently read my book, still knew nothing about astrology. Poor, misguided soul.

That particular book review however went on to include many, many more paragraphs that were favorable. The overall appraisal in *The Times* was more personable than the others, even offering an admission by the author, Mr. Thompson, a Pisces, that he did not, indeed, take dope. He was referring to my mention of Pisces in my book, such as Lord Roberts and St. Francis, as being the most prone to dope usage. Mr. Thompson's direct quotation resulted in much criticism from both Catholics and historians alike.

Nevertheless, another job well done. Although the life of the pre-publication manuscript lasted much too long; well over a decade, this book gave readers a chance to know and understand astrology straightforwardly. All was working in my favor. Every dream I'd had for myself, for astrology and for my astrological career had been actualized. According to my chart though, the best was yet to come. Communicating to people on a much grander scale, other than through books and newsletters, was on my future path.

☉  ☽  ✴

"I'm not ashamed to say that I adore the accolades." Time for another pat on the back, but since G.E. never touched me for any reason, I did it myself.

"*Of all the astrologists, no one is nearer to the stars than Evangeline Adams (Mrs. George E. Jordan Jr.), hardy and cultured Yankee, descendant of the famed Adams family (John, John Quincy, Henry)*," G.E. recited with verve, mostly with eyes absent from the page. His confidence never looked so supreme. I'd hoped my office was large enough to accommodate G.E.'s growing ego.

"No need to deliver anymore aloud. I've already read it numerous times."

"*TIME* magazine. It doesn't get any better than this. Nearly verbatim usage of the text I'd provided. Now we must turn to what's next."

"Similar to the last occasion, I presume."

"Precisely. But good. Good news. Good news for the masses," G.E. told me, stretching his arms far above his head while reclining lengthwise on my Austrian yellow velvet daybed.

"Politics. Economy. Religion."

"No, most definitely not religion. Nothing good about that. Too many conflicts there."

"I can't manufacture it, you know. It must be truthful."

Immediately after snapping a wad of Wrigley's Doublemint with his mouth wide open, G.E. said, "Believe me, we won't stretch it too far this time. How—"

"G.E., I have never stretched the truth to any extent. Not in the past, not now."

"May I finish?"

"Surely go ahead."

"How about casting a chart for the country as a whole? Again based on the birthdate July 04, 1776. Cancer sun."

"As I always do."

"Something good. Good for everyone."

"I'll certainly do my best. I can't deliver what isn't factual."

"Do some digging."

My digging needn't have been so deep, because I was able to discover exactly what G.E. was hoping for me to find nearly instantaneously. The coming of Jupiter in the second house brings nothing but good luck, prosperity, windfalls. ♃ was about to create radical change for all. This kind of news would be positive to every American wanting to become rich. It was so clear in my research what the stars predicted. The absolute best conditions within the Stock Market during the fall of this year: 1929. September third, to be most particular.

G.E., as usual, wanted me to announce my prediction via a press release. So, much preparation went into its development beforehand; minute details, such as the inclusion of "action" verbs that would have customarily escaped my attention. In a variety of ways our odd union made sense. I stopped thinking of our marriage as a counterfeit one because it took place for an obvious purpose, to make us both more prosperous.

Part of my reason for viewing G.E. this way had to do with the thousands of clients who'd entered my office. Some with arranged marriages, some blatantly fraudulent, some for business, some for inheritances, some for convenience, some for disguised fidelity. These were the majority. The couples that married for love were in the vast minority. Not for a second had I loved G.E., but I did love what he'd been able to do for me. I could imagine he viewed me in the same light. The perfect partnership.

In the pithiest manner, G.E. crafted a story that was written, edited and revised nearly a hundred times over. It was delivered to my thousands of newsletter subscribers, numerous reporters and went out over the newswire simultaneously.

"On this Labor Day, I inform you that within the next forty-eight hours the market could climb to heaven. One of the most advantageous days to make an investment in American history."

J.P. used to speak of this sometimes: a bull market. As the years passed, I'd come to know the importance of this trend. But in the scant few days ahead, my dear bull-headed friend's famous quote, "If you have to ask how much it costs, you can't afford it," would become obsolete. Labor Day was preceded by several months of financial productivity. And on September third it would climax.

With optimism and financial gain taking place nearly everywhere, feelings of invulnerability were evident on the faces of everyone in New York. Wide eyes, teeth that smiled their brightest, clear nostrils that took in only the air of sweet success.

On a late-summer evening Emma visited my home while G.E. was off somewhere "promoting." My soul's alter ego put on one of her favorite phonograph records, Gershwin's *Stairway to Paradise*. As she always did, Emma began doing a dance performance of it, looking just like the recently departed Isadora Duncan. Next, she did something different though, much to my dismay.

"Together. Come on," Emma told me softly while grasping for my right hand. She tickled me with the tip of the red feather boa she had draped around her neck. She wouldn't take no for an answer. I let Emma lead me into my first dance, something I'd never allowed myself to do.

As I felt my cheeks blush as brightly as the boa, I tried covering them up with my two hands, but Emma quickly brought them back down. "I don't know how—"

"Don't say a word, my dear. *I've got the blues, And up above it's so fair. Shoes! Go on and carry me there! I'll build a stairway to Paradise, With a new step ev'ry day.'...*"

Emma continued to give me a private concert while holding me next to her, both of our bodies now entwined in her feathery neckwear. My usual fears that G.E. would enter the room and ruin the perfection never materialized.

Only a few people in my inner circle knew that Emma and I were now living as a virtual husband and wife...in Westchester anyway. Residing together in Manhattan was still forbidden, too close to business, G.E. and prying eyes.

"I wish this evening would never end."

"It is bliss, isn't it? I guess good things do come to those who wait." Emma next spun me around like a top, and as she did so, I inhaled a waft of her newest perfume scent smelling of juniper berry. When I asked what it was, Emma said, "Marquis." Although spelled differently, hearing that word took me back to the corner of West 45th Street and Seventh Ave. when I stood there with Mrs. Brush in spring of 1899. Had it not been for that marquee we both stared up at, perhaps fate never would have delivered me to Emma.

"Evangeline, I never waited. We made this happen because we never went away. Our bond could have been created in the stars, but we're the ones who chose to never let it disintegrate. Hat's off to us. We did it."

As Emma slid off the Parisian sparkling indigo floral bonnet with cerise side bow from her head, I said, "Hat's off to us indeed."

Emma was most likely surprised by my conciliatory reaction to her "we, not the stars, made this happen" speech. But she never expressed it. After having experienced the greatest times of our lives together the moment had arrived for us to part. Emma back to her comfortably modest flat downtown, me back to my comfy yet spacious bedroom to retire for the night. We made the most of a magical evening and my spirit felt as if it was already in Paradise.

☉　☽　✸

My euphoria, which seemed evident to everyone who'd seen me, apparently never wore off. Instead it lasted and lasted as even more good news descended. Inside my residence after another days' work well done, G.E., dressed in a form fitting three-piece, charcoal grey cutaway tuxedo looked me up and down approvingly, the way a proud father would.

"Right on target. The Dow Jones Industrial Average closed at 381.17. Unheard of," G.E. said jubilantly. "We've got to toast this. Your accurate prediction has just made us a fortune, Evangeline."

"To the stars, G.E.," I told my husband as I raised a flute of Dom Pérignon high into the night air.

"We must celebrate. Go on the town. Whoop it up," freshly-shaven G.E. insisted.

I didn't resist at all. "Where shall we go?"

"It doesn't matter. All I want to do is show you off. You'll be the talk of the town."

"The Stork Club?"

"The Stork Club it is."

Just as G.E. himself had foreseen, my predictions had become the talk of the town. Never had so many joy-filled people joined forces in the streets, creating merriment on every corner. Newspaper stands revealed nearly the same words I'd foretold only a short while earlier.

I picked up and paid for a copy that I read aloud to G.E. with much enthusiasm and verve. "*Economist Irving Fisher proclaims stock prices have reached what looks like a permanently high plateau*.'"

"Look at the headline of this one. *Public Demand for Stock Appears Insatiable*.'"

"Just as I'd said."

"You're a star, my dear. *The New York Stock Exchange saw a near record 4,438,910 shares being traded. Call money was 9%. Commercial bank paper yields 6.5% while the Federal Discount rate is 6%. Good undertone, says those in the know*.'"

Once our coats were checked, we sat and witnessed the prosperity I'd known was to come. We, too, had made a fortune while taking full advantage of the financial advice I'd been delivering unto others. Investing in RCA Victor and the Ford Motor Company, then selling only a few weeks later, netted G.E. and I several thousands of dollars.

The Stork Club had never appeared finer. Every female diner was clad in the latest chic couture; spiral-cut, spiral-zippered taxi dresses as far as the eye can see, created to be easy enough to slip on while in the backseat of a cab. Even the palm trees inside, with top hats attached, seemed to have gone black-tie. After having ordered caviar, asparagus tips, vintage Cabernet Sauvignon and chateaubriand for two, the band played a familiar tune. G.E., not one for harmonizing, began without hesitation, *"I'll build a stairway to Paradise, With a new step ev'ry day! I'm gonna get there at any price; Stand aside, I'm on my way!"*

☉  ☽  ★

Seeing the configuration of planets following the bull market made my flesh crawl. Only a month had passed since the absolute best of times and now nothing but peril on the horizon.

Although President Hoover reassured everyone that the market was sound, financial ruin of catastrophic proportions was now before us all. On October 24, 1929, heavy liquidation took its toll on the economy as 12.9 million shares were sold. Paper losses that day reached five billion dollars. The press would later call this Black Thursday.

The pandemonium affected me personally, as hundreds upon hundreds of poor, scared souls actually arranged themselves outside, downstairs from my studio. In snake-like fashion they formed a line that stretched around the entire block surrounding Carnegie Hall. Some camping out overnight, while others, from what I was told, actually collapsed from panic and trepidation. My new mission was to accommodate as many people as possible while attempting to soothe their fears. In an effort to do so, I abandoned my regular practice of individual consultations and instead held group ones.

During one of my sessions I was interrupted by my own broker, unshaven, malodorous and wrinkle-attired Randall Wertheim, who'd burst into my office. Camouflaging his dread in front of the others by veiling his mouth with his left palm, Randy informed me that I was over one hundred thousand dollars in the negative. Not wanting to risk any additional losses, I advised him to sell everything first thing next morning. When he left my office, I apologized to everyone for the intrusion, took a deep breath, and went ahead with my work.

Good news came about though, when headlines only days later read, "Brokers Believe Worst is Over and Recommend Buying of Real Bargains." The spirits of many were lifted and skittish behavior began to vanish. Still uncertain myself, I cast a chart once more for the U.S. with focus on finance. My head began to spin by what the disenchanted stars had in store. Hopelessness overwhelmed my emotions and already sick stomach, overpowering melancholia was about take hold of my mental state, but this time I couldn't let it. Stronger than when I was a child, "this time I can overcome it," I said to myself.

To my many thousands of newsletter followers and to the best of our ability, G.E. and I attempted to warn everyone of what was to come in a matter of days. In the simplest way I said, "It behooves everyone to be extremely cautious in investment and money matters, and be prepared for this threatening configuration of planets." Knowing what was at hand, I felt the only remedy was to close my eyes and pretend none of it was happening. But it did.

On October 28, the stock market fell 22.6%, the highest one-day decline in U.S. history. To make matters worse, the press hailed this as Black Monday, while additional declines were experienced all over the world. I knew this would not be the worst of it all.

I saw the ghastliest drop taking place on a Tuesday, the very next day. October 29, 1929. Unfortunately, I was only too correct with my predictions. When this nightmare of a Tuesday was just about over, terror ruled the day as every investor, it seemed, made an attempt to sell off all their stocks at once. Over 16 million shares were sold, a new record for the Exchange. Over $14 billion in paper losses were recorded. The market went down thirty-three points in one twenty-four hour period.

The feel of impending doom must have affected everyone afterwards. I myself wanted to see with my own eyes what was happening, and in the afternoon, in the vicinity of the maddened masses, I saw a most peculiar display of destruction. An unexpected stroll took me once again through the Trinity churchyard at Wall St. and Broadway. Time and circumstances allowed me to view only one, time-worn blackened gravestone, mold covering the bulk of it. There it was as plain as day. Adams. The first name was invisible, but the rest remained. Tremors ran up my legs. An image of an older man scowling, pointing his finger at me ran through my mind.

I was suddenly struck by the thought that in over thirty years, all my endless hours of fervent drive and determination had amounted to naught; I had made no difference whatsoever in the world. My father would be so ashamed of me. I fled in tears.

As I finished weeping, I walked until I could walk no more. While standing on the corner of Wall St. and William St., I witnessed an entire flock of one to two hundred sparrows dive beak-first into a newly constructed skyscraper at 40 Wall Street, headquarters for The Bank of Manhattan. They perished instantly.

The plague continued as people followed suit. Suicides aplenty. For so very many, hope had vanished, and the end of the world was fast approaching.

# Sun @ 10° PISCES 41'14 (1930)

*G.*E. couldn't have been happier regarding the turn of events. The demand for me and my services had never been higher. Worldwide press was clamoring for my attention. I was working 'round the clock and G.E. was in ecstasy, even patted me on the back when the mood struck his fancy. I also discovered that offhand comments I happened to make turned newsworthy. In the gossip pages I was quoted while dining out one afternoon: *Asked for a tip about the market while lunching at the Plaza Hotel, Evangeline Adams gruffly replied to her waiter, 'You do not work for nothing, why should I?'* G.E. had turned me into a household name and I knew I'd be forever indebted to him.

My third book was now about to come out. Finding availability in my calendar to promote it seemed challenging. *ASTROLOGY: Your Place Among the Stars* turned out to be a bit more lengthy than the previous. Although eventually compensated for his contributions to both, Aleister continued to disparage me to anyone who would listen. Jealous or bitter or both, in one of his own books he referred to me as, "a grey-haired old woman of exceedingly shrewd expression."

"Well, happy days are here again, my dear," G.E. said, while opening up his office window in my honor. My lungs thanked him with a hearty inhale.

"If I'm able to help make anyone's life better as a result of my forecasting, yes, happy days are indeed here again."

G.E. snickered at my reply and said, "Before I begin referring to you as St. Evangeline, I know you're relishing in the glory just as much as I am."

"Part of me loves it," I said. "People looking up to me as if I were…"

Finishing my sentence didn't seem at all apropos considering the vast number of people suffering around me now without even a nickel in hand. After already having gone through five or six of my virgin Madeira embroidered bridal hankies, I knew I could yet again be brought to tears feeling the deep despair that was everywhere. Finding a happy and sensible medium of celebrating the needs the public had upon me and the compassion I should feel towards them, had become my restructured mission of the moment.

"Leverage. That's why this happened," G.E. explained.

"I see it as an opportunity as well, G.E. But I've got to show at least some empathy. People are killing themselves because of this."

"And you saw both. You told the truth, the noble thing to do. The upswing *and* the down."

"If I'd told them nothing of the bull market that preceded this all, some of them would still have their money."

Brushing his imaginary moustache with his right forefinger in a manner he probably thought J.P. would have, G.E. shouted out, "Balderdash! Isn't that what you told me Mr. Morgan would say about something like this?"

I laughed, because that's precisely what J.P. would have said. "Grab the bull by the horns," he'd commanded more times than I'd like to hear.

"OK, spill it, maestro," I said. "Or do you prefer 'Svengali?' Please do tell me what you have up your sleeve."

"Radio. I've got a whole lineup of sponsors ready to shoot their wad."

"Ready for *what*? You're not talking about *me* being on the radio. Are you?"

"Who else? It's what the world's waiting for, my dear. You and your talks about the stars. A match made in the heavens."

"Well, Emma once told me that I do possess the tonal qualities of a broadcast announcer."

"Damnit!" Squinting from the ray of direct sunlight in his eyes, G.E. bolted up to draw the roller blind, and said, "Emma. How'd she work her way into the conversation?"

"Remember our agreement, G.E. Not a bad word."

The agreement to which I was referring was one that meant a great deal to me. Not put into copy, but still binding nonetheless. After several years now of non-marital relations with my husband, most of the time without even a birdlike peck on the cheek, it had become terminally clear that ours was nothing more than a professional union. I loved, admired G.E. for the manly Midas touch he'd given to my career and my surge in popularity, but other than that we went our separate ways and lived apart. His advice to me though, which had now become a residual fright, was the notion that my private life would eventually become public. My time with Emma was still relegated to the hills of Westchester County. Our rendezvous in Manhattan were ever more shrouded in secrecy for fear of exposure.

"Actions speak louder than words, my dear," he said. "I can ruin you as easily as I've built you."

⊙　☽　★

Pretending she was Elizabeth Arden, my secretary, while nearly slapping me in the face with her pink powder puff, ordered, "More rouge on the cheeks, Miss."

"Sabine, this is radio. No one will ever see."

"For confidence. Looking your best."

I humored Sabine now just as I always had. She had nearly a basket full of cosmetic products at her disposal ready to paint me up like a flapper. A bit of red may have been charming, but my face soon became theatrical, clown-like as I readied for my time in this three-ring circus.

For the next hour prior to my rehearsal in the studio, Sabine plucked, painted and adorned me with artistic touches that would have rivaled those of Pablo Picasso. All her theatrics did was raise my anxiety level. At any given moment, I expected Rudy Vallee, Amos & Andy or even stars of the Camel Pleasure Hour, RKO Theatre or the Chase & Sanborn Choral to walk through the station's green glass doors.

"I'm never going to be Tallulah Bankhead. I think that's enough."

"Bite your lips. Bee-sting plump. And don't forget the—"

"Balanced breathing. Yes, I know."

All this effort for a simple sound check. A mere rehearsal for what's to come. When asked to speak aloud before the microphone, I couldn't think of anything else to say but, "Four score and seven years ago our fathers brought forth on this continent, a new nation, conceived in Liberty, and dedicated to the proposition that all men are created equal."

"That's rather dry, Miss Adams," the producer of the show, Mr. de Ropp, said to me with a slight lisp to his skimpy voice, whilst wearing trousers that lacked crisp creases.

"The recitation? Or the tone with which I read it?"

"Come to think of it, both."

"I'll try it once more. *Four score and——*"

"Deeper."

"Four score and seven years ag——"

"No, Miss Adams, radio today has to be seductive. Enticing every listener with not only provocative words but…gasps from time to time."

"Of course. Well then, I'll pretend I'm being choked."

"Nothing violent. Envision your listener as a prospective lover. Speak to them as if you're about to become intimate. Emote. Consider this an acting exercise."

"My imagination. I'll surely make the best use of it."

"Take in a few large breaths, Miss Adams, and begin once more, please."

After having paused a few seconds, I began thinking seductive and appealing thoughts. Pictures entered my head. Scenery. A startlingly handsome background of wildflowers in a meadow found only in the New Hampshire countryside. The smell of pancakes on the griddle. Boysenberry syrup. A roomful of luxury French furnishings, made of pitchpine, from the Second Empire.

"Four scccore and sevvven years ago, o——"

"This is going to take a while, I can just tell," Mr. de Ropp told me, after taking a conspicuous peek at the face of his pocket watch lying on the table.

"May I take a moment? I'd like to speak with my secretary privately for a second or so."

Now humoring me, the producer said, "By all means," as his eyeballs gave me the bum's rush.

Sabine and I stepped aside to an area where only caffeinated refreshments were available. As I began pouring nothing but hot water into my cup, my hands started to shake and their trembling became obvious to everyone. Sabine took charge from that point on and became the director I'd been needing from the moment I'd entered the recording studio.

"Miss, I will prepare the Postum. Instant. I brought some with me. A steaming hot cup of satisfaction that will make your mouth cry," Sabine said while kissing an invisible phantom paramour.

Noticing Sabine leaving her chair to stand behind me and mine, I asked, "What are you doing?"

"Trust me, Miss. Close your eyes and listen."

I obeyed my take-charge Scorpio leader and prepared to be entranced. Sabine next softly placed her hands over my shut eyelids and rested her chin gently atop my hatless head.

"You are in a room alone, longing to be with your lover. It has been five months and your loins ache with desire. After a rough knock at the door, it's then flung open by…Rudolph Valentino. He is undressed and—"

"Sabine. *Rudolph Valentino?* What are—"

"Oh. Right, right. After a knock on the door, it flings open by Jean Harlow. Her breasts are heaving. She—"

"That's enough."

With a mind that's perpetually in the gutter, Sabine attempted to seduce me into better diction. I instead thought of the best, most-sure fire remedy to my dilemma.

"Mr. de Ropp, you needn't worry. My closest and dearest friend is a dramatic instructor and coach. In no time, help will be on the way."

"Can he be summoned on short notice?"

"She. Emma Sheridan. Emma Sheridan-Fry."

"Of course…raven-haired Emma Sheridan, a divine voice from what I recollect. I saw her perform on stage many, many years ago. Why don't I give you a sample script, you take it home to study and have Miss Sher—, your friend work on it with you?"

But once home, as soon as I'd closed the doors to my sanctuary, I sat and did nothing. I couldn't. My fears, perpetuated by G.E.'s non-idle threats, prevented me from calling upon Emma.

On the second tier of my amboyna ebonised, ormolu and porcelain mounted breakfront credenza, staring me in the face, was an aged, somewhat less full, single bottle of malted Scotch whiskey. Not at all resembling the empties Father left behind that Mother kept as tokens of evil from which we children were supposed to be horror-struck. I walked over to the glass receptacle, picked it up and blew the dust off.

Housed in the darkest, unlit corner of my drawing room. Placed dead center on that buffet's middle shelf fifteen years prior. Never opened. Not for ornamentation, but as a remembrance. The manufacturer's label was tattered and discolored, but the personal label underneath was completely intact. 'From the cellar of J. PIERPONT MORGAN 1837-1913—A Souvenir to His Friends 1915.' The Scotch had been a staple aboard his privately owned luxury ship, the Corsair III. Our outing together on the previous incarnation of that very yacht, in 1909, was among many that had left an impression upon me for life.

Bold concepts, having to do with destiny or not, are ours to grasp, should we choose to do so. I remembered how J.P., wise behind his bravado, had offered a cryptically profound response to the Titanic tragedy that occurred nearly three years after our Orient trip: "Monetary losses amount to nothing in life. It is the loss of life that counts. It is that frightful death." These three brief sentences he'd uttered had made their way to print in nearly every periodical and publication known to mankind. It was to be the only time J.P. let the words "fear" and "death" slip out in the same sentence, in public. Privately, his shoulders shuddered every time he and I discussed mortality. Life's short.

⊙　☽　★

I placed the bottle back on the shelf and daringly chose to beckon Emma by telephone. She was more than pleased to take on the task of assisting me. While G.E. was "out for the evening," Emma joined me in my apartment. She offered a hundred and one ways in which to loosen me up, along with my larynx. Hours and hours upon hours repeating the same tongue twisters over and over and over again. By the time I was done with him, Peter Piper had picked enough pecks of pickled peppers to last a lifetime. In addition, I made "she" a rich woman with the multitude of sea shells she sold on the sea shore.

Into the late night we worked to the point where I began to develop an entirely new relaxed and confident manner of speech.

As I realized my mouth had turned numb, Emma, while gazing over to my antique pendulum wall clock, said, "It's nearly three. You must be tired."

"Thoroughly exhausted."

"I am as well. Time to go."

Although still looking as fresh as a daisy, not fatigued, it made no sense for Emma to walk the streets at this time of the early morning. Improper. Dangerous. "Please stay here. With me, Emma. It's too cold outside, you'll catch your death."

Emma told me she just needed a few minutes to rest her head, and before we knew it, Emma and I had so instinctively fallen asleep in each other's embrace.

⊙　☽　★

"Well, what have we here?" my ears heard a voice bellow out in an ersatz baritone fashion. Using a mocked tone of exaggeration, complete with all the melodrama of a silent picture show, G.E., not Rudolph Valentino nor Jean Harlow, flung the doors open to my bedroom and awakened Emma and I.

In the most unfazed way possible, Emma rose from the bed, outstretched her arms, slipped into a robe and stood only inches from my so-called spouse. "G.E., what a pleasure."

I could see in his face that Emma's lack of panic had left him speechless. I'd seen her do this with several others. Doing it, this time to G.E., made me want to applaud her. G.E.'s terror-inducing tactics no longer worked.

"Mrs. Fry. It's still *Mrs.* Fry. Isn't it?"

"You're absolutely correct, Mr. Adams."

This reply not only left me dumbstruck, but most likely G.E. as well. G.E. next looked to me for assistance, but I offered none. Emma matched wits with him just fine all by herself. After that, Emma stepped in front of the window I'd always kept closed and threw the drapes open wide for all to see. At this point, the volume of even the rain hitting the window pane had increased.

Yet a bit too timid to part from my security blanket, a sunshine yellow and white appliqued quilt, I said unobtrusively, "Emma's helping me with my diction dea—, G.E."

"I see," G.E. replied while scratching his forehead.

"Did you have something you wanted to tell us?" Emma asked with a broad smile on her face.

"Well…I only wanted to let you know that we've selected an opening song for your show."

"Who's we?" I asked G.E. with authority.

"Mr. de Ropp and I. I told him some of your preferences and we both agreed to *Ah! Sweet Mystery of Life.*"

Emma said, "A Victor Herbert tune. An excellent selection," before looking to me, possibly seeking my reaction.

"Now, make certain it's the phonograph recording version. The one that came out last year. By that tenor from Trenton."

G.E. looked at me sideways, obviously not knowing who I was talking about. "We didn't clarify that."

"Well then, you'd better be certain. After all, that's why we're in business together…so you can *get* things right," I said firmly.

G.E., rather than peering over in my direction, looked straight at Emma, who was still only inches before him. The energy about me felt so powerful, speaking with such conviction in front of Emma. She admired my courage, I could tell. Emma next reached out to shake G.E.'s hand, nearly inviting him to exit the door the same way he'd entered.

"That tenor from Trenton: Richard Crooks; such a handsome man. Almost as good looking as you, sir," Emma offered while tweaking G.E.'s cheek. Possibly not being too familiar with sarcasm, G.E. blushed.

G.E. stepped out and Emma and I prepared for my final rehearsal prior to my first broadcast. I should have known what was to come.

---

**The Ironwood Daily Globe**

IRONWOOD, MICH.
SATURDAY, MAY 24, 1930

**ASTROLOGIST NOW
RADIO PERFORMER**

———

**Evangeline Adams Considers
Horoscopes "Pure
Science."**

---

## BY PAUL HARRISON

**New York, May 24**—The oldest science in the world has found a new medium of expression in the newest. Astrology has adopted the radio, and unnumbered fans throughout the country have adopted Evangeline Adams as director of their individual destinies.

Others are amused, many are skeptical, as Miss Adams casts her tri-weekly horoscopes and predicts what the immediate future holds. But millions of the fans listen, whatever they think of astrology. For Evangeline Adams is the most celebrated of all children of the stars. The seers at the dawn of history, the Chaldaean magi, Manilius of Rome and William Lilly of England were apprentices by comparison.

Miss Adams has given half a million readings to seekers of the truth. Her mail order business and personal interviews during a career of almost 40 years have made her a very wealthy woman. And now, through the Columbia Broadcasting System, she launches her prophetic voice upon the ether.

Before she goes on the air, Miss Adams is announced by a blare of trumpets, music reminiscent of mystery, and a climactic clash of cymbals. But there is little trace of mystery about the Evangeline Adams who sits before the microphone, or even in her spacious studio, surrounded by her astral charts and tomes.

### "Stars Make No Mistakes"

She is quite short and plump, dresses in the most conservative style, has short, graying hair. . .

☉　☽　✯

With G.E. nowhere in sight, Emma said, "Isn't it something? No doubt about it. You're a true star now, deary," as we took turns preparing lunch in my kitchen. This time *I*, not Penelope, was wearing the apron that matched Emma's so perfectly. Floral print now obsolete, replaced with my much loved black lilies, embroidered on front.

"He didn't need to paint such an ugly picture of me. I stopped read—"

"You didn't finish? Here, let me see it."

I handed over the paper to Emma in a hurry so she could tell me more if there was anything worth hearing. "Where'd you leave off?"

"The gray hair, short, plump."

Appearing as if she just stuck her nose into a Chinese restaurant's back-alley trash bin, Emma said, "Oh, my heavens…yes, short graying hair *'and bubbling vitality which takes little account of her advancing years.'* You're reading it with prejudice, hon. It's a wonderful piece."

"From now on I'll only have you read them, Emma. I'm too discerning."

"You know me too well, Evangeline. If you expect me to edit out what you don't want to hear, you're mistaken. For better or worse."

"In sickness and in health."

# Sun @ 9° LEO 56'02 (1930)

The New York Times
August 3, 1930

## LISTENING IN

### ___By ORRIN E. DUNLAP JR.___

EVANGELINE ADAMS, astrologer, who reads horoscopes and studies the big swings in life as they affect the inhabitants of Mother Earth, has been on the air since April 23. And since that day radio has proved a revelation to her—it has surpassed the fondest expectations of herself and her sponsor at the microphone. She has received more than 150,000 requests for horoscopes. And each request was written on part of a carton which once contained a tube of toothpaste manufactured by her ethereal sponsor.

☉  ☽  ✫

"God Bless Forhan's For The Gums," G.E. shouted out in a slur.

"Because Four Out of Five Wait Too Long," Sabine replied back in perfect English, reiterating my sponsor's ad verbatim.

☉  ☽  ✫

"The letters come by the thousands," said Miss Adams. "The biggest day's mail brought 5,000 letters. When I began broadcasting eight stations were used. We plan to extend to forty-two stations in September going as far west as the Rockies." The company sponsoring the broadcasts has been forced to take over three more floors in its building to handle the mail. The letters are pathetically frank. Some must spend a half day writing about their problems. Radio has succeeded in getting astrology over to the masses and has given them a new outlet for their troubles and problems. The mail comes from men and women, and is about evenly divided among them. Their problems cover every phase of life.

"Many of the radio audience are anxious to make shifts in life. I warn most of them to be careful, because life is like a motion picture reel. If it is speeded up too much it does not show the picture as it is. I am a great believer in Old Dame Fortune in guiding our destinies, it is not wise to try to hurry her."

Miss Adams has a corps of assistants helping with the mail at her office in Carnegie Hall. She sits at a long table on the opposite side of which is the chair called "the seat of the mighty," because it has been used by financiers, army generals, society women, Presidential candidates, actors, publishers, priests, opera singers, ministers and leaders in all walks of life. They sit there as she "reads the bowl of the Heavens" to chronicle careers, to get an unknown glimpse into the future by way of the horoscope. They seek the answers to problems from the secrets of astrology, that will guide them in love, to wealth, fame, health and happiness. And now the radio audience is writing by the thousands to catch a look at the stars through Miss Adams "with more than a vague consciousness of their strange influence upon life." Thousands of those who listen in are asking her: "What shall I do with my life? For what am I fitted?" And this broadcaster on the air Monday, Wednesday and Friday nights at 7:30 o'clock over WABC and affiliated stations is endeavoring to reveal the listener's place among the stars...

☉  ☽  ✫

"Well, I'm happy," I admitted to Sabine and G.E. at a casual get-together in my breakfast nook. "Another Danish?"

Sabine must have heard me say the same words each time my name appeared in print. Still filing her nails with an Emery board, she said, "Me too, Miss. They got it all right. And, no thank you, Miss."

Wearing a frown as he placed his hands on his hips, G.E. leered at me and the cream cheese pastry I was about to stuff inside my mouth and said, "It's a mere launching pad. Very well put together, but now the hard part begins. This show's given you confidence. Let's make the most of it."

I could tell what G.E. had on his mind. Capitalize. Leverage. Maximize. Increase exposure. Because of G.E., his marketing know-how and copious connections to the press corps, horoscopes had for the first time begun appearing in most every newspaper the world over. Never had the average citizen been keener on sun signs and ascendants. Well over half of America was now preoccupied with the future as a result of my accomplishments. Sometimes, when not imagining I'd done all on my own, I felt as if I owed my life to G.E. On most occasions in public, I was gratified to call him my husband.

"Another speaking tour?" I asked.

"Oh, more than that. You'll be all over the place."

My calculations showed me that 730 days remained in my life. I hoped I could last that long. "My stamina, G.E. It's not what it used to be."

"What about your," G.E. began saying before wiggling his fingers to indicate effervesce; then went onto voice, "'bubbling vitality'? I wrote that. Had them squeeze it in, you know."

"The entire line read 'bubbling vitality which takes little account of her advancing years'."

"Well, yeah. I wrote the whole thing. It had to be truthful," G.E. said, as if he'd been under oath.

"G.E., I'm afraid my advancing self can't take it," I told my husband as I put back the croissant and jar of Smucker's apple butter I'd just taken off my Indo Persian silver platter.

"Miss still has all her clients, the newest book, the radio program. This is too much for anyone, if they're advanced or not."

All G.E. had to do was give Sabine a stern glare and she and her clingy black skirt that accentuated her streamlined hips left in a huff. It's amazing how persuasive the hand that writes the paycheck can be. G.E., Sabine's new employer in our reconfigured empire, and I went on to discuss his plans. Recalling her speech a few years prior about never allowing herself to be controlled by a man, any man, ever again, left me feeling weak, sad, a bit empty inside and more than all else, guilty. Sabine's freedom, along with a good deal of her joie de vivre, had diminished in my presence, and I felt responsible for that.

G.E. was most obstinate about a very lengthy tour that would take me to California and back, with a host of stops while en route. Looking for more Canadian Club whiskey to put into his morning coffee, through the wire mesh façade of the hutch, G.E. found only empty bottles, but beamed wide when coming upon one half full.

"The only way I can see doing this is if Emma comes with me. I'd need support of so—"

"You're *not* serious…not again, Evangeline."

"Yes, I know we ha—"

"Do you realize that more and more people see our marriage as a sham? Just the other day one of my gambling buddies told me we have a 'Hollywood' marriage. He even had to explain what that was."

"But, G.E., you know what? That's what it is."

After downing an entire cupful of his morning tonic in less than a minute, G.E. yelled out, "It absolutely is not. They see you as a diesel truck and because I'm twenty-two years younger than you they think I'm daffy. A daffodil."

"I have no idea what type of truck I am, but you're no daffodil. So…you needn't worry."

"When this all comes to ruin, don't come crawling to me," G.E. said while sounding like a despondent and neglected housewife.

"No, in all earnestness," I said to G.E., pressing my palms together as if to pray. I begged for mercy as I continued to tell him, "even if I accomplish a fraction of what you intend for me, I do need Emma's support. She told me that she'll be available to me whenever I need her."

"And why'd you have to pick her? A Suffragette. Those ladies' causes she's always muttering on about. Diesels," G.E. said while flexing his biceps.

"It doesn't matter what you say. I'm not the least bit concerned."

G.E.'s histrionics had given me a colossal migraine, not to mention a pain in the neck. After listening to his most recent sermon, I reached for my seltzer bottle like I'd done on during so many instances previous, and gulped down an enormous mouthful. Turning my back on G.E. and his propagandizing proved a better remedy for my throbbing skull.

Calling out for reinforcements after having been ignored by me, he yelled out, "Sabine…Sabine, would you come in here again, please."

I had no idea what G.E. was doing, but the belligerent tone in his voice was forceful enough to instill panic just as much as a lion's roar.

"Whatever you do, be nice to her."

"I'll be as sweet as honey," G.E. answered back from one of his many different personalities.

"Yes, Mr. Jordan. How can I assist you?"

"Sabine, precious. Evangeline and I know how deeply honest you are. Time and time again Evangeline has told you that honesty is one of the most admirable traits of a Scorpio, so we know you'll tell the truth when we ask you one persnickety question."

Trembling to be on the receiving end of G.E.'s uncharacteristic pleasantness, while most likely wondering about the word persnickety and its meaning, Sabine asked, "Am I in trouble, Mr. Jordan? Are you going to fire me again?"

"Oh, never, dear. You're a lamb," G.E. said, still as sweet as pie with a tad too much saccharin mixed in.

Sabine looked over at me quickly. I offered nothing back and her attention returned to G.E.

"Sabine, on your very first meeting with Mrs. Jordan, what did you think of her?"

"Who's Mrs. Jor— Oh, you mean Miss. Why do you—"

"No need to be afraid. We're playing a little game," G.E. said, while resembling Captain Hook, before laughing aloud and offering a menacing grin. When Sabine looked at me again for my reaction, I had not a one. By this time I'd grown a bit curious myself. Gripping Sabine by her shoulders, appearing fatherly, and in the most double dealing voice, G.E. said, "Everything's fine, dear. It's a game about first impressions we enjoy playing. Now, we'd like to know yours."

"The first time I met Miss. Very smart. Good with the numbers. Loves her astrology. Wants to make it big."

"And..."

"And what more do you want me to say?"

"What were your impressions of her...personal life? That's why the game's called 'First Impressions'," G.E. expressed to Sabine in a tone that's as honest as the day is short.

"It sounds to me like a game you're inventing."

"Oh, no. It's all the rage. Go ahead, dear."

"I didn't think much about it. I wasn't hired to know about this."

"Know about what?"

Putting her right hand up in front of her face to camouflage the words coming from the left side of her mouth, Sabine said in a whisper, "You know, her way. None of my business. I respect Miss, her privacy."

"So, you knew she was sapphic the first time you met her?"

"Saf— Well...I, perhaps..."

"And she never told you? I take it you automatically assumed."

"It was maybe a guess that told me."

Dispensing with his poker face, G.E. took out his grey tamponato leather billfold, opened it up, unfastened his sterling silver money clip and said, "Well, Evangeline. I think I just won the game. Pay up."

Not wanting to embarrass me, Sabine asked, "Did I say the right thing, Ma'am?"

"You told the truth."

For the millionth time, G.E. made me painfully aware, in the most humiliating way, that homosexuality is like concealed arsenic in the hands of a heterosexual society. Masquerading around; eating, breathing, living life as if it's normal, when in reality it's the furthest thing from it. My career, all my life long, exhausting hours of toil to be the world's best would crumble if I were exposed, I knew that for a fact. My back and forth with Emma all these years had been for naught. The decision simply wasn't mine.

⊙  ☽  ★

On the host of lectures that were in my immediate future, I took only a few staff members with me. They were my support system and I got along just fine. At an event in nearby Brooklyn, inside the smoke-filled Italo-American Club, I addressed a very vocal crowd of what ended up being mostly males, and the questions they posed were reasonably rousing. Fedora hats of every shade and size were visible everywhere inside the hall.

"Miss Adams, are polar opposites truly the best matches in matrimony?" a very astute young gentleman with only one, elongated eyebrow asked, while clutching a copy of *ASTROLOGY: Your Place Among the Stars* in his right hand.

"Well, much more goes into it than that. You're speaking

strictly of sun signs. It's wisest to compare full charts, not merely sun signs, ascendants, moons and the lot."

"How about signs of the same element?"

"My answer would be the same. But like elements do lend themselves to compatibility, yes."

"Identical to you and your husband. Aquarius and Gemini. Air signs. Is it true that you found him while creating his chart?"

"My, this story gets around. Yes, a businessman came to me and asked if he should join forces with another man. When I saw this other man's chart I noticed, quite by chance, a rather perfect complement to my own."

"How lucky you are to have been able to access it."

"Yes. Thank you. More questions?"

From the back of the room, an auburn-haired woman of thirty-or-so, showing much too much flesh of the bosom, said, "Word's out that he's over twenty years younger than you." Immediately my mind flashed back to the edict given to me now hundreds of times by G.E., "Reveal *nothing* personal."

"Yes. That's also correct."

"And he's your business manager as well."

"We're rather well matched in business. Correct."

"If I may be frank, are Geminis better or worse than Capricorns at love making? I'm trying to choose between my ballet-dancing Capricorn husband and my Gemini lover." After that comment two sounds of the same decibel level made their way through the crowd simultaneously. The few women in the room gasped, while the men chuckled.

Without being flippant I proceeded to tell the woman that only she could be the judge in that matter. I did happen to volunteer, on the sly, that Capricorns do enjoy an indulgence every now and again, while Geminis spend most of their time talking about it. The audience, this time men and women both, laughed, and I took only a few more questions. Another productive evening that even offered some showbiz value. What could be more satisfying?

☉  ☽  ★

On the eleventh and final stop on my current lecture tour I possessed mixed emotions. Confident on the outside, I still felt like a little girl attending her first day of school. I was headed for Ithaca, where I'd not only be speaking at Cornell University but before Emma and the fall-session dramatics class she'd be bringing with her. G.E., caught ill just before departure, decided to stay home. Instead I took my team of assistants and stenographers, should those attending wish to have charts created. Always thinking ahead.

My head was congested with thought and mucous while my muscles and joints ached with pain. Yet my stomach was less anxious than usual regarding the anticipation of seeing Emma after I'd, once and for all, surmised that our union was not meant to be. She'd taken the news of G.E.'s disapproval of her joining me on tour with more aplomb than I'd expected. I suppose she, like I, had simply become used to it and ceased worrying that outside forces had any impact on our feelings for one another as friends.

Having not one second before the speaking engagement to gather myself, I delivered my usual dialogue, gave a few demonstrations, answered a few questions when it was over and met with a few people in the back of the room. As anticipated, one of them was Emma. She reached out and hugged me deeply. Time may have made us appear differently to one another, but our embraces never changed. Forever warm, familiar and most sincere. "They adored you, Evangeline. I'd told them all about you," she whispered, pride in her eyes.

"Any Leos among the group?" I teased.

"Most certainly. But, to be fair, I'd told them it's not a prerequisite to becoming an actor."

At the moment I realized I was too tired to speak, Emma did it all for me. I'd now known her for so long that words between us had become utterly unnecessary. Masking my fatigue became tiring in itself. In the midst of her colleagues at co-educational-upon-its-inception-Cornell on its Red Maple-lined pathways made of brick, Emma took me by the hand, leading me to her on-campus home. While traveling, we encountered pencil-thin Professor So-and-so and dark-complected Dean What's-his-name and all the while my hand never left Emma's. I was with her, she with me and Emma seemed more than proud to show me off and what we meant to each other. Not a single Who's-its flinched at being among two mature women who cared deeply for one another. Within a matter of a few more worn-out steps, Emma and I were by ourselves.

Inside Emma's cozy pure white cottage with fluffy cotton pillows and knickknacks in every room, the fire was already roaring and I knew my hotel room nearby would not be my final destination as previously planned. In the warmth of the parlor Emma sat me down, laid a multi-colored woolen saddle blanket over me and brought three diversely fragranced candles; vanilla, orange blossom and pumpkin contained in antique teacups, inside the bathroom. There, she drew me a hot bath full of spices, the robust scent of eucalyptus quickly made its way to the depths of my nasal passages. During this process we shared no more than a handful of "ahhhs" and "oh, myyys."

Too cognizant of my caffeine aversion, Emma was brewing Postum with cinnamon, not hot tea, in her cubbyhole of a kitchen. The smells themselves were nearly enough to cure all that ails. In the bathroom, now as warm as the sitting room, Emma began removing all my garments one by one, neatly and as precisely as a Virgo, folding and stacking them on the knotty pine dresser. Not once did she snicker as she noticed the same shabby taupe pantaloons I've been wearing since the twenties. Without a stitch on, she took me by the hand and helped me into the bath. Emma directed me into comfort by mouthing, "Inhale."

"Exhale," I responded.

Pulling up a stool to be near me, Emma began to massage my sore feet. She even gave my bunions a harmless kiss. For a second or two, the pain that was making my life miserable had disappeared. This time together made it known that my relationship with Emma was not only natural, it was beyond natural.

"Soon you'll be living your own destiny once more, as it was meant to be. No longer controlled by anyone else and their wishes. I can just feel it."

A charge of adrenaline surged through my veins upon hearing Emma's words. In that moment in time, my body and soul felt invigorated imagining her prophecy turning true.

# Sun @ 2° SCORPIO 36'20 (1931)

"Are you back to your old self?"

"What do you mean by that?"

"Your virus. The reason you couldn't join me upstate."

"Oh, right," G.E. replied, right before he coughed. "I'm getting better."

Staring at G.E. upon my return home was like meeting a stranger. With his suit disheveled, his shirt red-tinged at the collar and his afterglow Tabu scented, G.E. plopped down a laundry list of things I must do, one of which included selecting a wardrobe for a photographic session upcoming. After rummaging through my clothes closet, scowling and cursing under his stale breath, G.E. immediately scheduled a shopping spree within a few hours from present.

"This is what's most pressing. New publicity photos. Make sure you get plenty of sleep before next Tuesday. Looking haggard is no longer in vogue."

"You needn't join me while shopping. I'll bring along one or two girls from the offi—"

"Negative. It's all set. Be ready at two."

Not to a Fifth Avenue gown designer but to the 3-way intersection of Sixth Avenue, Broadway and Thirty-fourth Street at Herald Square G.E. and I walked. Chestnuts were roasting on open fires all around us, but it was I whose eyes burned as we passed through the smoke of their scorched shells. An autumn chill was in the air and long, woolen knit winter scarves were making themselves known around the necks of New Yorkers everywhere. A time of year when horses snort frost. Even G.E. made sure I was bundled up, loosely, from scalp to foot. He insisted I wear an oversized tarp-like black shawl with frayed fringe—more appropriate for funerals—to mask my "midfield." When we stepped into Gimbels Brothers, my mouth watered at all things savory displayed in the entrance. Stacks and stacks of boxed chocolates. All my favorites: Fall nonpareils, Crunchies, Freddos, Snickers. Jars of jams, jellies, preserves and marmalades. Nuts. Even cartons of Butternut Mountain Farm pure maple sugar candy from Vermont.

"I'd love some salt water taffy."

G.E. scrunched up his face and pointed to my waistline. Next he stepped onto a wad of gum but didn't take the time to scrape it off. On the way to the garment section for women, he and I were approached by an attractive and exuberant redhead sales associate presumably in her twenties, eager to capture her commission. G.E.'s scrunch disappeared the minute he caught a glimpse of her "end zone."

"What might you like to see today, ma'am?"

"Something strong, business-like, somewhat conservative but stylish, suitable for a mature woman."

"My goodness, you certainly know what you're after, sir," the woman said with batted eyes.

Feeding off of the woman's moxie, G.E. said, "You're right about that, miss. It is miss, isn't it?"

It's as if I was invisible. Such a brazen display of disrespect in my very presence. In the back of my mind I'd heard Sabine's voice and all of her disparaging comments regarding G.E., minus the Bavarian accent of course.

"As a matter of fact it is. Your son surely knows good taste, ma'am."

"My husband, not my son."

Like a game of table tennis the young woman's befuddled head bobbed from side to side while examining G.E. and I together as a twosome.

"I beg your pardon, Mrs...."

Folded arms upon arrival, unfolded in the young woman's presence, G.E. said, "Mrs. George Edwin Jordan Jr. of Carnegie Hall, Miss," G.E. announced as if he was drawing up directions on a Rand-McNally road atlas.

"I'd personally like to see something with colors and frills. Tastes change over periods, G.E. It's about time I develop my own anew."

"Fine. Frills, bows, fringe...whatever you like."

"Please allow me to step to the back, ma'am, and I'll bring you a wide variety from which to choose."

As the girl in the tight garment began to saunter away from us, she peered at G.E. from over her shoulder. It was no mystery that he'd just been issued the invitation he'd been awaiting from one of his vixens-du jour.

"I'll go with you. Have to make sure it's...suitable. I'll be right back, dear."

G.E. and the sales clerk giggled in unison as they looked me over from head to toe while taking matching strides, approaching me upon their return. G.E. was carrying nothing but black dresses and suits, while the girl was toting the same exact styles in dark gray. "Try this one on first, Mrs. Jordan. I'll show you the way to the fitting room."

I took the dark gray suit with no frills, no color, no imagination from the young woman and said, "I'll find it on my own. Thank you."

"Of course, that's fine. I'll be waiting for you right outside the booth should you need me."

After placing the suit on the hook inside the dressing closet I began to disrobe. Somehow my breath became short being so boxed in. Claustrophobic, with nowhere to go. Now, only in my slip and stockings standing on faded, tattered flesh-colored carpet with no design, I saw my reflection in the looking glass, and was so startled that I couldn't move. Not a solitary inch. My eyes couldn't comprehend the sight; me, now thirty-two years older than when I came to Manhattan in 1899. Tired, wrinkled, sad, trying on clothing I didn't like, selected by a man I liked even less. Although my professional life had excelled far beyond expectation, my personal life was in shambles.

As I bent over to pick up the gray suit that had fallen to the floor, the golden Chai medallion on the chain Sabine had given me popped out from inside my slip. As I touched its smoothness I was reminded of time, timing and J.P.'s eternal message about taking action. I tucked the pendant back in with fondness emanating from my heart. Instead of retrieving the gray garment and placing it on its hook, I left it laying on the floor, crumpled, and chose to look into the mirror once more. There I was; me and my medallion. An object that represents life, placed around my neck by a woman who told me she'd always be near whenever I felt weak, frightened.

As I opened the door to the dressing booth the young sales associate, staring at her own reflection in a mirror nearby, not addressing me while speaking, asked, "Mrs. Jordan, did you see anything you liked?"

"Yes I did, as a matter of fact. At the House of Chanel on Park Avenue. Just the other day."

Wearing exactly what I came in with, I left the woman without saying "goodbye." I didn't bother to find G.E. Instead, I exited the entrance of Gimbels Brothers on Herald Square and I never looked back.

☉ ☽ ✴

On New Year's Eve of 1931, wearing a stunning cobalt blue Chanel Suit, two-tone pumps, a string of pearls around my neck and carrying a leather handbag, I made a grander-than-normal entrance at my Carnegie Hall workplace. Many of us in the office prepared to celebrate the many victories we had experienced throughout the year. Success and worldwide acclaim had been mine for decades now. My professional career had advanced in gargantuan proportions due to my ever-popular radio show, while a multitude of lectures were lined up in the year to come.

First things first. Only a handful of my employees had come in this holiday eve, but it was Sabine's being there that held my attention. From the moment she entered the studio, waltzing about with effervescent grace, her essence was radiant, face beaming from ear to ear. "It pleases me to see you like this, Sabine," I said.

"I am the one that is pleased, Ma'am."

"You've got to let me in on it."

"Karma, Miss. It has finally come around."

She prepared me some Postum with a sprig of fresh mint doting inside, and once I was relaxing at my desk, handed me the morning's *New York Times* and left. As I perused ads for new merchandise, I reflected on the joy I used to have for antiquing, discovering a discarded rarity under some discolored, sun-bleached everyday tarpaulin. Lifting it up to find a hand-knotted Turkish rug in perfect condition, a Perseus constellation map or even a George III sterling silver snuff box was for me like winning the Irish Sweepstakes. How I'd longed to do this again. Less time on the road and in the broadcast studio, more time discovering treasures cast aside.

While contemplating all the news that's fit to print, my eyes found themselves paralyzed once they had detected the following.

☉　☽　✭

---

### The New York Times
December 31, 1931

#### SEERESS' HUSBAND SUED.

#### G.E. Jordan Jr. Accused of Alienating Affections of Dancer's Wife.

George Edwin Jordan Jr., husband of Evangeline Adams, the astrologist, is the defendant in a $250,000 suit brought by Leo Chenko, the dancer, charging alienation of his wife's affections. Mr. Jordan's attorneys, Leslie & Martin of 72 Wall Street, made a motion in Supreme Court yesterday for a bill of particulars and submitted with it a copy of the complaint. David V. Cahill of 25 Broadway, Chenko's counsel, filed a memorandum in opposition. The decision is not expected for a few days.

Mr. Jordan, who is 51 years old and about twenty years older than Mrs. Chenko, was married to Miss Adams in April, 1923. Miss Adams said at the time that Mr. Jordan's horoscope proved they would be ideally matched. He has been serving as Miss Adams's business manager.

---

In his application for the bill of particulars, Edgar A. Martin, Mr. Jordan's counsel, asked that the complainant be ordered to file the circumstances of the defendant's alleged "wooing" of Mrs. Chenko. Mr. Martin denied last night that his client had more than a slight acquaintance with Mrs. Chenko.

☉ ☽ ★

After all these years of having been forced to keep my private life private, because of the fears G.E.'s instilled in me, now it was G.E. himself that had brought humiliation and shame to our lives. Anyone who knew him would never doubt the truth behind this lawsuit. Of course he was guilty. The evidence speaks for itself. Night after night in those speakeasies and clubs. A bevy of women surrounding him at all times, several of whom were employed by me.

No way in hell would he be able to access $250,000 of *my* money though, I assured myself.

His infidelities hadn't give me a colossal cause for concern, but the fact that he'd been caught so publicly. At my expense. For those who'd had qualms about our marriage being legitimate and above board, now they'd be fully convinced. The proof was now in print.

How could I face anyone after this? This dancer's wife twenty years younger than G.E.—truthfully forty-one not fifty-one— makes her approximately thirty to forty years younger than me. It didn't take a genius to see through the shameless fraud we've been perpetuating.

'Mr. Jordan's horoscope proved they'd be ideally matched.' It's too bad I never had the courage to clarify, make that statement more truthful. My declaration, now nearly decades old, should have read, 'Mr. Jordan's horoscope proved they'd be ideally matched *in business.*'

Now it all makes sense, I thought. Sabine's euphoria. From her perspective, Karma surely had come back around. He who had perpetually pointed fingers was now having it done unto himself. I wondered how Emma would see this. As soon as she entered my mind, the telephone rang inside my office. I didn't need to wonder who it was; I knew.

Nervousness invaded my "hello" at first. But when I heard hers, it receded.

"Emma. How delightful to hear from you," I said with a mountain of anxiety leaving my breath.

As calm as a cucumber, and with no audible inhales or exhales coming from the other end, my dearest said, "You must be so relieved. Finall—"

"Relieved? Emma, my husband is facing—"

"Dear, you have no husband. You never did. If people marry in the eyes of God, God sees only the truth. You and G.E. were never husband and wife. Just like my marriage to Alfred. Not one genuine vow exchanged."

"Emma. I'm devastated. What will people think?" Inhaling courage next came to my nervous system as an involuntary response. No need to question fate, or what destiny had in store, any further.

"Evangeline, you're now in your sixties. Why should you care what people think?"

"Fifties."

"The truth always comes out, dearest. I know your true age…I always have, and I've never wasted a second caring."

"Because you're still older than me."

"I don't care. I'm an actress and I don't care. I'm a wife and I don't care. I'm a lesbian and I don't care."

"Emma, you're saying all the right things."

☉  ☽  ★

The first weekend of the New Year, Emma and I made our way up to Boston while the sun was shining on a brisk day. Snow was glistening on the ground as usual and no one seemed to make note of that disgraceful article in the newspaper. All my worry for nothing.

Taking the most careful of baby steps on the icy streets we roamed in and out of three Back Bay estates and a host of high-quality shops that front the Public Garden carrying the finest antique cameos, collectibles and curios. The top finds of the day included a Victorian iridescent solitaire Akoya pearl eight-prong set 14k gold ring for Emma, size 6. A Victorian carved shell cameo rose 10k gold ring for me, size 7. Spending time together, without fear or worry, was the treasure for which I'd been searching. A time when our souls were finally at ease, in harmony, effortlessly together.

"Oh, look at that," Emma said, as we approached our final stop, a bohemian-style antique store on Newbury Street about to close. "You remember?"

Glancing over at a gem through the display case much less-cared for than mine at home, I said, "A Tiffany lamp. Now an antique." Full of cracks, scratches and faded colors. Old age hasn't been kind to this poor girl.

Yes, I recalled fondly the first time Emma and I had met...over one of those brand new Tiffany lamps nearly thirty years earlier. A time when my destiny had been placed squarely before my face, yet I'd done nothing about it. All my life I had deciphered the most favorable time for everything. All the advice I had given women as to when they should conceive to have the most favorable offspring. Only now had I learned that "favorable" was a meaningless word unless action, the desire to learn something along the way, was attached to it.

Now, closing in on what I'd foreseen as my final birthday back in Manhattan, I came up with the perfect celebratory gift for myself, one I'd longed to possess, but never had the courage to procure. The time had come for me to put fear and shame on the back burner. On February 08, 1932, 267 days 'til November, I asked Emma to be with me as a couple united in something as close to matrimony as either of us had known. She graciously and unconditionally accepted my proposal. The ease with which Emma consented made my heart full, my soul sing. Our gentle embrace that followed somehow managed to make a momentary imprint on my back, mine on Emma's. I felt relief in knowing that there was still room for me in her life, a heart that had patiently awaited mine for so many years.

With anxiety surrounding me, I'd spent the entire day before the ceremony writing, re-writing, editing and revising the vows I'd wished to share. Emma, the consummate literary composer, I'm sure, completed hers within the blink of an eye. Wanting or needing no one else around, Emma and I chose to have our private moment at my, our home, in Yorktown Heights right on Saint Valentine's Day. Before we began, an exceptionally light and delicate snowfall came upon us.

As I watched Emma shovel the few inches that had fallen on the front porch, I was amazed by her strength. For such a gentle soul she looked like a conqueror, a superwoman at that very moment, forever valiant, ready to do battle without ever lifting a fist. As Emma carried in a weighty armful of cut and split aspen firewood I watched her closely through the window after I'd rubbed off the condensation. I saw her trip on the ice. For a second or two the logs she was carrying jostled in her arms but never fell. This is how I'd always seen Emma. Forever secure in her footing, never clumsy.

Inside, all remained unembellished; a lit green Coleman gas lantern and its flickering yellow flame, our observance's only ornamentation. The scent of jasmine and rose filled my, our humble parlor. To be most accurate, it emanated from a perfume we both were wearing, Joy. Symbolic, one that was created specifically as a reaction to the '29 Wall Street crash. It was time to announce to Emma that I'd never again let misgivings, nor intimidation, overshadow the love I felt for her. Looking into Emma's eyes made me reflect on my days gone by, opportunities that had come and passed, success stories, fame, fortune and the pot of gold at the end of the rainbow.

"My beloved Emma, on this afternoon I find myself longing for no other. As you had told me nearly thirty years earlier, I am your soul mate and you are mine. The happiest moments of my life have been those spent with you. From this day forward I promise to honor my commitment to you and the love we share before all else. Life has blessed me with many riches, but none as dear as you."

Although I was quivering a bit during my recitation, Emma was still, absorbing every utterance of mine with what appeared to be nothing but sincerity and respect. I slipped the vintage gold ring I had bought onto Emma's finger. I let my hand linger on hers for a full minute, cementing the bond we were creating.

"Thank you, my sweetheart. The words you chose couldn't have been more perfect."

What surprised me next was the fact that Emma followed no script; she allowed nature to take over while allowing improvisation to guide her way through. I should have known.

"My dearest Evangeline, a writer speaks by way of prose on a page. An actress emotes via dialogue carefully scripted for her. Today, you are before me as my mirror image of what God has intended for us both. You are the half to my whole, I am the half to yours. Nothing more needs to be said. If you don't know and accept by now how much I love you, stand by you, support you, care for you and am here for you…you perhaps never will. I am your very own always, just as I have been the many days that preceded this very one. I will have and take no other, my beloved. I am yours 'til death parts us."

# Sun @ 18° AQUARIUS 1'14 (1932)

"*I*t feels strange being here, spending the night. Although it's really the second time, seems more like a first," Emma told me while being naked under the covers. Punching her fist into the middle of her European white goose down pillow made me laugh. The perfect dent for Emma's well-balanced head was now formed. In Emma, I saw a sixty-something schoolgirl reincarnated.

"Long overdue, my dear," I said back, cherishing this sight, longing to hold the image of my dearly loved in my mind, the way a photoscopic camera captures memories on film.

From this point on, my home in Manhattan became ours. Living together, unhindered, felt different from the time we'd spent in Westchester. This was where our lives were headquartered, the center of everything. Without worry of discovery, Emma and I strolled through Central Park and dined at New York's finest restaurants. Sometimes as far north as Turtle Pond just beyond The Lake, then a nice meal at the Parisian-themed Café Boulud on East 76th, while enjoying each other's company more than I thought was possible.

G.E., and his collection of occasional nighttime companions, still resided above Emma and me, and more than ever before, my marital relationship was never more clearly defined as 'business as usual.' With an abbreviated schedule of self-promotion, I had more time to myself, to Emma, but I began to tire of nearly everything I'd been doing since the end of the previous century. I'd accomplished all. G.E. and I were still contractually obliged by Dodd, Mead & Co. to complete a new book as co-authors, something novel. Titled *The Evangeline Adams Guide for 1933*. Occultist Manly Hall, who wrote *The Secret Teachings of All Ages*, would be penning its introduction.

For the most part, G.E. and I composed our respective chapters independently from one another. I'd deliver my pages to him by way of a member of my staff; he'd review them and add and/or delete what he felt appropriate. That seemed to be working out just fine. Running into him in the elevator happened rarely, but when it did, we remained cordial by saying "Bonjour," shortly before bidding each other "Adieu." On one spring afternoon as I was about to enter the elevator at the ground level, I found G.E. exiting with an attractive, younger, most likely peroxide-enhanced blonde. Times hadn't changed.

Expecting anxiety to take over our three-way encounter was my mistake. G.E.'s broad grin, and the serene demeanor he exuded when seeing me, told me all was well. The blonde with a black mole painted on her left cheek, who was preoccupied with the strap adjustment of her brassiere and seemingly incapable of multitasking, was unable to provide a smile.

"You go along, Miss...Miss..." GE said, uncomfortably attempting to straighten his too wide Herringbone navy solid tie.

"Faver. Ruthie."

"Yes, Miss Faver, of course. You go ahead and I'll meet you

at…our appointment."

"What appointment?"

"Mr. Jordan would like some time to speak with me alone…Ruthie," I said, not taking the time to doddle.

"Got'cha," the busty blonde uttered while cracking her pink Dubble Bubble immediately thereafter, without smearing her perfectly painted-on cherry red lipstick smirk.

As we watched Miss Faver saunter away from us, along with her tumultuous hip action that resembled a rumba, G.E. said, "It's not what you think, Evangeline."

I shook my head, because I initially felt a response unnecessary. Out of courtesy, out of loyalty, out of gratitude, I said, "I don't care. Do what you will, G.E. I want you to be happy."

G.E. looked over to me as if I were a surrendering soldier. No animosity whatever emanated from my being, my soul to his; no ill will, nothing until he wished me the very same. There we stood on the red carpet inside the Carnegie Hall lobby, as if we were long-time Swiss citizens, reveling in the country's state of armed neutrality.

G.E. was the man with whom I'd spent the most time in my life. I felt nothing but validation when he next asked me, apparently devoid of agenda or manipulation, "Are you happy? Having Emma around?"

"I couldn't be more so. I've longed for these days forever."

Utterly and completely out of character, G.E. outstretched his arms to their limits and embraced me like a long lost old friend unseen since childhood. His gesture comforted me to my core. Even made my toes tingle after I let go.

Still holding onto both my hands, G.E. said, "Emma's a fine person. You deserve such a reward, Evangeline. I can't imagine you not having earned this time in your life and then some. Your passion knows no bounds. I'm glad you now have another that's yours to keep. Live long and happy with her, my dear. And be afraid of no one."

$$\odot \quad \text{☽} \quad \text{✶}$$

As I continued my work on the manuscript inside my office into the early hours of the morning, I had the fictitious sensation that I'd had a blanket wrapped snugly around me, knowing that Emma was in the next room. It was a warmth I'd never known very often before and I wished I'd welcomed it much earlier.

"Emma, do you regret that it took this long?" I'd asked her the night before.

Softly, patiently, and taking time to ponder before getting the words out, Emma appeared to fill her diaphragm with air, then said to me, "Not for one second. Some people never know their purpose. Ours was, at some point in time, whatever point that may be, to be together. We belonged joined from the start, but because of fear, we never had the courage. Now, our destinies are our own. Not for a second."

"Better late than never, I surmise."

"I predict that we'll have many memorable years together...living life to the fullest," Madam Emma had said with an exaggerated Eastern European accent, hands hovering above an imaginary crystal ball.

It must have been my Pisces-rising that wanted to perpetuate a secret I had never shared with Emma. Two to three times past, unbeknownst to her I'd cast charts to determine my own death, resulting in my endless preoccupation with the findings, not to mention the fostering of numerous neuroses. Final predictions; something I had routinely summoned for so many others. Just as life begins, it ends when the stars say it does. Not recalling explicitly my two, make it three prognostications past, I always remembered having seen fall, autumn. Pictures in my head of orange and yellow leaves about to drop to the ground and wither. Mid-fall to be most precise. Mid-fall of the current year, 1932. The tenth of November, close to dusk.

While reflecting on my own mortality, I stopped my composition of the *Guide for 1933* at mid-paragraph. Setting my tablet and fountain pen onto my new African mahogany desk from the Ivory Coast, I next stepped into my parlor. There was Emma, reclined on the divan before the crackling fire, a crystal decanter of London Cream Canadian sherry on the table in front of her, her favorite lilac-scented candles casting their glow on all things gentle. Her being, as innocent and pure as when we'd first met decades earlier. What a sight. I couldn't see her face, so I tip-toed further into the room to find my beloved asleep on her cherished red satin, heart-shaped pillow. Even her snoring sounded delicate to my ears.

A wise angel was she. I allowed her slumber to be uninterrupted. I was only looking for a peek, nothing more than that. Emma's nap gave me the perfect and private opportunity to indulge in my own future for, now, a fourth time.

Opening up my ephemeris and decoding its data thereafter for what must be an incalculable amount of times by this point, there it was glaring right at me. So precisely. Even making sure that all transit aspects, when quantifying, have an orb of no more, no less than exactly $1°$, there it was. The day, date and time of my death remained the same as it has always been. Four weeks from present. Thursday, November 10, 1932, at 4:20PM. Three days prior to the full moon. Fatality during a fall afternoon, based on the position of Saturn in my Solar Equilibrium chart. My most recent results made it much clearer as to how exactly I'd depart. Strong indications that it would be a malady of the heart that would lead to my demise, and that the duration of my suffering would be minimal.

This re-discovery led me not to sadness; instead it made me

more aware of how I'd like to spend my final days. Spreading news of astrology to groups interested in the stars had always been my deepest passion. On my calendar for that time, early to mid-November, I was scheduled to speak on a 12-city tour, something G.E. had organized long ago. I shan't disappoint him, I thought. Without G.E. in my life, my career, my fame and fortune would be a fraction of what it had become, grander than anything I could have ever predicted or imagined.

Sitting at my lengthy desk, with no words coming from my pen, I laughed out loud. The picture of blond-Ruthie Faver adjusting her bra strap and munching on her bubble gum outside the elevator entered my mind, until the image was replaced by G.E. At my desk alone, now at sixty-four years of age, it was a most powerful sensation that came next. *The* most powerful. My mother's face flashed before me without warning. She was smiling at me lovingly and I smiled back without effort. It took a while for it to sink in, that profound chance meeting with G.E. at that elevator, the instant I chose to forgive. That was the moment I got my power back, and the destiny I had lost became mine once more.

G.E. and I both used each other equally for whatever reasons. No one person to blame more than the other. At sixty-four, only I am responsible for the decisions I make, the control I give away, the fears that had once immobilized me. At 64, rather late in life, I was reminded once and for all that I am my own woman. Independent. Strong.

Following my attempt to write a few more paragraphs of my newest book, I chose to instead prepare myself for bed. Still feeling the exhilaration of the peace I made with my chart, I let go of all preoccupation with thoughts of my remaining days. On that night I slept well, more than well, a sleep I'd been longing decades for. A wide variety of pleasant, comforting dreams about conclusiveness, having done it all had occupied my mind, and when I awoke the very next morning, I seemed to accept, not revoke, all the events that were before me. Still, overwhelmingly in sync, G.E. had entered my office to discuss what I'd been pondering only a few hours prior.

"You look so serene, happy, Evangeline."

Leaning in to catch a whiff of his newest manly cologne that smelled of musk, I said to my husband, "Thank you, my dear. I feel it. You as well."

"You know? Don't you?"

"Why you're here. Yes, I think I do."

"Practical matters."

"My Last Will & Testament."

G.E. seemed astonished at the accuracy of my presumption. For the next half hour G.E. and I discussed, in the most orderly manner, details of my imminent aftermath. He was most concerned with subsidiary rights transfers, permissions, trademarks, royalties, out of print provisions and copyright ownership. All having to do with the area of my life I found least important, book publishing. I not only agreed to everything he'd proposed to me, but I even offered more. G.E., after all, whether he be my husband legitimate or invalid, had multiplied my potential nearly single-handedly. Emma was never one to be concerned with overt wealth or riches. She'd be taken care of well enough.

Before parting, G.E. and I verbally shared many of the success stories we'd created together. Told with gusto and delight, they seemed endless. Like the time he penned a letter to Congress suggesting there be a "National Horoscope Day," thereafter receiving a serious reply. Our union was one I took pride in no matter what, one that needn't ever be judged by anyone. G.E. and I embraced genuinely as we set plans to meet with an estate attorney, only days away. He told me he'd ask Sabine to compile the paperwork once it had been received in my office. Taking forever to put his gloves on, G.E. left my company slowly with a grin on his face and camouflaged tears in his eyes.

A mere few minutes went by before my office doors opened abruptly.

Panic-stricken, blubbering and out of breath. Sabine was beside herself. She remained at a distance after having laid eyes on me.

"What on earth is wrong?"

"Miss…you are unwell? Mr. Jordan asks me to make…the arrangements. After you're gone."

With the onset of muffled sniffling and sniveling, Sabine's accent became thicker and thicker until I'd asked her to take a seat in my office. "It is the truth, Miss?"

"You and I'd talked about this before, Sabine. November tenth. It's approaching soon." The combination of saying this date again, out loud, and hearing Sabine now calling me "Mizz" for the millionth time, I, myself, began to get misty.

"I know. But, Miss. You must—"

Although I'd promised myself I'd not cry, Sabine broke me down. For someone who'd been there by my side as my right-hand woman all those years, Sabine had emerged as so much more than just my secretary. Recognizing her as one of the most passionate people I'd ever met, I had to say, "Sabine, you made me *like* Scorpios."

She laughed. "We are sex maniacs, but nicht so schlecht."

"Ja wohl."

Together we snickered. When my mind finished flashing back to the many merry moments I'd shared with Sabine, I told her as honestly as a Scorpio would, "You know I will miss you more than anyone."

Mouth open wide, she paused a second or two before saying, "Oh, but, Ma'am. Miss Emma…Mr. Jordan."

I could never have been more sincere. My words matched my

heartbeats when I said, "No, you. From you alone I learned the power of living life honestly at all costs. Never allowing yourself to be controlled by a man. I wish I'd been more like you years and years ago. You've never cared what anyone else thought about you or what you do. I marveled at this."

"Marbled?"

My head shook with delight as I once again attempted to play English-language translator. My speech to Sabine was sincere. My world would have stopped long ago had Sabine not been in it. Rescuing me daily from ireful zealots who call me a "sinner." Teaching me to accept human touch without guilt. Making sure I never take myself too seriously. Beautifying me when I didn't feel worthy. During the course of my life, the courage I'd learned, is what I was most proud of. Not just from Sabine, not only Emma, most certainly not G.E., J.P., Aleister or even Mrs. Brush. Not from the nearly one million charts I'd read of the clients to whom they'd belonged. I learned courage from each and every one of them combined. It took all these people to make me aware of the benefits of taking risks, living life fully, and forging new adventures while on the road to filling my soul with a purpose that belongs to no other. From all these factors combined, I, by myself, recognized my own, true strength.

When November tenth comes, I thought, I will have known that I'd put fear in its place. Emma'd taught me faith, and her life would go on courageously. I hoped that her son would know her as the pioneer she truly was. It was predicted long ago that I'd bear no offspring, yet my children were those who've put their trust in me. Those who scoffed at my practice of astrology had only made me even more obstinate, infinitely tougher and more determined.

"I've decided to cancel the speaking tour."

Inching her way closer to me at the dining table in one of our lavender Chinese Chippendale-style bamboo chairs, Emma asked, "All twelve cities? What did G.E. have to say about that?"

"I haven't told him yet. My instinct tells me that he'll understand. Copyright transfers and royalty payments are all he talks about."

"Business as usual. You know, Evangeline, I'm still not buying into it," Emma said while polishing her half of what had become *our* Tiffany lamp, the same one that brought us together at the Boston Museum during that premature summer of 1901. "November Tenth? Nope."

"I realize that, Emma. Look at it this way; I cancelled the tour so I could be with you."

"Great. Most appreciated," Emma said, seeming to do nothing more than humoring the requests of an old lady. "You missed a spot."

I smirked at her stubbornness. Emma smirked right back, presumably at mine.

"She's still beautiful. Isn't she?" I asked, rubbing my half of the lamp, which was resting on both our laps as we were seated facing each other, kneecaps touching.

"Forever lovely, sweetheart. Mmmm, the duckling smells divine. I'm going to check on it." Emma pushed the lamp onto the entirety of my lap, leaving me to complete the dirty work alone as she stepped into the kitchen. As she was busy clanging pots and pans together in the distance, I rubbed off the last speck of cleansing compound. Our beloved lamp now looked as good as new. Eager to show Emma the end result of our joint efforts, I took the lamp by both hands and carried it over to the kitchen for final inspection.

"Emma, come see," I yelled out through the closed kitchen

door.

Just as Emma swung it open in front of me, our faces met and my breath stopped. My back, arms, neck, chest felt instant, excruciating pain.

"Ev—" The look of fright on Emma's face nearly matched my own. I knew I'd soon become incapacitated. As my breath came and went, I felt I'd be a goner in next to no time. Before she could grab me, the Tiffany lamp I'd been holding onto with my weak hands fell to the floor, breaking apart into an immeasurable number of red, violet, amber, green, blue, brown and black fragments, all landing then dispersing at my feet.

I was able to mutter, "Help me," in between gasps for air. Just like the lamp, I fell to the floor. Emma clutched me to her side. "I need help." For the first time ever while looking up at Emma, she looked confused, seemingly unable to facilitate action, paralyzed. My left hand was able to point to the direction of the telephone. Pain prevented me from passing out.

Emma nodded. She set me gently on the floor and ran over to the phone. I could hear the dialing. The rest, a blur.

⊙  ☽  ✳

Close to eight o'clock that night, entering into the second week of November, I'd suffered a heart attack. The pain I felt was unbearable. Although I was mostly immobilized, my brain continued to function fully. Even with tears in her eyes, Emma did her best to show courage. She was wearing the dress I liked best. A chiffon print with pastel colors and bolero sleeves, her favorite as well, makes her look like she's still blossoming. Inside my hospital room, my mind still in a daze, Emma was there next to me, attempting to renew our conversation where we'd left off prior to dinner. This time with levity included.

"You see? You were *dead* wrong. Not November Tenth. Yesterday was the *Seventh.*"

I looked at her with love coming from my eyes and offered a non-verbal chuckle.

"That cancels out everything. All's well. And I didn't even need my crystal ball to prove it."

Emma took my hand, like she'd done so many times past. No more tears, no visible signs of sadness. Her disbelief regarding my departure didn't surprise me. "Living life in the moment is what God intended," she'd always said to me, solemnly, as if there's no other choice. I wanted so much to agree.

"I'm terrified."

No immediate reply. Still holding my hand, Emma did her very best to persuade me to abandon the stars, what I felt they had in store, by instead telling me stories. She regaled me with colorful tales about our trips to the New Hampshire countryside—the vows we'd recently exchanged in Yorktown Heights and the starry-eyed honeymoon we were planning in Venice—each one leading me into recuperative slumber. For the next two days of my convalescence, now back at home, through Emma's words I reflected on a remarkable life lived, lessons learned, cherishing my many accomplishments and wondrous moments, none more so than those spent with her by my side. My health started to show several signs of improvement. Color returned to my complexion, my pain subsided a bit and I could wiggle my toes without fear of them falling off. I felt invigorated.

Awakening to the early morning of the tenth in the solitude of my studio apartment, the sun outside my window was shining, and a nurse I'd never seen before, carrying in my breakfast, was especially cheery. Cheeks noticeably ruddy in blotches, skin bumpy, as if afflicted with rosacea. Her manner was comforting and the way she gazed at the sheen of her manicured fingernails waving in the sunlight made her, a stranger, appear so recognizable to me. As she was about to leave after having offered no introduction, I couldn't believe my eyes. Pointing to a sight atop the steel medical side table adjacent to my bed, took me back a few years. I asked, "Where did those come from?"

"Now, aren't those stunning. I've never seen any like them." The nurse picked up the vase containing black lilies and brought them to me for a closer look, along with what, at first glance, I thought was the morning newspaper. Instead, it was an old, rather tattered copy of *The New York Times*, opened to the financial section, with a familiar-looking and oft-repeated quote in bold print, circled in red ink, "Millionaires don't use astrology, billionaires do."

I could have easily asked myself, "Who brought these? Emma? Sabine? Why? Who was that nurse? How did the person know?" and more. But I simply smiled. I smiled at the fond memory of a man who, truthfully, more than anyone else, helped me achieve my lifelong dream of becoming the world's most famous and successful astrologist. I smiled recalling the closet fear we'd once shared, the one I swore never to divulge. Rather that wasting precious moments trying to figure out how and why these mementoes of J.P. Morgan had appeared before me, I elected to instead wonder.

No longer focused on how much time's left, I chose to savor life in the now. In a split second, while lying there in my bed, I chose to favor mystery over certainty. Perhaps some things are left best unknown.

Although it's my sincere wish to live on for many years to come, only time will tell if my wish is granted.

☉ ☽ ✯

# The New York Times
### November 11, 1932

# EVANGELINE ADAMS, ASTROLOGER, DEAD

### Her Radio Broadcasts Brought an Average of 4,000 Letters Daily, Many for Horoscopes.

## WAS ILL ONLY THREE DAYS

### Descendant of President Adams— Predicted Windsor Hotel Fire and Death of Edward VII.

Evangeline Adams, the astrologer, who claimed to have predicted the Windsor Hotel fire and the death of King Edward VII, died yesterday of heart disease in her studio apartment in Carnegie Hall at the age of 59. She had been seriously ill only three days. Her husband, George E. Jordan Jr., a former pupil to whom she was married in 1923, was at her bedside.

The death of Miss Adams will be a shock to thousands of radio listeners. She began to broadcast on April 23, 1930, and three months later she announced that she had received 150,000 requests for horoscopes. In January, 1931, when she was talking three times a week over the WABC network her representative stated that she received an average of 4,000 letters a day, almost entirely requests for horoscopes, the majority written on a side of the carton that had contained a certain brand of toothpaste.

Miss Adams was a descendant of President John Quincy Adams. She studied astrology under

J. Hebner Smith, later doing research in "Eastern lore." She was the originator of the Adams Philosophy, "a compound of truths of all truths, applied in the light of an intelligent optimism to the requirements of Western everyday life."

She published her autobiography in 1926, "Astrology, Your Place in the Sun" in 1928.

In "The Bowl of Heaven," the title she gave her autobiography, Miss Adams wrote that every sort of person from the highest to the lowest, in every form of occupation, had come to her for consultation. Among her clients she listed the late J.P. Morgan, Seymour Cromwell, Mrs. Oliver Harriman, Mary Garden and John Burroughs. With the generality of her clientele the chief interests, in a class by themselves for popularity, were love and money. Before the depression, love ranked first. Since January, 1930, money had taken first place.

# Acknowledgments

*T*o Caitlin Alexander, my exceedingly proficient editor, who remained sensitive and supportive while subtly curbing my urge to go slapstick. What a treat to work with someone so professional . . .

John Barker, book cover designer extraordinaire, for calling me "high maintenance" only on the inside so I wouldn't hear. The only thing that surpasses your talent is your infinite patience . . .

Sue Adams, who in the fall of 2012—when I thought I had long finished with writing—asked, "So, what's your next book about?" Thanks for your love, support and continued belief . . .

Jessica (Paul) Stanton, who first introduced me to Evangeline while we should have been rehearsing *The Trojan Women* at Cal . . .

Lisa Highiet for reading this book—analyzing its content and providing book cover feedback—when it was still in diapers . . .

Second stanza of German lyrics to "BRAHMS' LULLABY (CRADLE SONG)," written by Georg Scherer in 1849; melody to „Wiegenlied: Guten Abend, gute Nacht" ("Good evening, good night"), Opus 49, No. 4, composed by Johannes Brahms, published in 1868. In the public domain . . .

"FORTUNE TELLERS TRAPPED BY WOMEN" from *The New York Times*, May 15, 1914 © 1914 The New York Times. In the public domain (verified by Evelise Rosario and Victoria Vazquez of PARS International) due to copyright expiration; first published in the United States before 1923 . . .

"A CURIOUS KIND OF LIGHTNING.," written by Aleister Crowley, published by *The New York Times*, July 16, 1916 © 1916 The New York Times. In the public domain (verified by Evelise Rosario and Victoria Vazquez of PARS International) due to copyright expiration; first published in the United States before 1923 . . .

Jessica Stremmel of The YGS Group, for facilitating the following re-print:

"ASTROLOGY" from the Book Reviews *and* Literary Notes section of the *Oakland Tribune*, February 12, 1928 © 1928. Used with permission of The Oakland Tribune Copyright © 2015. All rights reserved . . .

"STAIRWAY TO PARADISE," music by George Gershwin, words by B.G. DeSylva, Ira Gershwin. Written for *George White's Scandals (1922)* © 1922 Harms, Inc., New York. All rights reserved. In the public domain due to copyright expiration (first published in the United States before 1923) . . .

Larry Holcomb, Managing Editor of *The Daily Globe* in Ironwood, MI, for generously allowing permission to re-print:

"ASTROLOGIST NOW RADIO PERFORMER" written by Paul Harrison from *The Ironwood Daily Globe*, May 24, 1930 © 1930 The Ironwood Daily Globe. All rights reserved . . .

Alex Reese, Intellectual Property lawyer, for well clarifying fair use; re-printing of a few words from an original work that make up a very small portion of *EVANGELINE The Seer of Wall St.* . . .

Benjamin J. Comin, Corporate attorney and friend, for so adeptly differentiating the public domain Content from the permissioned, copyright-protected Content appearing in this book . . .

Margaret R. Fortier, expert and meticulous genealogist, who verified once and for all that I'm *not* related to Morticia, Gomez or Uncle Fester despite my uncanny resemblance to Pugsley . . .

Sawyer Mahoney, impassioned photographer, the *best* at blending alpine lakes, pine trees, the Sierra Nevada Mountains and people; making it appear as if we all belong together . . .

Araby Greene, gifted eBook converter and more, for turning my methodically-formatted print edition into a tech-savvy read . . .

Lars Pfeiffer, Raquel Rull and Álex Vidal, for helping me get my books going in Spain. Hasta pronto en Barcelona. ¡Vamos! . . .

Ron Randall, for your friendship and the valuable criticism you offered in between ab crunches, power lifts and Cobb salads . . .

Samantha, who taught me to be unafraid of death and inspired me to write books about it.

# EVANGELINE